GIVING IN

"Here's a marshmallow. Put it on the stick, John, and hold it over the fire."

"We're roasting marshmallows? You're kidding."

"Now, you put my marshmallow on top and I'll cover it with the other graham cracker and you can pull out the stick. These are s'mores. Everybody knows about s'mores."

First, she gently squeezed the two graham crackers together, so that the heat from the marshmallow melted the chocolate a little, and the marshmallow itself sort of flattened and expanded, hanging over the edges of the graham cracker. She disposed of the excess marshmallow with her tongue, gave the crackers another squeeze, and started on the melted chocolate.

He took it for as long as he could, and that wasn't long.

"Okay. That's it," he announced, tossing his own s'more over his shoulder, onto the sand. "Jane Preston, I want to go to bed with you. Deal with it."

She halted in midlick and looked at him. "What . . . What did you say?"

"I said I wanted to make love with you. To you. Several times. In, oh, so many ways . . ."

Books by Kasey Michaels

CAN'T TAKE MY EYES OFF OF YOU

TOO GOOD TO BE TRUE

LOVE TO LOVE YOU BABY

BE MY BABY TONIGHT

MAGGIE NEEDS AN ALIBI

THIS MUST BE LOVE

Published by Kensington Publishing Corporation

THIS MUST BE LOVE

Kasey Michaels

ZEBRA BOOKS
KENSINGTON PUBLISHING CORP.
http://www.kensingtonbooks.com

ZEBRA BOOKS are published by

Kensington Publishing Corp.
850 Third Avenue
New York, NY 10022

All Kensington titles, imprints and distributed lines are available at special quantity discounts for bulk purchases for sales promotion, premiums, fund-raising, educational or institutional use.

Special book excerpts or customized printings can also be created to fit specific needs. For details, write or phone the office of the Kensington Special Sales Manager: Kensington Publishing Corp., 850 Third Avenue, New York, NY 10022. Attn. Special Sales Department. Phone: 1-800-221-2647.

Zebra and the Z logo Reg. U.S. Pat. & TM Off.

First Printing: February 2003
10 9 8 7 6 5 4 3 2 1

Printed in the United States of America

To Michael William Seidick.
Welcome to the world, sweetheart!

Everything is funny
as long as it happens to somebody else.
—Will Rogers

Chapter One

"Please, Janie honey, I'm desperate here. I have nobody else," Molly said, following her cousin into the small private office, the one with the child-proof plastic cover over the doorknob.

"No, Molly. No, nope, and most definitely not," Jane Preston said firmly, reaching for a bottle of waterless hand sanitizer. "I would not do this if I should, I would not do this if I could."

"Cute, Janie, really cute. And will you please stop talking like a Dr. Seuss character? You owe me. Plus, what you just said proves that you need to get out more. Heck, you just need to get *out*."

Tell me about it, Jane Preston thought as she tucked her straight, shoulder-length light brown hair behind her ears, sat down behind her well-ordered desk, and glared at her cousin through what she had always considered to be her extremely unremarkable hazel eyes.

She'd woken up that morning happy. Her business was thriving, her bills were all paid, and she'd found new sneakers on sale. She still fit in last year's summer clothes. She was actually looking at houses, thinking it was time, at age twenty–seven, to move out of her parents' home and take that last step toward independence.

And then—blam!—Molly had shown up. Marvelous Molly Applegate, who breezed into her life time after time after time, reminding Jane of everything she just might be missing in that life.

Was definitely missing in her life. Not that she'd let Molly know that.

"I owe you?" Jane glared at her cousin, shaking herself out of her impromptu pity party. "Now, that's just low, Molly. But you're getting better. It took you a whole five minutes to hand me that *you owe me* line. But it won't work, Molly. Not this time."

Molly Applegate, all five feet seven inches of her vibrant self—huge baby blues, a dark copper fall of thick, shiny hair—pressed both palms against the desktop and leaned closer.

Jane sighed as she was presented with a glimpse of Molly's great boobs as the top of her cousin's scoop-necked blouse gaped a little, wishing she didn't envy her cousin's height, her coloring, and most of all, her 36C cups. But, hey, a 32B cup, padded, must have some envy rights.

Molly grinned at her, flashing her perfect white teeth. "You think that's low? Hang on, Janie, I can get lower. Suzanne Hendersen? Does the name ring a bell? I seem to remember you wishing somebody would get her off your back when she was ragging you about your braces. I did that. Didn't I?"

Jane pulled a thick rubber band from the middle desk drawer and tied back her hair in a ponytail with a few quick, efficient, and slightly painful motions. "Nobody told you to give her a black eye and get us both suspended for three days. Besides, I don't want to talk about it."

"Oh? Really? You don't want to talk about it? Well, how about this one? How about the night I took the blame for you when your dad caught us sneaking home at three, carrying a speed limit sign?''

Jane pushed back her chair, folded her arms across her midriff. Did she look defiant? She hoped she looked defiant. Even fierce, although she wasn't sure she could pull that one off. Fierce would really be a stretch. "It was *your* scavenger hunt, Molly. You're the one who dreamed it up and then dragged me out at midnight.''

Molly pushed away from the desk, spun in a tight circle, then laid her palms on the desktop once more. "Details, woman, you're talking about unimportant details. I saved your sorry butt, took the fall for you.''

She leaned closer again as Jane pushed her toes against the plastic floor saver and tried to retreat even more. But the wall was behind her, and she was stuck, wishing for sunglasses to ward off Molly's bright smile and dancing, shining eyes. Because she knew, just knew, that her cousin was going in for the kill, any time now.

Molly pushed on: "And then there's Billy the Bod. Remember him?''

"I was fifteen," Jane said in slight relief, pulling her chair forward once more and busying herself with the few papers on her desk. Did she look nonchalant? If fierce or defiant didn't work, she'd go for nonchalant.

Molly still hadn't gotten to the Big One. Thank God. But it was coming. It was only a matter of time. Molly knew where to aim, when to fire . . . how to hit.

"Yeah, yeah, fifteen. And never been kissed, until Billy the Bod. And who arranged it? Huh? Huh?''

"He had breath like a camel on a diet of figs and sauerkraut," Jane said. "Okay, okay. Enough. I'm still not going to help you.''

"Only because you don't want me to talk about Sean, about the Big One.''

Jane knew you couldn't depend on Molly for much, but she could always depend on her to remember the Big One.

"There is no Big One. Just . . . just a whole bunch of

little ones, all of which I'd like to forget, including Sean Gentry. *Especially* Sean Gentry. I was eighteen, and dumb. He's in jail now, by the way, for cashing bad checks or something like that. And *you* threw me at him.''

''Ha! I didn't toss you anywhere you didn't want to be. Sean was your bad boy, Janie. Every woman needs one bad boy in her life. Maybe two. One to learn on, one to keep.''

''What a waste of a perfectly good virginity,'' Jane muttered with a shake of her head, then looked up at her cousin. ''A bad boy? Get real, Molly. The last thing I need in my life is a bad boy. I'm a grown woman now, Molly. I'm past those things. You should try it.''

Molly hopped up on the desk, then laid her head back so that it collided with Jane's lap. ''And be you? I don't think so.'' Then she rolled onto her belly, her legs bent and crossed at the ankle, her smile pure evil as she sprawled—but elegantly; Molly was always elegant—across the desk, like Salome asking for John the Baptist's head. ''Please, Janie? Pretty please? I need this. I really, *really* need your help. I'm begging here.''

Jane pushed away from the desk and stood up, walking to the window that overlooked the playground. Why was she fighting so hard? It could be fun. If she was totally demented, that was. ''Tell me about it one more time.''

''Yes!'' Molly said, jumping up and pumping a fist into the air. ''Okay, here goes, in a nutshell. Senator Harrison is driving everyone nuts. Will he run for president? Won't he? If he will run, when will he announce? If he won't run, *why* won't he? Is he being cute, wanting to be courted, or is there some great big scandal hidden there somewhere? Someone has to find out. Someone has to tell the world what he's going to do before he does, and scoop everybody else.''

Janie winced as April Fedderman zoomed off the end of the slidy-board and landed fairly hard on her rump, but one of the staff quickly scooped the girl up before the first scream, probably to take her inside and offer her a cookie. April would forget everything else with an offer of junk food, which was probably why her little rump was so well padded. She might even be getting so many boo-boos just for the cookie reward at the other end. That was it, Jane decided, no more cookies for April. The child would be on the apple and banana wagon as of this moment.

"Janie? Are you listening to me? I said, someone has to find out, tell the world."

Jane snapped back to attention, but still kept her watchful eye on the playground. "Yes, yes, I got that much the first time you told me. The public's right to know—which I think is pure hooey when it comes to a person's private life. I mean, do you ask your surgeon if he cheats on his wife? No, you only want to know how he handles the scalpel. Anyway, where do you come in?"

"Where do *you* come in, you mean. Okay, one more time—there's this party in less than a month . . . an affair . . . gathering . . . confab . . . whatever you want to call it. Week-long shindig in Cape May. That's in New Jersey, Janie, right down at the tip. You can see the sun both rise and set on the water there. Really, it was in the brochure."

"I know where Cape May is, Molly." God help her, she was actually getting excited about this thing. Hobnobbing with senators and other mucky-mucks, an all-expenses-paid week at the beach, fun in the sun. And such a switch from trying to get four-year-old Mason Furbish to stop taking off his clothes to show everyone his "wizzer." Oh, yes. She was weakening.

Jane turned her head for a quick peek at Molly as her cousin took command of Jane's desk chair, her long legs crossed at the knee, her great thighs showing as she lazily swiveled back and forth. Molly was in charge now, and obviously she knew it.

Jane knew it, too, suppressing a sigh as the playground outside her window seemed to somehow morph into a pristine, sandy beach edging an endless blue ocean. Maybe this time it might be fun, bailing out Molly. At the very least, she'd get some salt water taffy and a nice suntan before somebody lined her up in front of the firing squad.

"Good girl, Janie, you know where Cape May is. You were always great in geography. Anyway, this is some sort of annual intellectual, invitation-only retreat for brainy types and their guests. Sometimes the president of the moment even shows up, although the word is he probably won't be in Cape May. These big brains sit around and talk about Plato, and nuclear proliferation, the meaning of life, all that junk. The senator is going to be there. I *had* to get there. It was my big chance."

Janie faced her cousin at last as she leaned a hip against the windowsill after picking up a small rag doll, beginning to untangle its knotted red-yarn hair. "So you talked a friend who owns an escort service in Washington into pairing you up with one of the single attendees. That's spooky, Molly. I mean, who even *thinks* of stuff like that?"

"You *have* been listening. Good girl. Yes, it's all set. I go, hanging on the arm of some brainy type. Strictly platonic, there's no hanky-panky on these retreats—although if you hear about any, don't be a stranger, call me immediately. Anyway, and then I get all chummy with the senator, he tells me his plans, and I get the scoop of the moment and save my job. What could be easier?"

"Oh, I don't know," Jane said, frowning at the red-yarn tangles. "Curing the common cold? Getting Regis Philbin's face off television?"

"Regis Philbin? I really hate his ties, but love him. I wonder if he's going to be there. They've got people from everywhere. Politicians, professors, actors, even some reporters—sworn to secrecy, of course. You know those guys, the ones that call themselves journalists? But that's the thing, Jane, nobody is going to know I'm a reporter."

Jane put down the doll and did her best to glare at Molly. "Because you're not. You're secretary to one of the editors. And you're on probation."

"Lose one small phone message with the name of the guy trying to blow the whistle on some trucking company dumping hazardous waste ..." Molly said, sighing, then brightened again. "This will work, Janie. I get the scoop, and I save my job, get bumped up to reporter. Pulitzer Prize, here I come!"

Jane made one last stab at sanity. "So go. Have a ball. Send me a postcard."

"Janie," Molly said, sighing. "I told you. Senator Harrison is a widower. But he isn't bringing some woman he knows. He's not coming alone, either, as I found out yesterday. He's bringing his nephew." She wrinkled her elegant nose. "Dillon Holmes."

"The one you used to date right after college, when you were interning in Washington. I seem to remember you mentioning that."

"Exactly. And Dillon Holmes *hates* me for some unknown reason. I think he said I'm flighty, like it's some awful character flaw or something. But I'm still sending those Christmas letters to everyone, him included, about how I spent my year. You know how everyone loves my Christmas letters. Stupid computer. It churns out address labels for me, and I forgot to delete the man's name."

Jane bit her bottom lip. She *hated* Molly's Christmas letters. Chock-full of "I went here, and then I went there, and I met the Grand Pooba of Something-stan, and had a hole-in-one on the fifth of the desert course in Palm Springs, and wasn't it great fun to parasail in Bimini," and on and on and on ... all while Jane knew her Christmas letter, if she chose to write one, would be one sentence: "I made it through another year without having to trade in my Dodge Neon."

"Maybe," Jane said, trying not to sound snide, "he didn't bother to read your Christmas letter."

Molly rolled her eyes. "Janie, *everybody* reads my Christmas letter. Besides, Dillon sent me a card, too, or at least

his computer did. So I know he has to know that I'm trying
to get into the newspaper game.''

"*Life* is a game to you, Molly.''

"Janie, please. Even if Dillon didn't read my Christmas
letter, the man hates me. I wouldn't be able to get within
fifty yards of Senator Harrison the whole week. But *you*
could. We don't look anything alike—''

"Thanks for the reminder, *Legs.*''

"Oh, stop. You know you're so *cute*. People just love to
cuddle you.''

"I could be seriously sick any minute now,'' Jane mumbled under her breath.

"Yeah, yeah. Anyway, we don't look alike. We don't
have the same last name. Nothing. You go in my place, and
you get me the scoop. And in return I'll . . . I'll . . . Well,
I'll do something. What do you want?''

"A statement from you, signed in blood—also yours—
and then notarized, that this is the last time you ever ask
me to do anything for you. That, and naturally you'll have
to take over here.''

Molly swiveled the desk chair from left to right and back
again, her usually naturally pink cheeks having suddenly
gone rather white.

Jane knew what her cousin was thinking: The room was
piled high with kid stuff. Baby stuff. Outside the office
were the sounds of children. Laughing. Talking. Screeching.
Crying. Demanding. Their bottoms were bound to be wet,
their fingers all sticky. And she hadn't even met Wizzer
Furbish.

Molly had asked her, when Jane had bought the place, why
on earth she'd used her grandmother's bequest to purchase a
combination day care and nursery school. To which Jane
had answered somewhere along the lines of, "And what
was I supposed to do with Grandma's money—open a tattoo
parlor?'' That's when Molly had shown her the small butter-
fly tattoo on her left hip. Pitiful . . . and so sexy and daring.
Everything that Janie was not.

At last, Molly spoke. "How about a lung? Seriously, Janie. I've got two."

"No," Jane said, walking toward her cousin, pointing a finger at her chest, feeling in charge of her cousin, possibly for the first time in their lives. Oh, hell, she had to admit it, that would be definitely for the first time in their lives. And wasn't it fun!

Molly scooted the chair back against the wall. "No? Okay then, the organ of your choice?"

"Stop that. If I'm doing something for you, Molly, then you have to do something for me. Something *real*. And that's what I want. You ... here in Fairfax ... running Preston Kiddie Kare. We close for most of that week, because it's the Fourth of July and I always close for staff vacations that week and the next, so you'd only have to be here for two days. Two days. Even you can't mess that up."

"Wanna bet? Oh, hey, hey, don't make that face, Janie. I'll do it, I'll do it. And you'll get Senator Harrison to bare his soul to you?"

Jane was feeling powerful. Not quite omnipotent, but pretty darn powerful. "I've seen Senator Harrison on the news, and I don't want to see his bare *anything*. I'd rather he just talked to me."

"See? That's funny. You're already getting into this, aren't you, Janie? Loosening up. And we'll stay in touch by cell phone, every day. I'll feed you the right questions."

"And then we're even? Even if Senator Harrison doesn't talk to me? We're still even? You'll never come in here again telling me I owe you? Because I'm a grown-up now, Molly. I'm predictable, and practical, and stuffed full with common sense. I am not the same girl you led around by her nose and got into trouble when you visited every summer. I'm not."

"Of course you're not, more's the pity," Molly said, grabbing her in a bear hug. "And don't worry. What could go wrong?"

Jane looked up at the ceiling and whimpered softly.

* * *

It was a large, weathered gray wood and mostly glass house built into the side of a rolling green hill in a suburb of Fairfax, Virginia. The house looked as if someone had thrown several various sized boxes up against the hill, and miraculously they had connected to each other into a surprisingly attractive whole.

The huge windows at the rear of the house faced a tremendous view, the kind of view people paid a lot of money to see . . . which didn't explain why the man sitting in his battered, duct-taped black leather swivel chair had faced his desk against the wall.

But John Patrick Romanowski, the man just now sitting at that desk, had his reasons, the most important being that he needed to face a blank wall in order to create.

If he had a view to look at, instead of his computer screen, he'd soon produce nothing but sappy poems about deer and rabbits and bucolic vistas . . . which would mean he would soon no longer be able to afford the huge weathered gray wood and glass house on the side of the hill. Hell, he already had enough trouble every morning, breaking himself away from that damn Solitaire game that had come with his new computer and getting to work.

Okay, so maybe he wouldn't go broke. That would be pretty impossible, unless he suddenly decided to invest his millions in a dot-com fostering the notion that people really, really wanted to buy toothpicks on-line.

"Buy toothpicks on-line? Where the hell did that one come from?" John asked himself, staring at the mostly blank computer screen and that damn blinking cursor. "Maybe the cursor looked like a toothpick? Maybe I'm punch drunk?"

"I don't hear the tap-tap-tapping of nimble fingers, John Patrick."

John grimaced, then swiveled his chair around to see his Aunt Marion entering the room, carrying a rather large brown package. "Here, let me help you with that," he said, getting to his feet and taking the package from her.

"Look at this pigsty. Who's going to clean it up? Not me. I'm not your servant, you know," Aunt Marion said, smoothing down her ever-present white apron as John carried the package to a nearby table, pushed piles of books and papers out of the way, and set it down.

"The apron's just a prop?" he asked, reaching for the scissors.

"No, it's a weapon. I plan, one day soon, to choke you with it. I'm thinking a square knot, right on your Adam's apple. Would that work?"

"Possibly. I could research it for you, if you'd like," John said, grinning at his aunt, a short, plump, gray-haired woman with a liking for flowered house dresses and orthopedic shoes . . . and who looked less dangerous than any of the fuzzy creatures that gamboled on the hill outside his window. "What's for dinner?"

"It's a surprise. Mostly to me, because I haven't decided yet." She approached the table. "What's in the package? It's soft, so it can't be books. Unless they're paperback copies, I suppose. Do you think they're foreign copies? Oh, for pity's sake, John Patrick, open the darn thing!"

John raised one eyebrow at his aunt. "How old are you now? Sixty-five? And I still have to hide your birthday and Christmas presents. Shame on you."

"Yes, yes, shame on me. Now, open it. You've been getting the strangest things in the mail lately."

"I've explained that," John said, the package now open so that he could pull out the contents, which happened to be a pair of green-and-yellow-striped, baggy swim trunks—with a matching jacket lined in white terry cloth.

"Ohmigod," Aunt Marion said, grabbing the jacket. "Your Uncle Fred had one of these. In nineteen fifty-six! John, you can't tell me you're really going to *wear* this."

"Pretty bad, huh?" he said, holding up the swim trunks that went down to his knees and could probably double as a parachute, should he be dropped out of a plane at thirty thousand feet.

"You're a writer, John. I should think you could come up with a better word than just *bad*. How about atrocious, ridiculous, preposterous . . ."

"Nerdy?"

Aunt Marion shrugged. "Yes, I suppose that, too, if you insist on the obvious. *Nerdy.*"

John took the jacket from his aunt and rolled up both pieces, tossing them in the general direction of the rapidly growing pile of clothing in one corner of the office. "Then, they're perfect."

Marion Romanowski looked at her nephew. He was glorious. A shade away from six and a half feet tall, beautifully muscled, perpetually tanned. His eyes a marvelous cobalt blue, just like her dear departed Fred's eyes; she'd taken one look at those gorgeous blue-green eyes and fallen like the proverbial ton of bricks for Fred.

But, where her Fred had been rather blond, John Patrick was dark as sin. Fred had said their gypsy blood showed up every once in a while, and John Patrick had gotten it, in spades. Hair blacker than night. Lordy, he was a hairy man, but not apelike, like some she could name (from memory, as she hadn't always been in love with Fred, after all). He was just all . . . all male. And he had a five o'clock shadow by noon which, against all odds, just made him look even better.

Except now he was going to hide all of this glory behind, dear God, a green-and-yellow-striped circus tent!

Picking up several days' worth of newspapers from a chair, Aunt Marion sat down with a small thump. "I still want to go on record as saying that this idea of yours is ridiculous. You've never really been photographed, and I don't count that shadowy mess you insisted on for the back cover of your books when Henry wouldn't be put off any longer. It shows little more than that you have a full head of hair and your Uncle Fred's fine Roman nose. No one will know you anyway, unless someone recognizes you by the width of your shoulders, so why the disguise? And why—what did you call it? Oh, yes. Why *nerdy?*''

John opened the top drawer of his research desk and pulled out his latest bit of brilliance—thick, black-rimmed glasses he'd carefully wound with white adhesive tape at the nosepiece—and put them on. ''Because, dear aunt, nobody takes nerds seriously.''

Aunt Marion blinked at the sight of her handsome nephew in those outlandish glasses. ''Put those glasses with that swimsuit, and the rest of that nonsense you've been accumulating, and *I* wouldn't take you seriously.''

''And that's just the point,'' John said, removing the glasses and tossing them, too, on the growing pile in the corner.

''Don't do that, they could break.''

''All the better if they do. I could use a small paper clip to replace one of the screws. I think I'll do it even if they don't break. Call it my *pièce de résistance.*''

''You wouldn't have to talk me into resisting you, that's for sure,'' Aunt Marion said, getting to her feet once more. ''Oh, and by the way, I still don't believe you. You don't need a disguise to do your research. You never have . . . which doesn't explain all the times you've gone out of here with fake mustaches, tinted contacts, and all the rest of it. You do it because it's fun, John Patrick, because you're still a little boy inside that too-smart head of yours. And now you're doing it because of that monster, Harrison. But this?'' She swept one arm in the general direction of the pile of ''nerd'' in the corner. ''This is just too much.''

''Yes, ma'am,'' John said, grinning. ''I'm so ashamed.''

''Oh—drat you, John Patrick!'' Aunt Marion said, and swept out of the room, calling over her shoulder, ''You'll be having peanut butter and jelly sandwiches for dinner, since you're behaving like a child. I'll even cut the crusts off.''

John chuckled as he returned to his desk, sat down, and

picked up the brochure for the *Sixth Annual Intellectual Retreat*.

Part interesting, part—as Aunt Marion had said—a bunch of hooey, the retreat was a fairly well kept secret, thanks to a cooperative media who wanted to be included on the guest list.

John paged through the brochure, looking at the extensive list of workshops and seminars, some of them held inside Congress Hall, the retreat's choice of conference hotel in Cape May, New Jersey, and some scheduled to take place on the beach, weather permitting.

Communal meals, assigned seats at the tables. Night-owl bull sessions. Plain food, plain talk. No titles, no protocol, no egos—or at least that was the hype. An open exchange of ideas. A chance to recharge the old batteries, hear various viewpoints, rub elbows with some of the finest brains in the country.

A treasure trove of possibilities for J. P. Roman, *New York Times* Number One Best-seller of political thrillers.

Fortunately, the invitation had come to John Patrick Romanowski, college professor. Nobody knew John Patrick was also J. P. Nobody except Aunt Marion and Henry, and that was the way he wanted to keep it.

He was J. P. Roman, not J. D. Salinger—he wasn't a hermit or anything like that. He had a full life. His classes at the university, his house here in the hills, his motorcycle (when Aunt Marion didn't hide the key to the wheel lock), his work.

He loved his work. What had begun as a hobby and a bit of personal axe-grinding had grown into, to date, eight *NYT* best-sellers having to do with the ins and outs of national politics, usually with a murder or two thrown in to keep the story moving.

But now it was personal. Personal by way of the senior senator from New Jersey, Aubrey Harrison. Harrison was the original "hale fellow, well met." Popular, charismatic, even a sympathetic figure since his second wife had died.

Everybody's favorite son, and the probable candidate of his party for next year's presidential election.

The thought made John's stomach turn.

He closed his eyes, conjuring up a mental picture of his mother, dead these past fifteen years. His mother, who had raised him alone after his father had gone off to work one day and left his office with his teenage secretary, the two of them jetting off to Europe, never to return.

His mother, who had gone to work for the then junior senator from New Jersey, to put food on the table, keep a roof over her son's head. His mother, who had fallen so madly in love with Aubrey Harrison, the man who had promised her the moon, then dumped her to marry the daughter of one of his biggest contributors.

Maryjo Romanowski had never recovered from that second "dumping" by the man in her life, once again for a much younger woman. By the time John was eighteen, he was an orphan, having spent six years watching his mother deteriorate, be institutionalized, go off to live in her own tormented world, and die alone.

The senator's second wife hadn't fared much better than her predecessor or Maryjo Romanowski. Word was the woman was disillusioned with her philandering husband and drank, a lot, and that's why she'd fallen down the stairs at their Georgetown town house last year, breaking her neck.

Oh, the senator's connections had kept the woman's drinking all hush-hush, the media had never questioned the "tragic accident," but J. P. Roman had his sources, and pockets deep enough to buy information otherwise kept under wraps.

A few well-placed dollars, a few interesting talks with disgruntled employees, and he had learned all about the woman's love for the bottle, the loud arguments, even fights, between husband and wife.

He just couldn't print any of it if he worked for a newspaper. He could make up a character much like Harrison, use him in one of his novels, but that wouldn't be enough to bring the man down, not even with two dead wives also in his cast of characters. All that would get John, if a court thought Harrison was being unjustedly targeted in the book, would be one really major lawsuit.

How he wanted, wanted very badly, to catch Harrison in something scandalous, something the media couldn't ignore and the voters wouldn't countenance. He was pretty sure it would take a woman to do it.

Ah, yes, the women. John had learned all about the women in Harrison's life. All pretty, all young, all fairly interchangeable.

Horny Harrison, that's who John had learned about, using his own money, his own sources. The press called him Happy Harrison, but then the press wasn't always the "go for the truth, go for the throat" entity it liked everyone to believe it was.

Not when Senator Harrison and the media were such good friends, such great pals. Hell, the senator even had a condo in a Florida building owned by one of his biggest contributors, who was also the major sponsor of the highest rated Sunday morning talking-heads program. Harrison's was just one of the dozen or so million-dollar condos in the building that were also occupied by, among others, the head of one of the major networks, the dual anchors on that highest rated Sunday political talk show, and the news director of the largest all–news cable network.

Just one big happy family, each living out of the other's pockets—and covering each other's asses.

John had searched out the deeds for the condos, deeds all in the names of dummy corporations or idiot brothers-in-law, and found the selling prices that ranged from fifty thousand to two hundred thousand dollars. For million-dollar condos. Nice work if you could get it.

But John couldn't really care about any of that right now; that sort of thing was for the plots in his books. His latest, *Shallow Ground,* was set around the murder of a fictional congresswoman at a fictional Florida condo. That was as close as he could get without Henry putting on the brakes.

What he wanted, what he needed, was to get himself up close with Senator Harrison and then find a way to destroy him. For Maryjo, and maybe for the boy John Patrick Romanowski used to be.

Aubrey Harrison, President of the United States? Hell, no. Not if J. P. Roman had anything to say about it.

The retreat was the perfect opportunity, dropped into his lap out of the blue. Everyone who was there would be there by invitation. Harrison would feel safe, be off his guard. And that's when John would strike, find the man's soft underbelly and, somehow, some way, make it impossible for the man to run for president.

If he were writing one of his books, he'd know that his plot line was thin, his chance of success small. He could only hope his so-far sketchy cast of characters would provide most of the action.

Thinking of his cast of characters . . .

John put down the brochure and picked up the file card he'd used an hour earlier to jot down the information on his "partner" for the week.

"Jane Preston," he said, reading the name he'd penciled in after scratching out the name Molly Applegate. The agency had really sold him on Applegate, so he hoped that this Preston dame, her replacement, would be as suitable.

He needed pretty. He needed perky. He needed not too intelligent. He needed malleable morals.

He needed an attractive lure, to reel in the skirt-chasing senator, so that then he could go in for the kill.

"Jane Preston," he repeated, flipping the card back onto the desk. "Damn well better not be Plain Jane, or I'll have to go to Plan B, and there is no Plan B."

Chapter Two

Ah, the sweet voices of childhood.

"Was not!"

"Were too!"

"Was not!"

"Were too!"

"Children, children," Jane said, stepping between Zachary Balliet and Ian Turbetsky before Zachary, who thought pulling hair was a real fun thing to do, grabbed poor Ian by those bright red curls his mother seemed so reluctant to cut. Either the woman broke down and took him to the barber soon, or little Ian was going to have to learn how to fight, big-time. "What seems to be the problem?"

"He was looking at me. I was just coloring in my Scooby Doo coloring book and he started looking at me," Zachary said, his bottom lip pushing forward dangerously.

"Was not!"

"Were too!"

Jane sighed, then got down on her knees, so that she was eye-to-eye with the pair of four-year-olds. "Ian, honey?

Were you looking at Zachary while he was coloring in his Scooby Doo coloring book?''

"He was coloring Scooby purple, Miz Preston. I was looking at Scooby.''

"He was looking at me. And making faces.'' Zachary lunged, arms out, fingers curling, and Jane quickly gathered him into in a gentle bear hug. "Pig face. He's just a great big pig face.''

"Am not!''

"Are so! Piggy-piggy-pig face!''

"Toilet head!''

Jane whimpered under her breath, rubbed at her ear because Zachary had screeched "piggy-piggy-pig face'' right into it, then went into her "let's all be friends'' routine, rising to her feet five minutes later, having stopped what could have been an all-out war, and sending the boys off outside together to play in the sand box.

"Ah, détente,'' Molly said, watching the boys run off together. "You ought to sign up with the United Nations, Janie.''

Jane smoothed down her pink-and-white-flowered blouse and then brushed at her sensible light blue denim skirt. "And you'd better pay attention to my technique. I do détente about fifty times a day, at the minimum.''

Molly raised her eyebrows. "You expect *me* to—oh, you're kidding. I'm taking your place, sure, but that's in the office, right? You know, that nice safe place back thataways? The one with the lock on the door? Are the walls sound-proofed by any chance?''

"Molly . . .'' Jane said, dragging out her cousin's name. "We've discussed all of this on the phone, more times than I care to count. Either you take this seriously, or the whole deal is off.''

"Okay, okay,'' Molly said, holding up her hands in sur-render. "I'll be good. Heck, I'll be great. Just not today, all right? I told you, I took two of my vacation days early, so I could come down here now. Tomorrow I'll be all yours, all day, and you can show me the ropes. And maybe where you keep the whips and chains? Today you and I are going to the mall.''

Jane shook her head. "The mall? Why?"

Molly put one hand on her hip, then ran her gaze up and down Jane's form. "You're standing there looking like you just escaped from an eleventh period junior high home ec class, and you have to ask me that? You made that skirt yourself, didn't you? It's got loving hands at home written all over it. You could at least buy some designer labels somewhere, sew them on your butt, and *pretend* you're in style. Girl, in short, in long, no matter how you say it—you need work. I mean, serious *work.*''

"What's wrong with me?" Jane asked as she walked toward the nursery, where babies under the age of one year were closely supervised while their mommies were off banging their heads against glass ceilings. "I'm clean, I'm neat. I'm—"

"Bor—ring," Molly ended for her, reaching ahead of Jane to close the door on sixteen rather loud infants. "You can't go to the retreat looking this way, Janie. You have to . . . have to make an *impact.* Yes, that's it, an *impact.* A little zing, a little zip. Otherwise, how are you going to get Senator Harrison to notice you?"

Jane leaned back against the wall, folding her arms around her waist. "This is an intellectual retreat, Molly, not an episode of *The Love Connection.* Right?"

"Oh, yeah, sure. Right. Absolutely. You'll dazzle him with your intellectual ability. Uh-huh.''

Jane's eyelids narrowed. "I graduated from Penn State with a four-point-o, Molly. I can be . . . intellectual. I can hold a conversation. About politics. About child care reform. About the environmental crisis facing us.''

"Uh-huh, uh-huh, fascinating. Really. Honey, I'm sure you can hold your own in any conversation. But first you've got to get Harrison to notice you. Or maybe even Dillon.''

"Dillon Holmes? The guy who hates you?"

"Right. The senator's nephew. He's a god, by the way, in case I forgot to mention that. Green eyes, blond hair. Sort of a Brad Pitt slash Troy Donohue clone. Do you remember Troy Donohue, Janie? We used to watch him on the late movies, cavorting on beaches, flexing his muscles as he shoved back that sexy blond mop of his? Do you suppose he colored it? He could have bleached it."

"Would you shut up about Troy Donohue?" Jane said as she pushed away from the wall and headed down the hall and into her office. "I'm going to the retreat to get you a story and me a suntan, period. I am not going to get . . . get *tarted up* for you. Forget it."

"Oh, not for me, Janie, for Dillon and the senator. Now, come on. These little terrors can get along without you for a couple of hours, right? I've already scouted out the mall and know just what you need. I mean, there's this two-piece bathing suit that just screams 'take me to Cape May.' Padded cups, too. Besides, you have an appointment at four, with Angel."

"Angel? Who's she?"

"He, my love. Angel. One of the best hair stylists in the business. Well, at least here in Fairfax, according to my stylist. Now, if you want to go to D.C., we can do that, too, and I can set you up with Rafael—he's my personal stylist. But I figured you wouldn't want to be away from the Screamin' Meemies that long, so I got Rafael to recommend someone here."

"Stop calling the children Screamin' Meemies, if you please. And I can't leave. I have too much to do. I've got instructions to post, parents to contact, an interview with a prospective new client this afternoon."

"You don't trust your staff?"

"Of course I trust my staff," Jane said, stung. "But I make it a point to always interview prospective clients myself. And this one is complicated. I won't be meeting the parents, just the uncle, and the placement is only for two weeks, while the parents are off on a cruise or something. And then there's you. You've been observing me for all of ten minutes, Molly. You have to at least pretend to understand what goes on here, or I can't trust you to take over for me. So, no, it's impossible. No shopping, no Angel. I leave for Cape May in three days.''

''Not looking like that, you don't,'' Molly said, picking up Jane's purse and then grabbing hold of her cousin's arm and marching her out the door.

Aunt Marion peeked through the vertical blinds, then turned to look at her nephew as he walked in the front door. ''What in God's name is *that?*''

John tossed the key ring in the air and caught it, then launched it onto the marble top of Aunt Marion's latest acquisition, a black painted chest of drawers she'd picked up at a local estate sale.

''Don't *do* that,'' she said, grabbing up the keys, then running the hem of her apron over the marble top, checking it for scratches. ''Were you raised in a barn?''

He dropped a kiss on her cheek, because he loved his aunt, and because he was feeling pretty damn good, definitely pleased with his latest acquisition. ''Which question do you want me to answer, Aunt Marion?''

''The first one,'' she told him, heading toward the large, country-style kitchen. ''I already know the answer to the second one. You raised yourself, poor thing, until I took over. And if I didn't feel so sorry for you, I'd give you the full benefit of my famous lecture that has to do with how you're a grown-up now, and you should take better care of your things. And *my* things. Especially my things.''

''I'm sorry, Aunt,'' John said, pulling out one of the high stools that usually resided half under the serving bar and climbing aboard. ''I'm a slob, I know it.''

''You don't just know it; you're *proud* of it,'' Aunt Marion said, pushing a plate of homemade peanut butter cookies at him. "Now, tell me about that ... that *thing* in the driveway."

John bit one of the cookies in half, smiling as he chewed, then swallowed. "It's for the retreat. Part of my disguise. You like it?"

"I don't think so. What is it?"

"It, my dear aunt, is a Volkswagen Rabbit convertible. A bright yellow Volkswagen Rabbit convertible. A *vintage*, 1984, almost fully restored, zippy, zingy, bright yellow Volkswagen Rabbit convertible. A—"

"I get the point, John Patrick. I like your Ferrari much better. Even if the red is a little flashy. I almost even like your motorcycle better. Do you know what would happen if you rolled down a mountainside in that ugly yellow thing, with the top down?"

"Obviously, dear aunt, you didn't have that good a look at my vintage Volkswagen Rabbit convertible, or you would have seen the marvelous safety feature—a roll bar. Besides, I also don't think there are any mountains in New Jersey."

"Will that ... that *thing* even get you to New Jersey?"

"Oh, sure, and with great gas mileage. It only has one hundred and forty thousand miles on it. The back of the front passenger seat is propped up with a two-by-four, but other than that, it's solid. I borrowed it from one of my third-year students."

"Did you loan one of your third-year students your Ferrari?"

John smiled. "I would have, but he didn't want it. He said it was too class specific. Good kid, Bruce, but a little square. Okay, a lot square. Possibly cubed. Which is why I asked to borrow his car. It's perfect, Aunt Marion. The nerd's notion of a babe magnet."

"Humph!" Aunt Marion said, brushing past him, heading into the den. "Your new luggage arrived, too, while you were gone. I didn't think anyone even made plaid luggage anymore. With straps on it. You're certainly thorough, John, I'll say that for you."

"Nerds always pay attention to the details," John said, grabbing two more cookies before uncurling his length from the stool and following after his aunt. Sure enough, she'd unpacked the boxes the luggage had come in. There were wrapping paper, boxes, and twine all over the den, along with his five-piece matching set of truly ugly luggage. "Wow. This is even better than I'd hoped."

"You're a sick and twisted boy, John Patrick Romanowski," his Aunt Marion said, picking up a few other arrivals she'd unpacked.

A brown-and-tan tweed jacket, with brown suede patches on the elbows.

Four pair of baggy, pleated slacks, all brown. With cuffs on them.

Several white shirts, whose collars and material screamed, "Four for Forty Dollars."

Two pair of brown penny loafers. Beach thongs with thick black rubber tire soles. A pair of cheap high-top sneakers.

White socks with stripes around the tops.

And six bow ties.

Six.

Bow ties.

Aunt Marion held one up by her fingertips, then shuddered and tossed it over her shoulder.

"I wouldn't cross the street with you while you're wearing any of this," she said with heartfelt sincerity. "And you do know that brown is the one color you can't wear with your coloring. You'll look . . . muddy."

"And intellectual. And serious. And non-threatening. And nerdy."

"I'm learning to hate that word."

"I guess that means you aren't going to help me pack?"

"What? And ruin your fine wrinkling? You've been throwing clothes in the corner for weeks now, John. I'm assuming you *want* wrinkles."

"You know me so well."

"Yes, but you don't know nerdy. I've been checking,

John. Nerds are always compulsively *neat*. You're about as neat as that tornado in the movie we saw on video last month. You could successfully hide a dead cow in your office for weeks. And a tractor trailer in your bedroom. And stop grinning. And don't you dare tell me again that I'm Felix Unger to your Oscar Madison. We're an odd enough couple as it is, thank you. Of course, now that I've said all that about compulsively neat nerds, I suppose you'll want me to press everything for you?''

"Would you?'' he asked, giving her another kiss on the cheek before he began gathering up the last of his new wardrobe—rolling it up, actually.

"Give me that,'' she said, grabbing the tweed jacket as he began rolling it like a big ugly cigar. "Will you hang up everything when you get to the hotel?''

"In the closet? Wow, that's a stretch, Aunt Marion. Do you think I'm capable?''

"No, I don't. I think you're most at home in a pigpen. But if you're going to be serious about this nerd business, and from the looks of everything you've bought, I think you are, then you're going to have to be neat, for a whole week. Seven days, John. I imagine you'll have a nervous collapse by Wednesday, and I'll get a call to come shovel you into my car and drive you to the nearest funny farm. I'll leave a trail of carrots, and the Rabbit can find its own way home.''

He looked at the tweed jacket. God, it was bad. "This thing is going to be hot as hell, isn't it?''

"Yes,'' Aunt Marion said, grinning. "Do nerds sweat?''

"Ha ha,'' John said, heading for the stairs down to the lower level.

"You could have ordered a seersucker jacket,'' his aunt called after him. "Blue and white stripes. And a white boater straw hat. And wing tip shoes. And—''

John stopped on the top step of the spiral staircase and turned to grin at his aunt. "Is that a dare, old woman? Because I saw one at one of the on-line stores. Not the hat, but the jacket. I could order it now, have it shipped.''

Aunt Marion pressed her hands to her cheeks. "John Patrick. You wouldn't!"

"No, I wouldn't. But only because I leave for Cape May in three days and it might not arrive in time. Oh," he said, having turned away for a moment, then looked back at his aunt, "what's for dinner?"

"Whatever you pick from the menu, because you're taking me out. Somewhere that has a liquor license."

Jane looked at her reflection in the mirror, her bottom lip caught between her teeth.

"Come out, come out, wherever you are, and let me see how you look," Molly called to her through the door of the dressing room.

"There is no way I'm coming out there like this," Jane said, swallowing hard. "I'm naked."

"Don't exaggerate, Janie, you are not," Molly said as the knob turned and the door was thrown open. "Wow," she said, stepping back a pace. "I knew that suit was good, but this is even better than I'd hoped. You've got a nice tight little body there, Janie Preston. A very nice little body, a perfect size eight petite."

"Stop that," Jane said, dipping her head so that her straight hair covered her flaming cheeks. "I can't wear this in public. The top half of it isn't even me."

"It's partly you. Have you ever considered implants, Janie? I know this doctor in D.C. who—"

"I'd never consider implants. I have a perfectly good body."

"Yes, you do, and it looks great in that suit. That's the whole point I'm trying to get across. Pink is definitely your color. Put it on the we'll-take-it pile. Oh, maybe you want to try the cover-up? See how it looks?"

Jane looked at the beige mesh cover-up hanging over the door. Scoop neck, long, floppy sleeves, scalloped hem ending at about mid-thigh, and the mesh so loose that it looked like an upscale fishing net. She was surprised there weren't little corks sewn to it. "That thing doesn't hide much of anything."

"That's the genius of it, my dear. Conceal and reveal. I can get you another swimsuit if you want. You probably should have at least two. There's a great navy blue one out there I had my eye on. What do you say?"

"Does it have more than half a yard of material in it?"

"Close. With French-cut legs. I'll go get it."

Jane puffed up her cheeks and blew out her breath after her cousin closed the dressing room door once more. She turned sideways and placed a hand on her bare belly. Did it stick out too much? She didn't think so. She was just sort of a *rounded* person, that's all. Size eight wasn't so bad. It wasn't Molly's size four, but it wasn't bad.

She then looked at the pile of clothing on the chair.

It was a pretty big pile.

A-line skirts that ended above her knee. Little sleeveless sweaters, some which didn't even skim her bellybutton. Long breezy dresses that hit at her ankles—perfect for walking on the beach at sunrise or sunset, according to Molly. Short shorts. Not so short shorts.

A navy jacket with a hood. A white cardigan sweater meant only to be tied around her shoulders or waist. "Nobody actually *wears* them, you know," Molly had informed her.

And evening wear. A simple black sheath, a not so simple black sheath. A pink suit with a black silk shell. A butter yellow dress that would look better once she had been in the sun, picked up a bit of a tan. Several slacks with knit tops, silk blouses.

Six pair of shoes. Jane hadn't protested about the shoes. She was nuts about shoes.

She felt like a virgin being powdered and perfumed and dressed up to meet the sheikh . . . except she wasn't a virgin, and she'd given up on meeting a sheikh, or any fairy-tale prince, years ago.

But she was getting into the spirit of the thing. She couldn't lie to herself and say she wasn't.

An hour later, the trunk of Molly's Mercedes stuffed with boxes and bags, Jane was standing in the foyer of the largest beauty salon she'd ever seen, and a handsome, Latin-looking man in a skin-tight, sleeveless black T-shirt and matching black slacks (and the flattest stomach in the world) was approaching, his arms held out as he then gathered Molly into his embrace.

"Darling Molly! Raphael has told me so much about you," he exclaimed, kissing her cheeks. "You're right on time."

"For one of Rose's massages? You made it, and her, sound like heaven. How could I be late?"

That was Molly. She might live in D.C., but give her more than five minutes in any city and she knew the best hairdresser, the best salon, the best shops . . . and everyone adored her, wanted nothing more than to please her.

It was a gift from the gods, probably. One that Jane hadn't gotten when the gifts had been handed out. Her forte was her affinity for coping with children, children not even her own. Somehow, at this moment, that didn't seem quite fair. If she was going to have to snip bubble gum out of her hair, at least it should have been her own child who'd chewed it and then stuck it there.

Jane rolled her eyes at her fairly hysterical musings, then looked around the entry, which was decorated like the main saloon of a stately southern mansion. Fireplace. White leather couches. Antiques—real ones. Flowers everywhere. And not roses or carnations. Expensive flowers, the kind that were dramatic and not particularly pretty, but looked like they cost the earth.

"What does this place cost? I'll bet they charge just for looking, right?" she asked Molly out of the corner of her mouth once Angel had danced away, to call the massage therapist front and center.

"The same as the clothes, nothing. No cost at all. We've

been over this, Janie. You're doing me a *huge* favor, and me and my trust fund are dressing you for the part. Now, are you ready for your facial?''

''I don't know. I've never had one.''

''Oh, you poor thing!'' Molly said, gathering her cousin close for a quick hug. ''I didn't realize you've been so deprived.''

''Will you knock it off,'' Jane said, laughing as a reed-slim woman in a white coat, her hair impossibly red—almost purple—approached them, quite naturally zeroing in on Molly, who looked the part of someone who frequented salons like this . . . well, frequently.

''Ms. Applegate? Rose is ready for you. And this lady would be . . . ?''

''Janie Preston,'' Molly answered. ''Miranda is taking care of her. It's all arranged. Facial, manicure, pedicure, massage. But not the seaweed wrap. That's just for me, while Angel works his magic on her. Besides, if we tried to get Janie here into that big white tub and pile her with seaweed, she'd probably run out of here, screaming.''

''You're just a laugh a minute, aren't you, Molly?'' Jane said as she followed the white-coated woman, looking around nervously at the lush surroundings. What was she doing here? She didn't belong here.

Okay, so maybe she could get used to this, Jane thought ninety minutes later as, face tingling, muscles relaxed, nails painted a pretty pink, and still with cotton between her toes so that she had to walk on her heels, she followed Angel into ''the color room.''

''Aren't you the lucky one. You have lovely hair, sweetie,'' Angel said, running a hand through Jane's mop of shoulder-length, stick-straight hair. ''Healthy, thick. The basic style is enchanting, if a little overgrown. We'll keep it simple, no bangs, an off-set part, and then just a sleek sweep of hair to that wonderful chin. You'll adore it. Perfect for summer, very low maintenance. But it needs . . . something else. Don't you think?''

"It does?" Jane asked, sliding her eyes to the left, to look at the strands of plain, light brown hair he still held out in his manicured fingers. "Like what?"

Angel let go of her hair and stepped back, looked at her consideringly. "Texture," he pronounced. "Shading. Highlights. Yes, that's it—highlights. A little . . . boost."

"A little boost?" Jane repeated nervously. "How little a boost? I don't know . . ."

"Look here, sweetie," Angel went on, taking her hands as he led her beneath one of the bright lights in the ceiling. "Do you see my hair? Do you see the color? Black. Unremitting black. So . . . dull. So I fixed it. But the changes are subtle. I'm too tall for you to see the top, aren't I? Let me step under this light to show you. See? Just a bit of highlighting here, on top, very understated, and the whole look changes. Do you see it now?"

Jane stood on tiptoe and looked at the top of Angel's head. "Nice," she said, her vocabulary having pretty much shrunk to words of one syllable beginning the moment she'd walked into the salon. "But that's red, yes?"

"Yes, sunburst red. Not for you, darling, definitely not for you. But look here," he said, indicating a large chart on the wall and the swatches of differently colored hair. There must have been a hundred different shades, a rainbow of hair.

"You want me to get a dye job," Jane said, nodding.

Angel winced as if in real pain, then leaned close to whisper, "No, no, never say that word, darling. You'll be getting a *color*."

"Uh-huh," Jane said, biting her lip once more. "Okay. If you think so. What dye, um, color am I getting?"

"What do you like? What catches your eye?"

Jane panicked. "You're not going to help me?"

"Certainly I'll help you. Here. As your own hair is a fine light brown, I'd say we choose from these," he said, waving one hand over a collection of about two dozen shades of light brown that lightened all the way to blond. "Not red, not with your coloring, although you certainly do look pretty in pink. Oh! That was a movie, wasn't it? And wouldn't you just *die* to have Molly Ringwald's lips?'' He pushed out his own lips, pouted at her.

Jane didn't say anything, because she was pretty sure all she'd be able to come up with would be, ''Huh?'' Angel fascinated her, and she was already half in love with him.

He gave a shake of his head. ''Never mind that, sweetie. I'm rambling, shame on me. Shall we go on? We want to go cool blonds. Pick two, darling. The more shades we use, the more natural the end result. Definitely lighter shades. Especially for the summer. Sun washed. Subtle, but sun washed.''

Jane leaned close to the color chart. ''In high school, I used to comb hydrogen peroxide through my hair in the summer, then go out in the sun.'' She looked at Angel, who had gone rather pale. ''That probably wasn't a good idea, huh?''

''No, sweetie, that wasn't a good idea. Now, what do you like?''

Jane looked at the swatches again. Ran her fingers over them, wondered if they were real hair. ''I kinda like this one,'' she said nervously. ''And this one.''

''Caramel! And Butter Cream!'' Angel grabbed Jane in a hug that nearly lifted her off her feet, then put her down, cupped her shoulders in his hands. ''Oh, sweetie, you're going for *drama!* And you're *so right!* Subtle?'' He gave his own cheek a small slap. ''Shame on me. What could I have been thinking?'' He took a deep breath, closed his eyes, then let out his breath in an ecstatic sigh. ''We'll do chunks.''

''Chunks?'' Jane said, trying to imagine chunks of caramel and butter cream. Were they coloring her hair, or making candy?

''Yes, yes, chunks! Not subtle shadings. Splashes of color. Startling. Full of pizzazz. Chunks on the crown and sides, thick swatches of color, lightest at the face, then more subtle in the back. I can already see you.''

He let her go, then struck a pose, one hand on his hip, the other high in the air. ''Look at me, I'm here! Fake and proud of it! Oh, sweetie—*drama.*''

''Oh. Drama,'' Jane said, closing her eyes and giving in to her fate. ''Well, okay. If . . . if you say so . . .''

Marion Romanowski was watering the red and white geraniums she had planted out front when John emerged from the house, carrying three of his five new suitcases. She blinked, thinking the sun had distorted her vision, then said quite slowly and distinctly, ''Oh . . . my . . . *God.*''

John put down the suitcases and turned in a full circle for his aunt's benefit.

He knew what he looked like: six feet six inches, two hundred and forty pounds of pure, unadulterated *nerd.*

He had chosen to wear a pair of his new brown, just a tad too short cuffed slacks, and topped them with a brown-and-pink-plaid, short-sleeved dress shirt buttoned to the neck. His belt was black and had a silver horseshoe buckle with a horse head on it. His shoes were the brown penny loafers, with white socks.

He wore the plastic, black-rimmed glasses with the white adhesive tape on the bridge, and he had slicked down his thick black hair with some greasy stuff he'd found in a jar in his aunt's bathroom, finishing it with a side part.

He'd put on a brown bow tie spotted with pink, but decided that might be pushing it, so the bow tie was now stuffed in his pants pocket, in case he changed his mind.

Aunt Marion continued to stand there, drowning the geraniums with the garden hose, her mouth dropped open.

''Hello, ma'am,'' John said in a faintly nasal, sing-song voice as he smiled at her. ''I'm Professor Romanowski, here for the Sixth Annual Intellectual Retreat? I've reserved a suite. No-smoking rooms, of course. And I do hope you have unscented soap? Allergies, you understand. I checked on-line, with the Weather Channel, and the pollen count seems manageable here in New Jersey, and I've got my inhalers, but scented soap invariably increases my mucus production."

Aunt Marion turned off the hose, then covered her mouth with one hand as, her eyes wide, her shoulders began to shake. She made a few unintelligible sounds, then gave in and burst into laughter. "You . . . You can't really plan to say that," she got out between giggles. "Inhalers? Mucus production? Oh, John, no."

"Too much?"

"You were miles beyond too much before you opened your mouth," Aunt Marion said, shaking her head. "Seriously, John, I think you've gone too far. Senator Harrison won't recognize you, connect your name with Maryjo. I barely recognize you myself. And I mean, those slacks, that shirt—and the mucus—have all got to go."

"I've got a sweater vest I could put over the shirt," John suggested, reaching for one of the suitcases. "It's one of those that's sort of checked all over. You know, it looks like a big argyle sock?"

"Don't you dare," Aunt Marion said, pointing at him. "You just march yourself back inside and let me see what you've packed. Because you've forgotten something, nephew. You aren't *built* like a nerd. I mean, look at your forearms. Muscles. All right, hair and muscles. And those shoulders? Your body looks like what you are, a man who works out every day. Nerds don't work out, John. I'm sure of it. You don't get muscles typing on keyboards or moving chess pieces. Someone with half a brain will spot you for a fake the moment you get into that terrible swimming suit."

John looked down at his forearms, sighed. "You really think I'm over the top with this?"

"Over the top, over the mountain, over the *moon,*" Aunt Marion said, pushing him toward the door. "You've had your fun, John Patrick, and I've stood back and let you play because it took your mind off Senator Harrison and Maryjo for a while; but now it's my turn."

"I'm doing this for the sake of a country that doesn't deserve a bastard like Harrison. This has nothing to do with Maryjo."

"Lie to yourself, John Patrick, but don't lie to me."

He picked up the suitcases, knowing there was no come-back he could conjur that would make his aunt believe his lies. "Can I at least keep the glasses?" he asked as his aunt gave him another push toward the door.

"If you lose the tape, yes," she said, the voice of authority, and sweet reason.

"How about the hair?"

Aunt Marion rolled her eyes. "You can keep the hair *and* the glasses. You look like the gypsy king version of Clark Kent, and that's not so bad. But that shirt has to go, and the slacks, and those white socks. Definitely the white socks. You can donate all those new clothes to a home for homeless nerdy persons, or give them to the Rabbit's owner, or some-thing like that. You're going there in disguise, John, not in costume. This is a retreat, not a Halloween party. Surely you can learn how to be dull and boring and nonthreatening without all the rest of this nonsense."

"Yes, ma'am," John said, and let his aunt take charge. "As long as I'm out of here in about twenty minutes. I'm meeting my companion in D.C. at eleven."

"Yes, and if you don't want her to run screaming into the mists, you'll let me repack for you."

"You're a real spoilsport, Aunt, you know that?"

"Somebody has to be with you, John Patrick," she said, removing his glasses and beginning to unwind the adhesive tape. "Somebody has to be."

Chapter Three

Jane was sure she had been more nervous sometime in her life, although, at the moment, she couldn't remember when, or for what reason.

She was so nervous that she actually opened her mouth to call Molly back as her cousin walked to her Mercedes illegally parked at the curb, to drive off to her weekly salon appointment, leaving Jane standing just inside the large window of Taylor's D.C. Escorts, trapped like a mouse in a cage.

Molly, in her usual dramatic fashion, had only moments earlier enlisted the agency owner, Imogene, in a rousing rendition of "I Am Woman," urging Jane to roar.

"Roar," Jane had bleated quietly, knowing Molly wouldn't quit unless she answered her.

"Oh, that's pitiful. Imogene, isn't that pitiful? *Roar,* Janie. You are woman, you must *roar.*"

So she'd roared. Sort of. And Molly, satisfied at last, had deserted her for Rafael, and Imogene was busy now, on the phone with another client.

It was Saturday, the opening day of the New Jersey retreat.

In two days, Molly would take charge at the day care and nursery school, which would be open only until Tuesday evening, then close for the next twelve days. Two days with Molly in charge. What could even her scatterbrained cousin do to destroy six years of hard work in just two short days?

Jane's stomach did a small flip.

Okay, so she'd never been so nervous before in her life.

At least she looked good. Molly had told her she looked good, and that really meant something, passing Molly's fashion acid test.

She had on a short, flowered skirt and a soft lime green sleeveless sweater thingie that barely covered her belly button. Little "skimmer" sandals made of the world's softest leather. Herringbone weave gold chain at her neck, one circling her right arm, another around her left ankle. Not flashy, just "rich looking," as Molly had said.

Molly had even commandeered her watch, the one with the alligator band and large round face with the second hand—which, being waterproof, glue proof, and mostly plastic, was so right for the nursery school—and replaced it with a fourteen karat gold sliver of a thing that left Jane's wrist feeling almost naked. And definitely expensive.

But it was the hair. Angel's fantastic cut and those "chunks" had kept Jane looking in any mirror she passed. Mirrors on the wall, the little mirror on one of the infant activity centers hanging over the cribs, the mirror in her car—even her reflection now in the window of the escort service.

She loved the way her hair now "swung" with her whenever she moved, then sleekly fell back into place. She loved the way she could even tuck it behind her ears as she leaned over one of the babies, changing diapers. And she especially loved the colors. Caramel and Butter Cream. Bands of both colors, mixed with her own unremarkable hair, giving her hair a whole new look, her face a whole new look. Caramel and Butter Cream? Who knew what a little color could do? Angel, obviously.

There was also her makeup. Once Angel had finished with her, he'd escorted her to the very private makeup area and placed her in the care of Yvette, another genius with color. Jane now had a whole makeup bag filled with goodies Yvette had selected for her, then taught her how to apply so that she looked "natural." It was amazing how much makeup a person needed to put on to look "natural."

But Jane had practiced with the products, and she had to admit that the time spent seemed well worth the effort.

She was smoothed and painted, cut and styled, powdered and lipsticked, and dressed head-to-toe in casual clothes that had nothing casual about their price tags.

Armor. That's what it was. Protective armor as she went forth into battle, to slay big bad Senator Harrison and come home with the trophy of Knowing What The Great Man Is Going To Do.

Jane could have been nervous about her assignment, but she wasn't. Not really. For one, she didn't have to succeed, just try, to satisfy Molly. And two, she was a good conversationalist, and she certainly had always been the sort people seemed to like to confide in, tell their innermost secrets to— whether she wanted to hear them or not.

It was John Romanowski who scared her.

Scared her no matter how many times Molly and her friend Imogene had told her that Romanowski only wanted a female to hang on his arm because everyone else would come as a couple—sort of like Noah's Ark, Molly had said. He wouldn't expect anything else. No hanky-panky. No groping. Separate rooms. Purely business.

On and on and on, they'd assured and then reassured her. It was just business as usual. Why, Imogene's agency had provided a total of five companions just for this retreat.

So why was she so nervous? Had she actually not given up all her dreams of an adventure somewhere in her humdrum life, dreams of a handsome prince riding up on his sleek white stallion one fine day (okay, driving up in his BMW) and carrying her away? Did she still harbor romantic fantasies, believe in fairy tales? Did she really hope, some-where deep inside her, that this week could be magical in some way?

Was she that silly? Had the caramel and butter cream somehow seeped inside her head and turned her brain mushy?

Anything was possible.

Or maybe just being around eighty children, five days a week, ten hours a day, had finally gotten to her. She probably should stop showing the *Cinderella* and *Sleeping Beauty* videos to all those impressionable young kids.

So, no Prince Charming. Just a man. And, just like a man, he was late.

Jane looked at her new watch yet again, had to squint, actually, to see the little gold hands on the mother-of-pearl face, and then looked out at the street once more. Oh, yes, he was late. A good forty minutes late. So late that even Molly, who'd really wanted to see him, had had to leave. She couldn't miss her standing appointment at the salon, Lord knew. The poor thing might have to spend a week looking only ninety-nine-point-nine percent gorgeous.

"He's probably been held up in traffic. He's coming in from Virginia, just like you did. I told you that, right? Good thing you drove up to stay with Molly last night. Would you like a cup of tea?" Imogene asked as she walked by, carrying a stack of folders that probably held names of clients, most of them government types, Molly had told her, who were always looking for a "female to drape on their arm" for political functions.

What a world. A guy could get enough votes to earn himself a trip to Washington, but he couldn't find a date on his own? It sort of shook her confidence in the men who voted up or down on important domestic issues like roads, and school lunch programs, and welfare moms. Wasn't one of the new "brilliant plans" to get welfare moms to marry? And this from a bunch of guys in powerful places who couldn't even find themselves their own Saturday night dates?

What a world. . . .

Jane leaned closer to the glass as a car pulled up and parked in the same illegal space outside the agency. She had bought a used one very much like it when she'd turned sixteen. Bright yellow, just like this one. A fully restored 1984 Volkswagen Rabbit convertible. Man, she hadn't seen one of those in years. The black convertible top was up, making the thing look somewhat like a bumblebee with a VW logo on its nose, and she couldn't really see the driver.

Had to be a kid. Who else would drive one of those things?

The driver side door opened, and one long leg came out, followed by the rest of a slowly unbending male body.

Nope. Definitely not a kid. This was a man's body. Absurdly tall. Muscular. And, when he bent over, reaching back into the car for something, a darn nice butt.

Oh, yes, the body was good, if too big. How many times had the guy heard the joke, "How's the weather up there?" Probably a *lot.*

But there was something a little off about the clothes. No socks and tan docksiders. That was okay; she'd always wondered how people could stand having their bare feet stuck against equally bare leather, but it was okay. She'd even tried it once herself, except that she had felt the need to sprinkle some baby powder inside her shoes, and every time she had taken a step she'd sent up little clouds of white powder.

But black dress slacks? Pleated dress slacks? And his green-and-blue-striped cotton shirt buttoned all the way to the neck?

He looked . . . uncomfortable.

Designer clothes (Molly could be blamed for getting her to look for such things), but too neat and pressed, and too formal to ever be thought casual. *Wrong* somehow. The clothes didn't match the body. He had the kind of body that would have looked great in khakis and a soft knit shirt opened at the neck. He was . . . He was just too buttoned up . . . as if he were trying to look casual, but just didn't quite know how.

But it was the face that got to her. Good face. Handsome face. Except he had on these really ugly black-rimmed plastic glasses. And that shiny black hair? What did he slick it down with? Axle grease?

He looked to be in his early thirties, definitely too old to be driving a Volkswagen Rabbit unless he was a vintage Volkswagen aficionado—and were there really many of them in this entire world, unless they were overage hippy potheads in search of a psychedelic VW bus?

Look at those arms. Hairy arms. Nicely muscled arms. Good shoulders, too. A stomach as flat as Angel's.

Definitely not her type. She liked blonds. She liked her men a little shorter, their builds less athletic. Less hairy. Less, okay, less overpoweringly *male,* even if it was in a nerdy sort of way.

The guy slid back into the driver's seat, and Jane relaxed. Good, he was leaving. She'd begun to worry that he was Professor John Romanowski, but obviously he wasn't.

He reached for the overhead roof release latches, then pushed the button that would slide the roof back into the boot, the well built for it behind the backseat. Jane knew what he was doing, and it was a good day to have the top down, bright and sunny. He'd just pulled over to stretch those absurdly long legs and put the top down.

She also recognized the slight hesitation as the mechanism struggled to work, then finally quit with the top only halfway down.

Her roof had stuck, just like this one. Was this her old Rabbit, the already vintage one she'd traded in at seventeen for a much zippier Mustang after Molly laughed for a full ten minutes when she was tossed out of the latest summer camp her parents had sent her to and she saw the Rabbit? Or did they all do that?

The guy got out of the car again, his lips moving in what Jane was pretty sure were some choice curse words, and began pushing at the roof.

"Hey, don't do that! You'll just make it worse," Jane said, banging on the window. But he didn't hear her, so she grabbed her purse, nearly tripped over her luggage, and headed out to the pavement to repeat, "Hey, don't do that, you'll just make it worse."

He didn't even turn around. "Not yet, I haven't. Wait until I rip it off and throw it in the street. *That* will make it worse."

"Just like a man," Jane said on a sigh. "Okay, break it. Take a beautifully restored 1984 Rabbit and destroy it. Why not?"

Now he turned around and looked at her owlishly through the thick lenses of his ugly glasses. "You know what this is?"

"Of course I know what it is," she said, using her calm, unflustered Miss Jane voice, the one she used when one of her little charges presented her with a dead bug for Show and Tell . . . or even a live one. But it wasn't easy. Up close, the man was even bigger than she'd thought. Really big.

But she pressed on: "It might even be mine, if you bought it in Fairfax, which I doubt. But the mechanism is still probably the same. Now, move away like . . . That is, now move away, please, and let me help."

Good Lord, she'd almost said "move away like a good boy." Molly was right, she'd been knee-deep in kids *way* too much.

The not so good boy looked at her as if ready to say something smart—as in smart-assed—and then looked at the window of the agency.

Jane turned around as well, in time to see Imogene pointing to the Ape, and then to her, and smiling.

"You're John Romanowski?" Jane asked, just as he asked, "You're Jane Preston?"

Each question pretty much answered the other, and they both continued to look at each other for a few moments.

"Good. Very good," John Romanowski said at last, nodding his head.

Bad. Very bad, Jane thought to herself, even as she pinned a bright smile on her face. *I wanted a prince and didn't get one. I didn't even get a frog. Oh, no. Look what I got. Me and the Ape, for a whole week, in New Jersey. Him Tarzan, me Jane. Oh, God! Where was my brain when I said yes to this? What could I have been thinking?*

"Hello? Knock, knock. You in there?"

"Oh," Jane said, shaking herself back to attention. "I'm sorry, did you say something?"

"I did, yes. I said, so," the Hairy Ape said, standing up very straight, almost as if he was both horse and rider and had just reined himself in, "you're to be my companion for the week. And you know something about Baby? I must say, that's wonderfully fortunate."

Jane looked at John, then at "Baby," and sighed. "Let me guess. We're going to drive all the way to New Jersey in that, aren't we?"

"Not as it is, no," John said, pushing at the bridge of those awful glasses. "But as you've so kindly volunteered your services as mechanic?"

"Oh, brother," Jane said, wiping her hands together. "Okay, okay, I'll do it." She gave John a sickly smile as he held open the driver's side door for her, and she slipped behind the wheel. "This might not work the way it did with my Rabbit, but God knows somebody has to give it a shot."

So saying, she measured two hands' widths from the steering wheel, then with the side of her fist, gave the dashboard three hard whacks, then hit the lever again.

The top went down.

"Amazing. Something to do with physics, I'm certain," John said as she got out of the car, dragging the boot cover with her from the backseat.

"It's nothing," she said, tossing the boot cover at him.

"Just a little something I picked up from The Fonz on *Happy Days* reruns. If it worked for a juke box, why not a convertible top? The rest is up to you. I'll go get my luggage."

And, if she was smart, bribe Imogene to show her the back door of the place so she could make her getaway.

"He's not so bad," Imogene said when Jane pushed her way into the agency, still muttering under her breath.

"Yeah. His knuckles don't quite drag on the ground," Jane grumbled, grabbing her luggage, piling one of the two smaller cases on top of the large, wheeled one. "So much for any thoughts of this woman doing any roaring this week. And did you see those clothes, those glasses? That *hair?* Not just an ape, but an uptight ape. All he needs is a plastic pocket protector full of leaky pens. To think that Molly worried that my wardrobe wasn't up to snuff. If she got one look at that guy out there, her American Express would get whiplash, she'd be pulling it out of her purse so fast."

"I'm sure you know what you're talking about, dear," Imogene said. "But don't be in such a rush. You still have to sign these contracts."

Jane let go of the handle of her suitcase. "Contracts? What contracts?"

"Oh, nothing big. Just a list of ground rules, meant to protect you mostly, Jane, and even to protect me, in case Professor Romanowski decides you don't fit his needs. That's the agency contract, and the professor has already signed his copy. Then there's his."

"He's got needs? Like what? What exactly are his *needs?*"

"A pretty, smiling face. A good conversationalist. A good dancer, hopefully. And that you sign this confidentiality agreement he drew up, which says that you will not in any way try to profit from this week, other than your fee."

"Gimme those," Jane said, taking the papers Imogene held in her hands. It took only a minute to read through the agency contract, which seemed pretty standard, if selling yourself as a companion to a stranger for a week could be considered anybody's notion of standard operating procedure. She bent over the desk, using the pen Imogene had handed her, and signed the agency contract.

It was the second sheaf of papers, the ones stapled together under the letterhead of a Fairfax law office, that worried her. There were a lot of "whereas"es and "whatfor"'s and "in consideration of"'s, but the bottom line, Jane was pretty sure, had to do with the fact that she would be open to civil litigation if she ever breathed one word of anything that had gone on during the retreat.

She was not to profit from any information that might come her way, reveal any secrets she might learn, or take any photographs or confiscate any other "evidence" to prove that she had been to the retreat at all.

Was the guy nuts?

What would Molly have done? She'd planned to go to the retreat to get a story, certainly to "gain" from that story. Would she have signed this agreement?

In a heartbeat. To Molly, consequences were what happened to everybody else, not her.

Jane, who knew she'd never gotten away with anything in her entire life, threw the papers on the desktop. "I'm not signing this."

"Why?" John said from behind her. "Are you planning on selling the story of your week to the tabloids?"

"Don't be ridiculous," Jane countered, whirling to face him . . . one frivolous brain cell in her agitated head taking note that, yes, her hair did swing back into place quite nicely. "I will not—repeat, will not—sign this ridiculous agreement. Either you trust me, Professor Romanowski, or you don't."

Just to make herself perfectly clear, she then picked up the three-page agreement and ripped it neatly in half. She thought the act to be very dramatic.

And then she panicked.

For someone who had wanted to bolt moments ago, she'd

suddenly realized that she wanted this. Wanted the week, wanted the possible intrigue, wanted the adventure. So she waited, her heart thudding in her throat, for the man to speak.

John lifted one hand, undoubtedly to push his fingers through his hair, but stopped as his fingertips initially contacted his slicked-down patent leather head, instead balling the fingers into a fist and slowly lowering his arm.

"I have my computer with me and can print out another copy."

"And I can rip up another copy," Jane said, knowing her lower jaw was jutting out, so that she probably looked very much like little Merilee Chapman, whose middle name should have been Belligerent rather than Belinda. At least she didn't add "So there," as Merilee would have done. Would she get a gold star for restraining herself? Probably not.

"All right, Ms. Preston. You seem an honest sort, and I am desperate, unfortunately. I'll take you at your word."

Jane blinked twice and swallowed hard, trying to get her heart back down her throat. "You will? Wow, Merilee may have something there."

"I beg your pardon?"

Jane grinned, feeling pretty proud of herself. Although she restrained a roar. "Did I say something? I'm sorry, I guess I was just talking to myself."

"You do a lot of that?"

She shrugged. "I'm used to holding one-sided conversations, yes. With the babies, you understand."

John sliced a look at Imogene. "Explain, please."

"Certainly, Professor. I didn't have a chance to give you much in the way of background information on Miss Preston here, did I?"

"You said she was Ms. Applegate's cousin. I assumed she lived here in the District, possibly even worked with her in the Senate."

Jane's ears perked up. "In the Senate? She told you that? I mean, Molly told you about that?"

"Yes," John said. "That's what was on her information sheet. A junior member on one of the Senate staffs, although she wouldn't say which one, which is commendable, as it shows discretion."

"Or that she's smart enough not to make her fibs too specific," Jane mumbled under her breath as she bent to retrieve her overnight case. Nothing, not a single thing she could do this week could so much as put a patch on Molly and her fast and loose way with the truth. The last of Jane's fears disappeared.

John took a step closer to her. "I'm sensing that you're not happy?"

"Me? Hey, I'm happy. But I don't work with my cousin, I'm afraid. I live in Fairfax, where I own a combination day care center and nursery school. The center is closed next week, which is why I was able to step in and help when Molly couldn't . . . couldn't fulfill her obligation. Is that a problem?"

His frown told her it was. Well, tough beans.

"No. No problem. I reside near Fairfax myself. Teach a few courses at one of the local universities."

Jane would have asked which one, but she really didn't care. It was enough that the man was a college professor. It even made sense, a little. He dressed in what many would think of as a college professor's idea of summer vacation clothes. It was only the body that was so jarring, so very "unprofessorlike."

"Really," she said, putting on her professional voice. "What do you teach?"

"Political Science," John said, picking up the remainder of Jane's suitcases as if they'd been packed with feathers. "Shall we go?"

Jane wondered if the man ever spoke more than three words at a time; getting information from him was like pulling teeth. She gave Imogene a weak wave, then followed John outside to the Rabbit. "How did you get to be invited to the retreat, Professor?" she asked as he stowed her luggage in the trunk, beside some truly horrible luggage that had to be his.

"I'm not sure. I have written a few articles for some journals. Perhaps that's it. And, please, call me John. A week is too long a time to remain formal."

Okay, he'd given her—she did a mental recount—five whole sentences. Was this progress? She'd try to get him to say something else. "How interesting. Would these be political articles?"

"No, organic gardening," he said, then seemed to bite the inside of his cheek, trying to take back his wiseacre response. "I'm sorry, Ms. Preston—Jane. My . . . My allergies are acting up, and I seem to be in a foul mood. Forgive me. Yes, of course, political articles. Although I am far from being in agreement with the current administration. I believe I may have been invited for just that reason—as this week will be centered on a free and open exchange of ideas, you understand. It's a commendable approach to governing."

"How . . . interesting," Jane said, settling herself in the front passenger seat, wishing she'd brought a scarf, because Angel's free and easy hairstyle was really going to be put to the test once they were out on the highway, going at least sixty-five miles per hour . . . or however fast the Rabbit could hop.

"Are you very political, Jane?" John asked as he slipped the key into the ignition, the engine turning over after only three tries.

"Should I be?" she answered carefully. She was trying to get this man's measure, but it wasn't working. It was as if he were two different people, each vying to be in charge.

"Probably not," he said, and turned to smile at her.

Her stomach did a small flip. She hadn't noticed his eyes until now. How had she missed them? They were glorious. Not cornflower. But, then again, not teal blue, either. Blue-green was one of her favorite Crayola colors, but they weren't quite that, either. Turquoise blue? That was closer. It was difficult to believe, but Crayola, even in its "Big

Box'' ninety-six crayon pack, hadn't quite captured the color of John Romanowski's gorgeous bedroom eyes.

Jane gave herself a small mental shake, knowing it definitely was time to get her mind out of the Crayola box, and the bedroom, and pretend to be interested in this guy's mind instead of his eyes. "You, um, you said you aren't in agreement with the current administration? Is the President going to be at the retreat?"

"So far, no, but that could change at any time." He grinned at her again. "But don't worry, I won't tackle him and hold him down until he agrees not to allow any more off-shore drilling."

"Too bad," Jane said, settling back against the seat, which shifted ominously, as if it might collapse into the backseat, but then seemed to steady again. "You could hold him down, and I could describe the damage to sea life and bird sanctuaries. If you can find me some crayons, I could even draw him a few pictures, although I'd probably need an extra-black crayon."

"That's also probably not a very good idea."

Jane managed a weak grin. "No, I didn't think so."

It was quiet inside the Rabbit for a while, until they'd been on the highway for at least ten minutes.

"I want to thank you for not making me sign that agreement," Jane said at last, over the sound of trucks whizzing past on their way north.

"I decided I could trust you," he answered, changing lanes, as if the Rabbit could actually keep up with the vehicles winging by at eighty miles an hour. He just as quickly returned the car to the right lane, his lips tight, his knuckles white on the steering wheel, when a truck honked at him long and hard. "Guess I forgot myself for a moment there. Sorry."

"Forgot yourself?" Jane asked, looking over at the truck as it zoomed past them. "How? Isn't this your car?"

He shot her a quick look. "No, it isn't. My real car is a Ferrari."

"Okay, sure it is. I'll bet it's red, too. Be careful, John. If you tell lies, your nose will grow," Jane grumbled, and turned on the radio, hoping to fill the hours between D.C. and Cape May with something other than her perfectly natural questions and his smartass answers.

By the time the Rabbit was heading up I-95, John was beginning to think he'd made a mistake. All right, lots of mistakes. That's what happened when someone lived so long and so closely with a fiction writer's imagination. They began to see the whole world as a book plot.

Except, with his plots, he could maneuver the characters around, regulate the action, and come out at the other end of a million improbabilities, all appearing seemingly logical, and even smelling like a rose, all the way to the *NYT*.

If Aunt Marion were here, and sometimes he could swear she'd found a way to shrink, become invisible, and perch on his shoulder, she'd whisper those mistakes into his ear.

One, the nerd idea, even downplayed to only seminerd. It really wasn't him. He couldn't carry it off for a whole week. Hell, he couldn't carry it off for ten minutes. It was one of those good in theory, lousy in execution ideas.

Two, bringing along a companion.

Three—and only a hop, skip, and a jump from the nerd part—trying to remember to rein in his smart mouth, which he hadn't been able to do in thirty-three years.

Four, lying to this very cute little teacher-lady beside him.

Finally—and this was his part of the list, the solving the problem part—giving serious thought to telling her the truth, parking this heap at some car rental agency and picking up a vehicle that actually had some acceleration, stopping at a store and buying all new clothes, and starting over from scratch.

But that would mean he had to, one, reveal who he really was, which he never did and, two, hope prim and proper little Miss Nursery School Teacher would still agree to going along for the ride.

He'd give it until they were off I-95, then either bite the bullet and stay in character (which he wasn't pulling off so well to this point), or tell her the truth, lay it all out, and hope she was intrigued by the idea of being a "research assistant" to a best-selling author.

Tell her he was J. P. Roman?

He'd really do that?

Hell, no.

Okay, so he wasn't going to tell her the *whole* truth. But he could tell her some of the truth and sort of massage the rest. He wrote fiction; he could do this.

He'd keep thinking about it, maybe all the way to Cape May.

They'd just turned onto the Atlantic City Expressway when the sun scuttled behind a single large black cloud that immediately opened up, sending a downpour that seemed to be specially aimed at the Rabbit.

John had two choices. He could ignore the rain, hoping it would stop in a few minutes, or he could pull over and let Jane put the top back up.

The John he was, really was, would rather chew nails than let a woman show him up mechanically. The John he was pretending to be, the now only slightly nerdy professor, would be oblivious to the rain, until he was sitting ankle deep in it.

"John?" Jane said, breaking into his latest thoughts that suddenly had a lot to do with the fact that in his Ferrari, they would have been in Cape May at least an hour ago. "It's raining, John."

The woman seemed to be in total command of the obvious.

"Really?" he said, smiling a teeth-gritted grin as he blinked raindrops out of his eyes. "I hadn't noticed."

"You've turned on the windshield wipers," Jane pointed out reasonably, and for the twentieth time, John wished

Molly Applegate hadn't backed out on their deal at the last minute.

A Senate staffer he could use; she was going to be the perfect "in" for him. A nursery school teacher, however physically appealing, was about as useful as the canvas top was, folded down in the boot; and the only way she could help him would be if he had some burning desire to refresh himself on counting to one hundred or relearning how to tie his shoes.

Since he had a calculator, and wore loafers, that meant that Jane Preston was no use to him. No use at all. And he'd been thinking about telling her the truth? She'd probably look at him with condemning teacher eyes, rap his knuckles with a ruler, and send him off to stand in a corner.

Although she might also be able to put up the top before they were both soaked to the skin.

He pulled over to the right shoulder and stopped the car. "I'm sure the rain will stop soon, but I'll unsnap the boot cover for you," he said, getting out of the car.

"And I'll push the button," Jane said, wiping rainwater from her cheeks.

She looked kind of cute. Her hair all damp and her eyelashes sort of clumped together in the rain. Although maybe he ought to tell her that her mascara was smudging under her eyes, and she was beginning to look like a cute, fairly unhappy raccoon.

Nah. Let her figure it out for herself.

He ripped off the boot cover and tossed it into the backseat, then crawled over the trunk, across the backseat, and neatly swung under the roll bar and into his own seat again. "You may fire when ready, Gridley."

"I have been," Jane told him, pushing her damp hair back behind her ears. "Firing, that is."

"You have? Okay, then thump on the dash."

She sent him a look that should have dried his wet hair and damp shirt. "I did."

"You did?" he asked, wondering how a nerdy professor

would handle this one. On his own, being himself, he'd be banging both fists on the dashboard by now. Maybe jumping up and down on it.

"It isn't working. Nothing's working. How much farther do we have to go?"

He shrugged, then reached across her and pulled the map out of the glove box. The map was wet within moments, and she helped him open it, holding it open against the wind and now-driving rain.

"About an hour," she said at last, as he pretended to have no clue how to read a map. "But in this thing? Maybe twice that long. We're going to drown."

"You're being both pessimistic, Jane, and inaccurate. The sun may come out again any moment, for one, and the amount of precipitation necessary to fill this entire car would mean at least, conservatively, thirty-six inches of rain falling in two hours. Not to mention the fact that we're roofless, so that our chests and heads would not be submerged in any case. Therefore, I think—"

She balled up the sodden map and threw it at him . . . and he suddenly liked her again.

"I do hope you'll be able to better contain your temper while we're at the retreat, Jane," he said, stifling a smile as he wadded up the map even more and tossed it into the backseat. "We'll be in the presence of very distinguished and probably quite straitlaced persons, you understand."

She folded her arms across her waist. "I promise not to drip on any of them, *John*. Now would you please just shut up and drive?"

"Is that how you talk to your students?"

"They aren't students. They're children. And they know enough to get in out of the rain, which is more than I can say for you. I'll bet you're Mensa. Brains out the wazoo, but without the sense to get in out of the rain. And, in case you're still not sure how I feel, let me say it outright—I don't like brainy types. Especially hairy ones."

So saying, Jane pushed her hands through her dripping

hair, turned face front, crossed her arms, and sort of *slammed* her body against the back of the seat . . . which completely gave way, so that she was suddenly lying prone, staring up at the rain.

"Don't . . . say . . . a word," she gritted out from between clenched teeth, her arms still folded at her waist, her marvelous eyes locked on his like twin laser beams.

"I wouldn't think of it," John answered, trying not to choke on his suppressed laughter.

"Good. Now drive. Just . . . drive."

"Don't . . . Don't you want to see if I can fix the seat?"

"No, thank you, I'm fine," Jane said, still lying on her back, blinking at the rain.

"Are you sure? Because it's held in place by a two-by-four, and I could just—"

"*No,* thank you."

Stubborn little thing.

"Do you think it's safe to ride like that?"

"I've got my seat belt on."

"Well, yes, you do, but . . . but you're flat on your back. Wouldn't it be better if you hopped into the backseat? I mean, the part that's behind my seat?"

"No. I like it here. The rain's slowing up, the sun's coming out, and there should be a lovely rainbow any moment now. I like rainbows."

John ran his tongue over his bottom lip, then said, "You hate me, don't you?"

Slowly, she turned her head, looked up at him again with those huge raccoon-ringed hazel eyes. "Don't be ridiculous. You couldn't have known the top would break, or the seat would break. Could you? Oh, wait a moment. Yes, you could. Because it's *your car.*"

"You're raising your voice now, Jane," John pointed out, trying so hard not to laugh. "Do you raise your voice at the children in your nursery school?"

"No. I just boil their little butts in oil. Now, would you please drive?"

John shifted into Drive, then slid the gear back into Park. "No. I can't let you ride all the way to Cape May like that. Let me at least try to fix the seat."

"If you insist," she said at last, and undid her seat belt, hauled herself forward, opened the door, and stepped out onto the shoulder of the road. Dare he tell her that her sodden sweater was clinging to her in a way that made him appreciate rain more today than he ever had in his entire life?

Probably not.

Keeping his mouth firmly shut, he got out of the car and walked around, looking for the two-by-four and then trying to figure out just how it had been braced under the back of the front seat.

While he was wiping rain from his face, and cursing inside his head, Jane got in behind the wheel and put the car in Drive. "Coming?" she asked, and her smile was so sweet and yet evil that John knew he had two seconds, tops, to get in the passenger seat or be left by the side of the road.

"They let you with children?" he asked as she sped down the shoulder, then neatly merged back into the traffic. He was holding on to the dashboard, doing his best not to slide into the backseat.

She turned to him and grinned, wickedly. "Your glasses are about to fall off."

He instinctively reached for them, taking both hands off the dashboard, and Jane put the gas pedal to the floor. The Rabbit didn't have a lot of acceleration, but it was enough to send John sliding into the backseat, where he stayed, quietly looking up at the rainbow overhead, because he was a smart man, and a smart man knew when he's been outsmarted.

Chapter Four

You're a terrible person. You've got a here-to-fore unmined streak of pure nasty in you, Jane told herself, even as she tried to pretend that John Romanowski wasn't sitting propped behind her in the backseat, his hairy bare ankles and Docksiders visible as he rested them on the laid-down front seat.

The sun had come out once more, and between the warmth of the day and the constant breeze circulating inside the car, she'd pretty well dried out.

But she hadn't really cooled down.

There was something going on here with John Romanowski. She wasn't sure what, but something was going on. He was like two people. One, a nerdy professor, dressed all wrong, talking like a very dry textbook. And the second, a sometimes funny, always sarcastic hairy hunk with laughter in his gorgeous eyes . . . and a way about him that all but screamed "I'm having fun here, but I'm the only one who knows the game we're playing."

Did he really think she hadn't noticed? That she was so

stupid that she couldn't sense that something was just a little bit "off" about him?

Did the man have no idea what sort of nose for mischief a woman had to develop when dealing with children? Children who could make Machiavelli and the Medicis look like playground losers?

Did she look as though she'd just dropped off the turnip truck? Fallen to earth in the last rain? Cut her wisdom teeth only yesterday? And any of the other ways her terribly polite and yet wonderfully sarcastic grandmother used to describe blooming idiots?

No, she didn't look like that. She didn't think she did, especially after Molly and Angel and Yvette had gotten hold of her. But she could. So she sneaked a quick glance at herself in the rearview mirror.

"Rats."

Okay, so she looked like a blooming idiot. The rain had teased every bit of natural curl back into her hair. It wasn't much, just enough to bend the hair in some places and frizz it in others. And her mascara was halfway down her cheeks. She looked like a madwoman.

Well, she was a madwoman.

Keeping one hand on the wheel—the Rabbit seemed to like to shimmy between forty and fifty miles per hour—she reached for her purse, then rooted in it for the feel of her handy travel pack of tissues.

Got it.

Ripping it open with her teeth—Easy opening packages? Who goes for patents on these things? Sadists?—she wiped at her cheeks. Spit on the tissue, wiped again.

Great. Not waterproof mascara, that was for sure. But indelible on the skin? Oh, yeah. She should have let Yvette talk her into new mascara while she was selling her everything else. But she'd had to put her foot down somewhere, pay for some things herself, and her own mascara was perfectly fine ... or at least she'd thought so.

Jane tossed the tissue back into her purse and concentrated on the road, and what she'd do next.

Behind her, John Romanowski *hovered*. Hunched. Hulked. And any other "H" word she could think of. She could write her own book: *Horton Hears A Hulk*.

Except she didn't hear anything. The Hulk was quiet. There was nothing but quiet from the backseat, and that's all there had been for almost twenty minutes.

What did the movie soldiers say just before the mortars came lobbing into their foxholes or the bad guys came storming up over the hill? She remembered. *Quiet, yeah. Too quiet.*

"What are you doing?" she asked, trying to catch a glimpse of him in the rearview mirror.

He didn't answer.

Oh, this was good. She'd killed him. He was probably at least unconscious, suffering hypothermia or something. It was always windier in the backseat of a convertible, right?

"John? Answer me."

Nothing.

"Not funny, John," she said, taking her eyes off the road only long enough to take a quick peek behind her.

Asleep.

How dare he fall asleep!

He should be angry. He should be yelling at her to pull over, change places with him, "let the *man* drive." He should be telling her she was fired, if not for commandeering the driver's seat, at least for that "Your glasses are going to fall off" stunt.

He should be telling her where the heck they were going, because she didn't have a clue.

Jane turned down the radio and, over the noise of the traffic—which now seemed to be made up mostly of huge, hulking and speeding buses on their way to the casinos—listened again.

Was that a snore? Was the man snoring?

He wouldn't dare!

Her fingers gripped the steering wheel with enough pressure to turn her knuckles white.

"Let's recap," she said out loud, since her only possible audience was unconscious. "You're on the Atlantic City Expressway, which leads to Atlantic City, not Cape May. You don't have a map anymore because the Incredible Hulk is sleeping on it. You look like you fell into the washer in the middle of the spin cycle, and you're not drip-dry. You've got that aforementioned comatose hairy hulk in the back seat, and you think you might just like him better that way. The top's still stuck in the boot, and it looks like it might rain again at any moment. So, Jane Preston, now that you've been named Most Oppressed Player in this little farce, what are you going to do now?"

She chanced a quick look at a large sign up ahead. "Ah, eureka, and all that good stuff."

The fates had answered all her questions for her, by way of a sign announcing that the Frank Farley rest stop was located three miles ahead. Food. Fuel. Restrooms.

All three of them sounded like a plan, if not necessarily in that order. She put the pedal to the floor, which meant the Rabbit could get to seventy, which seemed like the average cruising speed on the expressway; at least one decision made.

"I keep the keys," Raccoon Eyes said once she'd parked at the rest stop and John, who had been enjoying the ride, and the one-sided conversation, finally lifted himself from his prone position and looked around the parking lot.

"That sounds trusting," he said, grabbing the roll bar and levering himself out of the car without bothering with the door. "Where are we?"

"A rest stop outside of Atlantic City. Since Atlantic City is on the water, the next one isn't until Paris, so I figured we should stop here."

"Oh," he said, looking around the large parking lot. "I thought for sure we were going to Disney World."

He counted to three—that's all it took—before Little Miss Talks-to-Herself exploded.

"You . . . You weren't asleep!"

"And you like me comatose. Nice."

She narrowed her eyelids, which might have been less cute and more intimidating if she didn't still have mascara smudges under both eyes.

"I quit."

"Suit yourself. Funny. You didn't strike me as a quitter," John said, stepping past her and heading for the large brick building.

Just as he'd thought, she was after him in a second, all pent-up fury and tousled hair . . . and really cute. Really, really cute. Somehow even cuter, and more real, after the rain.

"I am *not* a quitter, John Romanowski. I have outlasted mothers who think their little cherubs came equipped with halos instead of pitchforks, and lived through finger painting with a group of twenty homicidal three-year-olds. I am a brick in a crisis, a refuge in times of trouble, and I can diaper a toddler as I'm chasing him across the room—one-handed, if necessary. What I do not do, John Romanowski, is continue beating my head against a brick wall once I've figured out that it hurts."

That stopped him. Maybe he'd misjudged the little dynamo and her one-sided conversation in the Rabbit. "You aren't enjoying yourself?" he asked, then waited for another explosion.

It never came.

She looked at the ground, then up at him, her bottom lip caught between her teeth. Then she sighed, smiled. "Actually, it's kind of funny, isn't it? I mean, the top stuck, the rain, tricking you into letting go of the dashboard?"

"Yes, I thought you probably got a real kick out of that last part," he said, taking her elbow and guiding her toward the building. "Come on, let's find ourselves something to eat. Then, once we're fed, we need to talk."

"Talk? About what?"

"Not cabbages and kings, I can tell you that. But there has been a change in plans. My plans, that is. Hear me out, and then we'll see if there's a change in yours, all right?"

"If you think you've just made any sense," Jane said, almost skipping to keep up with his longer strides, "let me be the first to tell you that you didn't. Although I must admit that I've been thinking that something didn't quite fit ever since we left D.C. Something about *you*, John. At least tell me this. Are we still going to Cape May?"

"I am," he said, holding open the door for her, rather pleased that she already had suspicions about him. This was a cute lady, and definitely not a dumb one. "Once we've talked? Well, you can tell me your plans then, okay?"

She stood inside the busy rest stop, people brushing past the two of them, heading for the restrooms, for the various food stands, the gift shop. "Am I going to like this?" she asked him.

"I wouldn't have thought so, no, at least not until your little soliloquy while you thought I was sleeping. But I'm betting now that you will. Finger painting? Diapering other people's kids? You'd like a little adventure in your life, wouldn't you, Jane?"

"That depends. Would it involve getting wet again?"

"I don't think so. I promise, I'll get the top back up, even if I have to call a mechanic and haul him out here. No, this has to do with Cape May and why I'm going there. Why, if you decide you still want to come along, you have been hired."

"You weren't telling the truth?" Jane put out her hands, waggled them as if erasing her question. "No, don't answer that, not yet. I already figured that out, about thirty miles back. Well, sort of. I figured out something; I'm just not sure what it is. I've got to go . . . wash my hands. Meet me right here in five minutes, okay?"

"It's a deal," John said, then watched as she walked toward the restrooms. Then he headed for the gift shop, to ask a few questions of one of the employees ... starting with finding out the location of the next exit and the nearest shopping mall and car rental agency.

When Jane rejoined him, he handed her a penny he'd put through a machine that elongated it into a bent oval. Why anyone would want to have a penny elongated into a bent oval escaped him, but there hadn't been anything else to do while he waited.

"What's this?" she asked, holding the coin in her outstretched palm.

"A peace offering?" he asked, shrugging.

"Well, thank you. But I'd rather have a hamburger if you're treating," she told him, heading for the food stand. "And a Coke. And whatever it is you're going to tell me."

He ordered for both of them and carried the food outside to the car. "We can have a picnic," he told her as she got into the driver's seat once more. "All the ants have drowned."

"You have ants in your car?" she asked as he handed the food to her, then shoved the two-by-four back under the passenger seat.

"Okay. That's a good enough place to start," he said, settling gingerly against the seat. "This isn't my car."

Her hazel eyes got round as saucers. He'd never quite understood that metaphor, or analogy, or whatever the heck it was—he was a writer, not an English major—but he understood it now. Jane Preston had huge eyes, adorably placed in her small face. He bet all the kids at the day care and nursery school adored her. If he were a kid, he'd be bringing her an apple every day. "This isn't your car? You *stole* it?"

"Borrowed it," he corrected, taking his hamburger and soda from her. "From one of my students."

"You borrowed it. From one of your students. At the college. O-kay." Jane unwrapped her hamburger and took a bite, offering her next question around a mouthful of meat and bun. "Why?"

He grinned. "Good question. And I have to tell you, Jane, I wish my answer was more logical."

Jane patted at her lips with a paper napkin, then ran her tongue over her top lip, probably to make sure she didn't have ketchup on her mouth. Oh, boy. Make that two apples every day, and tickets to a show, and maybe even dinner. Definitely dinner. He could spend hours watching her eat.

"That's all right, John," she then said, putting down the napkin and looking at him levelly, inviting his trust, he supposed. "Just tell me the truth. You'll feel much better, really, once you get it off your chest."

John pressed his own lips together, trying hard not to laugh. He was getting the hots for the schoolmarm. Who would have thunk it? "I didn't just stick some little girl's pigtail in an ink well and then lie about it, teach, honest," he said, chuckling.

A delightful pink blush invaded her cheeks. "Sorry. Old habits die hard, I guess. You were saying . . . ?"

"Right. Let me do this quick, okay? I mean, if I had hours to massage everything to where it makes me look good, I could do it; but I think I'd better just get this over with, and you can yell at me, and then we can sort out any details afterward."

"Then, you *did* steal this car?"

He waved both hands at her. "No. I really did borrow it. Scout's honor."

"Uh-huh. And your *real* car is a Ferrari."

"A red one, just like you guessed, yes."

"On a professor's salary?"

It sure hadn't taken long to get to the lying part, and John voiced the first one quickly, and probably too meekly. "I . . . I have inherited money."

Jane reached for the door handle. "Okay, I'm outta here," she said, and he quickly grabbed her arm.

"Hang on, Jane. I'm telling the truth now. Hell, I was

telling you the truth then; you just didn't know it,'' John said, still pretty sure he was much too amused for his own good, except for one small part of his conscience—the Aunt Marion part, probably—that told him his lie about the source of his income could be digging him an even bigger hole down the line.

Did he want to ''go down the line'' with Jane Preston? He didn't know the answer to that. He should know the answer, and the answer should be a quick and emphatic *no*. But as long as it wasn't, he wanted to keep her around, until he figured out *why* it wasn't.

''Please, Jane?''

She looked down at his hand until he removed it from her arm. ''You own a red Ferrari, and you decided to borrow this heap instead? And I'm supposed to believe you?''

''When you hear the rest of it, yes. And I know it's going to sound stupid, and it is stupid, so just please stay in the car and hear me out.''

She nodded. ''Okay. And I promise not to interrupt again, if you promise not to grab me again if I try to leave this car once you're done.''

''Deal,'' he said, his hands in the air. ''Totally hands-off, I promise.''

''Good, because you're an awfully big man, and I think I could be afraid of you.''

John pointed to his own chest, surprised. ''Me? You could be afraid of me? Man, I knew this nerd disguise could be tricky, but I didn't think I came off looking like a serial killer.''

''Back up,'' Jane said, twirling one hand at him. ''Nerd *disguise?* You mean you did—did *this*—on purpose?''

''Yeah. Pitiful, huh,'' he said, pulling off the eyeglasses, and feeling as stupid as he was pretty sure he still looked. ''But Aunt Marion toned it down before I left home. If you think this is bad, you should have seen me in my brown cuffed slacks and the adhesive tape around these glasses.

And the bathing suit I bought on-line is a real gem, I promise you.''

She ignored everything he said but one. ''Who is Aunt Marion? Your keeper?''

Now John put back his head and roared with laughter. ''Bing-o,'' he said after a few moments. ''Aunt Marion is my keeper. Look, just listen, all right?''

''I said I would, didn't I?''

''Yes, but then you—oh, never mind. Here goes. I'm a professor, just as I said. I got this invitation, just as I said. And I want to go to the retreat to gather information to write a book''—he sighed—''just as I didn't say.''

''A book,'' Jane said, folding the paper over the rest of her hamburger. ''You want to write a book. Everybody's writing something these days, aren't they? About what? I mean, what about? No, that isn't right, either. What do you want to write about in this book? Is that better?''

''I guess so. And the book would be nonfiction. I'm . . . I'm thinking about a political exposé.''

Now it was Jane's turn to laugh. ''An exposé? You're kidding, right? A professor writing an exposé?''

John forced a sheepish grin and let his fiction-writing mind go berserk. ''Yes, silly, isn't it? But I had this student in one of my classes last year, and he told me that his cousin's friend's father worked in the Senate and said that Senator Harrison is sitting on some sort of scandal that could ruin him politically, even personally. I've been researching him ever since. Extensively. For my book,'' he ended, eyeing her hopefully.

He watched as Jane's smile faded, along with all the color in her face. ''Senator—'' She coughed, twice. ''Did you say Senator Harrison? Senator Aubrey Harrison?''

John nodded. ''Yes, the senior senator from New Jersey. You know who he is?''

''Me?'' Jane made a face, shook her head. ''I mean, sure, I know he's a senator from New Jersey, and that maybe he's going to run for president. Everyone knows that—right?''

"Anyone who doesn't have their head up their—yeah, everyone knows that."

"Yes . . . yes, of course."

He looked at her curiously for a moment, something making his well-developed snoop senses tingle, then shook his head. The woman taught nursery school. You couldn't fake the way she just about *oozed* nursery school teacher from every pore.

Except when she was eating, like the way she was eating now. Ketchup had squeezed out from the hamburger bun, and she was in the process of licking it off her fingers, her palm. She was a very oral, very sensual woman . . . but he doubted she knew that. Which only made her more intriguing.

"Anyway," he continued, dragging his gaze away from her tongue, "I've been wanting to write a book for a long time—this book, on Harrison, actually—and then this invitation came to me through the college, and I found out he's one of the guests, and I thought, hey, here's my big chance to do a little more investigating of the man."

Jane cocked her head to one side, looked at him from between narrowed eyelids, then sighed. "Nope. You're still not making sense, John. Or does Senator Harrison know you, and that's why you dreamt up this . . . disguise?"

Okay, so he'd forgotten how smart the woman was, damn it. He couldn't tell her that the nerd disguise was in case someone just might recognize him as J. P. Roman, either before or after the fact. And then, even more importantly, there was Harrison himself, even though John hadn't seen the bastard since he'd been about twelve.

But he wrote fiction, which meant he could be a world-class liar, without breaking a sweat. "No, I don't know him, but I have been introduced to his nephew, Dillon Holmes, at a political seminar in Fairfax about five years ago. He's also going to be at the retreat, as the senator's guest. I . . .

I wasn't sure I wanted him to remember me. Although I doubt he would. I mean, I was just one more person in a sea of people, although I did engage him in a small debate over campaign finance reform. So maybe I just wanted to play at disguising myself. I guess I should be ashamed, huh?''

He shot her a quick look, to see if his sheepish idiot act was going over, but Jane didn't seem to be paying him or his act any attention. She had pressed both hands against her midsection as he spoke, and from the paleness of her cheeks, he was afraid for a moment that she might be really sick.

''Hey, are you all right?''

She nodded, then slowly raised her head to look at him. ''I don't think that hamburger agreed with me. But, yes, I'm all right. Except . . . except maybe for this buzzing in my ears. So now we've got the senator, and his nephew, and your book. Are you done yet?''

''I don't think so, no,'' John said, really worried about her now. ''I think I got a little carried away with my idea of being an undercover journalist type, getting the big story for my exposé. Not only did I take the nerd thing too far, I forgot that I'm just not the nerd type.''

''No kidding,'' Jane said, seeming to rally a little. ''You're built more like a jock than a nerd.''

John smiled. ''Why, thank you, ma'am. I did play a little football in my day.''

She rolled her eyes. ''Oh, please, it wasn't a compliment. You tried to trick me, John, draw me into your plan, and you're going to the retreat under false pretenses. You should be ashamed of yourself.''

Then she sort of flinched, probably because she'd attacked his ethics.

''Oh, I'm crushed, really I am,'' John said, grinning at her. ''But, now that I've decided to tell you the truth, because I trust you, and because if I don't get into my own kind of clothes and behind the wheel of a real car in the next hour,

I may run howling into New Jersey's famous pine barrens—well, are you okay with this?''

"Am I okay with this? May I remind you, John, that I nearly *drowned* back there?''

"You did not,'' he said, rather proudly. "You started to have *fun* back there. And we could have a lot of fun, Jane, if you agree to help me.''

"Agree to help you what?''

"Help me get close to Harrison, either by batting those big eyes at the senator or even at his nephew. Get us close—get me close, I should say—and let me watch the great man for a week, pick up on some of his body language, stuff that will make my book seem more real, maybe fill in some of the bare spots on my research on the man. Nothing too daring, nothing kinky, just get the man's attention. I understand it isn't all that difficult for a beautiful woman to do that.''

"So I bat my eyes at him, as you said, get us close to him, so you can get information?''

"For my book,'' he added, reminding her yet again that he was writing a book. In his mind, he had already ditched any idea of pushing Jane too hard at the senator. A woman of the world, he knew now, Jane Preston was *not*. There would be other women at the retreat. Willing women. But a couple got invited to more social affairs at these things than did single men. They were safer. All he had to do was get close enough to Harrison to watch the man screw up, then make sure he was caught in the act. Good-bye presidential aspirations.

Jane spoke again. "That's why you wanted me to sign a contract, isn't it? In case you actually get this book published? You wouldn't want anyone to know you went to the retreat under false pretenses?''

"Right,'' he answered, as willing to let her think that as anything else she might think.

"And you hired me—hired Molly first—as a *lure?*''

"Guilty as charged,'' he said, grinning.

"But you're dropping the nerd look?"

"I have to, Jane. If I couldn't fool you, I'm not going to be able to fool anyone."

"Well, gee, thanks. It's nice to know what you think of my intellect, or powers of deduction, or whatever."

"I also think that you're beautiful enough, and charming enough, to use as a lure, remember. Does that redeem me at all?"

"Good-bye, John, have a nice life, and seek therapy. Seriously," Jane said, reaching for the door handle once more. Then she turned back to look at him. "Aren't you going to stop me?"

"You said I shouldn't touch you again, and I wanted to show you that I'm not the brute, Neanderthal type with women. I want you to know the truth, and I want you to feel safe with me, safe enough to help me and have yourself an all expenses paid vacation while you're at it."

He grinned, and sort of waggled his eyebrows at her. "So? Did it work?"

"Molly?" Jane spoke into the cell phone her cousin had bought for her, one eye on the men's clothing store across the mall, where John Romanowski was presently ditching his nerd disguise and replenishing his wardrobe.

"Janie! Are you there yet? What's the professor like? Do you have a room overlooking the ocean? I looked at the weather forecast for the shore areas, and you're not supposed to get any rain all week, which is—"

"Shut up, Molly," Jane hissed, turning her back on the mall. "We've got a problem."

"We do? Funny, I don't feel like I've got a problem. But I did get a new nail color after I left you. Knock-em-dead-red. You have to see it, Janie, it's—"

"John Romanowski is a professor who thinks he's a writer, and he's going to Cape May to get information to write some big political exposé-type book on—get ready for it, Molly—Senator Harrison.''

"*Our* Senator Harrison?"

Jane was pretty sure smoke had begun pouring out of her ears. "How many Senator Harrisons are there?"

"Wow, Janie, how about that? I mean, what are the odds that you'd hook up with—"

"I don't care about the odds, Molly; it's the *actuals* I have to deal with," Jane all but shouted into the phone. "I'm supposed to lure Senator Harrison close enough for John to pounce on him. That's why he went to Imogene's escort service in the first place. He's . . . He's all but *pimping* me, Molly."

"Well, honey, when you get down to it, I was doing pretty much the same thing, in a PG-13 rated sort of scenario, or have you forgotten the pink bikini? And, hey, this is great. I mean, anything the professor learns, you can then just forward to me, right? It's like now I've got a *team* up there."

"Would you please stop thinking about *you* for a minute! Contrary to what you've always thought, everything isn't always about *you.*"

"Well, that's gratitude for you," Molly said in obvious insincerity. "I'm hurt, Janie. Really hurt."

"Yeah, yeah, tell it to someone who cares, okay? Molly, help me. What am *I* going to do?"

"Do? What do you mean, do? This is manna from heaven, Janie. Why are you looking the proverbial gift horse in the mouth? I need you near Harrison—did I mention that I told my boss about you and our plan when he got a little snarky about me taking so much vacation time, and that my job is now hanging on how well you do this week?"

Jane's heart sank. "No. You didn't."

"I didn't? Well, consider it mentioned, not that I want to put any more pressure on you."

"Yes, you do."

"Oh, okay, I do. Anyway, this Romanowski guy also

needs you near Harrison; that's what you're saying. Popular guy, the senior senator from New Jersey. My boss already has one of his top guys there as an invited guest, just to feel out Harrison. In fact, I'll bet half the people at the retreat only showed up to get to Harrison one way or another, find out what he's up to. Even your professor. It couldn't be better. What is that? Kismet? Karma? The two of you can just work together.''

Jane shot a look toward the entrance of the men's shop. "I didn't tell him I'm here to help you keep your stupid job which you'll probably quit in another month anyway.''

"You didn't? Why not?''

If she could crawl through the phone lines from here to Washington, Jane was pretty sure she'd still have enough strength left to shake her cousin senseless. Well, more senseless than usual anyway.

"How could I do that, Molly? He wouldn't believe me, for one thing, and he trusts me, for another. If I told him I was working undercover for an employee of a big D.C. newspaper? I'd be on a bus back to Fairfax before I could say, 'Molly I'm going to kill you.' This was supposed to be my *vacation,* remember? Ha! Some vacation. I've got chunks, I've got a great wardrobe—and now I'm playing Natasha to Romanowski's Boris, for crying out loud. But even that would be over if he found out that the *two* of you are *pimping* me.''

Jane suddenly realized that a child had stopped in front of her—kids always were drawn to her, for reasons she would never understand. He'd tugged his mother to a halt as well, and obviously both had been listening to everything she said. "Oh, God,'' she groaned as the child's mother lifted her chin and said, "You should be ashamed of yourself. Don't you have a corner to stand on?'' Then she picked up her child and stomped off . . . probably to call Security.

"Molly, I think I'm losing it here.''

"All right, all right, calm down, I get the picture. And you're right. Don't tell him. But a professor writing an exposé on Harrison? What's it going to say—that the great man doesn't floss after eating? I mean, come on. A professor digging for dirt? He wouldn't know where to start. What's he like, anyway? What does he look like?''

Jane began to tell her cousin, but only got as far as "He's ..." when the professor himself walked out of the store, holding about four large plastic bags, a zippered suit bag, and wearing casual khakis and a thin black pullover tucked into his slacks. No glasses, his hair recombed and looking as if he had rubbed most of the grease out of it, his pecs a marvel, his forearms bulging under the weight of the bags. The testosterone wave hit her from fifty feet away. "Oh, boy ..."

"Janie? Janie, are you still there?"

"Huh? Oh! Oh, Molly, I'm sorry, I was ... distracted for a moment. Look, I've got to go. I'll call you from Cape May, once I'm in my room, give you the number there and all of that in case my cell phone's turned off, or in case I go missing, or if I land in the pokey for impersonating a sane person."

"No, don't go yet. You were going to tell me what this Romanowski looks like. Bet he has thick glasses and a pencil-thin neck, right? Tweed jacket with suede elbows? Has the whole college professor nerdy thing going?"

Janie whimpered, thought, *This is the way Jane's world ends, not with a bang, but a whimper,* then pulled herself together. She owed Molly one, and her cousin was going to get it. "What does he look like? Let me see, how can I explain him? Okay, I've got it. Picture Hugh Grant, Molly. Taller, and on steroids."

There were four seconds of silence—Jane counted— before Molly said, "Huh?"

Jane was getting into it now, watching John as he stood near the railing of the opening in the middle of the mall, looking for her. "Hugh Grant, Molly, at least for the hair and eyes. And maybe the smile. And not Arnold Schwarzenegger-type pumped, but just nice muscles. And hair. He's all tanned and . . . hairy. One hundred and twenty percent man.''

"Oh. Not your type," Molly said, sighing. "Too bad, Janie, I was hoping you'd have a little romance in Cape May. But don't worry. Dillon is right up your alley. Slim, blond, sophisticated-looking. Nonthreatening," she added on a giggle.

Jane pulled the phone away from her ear and glared at it a second before pulling it close again. "I do not like non-threatening men."

"Do so," Molly countered. "Think about it, Janie. Who did you date in high school? Captain of the chess team, that's who. And in college? Captain of the debate team. Bor-ring. You should have tried for the captain of the football team, Janie. But you don't like your men to be manly. You like wimps."

"I do not. I—oh, okay. I'm not going to argue with you. Just be in my office at six-thirty Monday morning, ready to work."

"There's a six-thirty in the morning?" Molly countered. "Who knew?"

"Just be there," Jane said, and hung up as John saw her, waved one arm laden with bags, and headed toward her around the railing.

"Hi," he said, smiling down at her. "I thought I lost you there for a moment."

"No . . . um, I was just phoning my . . . my mother. I said I'd call her from Cape May, and as we aren't there yet, she might have been worrying about me. You . . . You look nice."

"I look human again," he agreed. "And when I can wash the rest of Aunt Marion's hair cream out of my head, I'll feel human again. Give me five minutes in that J. C. Penney's over there to buy some new luggage for this stuff and we'll be out of here, unless you want to do some shopping. Or are you ready to go to the rental agency, pick up our car, and head to Cape May?"

Jane took a deep breath and smiled. She'd had her chances to bail, to run away, and she hadn't taken them. One day, maybe when she was eighty, and in her rocking chair, she'd figure out why. "Ready when you are, Gridley," she said, and he laughed.

How nice that one of them found this all so funny. . . .

Chapter Five

Congress Hall was beautiful. Jane lingered outside, admiring the large brick building painted a soft yellow, the three-story high, huge white pillars that marched the length of the building, holding up a seemingly endless porch roof.

There were old-fashioned rocking chairs on the long verandah, and the whole place seemed like something out of an earlier time, a quieter time, a simpler time.

Cape May was, she had read on a sign coming into the town, on the Historic Register, and in truth it didn't look like the typical shore town. The buildings were mostly Victorian: huge, many-gabled houses surrounded by ancient trees, many of the lovely structures turned into bed and breakfasts. Small shops lined streets closed to all but pedestrian traffic.

She could smell the ocean, but not see it, because it was on the other side of the hotel. But the ocean breeze was here, the laughing gulls were overhead, and if she closed her eyes and concentrated, she could almost taste the salt water taffy that would be her first purchase once she was on her own for five minutes, away from John.

On the remainder of the drive, she had fairly well convinced herself that she could do this; she could pull this off, in this place, in this time. After all, what could go wrong in such a lovely setting? All she had to do was pretend she was Molly, not Jane. Yes, she could do this. She could even enjoy this.

She could have an adventure. She *deserved* an adventure.

This was a moment out of time, a week out of her life. She could do what she wanted, without fear of consequences, and then head home to her humdrum life, to sanity.

With her memories.

Even nursery school teachers should be able to go on a lark, shouldn't they? Even Plain Janes—and their chunky highlights and their pink bikinis with the padded cups.

She wouldn't even be herself. She couldn't be Molly, not completely—nobody could (or should) try to be Molly. But, darn it all—no, *damn* it all—she could try!

The mood, possibly hovering near a dangerous euphoria, lasted as she entered the building, stepped into yet another fairy world of another time, another place. High ceilings, Victorian furniture, a coolness and quiet that was both welcoming and still oddly formal.

Her last vacation had been two years ago. In the mountains. Where it had been unseasonably cool. And the heat in the cabin didn't work. And there were bats in the trees. And she had gone there with her parents.

Pitiful.

But this would be better. She'd make sure of that!

She saw John standing at the reception desk and joined him, leaning against the hand-rubbed wood, smiling at him. She was being free and easy. She was being not-quite-Molly. She was Having An Adventure—suddenly seeing the words capitalized, for emphasis. Jane's Great Adventure.

She was going to relax, let her hair down, hang loose. She was going to have fun . . . if it killed her.

"How are we doing?" she asked, because John didn't look happy. Not that she knew how he looked, happy, unless she counted that moment when he'd remarked that he was surprised they hadn't arrived at Disney World, the rat.

John was leaning his elbows on the high counter and sort of lowered his head as he turned it to look at her. "We're not."

"We're not what?"

"Doing. We're not doing. Somebody screwed up the reservations."

"Sir, as I explained to you," the neatly dressed young woman behind the counter said, "there are only a limited number of suites in the hotel, and somehow the one for the president wasn't held out of the mix. Those who arrived first received their suites, but as you're the last, unfortunately, and we've just gotten word that the President will attend the retreat one day this week, I'm afraid you've . . . Well, you've been bumped, sir. I'm so sorry."

"Oh, that's too bad, John," Jane said, feeling faintly smug. All she was going to have was a normal hotel room, but he'd reserved himself a suite? Served him right. "A suite would have been so nice for you."

He looked at her levelly. "You're not getting this, are you, little Miss Sunshine? The suite was two rooms, one of them yours."

Jane felt her stomach do a little flip. "I didn't have my own room?"

"Sure you did, but it was part of the suite."

"Oh, that's not good."

"No kidding," he said, looking back at the desk clerk. "Do you have two more rooms?"

"No, Professor, I'm sorry. We did, however, have a cancellation just this morning, so there is a lovely room available, with the compliments of Congress Hall, to make up for any inconvenience. We'd only need an imprint of your credit card in order to allow you to use long distance on the phone. It has a lovely restored bath," she added with a bright smile, punched a few keys on her computer, then turned that smile on Jane. "And, yes, I'm right, two double beds."

A short, rather hysterical snort escaped Jane before she could silence it, and she turned to John and spoke with her jaw clenched. "Think of all the ways a person can say no and pretend I just said them."

"We'll take it," he told the young woman, tossing his charge card at her, then quickly grabbed Jane's elbow and all but dragged her toward the rear of the hotel and the double doors that led out onto a second verandah, the pool, and the beach and ocean beyond it. "Look, Jane. Look at that ocean. Smell that breeze. You don't want to give all this up, do you?"

"I am *not* going to share a room with you," she told him, looking at the ocean, watching her dreams wash out to sea.

"Two beds, Jane. Big room. If I can live with your pantyhose over the shower rail and you can live with my snoring— and I don't really snore, honest—we can do this. We've come too far to give up now."

"No, *you've* come too far, with all your secret plans and ridiculous intrigue and . . . and Rabbits. I'm just along for the ride, remember? This is all your fault," she said, tearing her gaze away from the ocean. "If you hadn't done . . . done that stupid *nerd thing,* we'd have been here in plenty of time to get a suite. The Ferrari, remember?"

"I know, I know, and I'm kicking myself about that."

"Oh, no, John. Don't kick yourself. Let me do it for you."

"Now, Jane," he said, sounding so condescending that her right foot actually itched, she so wanted to kick him in the shin. "Let's be calm, not go to pieces. You said you were a brick in a crisis, remember? You said that, right out of your own mouth, and I heard you. We're here, Jane. The sand, sun, and surf are here. Harrison is here. I asked at the desk, and he checked in a couple of hours ago."

"Probably into our suite," she said, feeling her lower lip jutting out, knowing she was close to throwing a real first-class hissy fit. That wasn't like her. She was a trouper, usually. But, then, she'd had a long day.

"Probably," John agreed, being entirely too calm and logical for her. She wanted yelling, she wanted shouting, she wanted demanding, she wanted stamping of feet and pulling of hair. She wanted her own hotel room. She wanted her salt water taffy, damn it!

"How can you be so . . . so *calm* about this?"

"You prefer hysterics?"

"Yes! I mean, no, of course not. But I'm not in the habit of sharing a hotel room with a man."

"Gee, color me surprised," John said, showing some first small hints of anger.

"And what's that supposed to mean?" she asked, jamming her fists on her hips as she glared up at him. If she stayed for the whole week, she'd have a permanent crick in her neck from staring up at him. "I mean it, John—what is that supposed to mean?"

"Whatever you want it to mean, teacher-lady, okay?" he said, stabbing his fingers into his hair, dislodging one still-greasy lock that fell forward, over his forehead. "For crying out loud, Jane, you know why I'm here, why I hired you. I'm not here to . . . to fool around."

"So then you *have* thought about it," she said, knowing she was jumping off the edge, emotionally, but she hadn't eaten since that half a hamburger two hours earlier, and she, all in all, just hadn't had a real good day, you know? She was entitled to a little hysteria, a little pigheadedness.

"Thought about it? Oh, for crying out loud, what kind of person do you think I am? No, don't answer that. I already know. That's it. Where's the nearest bus station? Because you're gone, lady."

Jane sobered immediately. She was up for an argument, champing at the bit for one, if she was honest with herself, but she hadn't thought he would go this far. "Gone? You mean *fired?* You can't do that. You can't fire me. I quit."

"You quit at the rest stop," John reminded her. "Now I'm firing you."

"But . . . but . . ."

"Oh, shit," John said, grabbing her arm, pulling her back behind a thick, round pillar. "There's Harrison."

She shook off his hand. "Don't swear, it isn't polite. Where?" Jane looked toward the swimming pool. "I don't see anybody."

"To your right, walking down the verandah, or porch, or whatever you want to call it."

"Verandah. I think that sounds pretty," Jane said, peering around the thick pillar. Sure enough, there was Senator Aubrey Harrison, heading straight for them.

Not that it mattered. She'd been fired. She had been canned, dumped, relieved of her duties . . . locked out of her dream of having one great adventure to keep her warm for the next fifty years of lonely nights, after all her nifty chunky highlights grew out.

Fired? Yeah, well, that's what John Romanowski thought. She'd show him! This may have been a nutty idea from the moment Molly had first walked into Preston Kiddie Kare, but she was in Cape May now, and John was right: the sand and the sun and the surf were there—calling to her—and she'd be darned if she was going to be sent home. Think! Think! What would Molly do in this same position?

Yeah, she probably would do that, Jane thought as an idea hit her. And, darn it, anything Molly could do . . .

Before John could grab her arm again, or her own usual common sense could put on the brakes for her, Jane stepped out from behind the pillar and began walking toward the senator. Strolling, actually. Using a lot of hip.

He was a fairly good-looking man. Tall, with a shock of snow-white hair. Lean and trim, and with a golfer's tan. He was sixty-two, Molly had told her, but he looked younger, with smile lines around his mouth and eyes. A face born to grace a campaign poster.

Jane kept walking toward him, biding her time until the

senator was only about six feet away from her, before deliberately overturning her ankle and dropping to one knee.

"Ouch!"

"Oh, here, here, let me help you," the senator said, rushing to the rescue. Such a gentleman. "Come along, there's a chair right here. Sit down, and let me see that ankle."

"No, no," Jane protested feebly, "that's all right, really. I knew I shouldn't have worn these new sandals. I'm so clumsy."

She sat down, then looked up at Harrison and smiled, batted her eyelashes—thank heavens she'd done a repair job at the rest stop—telling herself she was Molly, she was as good at this as Molly, and boring Jane Preston was on the moon somewhere, being her usual well-behaved self, a Do Not Disturb sign hung around her conscientious, good-girl neck.

"But very pretty sandals," the senator was saying, and Jane tried not to groan.

"Thank you. I'm Jane . . . That is, I'm Janie Preston, and I'm here for the retreat. I'm not anybody; I'm just here with Professor Romanowski. Are . . . Are you anybody?"

That last bit was so bad she couldn't even work up a groan.

But the senator seemed enchanted and smiled down at her. "No, I'm nobody, just like you. Just Aubrey Harrison. You can call me Aubrey, Janie. Please."

Okay. This was almost too easy. But it was time to go for the gold.

"Oh, thank you, I—oh, dear! You're *Senator* Harrison?" She forced her eyes wide, but didn't have to fake the way her chest rose and fell rapidly. She was pretty sure she was hyperventilating and would probably pass out at any moment. Quick, somebody, get her a paper bag to breathe into!

"Professor!" she called out, looking to her left. "Oh, drat it all, where is he? He was here just a minute ago. The professor will be *so* delighted to meet you, Senator. He was just telling me on our drive here just how much he, well, how much he *admires* you.''

''Really. How nice.''

''Oh, yes, he's very ... nice. I really don't know him, you understand. I'm just a hired escort because the poor man doesn't have anybody.'' She made a face. ''You know how it is with these brainy types. Poor thing. Anyway, this is just sort of a lark for me, you understand. My ... My cousin said it would be a wonderful way to meet eligible— er, new people.''

She sort of scrunched up her nose and said conspiratorially, ''I think he's a little shy, you know. The professor, that is. Probably doesn't get out much. But he's very smart. I mean, he's a professor, so he must be smart, right, Senator? So, anyway, it's quite platonic. No hanky-panky, I'm just his escort. But, just like I said, I do hope to meet so *many* interesting people here this week. And just look, I've only been here for ten minutes so far, and I've already met you— the next president of our own great United States.''

''Well, thank you, Janie, but that would be up to the voters, now, wouldn't it?'' Harrison preened a little, touching a hand to his opened collar, as if to straighten an imaginary necktie. ''Too bad your professor isn't here right now, Janie. But tell you what. I was just going to sign up my nephew and myself for a table in the dining room. How about I add your name, and the professor's, of course, to those sitting at our table for the week?''

''Oh. Oh, my, wouldn't that be wonderful! Aren't you just the sweetest thing? I'm Janie, like I said. Janie Preston. And he's John Romanowski. Professor Romanowski. That would be Roman ... and ... and an *os-key?* I really don't know how to spell it. Thank you, Senator.''

''You're quite welcome, my dear. Now, are you sure you won't need assistance getting to your room?''

''Thank you, no, I think I'm all right now,'' Jane said, getting to her feet, faintly surprised to find that she wasn't standing in a good six inches of horse manure, she'd been laying it on so thick. "I'm from Virginia, you know, Senator."

"Yes, I had thought I heard a hint of our great south in that lovely voice of yours."

Jane nodded, but didn't have to work hard to force a blush. "Well, I may be from Virginia, Senator, but I do believe courtesy is far from dead here in the north," she said, darn near drawled, then giggled.

And nearly threw up.

"Now I thank you, Janie. Dinner, I'm told, is promptly at six. I'll see you then? It will be my pleasure to get to know you better this week, and tell you all about my home state while you're a guest here."

Jane watched him leave, also watching as John sort of shuffled around the large pillar, keeping out of sight as Harrison passed by.

"That was pretty generally disgusting," John said when he joined her.

"Yes, I thought so, too, but it worked. Of course, now that I'm fired, I won't be at dinner, which means *you* won't be at dinner, so—"

"You're hired again," John said, leading her back into the lobby of the hotel, one hand clamped around her elbow.

She had to hurry to keep up with him. "I do want you to know that I'm usually not so forward. I don't know what got into me, but I will tell you that it was sort of fun, flirting like that, except for the nearly gagging part, which was pretty powerful. Can you believe the man was that easy?"

"Yes, I can believe it. He was undressing you with his eyes, the bastard," John spat as they slowed in front of the check-in desk and he quickly signed his name, gathered his charge card and the room keys, then did a U-turn, heading for the elevators.

"He was?" Jane stopped dead, and grinned. "I didn't notice."

"You didn't notice," John repeated flatly. "Sure. Like it doesn't happen to you every day."

"Happen every—you think this sort of thing happens to me every day?"

He sliced her a quick look, then stabbed the button once more as he glared at the closed elevator doors. "We're business partners in this, Jane. Or should I say *Janie?* Don't try flirting with me now, because it doesn't work."

"You think I'm *flirting* with you?"

"Flirting? Fishing for compliments? Yes, I do. I gave up my nerd act, and you've given up your Goody Two-shoes act. We're even."

Jane opened her mouth to say something . . . say anything; but it appeared that her brain had lost all control over her voice box, and all that came out was a squeak.

The doors opened, and she stepped in ahead of John, avoiding his eyes as he joined her, followed by a bell person pushing a cart holding their luggage. The car rose to the second floor.

They followed the bell person down the hallway. When John opened the door, they all walked inside the room that was pretty well dominated by two double beds with white hobnail bedspreads.

John slipped the bell person five dollars. The man thanked him, then said, "You and the missus have a nice time, sir," and backed out of the room.

"He thinks we're married," Jane said, retreating to the far side of the room, to see that the windows overlooked the ocean. There was even a balcony.

"That's because we act married," John said, heaving her largest suitcase up onto one of the beds.

"We do?"

"Yeah. Only married people act like they hate each other."

"Oh," Jane said, sighing, as she turned to examine the room. "We can do this, you know. I don't know why I panicked. I even saw this old movie one time, where the guy hung a blanket between two beds. We could do that."

"Dream on. We've got room service, Jane. I'm not going to do anything that brings attention to us."

"All right, all right, don't get all hot under the collar again, for goodness sakes. I'll just make up a schedule, and we'll go with that."

He flipped his new—newest—suitcases onto the other bed. "You're going to make up a what?"

"A schedule. You know, like I'll shower at night and you can shower in the morning. Things like that. I like schedules. They keep things neat. I like things neat."

His grin was positively wicked. "Then, you're going to hate it in here."

"Excuse me?"

John looked at her for a few moments, muttered something under his breath, and headed into the bathroom, slamming the door behind him.

"Well, that was rude," she told herself, then finally let her bottom lip begin to tremble as a bubble of laughter—hysterical laughter she was pretty sure—escaped her.

Plain Jane? She gave her head a shake and let Angel's glorious creation swing back into place. Heh, heh, heh. Not this week, baby!

John stood under the shower, shampooing his hair for the third time, at the same time cooling off his temper, which had risen the moment he had seen the look in Harrison's eyes as Jane flirted with him.

Bastard.

If he hadn't already had first-hand knowledge of Aubrey Harrison's skirt-chasing proclivities, thanks to his mother and the results of his quiet research, he certainly would have to believe now that the man had never seen a pretty woman he didn't try to hit on.

Bastard.

But he wasn't angry only with Harrison, pissed at Harrison.

It was Jane who had really upset him.

She'd seemed like such a nice kid. A good kid. A nursery school teacher, for crying out loud. The sort of nice, neat, organized person who made schedules, for crying out loud.

But it would appear that even nice kids could be turned on by the powerful and famous, like Aubrey Harrison.

Either that, or she was the world's best actor. But when was she acting? When she was playing the nursery school teacher, or when she was batting those big eyes of hers at Harrison?

Finally satisfied that his hair was now completely free of all the grease he'd slathered on it, John stepped from the shower and came face-to-face with himself in the mirror.

He stood there, looked at himself for several seconds, then shook his head.

"You know what, John Patrick? You're an ass. You're lying through your teeth to the girl, and you're complaining about the way *she's* behaving? Face it, you're attracted. Very attracted. And, to paraphrase the lady, now that you've been named World's Greatest Ass, what are you going to do?"

For starters, he dressed again in the clothes he'd bought only an hour ago and opened the door to the bedroom. "I'm calmer now," he said, stepping into the room, prepared to be magnanimous, an all-around nice guy. What a sweetheart he was.

She wasn't there.

A shot of pure panic rammed John in the gut, until he saw that Jane's suitcases were stacked in the bottom of the closet, her clothing all hung neatly on hangers. Even the hangers were neat—all hooked over the rod front to back, all in the same direction. Scary.

So where was she?

He stomped around the room, knowing he was still pretty much stuck in Idiot Mode, and then saw the message on the notepad next to the telephone. Neat handwriting, very precise. More and more, he was getting the feeling that Jane was a very precise, very controlled person—except when some devil gave her a poke and she did things like trick him into letting go of the dashboard or flirting with Harrison.

Gone to find salt water taffy, be right back. Jane.

"She's got to be kidding. Salt water taffy? *Now?*" He searched in his new luggage until he found the toiletries case he'd transferred from the plaid luggage and quickly ran the electric shaver over his face, lifted his shirt and wiped some deodorant under his arms, then combed his hair in front of the mirror.

He looked better. He felt better. But he wasn't a happy camper.

Sticking his key card in his pocket, he left the room, headed for the front desk, and asked the location of the nearest salt water taffy store.

"We have taffy in the gift shop, sir," the same young woman who had registered them said, pointing down one of the hallways. "Your . . . companion was just here about ten minutes ago and asked the same question."

"Thanks," John said, wishing the young woman hadn't hesitated over the word *companion*. It would be all over the hotel by dinnertime—Room 217 was the one with the illicit lovers, except they're fighting, so this ought to be fun to watch all week.

Just what he didn't want to be, the subject of gossip or the center of attention.

Oh, he was tall enough, big enough, that he'd never quite been able to blend in with the woodwork anywhere he went, but it was one thing to be noticed, and another to be *noticed*.

After scoping out the gift shop and coming up empty, John headed out toward the beach, pretty sure Jane would be drawn to the ocean, but spied her relaxing on one of the chaise lounges that edged the pool, reading a small book whose title proclaimed it a guide to New Jersey vacations.

He sat down beside her, and she looked up from the book. "Hello, John. Calmer now that you've had some alone time?"

"If you'd been waiting in the room, where you should have been, you'd know that I was—until I saw that you were gone."

She reached into the open box beside her and lifted a paper-wrapped candy. "Taffy? This one's cinnamon. It's really good, although I've always liked the molasses-mint best. Except for the licorice ones."

He glared at her, then snatched the paper-wrapped stick of cinnamon taffy from her fingers. "We have to talk."

"We do? I thought we had to mingle. I mean, we've snared Harrison pretty well, but then I got to thinking. If you want to write a book, you should do as much research as possible, especially with all the powerful people attending this retreat. So I picked up a list of attendees at the registration desk. Here you go."

He took the folded pages she slid out from beneath her and quickly scanned the pages. "Oh, boy. I knew about most of these people, but not all of them. Brandy Hythe? That's one I hadn't been expecting."

Liar, liar, pants on fire. . . .

"The actress? Why not? There are several people representing film and television here. See," she said, sitting up, pointing her finger on the first paper. "There are titles and occupations listed in short bios beneath every name. I counted four other writers—who actually admit to being writers."

"I think I liked you better when you didn't know what was going on."

"I liked you better then, too," Jane said, avoiding his eyes. "But we're here, just as you said, I'm being well paid for the week, so I think we ought to just try to make the best of it. Now, although I'm sure you'll want to attend every workshop or seminar or whatever it is that the senator attends, I think we should also take advantage of this opportunity to see something of Cape May. Don't you? There's a lighthouse, and a zoo, and a—John? John, are you listening to me?"

"Huh?" he asked, swallowing hard as his gaze traveled the length of the dark-haired beauty standing on the other side of the pool, stripping off her cover-up. Tall, at least five-foot-nine, and willow thin. But with all her curves in the right places. Hair down to her shoulders, looking a little mussed, as if she'd just climbed out of bed. Black one-piece suit that made her skin look whiter than white. And that face. Damn. That face. Slanted eyes. Lush, full lips. Yeah, yeah, and the body. Let's get back to the body. . . .

"John," Jane said, giving his arm a nudge. "It's not polite to stare."

He blinked, shook his head, and tore his gaze away from Brandy Hythe, star of three of the top box office grosses of the past year.

"That's better. For a minute there, I thought you were in a trance. Beautiful, isn't she? Even prettier than on the screen. But, if you'll notice, her short bio on the list of attendees says she's an honor graduate of Princeton. Political Science major, just like you. In other words, not just a pretty face."

"Princeton? That's here, in New Jersey." John grabbed the papers again, found Brandy's name, pretending he didn't already know all about Brandy Hythe. "New Jersey native, huh? I wonder if Harrison had anything to do with her invitation to the retreat."

Jane swung her legs off the chaise lounge. "And that would be a bad thing?"

John nearly slipped, nearly said something on the order of, "Yeah, if he's brought his own talent, it's going to take a lot more than a twisted ankle and an overdone southern drawl to keep Harrison close."

But he didn't say that. Because he wasn't entirely stupid, although he knew that his behavior so far today wouldn't put him in the top three of any Greatest Brains Of The Century contest.

"No, no, it's not a bad thing, Jane," he said, taking another look at the actress, who was now moving her long form through the pool in a graceful sidestroke. He watched her legs do the scissors kick just under the water and tried to imagine those long legs wrapped around Harrison's back . . . and had to break the image quickly or else lose his lunch. His research hadn't proven an affair, but it hadn't disproved it, either.

"Good. Now, while you were showering I took a walk and found the ballroom. It's painted a lovely Tiffany blue. Just beautiful. Anyway, I saw the board with the tables marked on it and the list for who else is sitting at our table. We only have six, although all the rest seem to have eight. That may have been the cancellation this morning, don't you think, combined with the fact that we arrived so late in the day? I wrote all the names in my notebook. Wait, I'll get it out of my purse."

John stared at her. "Are you always this efficient? Because you're starting to scare me."

She pulled out the notebook and opened it. "I work with children, John. If I'm not on top of everything, every moment, the children can turn the most orderly world into chaos. I think they're born with the talent. Okay, here we go. There are you and me, of course, and the senator and his nephew, Dillon Holmes. Ms. Hythe—so you might be right, and he did get her the invitation. And a gentleman named Henry Brewster. He's listed as a publisher. Oh, do you suppose that would be Brewster Books? I'm sure that's it. John? Are you all right? You aren't choking on the taffy, are you?"

John held up one finger as he used his other hand to press against his mouth as he coughed, for yes, he had damn near choked on his taffy. To make things worse, Jane hopped up from her seat and began beating him on the back, as if trying to burp him or something. Henry? Here? Damn it, couldn't the man keep his nose out of this?

"I'm . . . I'm okay. Swallowed wrong, that's all."

"Perhaps you should have something to drink? Some water? I can go get—"

"Jane. Sit. I'm fine, really. And, no, scratch that, don't sit. We can't talk here. Come on," he said, helping her gather up her belongings—she had acquired quite a few in a very short time. "Let's head down to the beach."

"Oh, all right. But shouldn't we start thinking about getting changed for dinner? It's nearly five, and dinner will be served promptly at six o'clock, just as the senator said earlier. It says on the registration handout that meals are informal, but—"

"If Brandy Hythe has time for a swim, we have time for a walk on the beach," John said, taking Jane's hand and leading her toward the wide stretch of sand.

"Sure," Jane muttered, hanging back a little. "She doesn't have to spend twenty minutes in front of the makeup mirror to look natural. The woman didn't have so much as lipstick on back there, John, and she looked like she could pose for the cover of *Cosmo*. Me, I need time to work."

"You're fine," John said, turning to smile at her. "And you're getting a few freckles on your nose."

She pressed a hand to her nose. "No! Oh, darn it. My sun screen probably washed off in the rain. I hate freckles."

"I think you look cute."

She did a quick two-step to keep up with his longer strides. "Whoopee, I look cute. Did it ever occur to you, John—to any man—that a grown woman wants to look a lot of ways, but cute isn't one of them."

"Really?" She really was a funny little thing. "What ways does a woman want to look?"

"You want a list?" Jane stopped as they reached the beach and bent down to remove her sandals. Nice gold chain around her slim ankle. He'd noticed that before . . . the ankle, that was.

"A list might be good. I'm a firm believer in continuing education, remember."

"Okay, a list. Sexy. Beautiful. Sultry. Kissable. Exciting. Seductive. I could go on, but I won't. But did you hear the word *cute* anywhere in there? I sure didn't. And let me tell you, *nice* wasn't in there either. Nice and cute equals great pal, always a bridesmaid, and alone on Saturday nights, talking to your cat. Trust me.''

"You've given this a lot of thought, haven't you?"

"Yes. I've had a lot of Saturday night conversations with my cat about it. And I can't believe I just said all of that to you, along with telling you that I need a lot of time with a mirror and a makeup bag before we go to dinner, or else I won't be able to order a drink without the waiter carding me. And, no, before you ask, that isn't flattering, either. What grown woman wants to look like a teenager? See how much you're learning? Maybe you should be taking notes. Us nice and *cute* girls, with the freckles, we're also honest. Too honest. But, hey, we're going to be pals, right?''

"Pals?" He nearly stumbled. "God, I haven't heard that word since I was a kid.''

He stared at her, trying to take in everything she'd said— confessed. And then he figured it out. "So that's it? That's how you've worked it all out, how you're justifying the two of us sharing a hotel room all week? You're planning on the two of us being *pals?*''

"Why not? I'm certainly not planning on anything else. And neither are you, not when you were looking at Brandy Hythe as if you'd like to pour chocolate syrup all over her and then lick it off. Oh—and that's the one benefit of being cute and nice, in case you were wondering. We can say things like that and get away with it, because it's so *cute*. Gag me. Anyway, I'm much more relaxed now, John, actually, knowing for certain that you see me as nice. You aren't going to try to . . . hit on me. I'm just a handy tool to you, doing a job and all of that. We certainly couldn't be anything more than friends. I'm not your type and . . . sorry, but you're not mine, either.''

"I was only looking at the woman, for crying out loud. It doesn't mean—oh, hell. Never mind." John slipped out of his Docksiders, then relieved Jane of her sandals and piled shoes, taffy box, guide book, and papers on the sand.

"These should be safe enough here with all the other people out on the beach. Come on, let's play tourist and dabble our toes in the mighty Atlantic while I try, very hard, to forget everything you just said."

He took her hand once more, and she let him, which surprised him this time as much as it had surprised him the first time. Maybe she thought pals held hands. Or maybe she thought he was one of her nursery school kids, and she was holding his hand because a semi loaded with bricks was going to come barreling down the sand and she wanted to make sure he looked both ways before crossing the beach.

Hit on Jane Preston? He couldn't hit on her. He'd never made love to any woman he'd feel he might first have to ask "Mother, May I" or check to see if "Simon Says" before making his move, and he wasn't about to start now.

Aunt Marion would be amazed to know how nonthreatening Jane considered him. Not that he'd ever tell her, because he would never live it down. J. P. Roman. Nonthreatening, and not her type. Jeez.

He should be insulted, or maybe relieved. Instead, he was intrigued. Nice little Janie Preston was intriguing as hell. He may only have minored in psychology in college, but he knew darn well that being told you don't want something, with the unspoken addition of "you can't have it," only makes a person want whatever it is more. Maybe he should mention that to Jane.

No. Maybe not. As long as she believed they were pals, she'd stick around, and he wanted her to stick around. He really did. And exposing Aubrey Harrison didn't have a thing to do with it.

He wouldn't mention that to her, either.

The beach wasn't very crowded. Just a few blankets spread on the sand, a few people walking along the shore, also dipping their toes in the mighty Atlantic. He recognized three of them, men he'd also been researching: a congressman from Pennsylvania, the CEO of a major oil company, and one of Harrison's newscaster buddies from the Florida condo. They seemed deep in conversation.

That the attendees were mostly from the East Coast wasn't surprising, as there were a total of four of these retreats held every year, all in different areas of the country. But to already see so many of Harrison's cronies in one spot made John wonder if there wasn't more happening here than a simple intellectual retreat. Were people like himself being used as a convenient "cover," while there was something bigger going on that Harrison didn't want the media types to know until he was ready to tell them?

He'd have to study the list Jane had picked up and check the names against the notes on his computer.

Jane bent to pick up a shell, then frowned and dropped it again when she saw that it was broken. "It's nice here, isn't it?"

"I thought you had a thing against *nice*," John said, realizing that he may have been thinking about Harrison and his cronies, but he'd also been admiring the way the sun lit small golden fires in Jane's hair.

"Right. I'll try to think up another word."

"I like your hair, you know," he said, surprising himself. "I guess the sun does that to it?"

"Nope. Angel did that to it—my new hairdresser. I'm actually mousey brown." She sighed, pushed her hands through her hair. "God, it's good to be honest. I mean, it *feels* good. I can see why you couldn't carry off that nerd thing, John. I can't carry off the chunks, either."

"Chunks?"

"Never mind. Now, are you going to tell me why you started choking when I mentioned that publisher's name? Something Brewster, right?"

Okay, time to mount his trusty steed and take yet another ride to Liarsville. He'd blend a little embarrassing truth, a few fibs, and she'd never suspect. "That's Henry Brewster, right. I submitted my first and to date only book to him directly, right after I got out of college. He said it was lackluster. *Nice,* huh?''

"I'm beginning to really hate the word *nice,*" Jane said, lightly dancing out of the way of a particularly energetic wavelet. "What was the book about? I mean, what subject.''

"It was fiction. Remember *Love Story?* A professor wrote that. I don't know who wrote *Bridges of Madison County,* but I guess it doesn't matter. They both got published. I didn't.''

"You . . . You wrote a *love* story?''

He suppressed a grin. "Don't look so shocked. Shakespeare wrote love stories.''

"Okay, I'll back off. Obviously this is a sore subject with you.''

"It still pisses—rankles, yes. I mean, I put all the ingredients in there. Star-crossed lovers, lots of imagery, an uplifting ending.''

"Uplifting? I hate uplifting. And you called this a love story?''

"It worked for those guys,'' John said, pushing his hair out of his eyes.

"It wouldn't work for me. If I'm going to read a love story, it had better have a happy ending. If I want to cry, I'll rent *Free Willy.*''

"That has a happy ending. The whale is set free.''

"Exactly. I like happy tears. But I sure don't want to invest my time and emotions in getting to like people who are going to make me cry *sad* tears.''

"I'm not even going to try to understand that one.'' John stopped, pulled her around with him, and headed back up the beach, toward the hotel. "Ah, hell, there's some bum checking out our stuff.''

"He is? Where? Oh, I see him. He's not a bum, John. He's . . .''

"A bum. Wearing a dirty trench coat and combat boots. You want to take notes, take notes on this. This is not a stockbroker. This is a bum. He probably wants to snag your salt water taffy.''

"Well, if he's hungry . . .''

"Hey, buddy!'' John called out. "Move along, okay?''

The bum looked up, gave a grin and a wave, then shambled off.

"Are you happy now? I wouldn't have minded if he took the taffy.''

"Really? Next time, why don't you leave your wallet with your shoes and really make yourself a new friend.''

"I know you think you're being funny, but you're not.''

"Pretty place, isn't it?'' John remarked, changing the subject as he looked at the sprawling four-story hotel that dominated the beach. "But not exactly the Helmsley Palace, either. I wonder how long all the big mucky-mucks are going to hold out before they start skipping the no-protocol community meals and screaming for twenty-four-hour room service.''

"Has anyone ever told you that you're a cynic, John?'' Jane asked as she picked up her shoes.

"There have been rumors,'' John admitted, letting her balance herself against him as she swept drying sand from her feet, then slipped into her sandals.

"I'm surprised there haven't been billboards,'' Jane told him, brushing sand from her hands as he put on his own shoes, then picked up the taffy box and the rest. "And you help form young minds. I don't know that I think much of that.''

John grinned at her. "You form young minds, Jane. I get them when they think they know everything, are smarter than anyone else. What I give them is the real world.''

"Maybe. But you're still a cynic. For instance, Senator Harrison seemed like a very nice man.''

"Who was undressing you with his eyes,'' John reminded her, and himself . . . which pretty much wiped out the good mood that had only been getting started. "Be careful around him, Jane. Don't let him back you into any dark corners.''

"Oh, for pity's sake! A *senator?*"

Okay, the good mood was back. "What tuffet do you live under, Little Miss Muffet?" he asked, bending down to peer into her eyes. "Of course, the senator. And probably the CEO and the TV anchor, and all the rest of them. They're powerful people, Jane. Sex, money, influence, it all comes with the territory. And powerful people think they don't have to play by the rules. Mostly, and sadly, they don't."

Jane tilted her head to one side and sighed. "I don't believe that. At least, I don't believe they're all like that. Look at George Washington."

"I can't, unless I can dig him up. We're in a different age, Jane, and power is in charge."

" 'Power tends to corrupt, and absolute power corrupts absolutely,' " Jane said, nodding.

"Lord Acton," John said, smiling. "You're a constant amazement to me, Janie Preston."

She tucked her hair behind her ears. "Yes. Sometimes I even amaze myself."

Chapter Six

Jane stood in front of the mirror hung over the dresser, combing her hair one last time. She'd showered, washed and blow-dried her hair, dressed, and put on her makeup in the bathroom, where John couldn't see her trying to work the eyelash curler without pinching herself.

It was bad enough that she'd blabbed all that *cute* and *nice* stuff to him . . . even if she did feel better now that the air had been cleared. This was strictly business, although they could be friends, pals.

Pals?

Was she out of her tiny mind?

But still, no hanky-panky, as her grandmother would have called it.

Now John was in the bathroom, and she could hear his electric razor buzzing as he shaved his five-o'clock shadow. It was a nice sound, homey and domestic, the way it would sound if her husband had been in the next room, shaving so that they could go out to dinner, with her mom already downstairs, ready to baby-sit the kids.

Not that she thought of John in that way.

She wondered if John ever thought about growing a beard. It might be easier than trying to stay clean-shaven for more than four hours, poor hairy man.

Maybe he'd look more like a college professor with a beard, instead of a pirate, a buccaneer. Less dangerous. Then again, Bluebeard the pirate probably had a beard, or they wouldn't have called him Bluebeard, now would they? Or was that Blackbeard? Or were there two of them? And hadn't she just read in the guide book that Bluebeard or Blackbeard had sailed from New Jersey?

And who cared? The important part, the unnerving part, was that John looked dangerous.

She was trying very hard to keep up her "sure, I'm game, I'll play along" facade, keep her secret, but when John looked at her with those killer blue-green eyes, she felt certain she'd be making a full confession with her next breath, then running for the hills.

Frankly, she still wasn't sure just what had stopped her so far, why she was still here. It certainly wasn't because of her promise to Molly. Even her cousin wouldn't want her to share a hotel room with a stranger. A big, hairy stranger with bedroom eyes.

Okay, scratch that. Molly would think that was a real hoot, and probably a nifty challenge.

No, she was here because here was where she wanted to be. That was the reason in a nutshell.

She sensed intrigue, secrets . . . and since the last time she'd sensed intrigue, it had turned out to be Jeremy and Jason, the four-year-old Stemple twins, planning to escape the playground under a hole they'd been digging beneath the chain-link fence behind the playhouse, and the last time she'd had a secret had been when she was seventeen and had gotten deathly ill trying to smoke a cigarette Molly had given her—and had been forced to hide the truth from her mother, who was serving greasy, cheesy lasagna that night— well, maybe it was time for a little excitement in her life.

She might have protested to John that Senator Harrison

was a nice guy, but she'd felt vibes—something—coming from the man when he'd looked at her ankle, when he'd smiled at her. The guy was oily, no matter how well his hair had been blow-dried. His smile, which some might call open and honest, had been more of a know-it-all sneer when he'd looked at her. She'd felt it, tried to ignore it, but then relived it once John had gone off in a huff to take his shower.

Molly had said there might be some reason Harrison wasn't going to run for president. John had said that he was pretty sure Harrison was hiding some scandal. And the man had leered at her.

Leered, sneered. One of those.

Was that enough for an intriguing week at the beach?

Probably not, but it was all she had to work with, and it was certainly more fun than her usual trek to the mountains with her parents, lugging insect repellant and binoculars for bird-watching, and complete with a July Fourth picnic topped off by lighting a single sparkler each once it got dark. *Weeee!*

She put down the comb, then took a last look at her reflection in the mirror, believing the black dress looked pretty good, or at least it would until Brandy Hythe came strolling into the dining room draped in an Armani something-or-other.

Turning around, just to check on her side of the room, pick up her shoes, and put them in the closet, Jane shook her head at the mess on John's bed. He'd opened his suitcases, rifled through them, but hadn't unpacked them. His shoes were on the floor, his toiletries spilled all over the mattress.

Well, she could fix that.

Sure she could. But not in this lifetime.

Her side of the room was neat and orderly. She'd hung up all her clothing, then used the area to the left of the sink for her toothbrush, toothpaste, and dental floss, and hung the rest of her toiletries in a bag on a hook behind the door.

She'd folded her damp towels and placed them on the floor under the sink.

The guide book she'd bought, along with two novels she'd brought with her, and her box of salt water taffy, sat on the left edge of the nightstand between the two beds. Her clothing, all on padded hangers brought from home, hung on the left side of the closet, leaving plenty of room for John's things.

Her shoes, five of the six pair she'd brought with her, were lined up in a double row on the left side of the closet floor.

Her mother would have been so proud.

Not that her mother would know about any of this, because if she knew her only daughter was sharing a hotel room with a man, however platonic the arrangement, she'd run screaming to Jane's father: "Daddy! Where did we go wrong?"

Yes, well, she wouldn't think about that, either.

She'd just sit on the edge of the bed—her bed, the neat one—and wait for John to take her down to dinner, where she'd cozy up to Senator Harrison and try to find out if he was going to run for president or not.

Like he was going to tell her. Sure. That was the one huge flaw—okay, the largest flaw out of many—in Molly's plan. Molly, he might have told. Molly could compete with Brandy Hythe. Heck, she could compete with anybody.

But she was Jane, not Molly, no matter how many times and ways she tried to convince herself that some new clothes, makeup, and a killer haircut could turn her into Mata Hari.

Which left John. John the professor and his cockeyed idea about writing a political exposé on Senator Harrison. What John might learn would be what she learned.

Jane squeezed her eyelids shut and rubbed at her forehead. She really didn't like thinking about that part. Because, if John really did learn of some scandal in the senator's past and told Jane, and Jane went running to Molly, and Molly went running to save her job at the newspaper . . . ?

It was like the game she played with the children, the one about consequences. "If I pinch my baby sister, and she cries, then Mommy will come into the room and ask why she's crying, and then I'll . . ."

What had Billy Haskins answered the last time she had played the Consequences game? Oh, yes. "Then I'd be in deep doo-doo, Ms. Jane, right?"

Consequences. Following through from action to reaction.

So, if Senator Harrison had a secret, and Secret Squirrel John found out and told Jane, and Jane told Molly, and Molly's newspaper broke the story and pretty much ruined John's chance to publish a book (his "uplifting" love story didn't count), then John would know that Jane told Molly, and John would come after Jane and . . . Hooboy, she didn't want to think about it, but it would be Doo-doo City, that's for sure.

She was reaching into her purse for her cell phone, to call Molly and tell her, sorry, but their deal was off and she'd pay her back every penny for her clothes and hair and stuff, but she was staying for the week to have an adventure (so there!), when the bathroom door opened and John walked into the room.

"Excuse me," he said as her jaw dropped.

Where were his clothes? All the man was wearing was a small white towel and a smile. Not even a sheepish smile.

Jane squeezed her eyelids shut once more. "Get dressed," she ordered tightly.

"Sorry. I stripped off, then realized I'd forgotten my clothes," he said, and she could hear him messing about in his luggage, hopefully to find his boxer shorts or jockey shorts or—oh, who cared, just let him put something on!

Behind her closed eyelids, Jane was having trouble blocking out the sight of John's body as he'd walked into the room. It was sort of like staring at the small black and white tiles on her parents' bathroom floor. Stare at the tiles for a while, then close your eyes and you could still see the pattern of the tiles.

She could still see the "pattern" of John's body behind her eyelids.

She thought men only had bodies like that in those exercise machine ads on television, those "You, too, can have this body if you only give us three thousand dollars and eighty hours of exercise a week for ten years."

Oh, well, as long as the image was there, she might as well take inventory:

Not Arnold Schwarzenegger, but more muscular than, say, Tom Cruise.

Hairier than both of them.

A great overall tan, except for that hint of lighter skin just above the line of the towel that had been hanging pretty darn low over his hips.

Straight legs, hairy legs. Just that all-over look of muscles, tan, and dark hair that was far from ruglike or bearlike—so that she had to take back her mental Ape Man and replace it with, oh, who knew? Masculine? Manly man?

Hunk.

Horton Hears a Hunk?

Okay, forget the body. Go to the face.

There were those eyes. She'd never forget those eyes. But now there was also that hair, once parted and slicked down, but now a dark, rich fall of slightly unkempt ebony glory that made him look almost boyish—if big, bad hunks could look boyish.

Most of all, he was overpowering. Yes, that was it; overpowering. He *filled* the room. Took all the air out of it.

Some people might call that a presence.

Jane called it strutting around without a care in the world, with darn near no clothes on.

What would Molly call it, call him? Bad boy?

Probably.

"You can open your eyes now," John said, interrupting her thoughts just before she could examine her reaction, try to figure out why she was still primly sitting here with both feet on the floor and her hands neatly folded in her lap, and not running for the nearest exit.

"You're decent?" she asked, still keeping her eyes tightly shut.

He laughed. "God, I hope not."

Bad boy. Definitely a bad boy.

Jane opened one eye and turned to look at him.

He had his slacks on, but that was about it. "You still have a tag hanging off the back pocket," she told him, already reaching for her purse and the small sewing kit with the folding scissors that one of the mothers had given her for Christmas last year and that she'd never be able to take on an airplane again—not that she'd ever *been* on an airplane.

"You come prepared, don't you?" John asked, standing in front of her, then turning his back, so that she was just about on eye level with his backside.

Urp.

Jane spoke quickly to cover her embarrassment and hoped he didn't notice that her hands were shaking so badly she could barely open the scissors. "I get Christmas presents from all the students. I think I have five sewing kits like this. Along with three dozen scarves, more perfume than any one person could use in two lifetimes, a zillion embroidered handkerchiefs ... oh, and one knotty pine placard for my desk, with my name burned into it. Scotty Klein's father likes to do woodworking, you understand. I think it's because then he can stay in his workroom rather than be with Mrs. Klein, who really is a bit of a—there. Tag's off."

She resisted giving his rear a little pat, the way she would have patted the behind of one of her small charges to send him on his way.

John twisted around, trying to look at his backside, she supposed, then grinned at her. "Great. Keep that out, okay? I've got a lot of tags to get rid of."

"And here's the scissors to get rid of them. I'm not doing it for you," Jane said, resisting the urge to fan herself, because it was suddenly very hot in here. "I'm going down to the gift shop, to look at the postcards again. I should send some soon, or I'll be home before they are."

"All right. Don't wander off."

That stopped her, and she turned around just in time to see him ready to pull a tag from the cuff of his navy blue sports jacket.

"Stop that! Give it to me," she said, grabbing the jacket from him. "You *cut* these things off; you don't *pull* them off."

"Yes, ma'am, thank you, ma'am, and may I say, ma'am, that you look very *nice* this evening."

She looked up from her task and glared at him. "I'll bet you were a teacher's pet all through school. I'll bet you never did your own homework. I'll bet you—oh, here, take this."

She threw the jacket at him and, scissors in hand, approached the suitcases. "Which shirt are you going to wear? This white one?"

"If you want me to, ma'am," he said, standing close beside her.

"Cut that out," she ordered, giving him a slap on the arm. "You're not funny."

"You are, teach. I think I like you as a roommate," he said, taking the shirt from her as she was still trying to remove the last bit of cardboard tucked under the collar. "You . . . ruffle well."

"I do *not* ruffle. I am unflappable. I am—"

"A brick in a crisis. I remember."

"Shut up," she said, and slammed out of the room. Well, nearly slammed out of the room. She had to stop at the door, turn around, go back, and get her purse. But then she slammed out of the room.

"See you downstairs, teach," he called after her.

Jane muttered to herself, all the way to the elevator.

* * *

There was a line outside the ballroom as John and Jane approached, the bottleneck being the registration table, where information packets and name tags were being handed out.

John took the time to look around, trying to match names on the list Jane had picked up with the faces that passed by.

Captains of industry, movie stars, politicians, scientists, economists. Some of them talking, some of them sulking, some of them looking around just like he was—those would be the lesser lights, like him, checking out the VIPs.

There wasn't an equal division of men and women, not that he had expected it, not with the current administration, but the women he did see were divided into two categories: serious thinkers, and arm candy.

He wondered if Jane knew she would automatically be put in the arm candy category by the other men attending the retreat.

Slowly, they made their way to the registration table, where Jane quickly located their packets and name tags, laughing as she saw that the ''owski'' on Romanowski sort of slid down the side of the handwritten badge, clearly written by a person who didn't ''plan ahead.''

''I'm not wearing that,'' John said as Jane eased the name tag off its backing and aimed it at his chest.

''Don't be silly, you have to wear it. Everyone else is wearing one, John.''

He made a face. ''And if everyone else jumped off a cliff . . .''

''Very funny. Look, there's the board with the table listings.''

He followed after her, trying really hard not to feel like a puppy coming to heel, and she located their table: Table 2.

A quick scan of the board located the three men on the beach, Harrison's condo buddies. Funny they hadn't all taken a table together. Or maybe not so funny; maybe planned.

"Sounds like we're right up front," John said at last. "Well, we're not. Harrison is. But we get the benefit."

"What's the benefit? Are there going to be dinner speakers?"

"Not if we're lucky," John said, taking Jane's elbow and guiding her into the large ballroom. "No, the first tables always get served first. I don't know about you, but I'm starving."

They continued to thread their way through the crowd, until they bumped into the largest knot of people, the one around Brandy Hythe.

"She's very popular," Jane said as everyone around Brandy—and they were all men—laughed at something the actress had said. "I imagine she'll be sitting next to the senator."

"Yes, and you'll be sitting on his other side, since you're the only other woman at the table. Got your southern belle drawl all wound up and ready to go?"

"I do not drawl," Jane said, putting her purse down on one of the chairs. "And I'm sitting right here. If the senator wants me, he's going to have to come and get me. Oh— fruit cup, and it looks fresh, not canned."

John smiled, shook his head. "I guess that means I can't ask you to give me your strawberry?"

"Not a chance," Jane said, then seemed to stiffen, her smile locked in place. "Oh, my . . ."

John turned to look where Jane was looking and saw Dillon Holmes approaching the table. Tall, but a good six inches shorter than John, Holmes was slim, with a narrow, almost aesthetic face, green eyes, and carefully combed blond hair. His light gray suit looked tailor-made, his smile professional, and his overall attitude one of "Here I am, and aren't you glad."

"You like that?" John asked, hitching a thumb in Holmes's direction.

"What's not to like?" Jane whispered out of the corner

of her mouth. "He's so . . . so *urbane*. So sleek, so sophisticated."

"Domesticated, you mean. Like a house cat."

"You prefer shaggy lions?"

"I don't prefer either. I like long legs in short skirts. That's Dillon Holmes, by the way, Harrison's nephew and general dogsbody. You should probably suck up to him, which would be easier if you weren't staring at him like he'd just dropped off a cloud to grace all us mortals."

"I am not—ohmigod, he's coming this way. Quick, is my hair all right? Do I have enough lipstick?"

"Oh, for crying out loud," John muttered under his breath. And here he thought the girl had some intelligence. "What am I, your pal or your pimp?"

She looked up at him. "Well, as a matter of fact, I had thought of that. But, no, we're . . . We're on a case, a project, a . . . a mission. Right? I really should get to know the man if I'm going to help you."

"Help me by getting close to Harrison, and leave the little puppy dog alone."

Jane blinked at him. "What's the matter with you?"

He had no idea. "Nothing's the matter with me, damn it. I just didn't bring you here to be some groupie."

She shook her head. "You're such a jerk," she told him, pinning a smile on her face again. "Now, here he comes. Introduce us. Remember, I'm just your friend."

"You got it," John said, and slipped his arm around Jane's waist, drawing her close against his body with enough force that he could hear her breath *whoosh* out of her.

"Excuse me?" he said, extending his right hand. "You'd be Dillon Holmes, wouldn't you? Assistant to Senator Harrison, who is also your uncle? I believe we met a few years ago, at a seminar in Fairfax? I'm John Romanowski. I teach political science at the university."

Holmes looked at John's hand for just a split second, then quickly extended his own. "Forgive me, I meet so many people. How are you, John?"

"Fine, Dillon, just fine," John answered, his fingers closing around Holmes's hand in what would only be called a politely firm handshake by someone wearing an iron gauntlet. "And this is Janie Preston, my . . . companion. Janie owns a day care and nursery school in Fairfax. She'll be invaluable to the senator, should he want to know a woman's views on day care in this country. Isn't that right, Janie honey?"

Jane dug her elbow into his side—rather like a mouse attacking an elephant and hoping to make an impression—and somehow extracted her arm enough to hold out her hand to Holmes. "It's a pleasure to meet you, Mr. Holmes."

"Dillon, please," Holmes said, grabbing his hand back from John and offering it to Jane. "I believe we'll be table mates this week?"

"Yes, indeed," John said, corralling Jane once more. "Janie here twisted her ankle this afternoon, and Senator Harrison was nice enough to come to her rescue, then invite us to join his table. I'm anxious to thank him. Can't have anything happening to my little Janie girl, you know."

There was the elbow again. Not quite jabbed, but just being pushed, ground, into his ribs. She was probably wondering what the hell he was doing, and if he knew, he would tell her. But he didn't know. He just knew he didn't want Jane and Holmes spending the week making googly eyes at each other.

Holmes looked at John for long moments, then sort of shrugged. An elegant shrug. Everything about the man was sleek, elegant. "So, you teach political science, John? Freshman level?"

"Graduate level, actually," John said, wondering if anyone would notice if he ripped Holmes's aristocratic nose clean off his face, then fed it to the man.

What was the matter with him? Holmes was a nothing. He shouldn't care if Jane was attracted to him, went to bed with him, married him, and bore his kids while he kept a mistress in Bethesda. It wasn't his problem.

So what was his problem?

"Will you be managing the senator's presidential campaign, Dillon?" Jane asked, and John silently gave her points for getting the conversation back on track, if it had ever been there.

Holmes's smile showed straight white teeth that had probably cost his parents a few cool thousand. "That hasn't been decided yet, Janie."

"That he's running, or that you'll run the campaign?" Jane asked, and now it was John's turn to jab her in the ribs, because she was moving too fast. Did she expect to get all the information this first night?

Holmes's smile grew even wider. The guy had to practice in front of a mirror. "Why, Janie, I didn't know you were interested in politics."

"Oh, I'm not," Jane said brightly, looking at John. "But John told me that the senator is going to run. Didn't you say that, Johnny?"

Johnny? He was going to have to kill her. Too bad; he really liked her, at least sometimes he liked her. "No, Janie, I said that he *should* run. The country needs more men like Senator Harrison."

"Ah, just what I like to hear," Holmes said. "An unsolicited and highly intelligent, informed opinion. That means a lot, John, coming from someone of your stature and background. And have you shared your views with your students?"

"I always share my views with my students," John said, pretending he didn't hear Jane's small sigh. "Of course, that doesn't automatically mean that my students agree with me. For instance, a few of them, when they learned I was coming here, were rather vocal in their objections to the senator as a presidential candidate."

"Really," Holmes said, obviously losing interest. "We'll have to discuss that, won't we? One has to keep one's finger on the pulse of young America, whether the senator decides to run or not. Ah, here come the senator and Ms. Blythe at last. Even here, even in this supposedly august gathering, the autograph seekers line up for both of them.''

"For Brandy Hythe, certainly,'' John said, but quietly, because he knew he was letting his temper rule his tongue. Okay, and yes, he was a little nervous. Only a little nervous.

And then the moment was here, and John was being introduced to Aubrey Harrison (Brandy was busy speaking into a cell phone), the man who had put the last few nails in what would end by being the coffin of Maryjo's mental breakdown.

"Senator,'' John said, feeling his large hand being enveloped by an even larger one, although this one was soft, without calluses, and the nails were professionally cut and polished.

"Hello, good to meet you. And you'd be—?''

He hadn't needed the nerd costume after all. The man didn't recognize him. John didn't know if that was a good thing or a bad thing, because he wanted any excuse to take the man apart. No, it was better the senator didn't recognize him. But the bastard could have at least commented on his name. How many John Romanowskis did the man meet?

Dillon deftly made the introductions. Just a helpful, helpful guy.

"Professor, or may I call you John? Let's make it John and Aubrey, shall we? We're supposed to dispense with titles this week, as part of the charm of the retreat,'' Harrison said, already looking at Jane. "Hello again, my dear. How lovely to see you. How's the ankle?''

"Oh, fine, sir, just fine,'' Jane said, seemingly caught between a bow and a curtsy before she, too, offered her hand. "And I can't thank you enough for inviting the professor and me to sit at your table. I'm *so* honored.''

"That honor is solely mine, my dear. Now, as Brandy is finally off the phone, let's finish these introductions and sit down. I think the servers are anxious to pour us some wine and start the meal.''

John and Jane said hello to Brandy Hythe, who seemed

truly happy to meet them—but, then, she was a very good
actor—and John shook hands with Henry Brewster, who was
an even better actor as he said his hellos, then immediately
mispronounced John's last name.

Henry looked good, for Henry. A fairly short man who
liked bow ties could only look so good. But his once carrot
orange hair had finally darkened a little, so at least he looked
more his age, which was the same as John's. His waistline
was running a little to fat, because the man did enjoy his
food, and he hated exercise. Henry's idea of a good time,
even in college, was a table by himself in a good restaurant,
a book open in front of him, and two desserts.

John liked Henry. Had always liked Henry.

He couldn't wait to get the man alone, stuff him in a
suitcase, and air mail him back to Manhattan.

There was more room at their table than at the others,
which all seated eight, but still the atmosphere was pretty
thick. The feeling of being too close for comfort made John
want to loosen his tie and open the top button of his shirt.

Jane did end up on Harrison's left side, with Brandy to
the man's right. John decided to ignore Jane, because every
time she caught his eye, she glared at him.

Beside Brandy was Henry Brewster, then John—almost
directly across the table from Jane—and lastly, beside Jane,
Dillon Holmes.

Just one big happy family.

Maybe he should pair up Jane with Henry; the man would
be safer than Holmes, and less upsetting to John's own
stomach.

Then again, no. No way. Let Henry find his own girl.

Harrison took charge of the conversation with the first
bite of fruit cup and held center stage throughout the dinner,
telling everyone more about New Jersey than anyone not
writing their own guide book would ever want to know.

Cape May was America's oldest seaside resort, and this
very Congress Hall had served as the summer White House
for four presidents.

John Phillips Sousa played his march tunes right here, to admiring audiences.

More than one hundred battles took place in New Jersey during the war for independence, making it known as "The Crossroads of the Revolution."

Thomas Alva Edison invented the incandescent lightbulb, the movie camera, and phonograph in his West Orange and Menlo Park, New Jersey labs.

New Jersey was the home of the Meadowlands sports complex, which was the home of the Giants and the Jets.

"And Jimmy Hoffa, who's buried in one of the end zones, if the rumors are right," John whispered to Henry Brewster, who discreetly coughed into his napkin.

The Hadrosaurus foulkii was the state dinosaur.

"Right after Harrison," Henry whispered to John, because it was his turn.

Over one hundred and fifty types of fruits and vegetables were grown in the Garden State, and New Jersey was fourth in asparagus and fifth in head lettuce.

"I wouldn't touch that one with a five-foot pole," John whispered to Henry, then beat down a wince as Jane frowned at him with that never to be forgotten "Shame on you, Johnny, now be a good boy and behave" teacher face of his youth.

Alexander Hamilton, first U.S. Treasury Secretary, shot in a duel by Aaron Burr, died right here in New Jersey, in his beloved Weehawken.

"Not the first political career to go belly-up in New Jersey."

John's head snapped to the right, because it had been Dillon Holmes who had said that one.

"Bored, Dillon?" John asked him as the server removed the half-eaten block of chocolate, vanilla, and strawberry ice cream from in front of him.

"It's not like I haven't heard it all before, you know," Holmes said, waving away his own melting, barely touched ice cream. "He's got to start talking more on a national stage, not just about his beloved New Jersey."

"I didn't know anyone loved New Jersey, to tell you the truth. I mean, think about it. I'm willing to bet you never heard a song like *I Left My Heart In Newark*. My spleen maybe, but not my heart."

"The state is the butt of some bad jokes, I'll grant you, but we're known for more than our beaches, casinos, and Frank Sinatra."

"Yes," Jane said, and John looked up to see that she had left her chair and was now standing behind him. "According to the guide book I was looking through earlier, New Jersey is also home of the first condensed soup. Who keeps track of these things?"

"We do, obviously. Every state delights in listing its firsts, its important citizens, things like that," Dillon said, standing up, so that John knew he had to stand as well, as did Henry Brewster. It was that politeness thing, drummed into young men by women like Aunt Marion, and one of the reasons John spent a lot of time alone, because then he didn't have to be polite while his coffee got cold.

"I'm sure you're right, Dillon," Jane said, then shrugged her shoulders. "But, to tell you the truth, I think I've heard enough about New Jersey for one evening. I'd much rather take a walk on the beach and *see* New Jersey."

"Just let me drink my—" John began, but Dillon cut him off with an offer to escort Jane on a walk along the shore.

"Oh, that's so *nice* of you, Dillon," Jane gushed, and the next thing John knew, he was standing alone at the table except for Henry, as the senator and Brandy had gone off to visit other tables, Brandy just being nice, and Harrison openly working the room, like any politician.

"So. John. How goes it?"

He turned to look at the last of his dinner companions.

"Henry. I see you. I've been talking to you. I passed you

the rolls, and the salt. But I still don't believe you're here. So—why are you here?''

''Would you believe that a few weeks ago I decided to use my own invitation just so I could watch my good friend, old college buddy, and best-selling author at work?''

''No,'' John said, motioning for his editor to follow him outside, onto the verandah. ''But I do believe you might be here because somebody whispered something into your ear and you've come to make sure I behave myself, don't land in jail for busting Harrison's face, or something like that. So, what else did Aunt Marion tell you?''

''Well, there was something about slicked-down hair and black-rimmed glasses.''

''I ditched that as a bad idea,'' John said as they walked along. ''I couldn't carry it off. Jane saw through me right away.''

''And she's still here?''

''Yeah,'' John said, jamming his hands into his pants pockets. ''I told her I'm a college professor with a chance to write a big political exposé book on Harrison, and I needed her along for cover. We've decided to be pals.''

''You're kidding. Pals?''

''Yeah, pals,'' John said, looking toward the beach, looking for Jane. ''What's wrong with that?''

''John, John, Johnny-boy, I know you, remember? You've never been pals with a woman in your life.''

''There's a first time for everything.''

''Sure. The first lightbulb, the first condensed soup. But J. P. Roman as a pal to a beautiful woman? And lying to her on top of it? Quick, where do I go to bet against the two of you ever exchanging friendship rings?''

Chapter Seven

Jane slid her key into the electronic lock and stepped inside the dark hotel room. She fumbled along the wall a little, looking for the light switch, one hand holding her shoes by the heel straps, part of her wondering what time it was, and most of her wondering where John was.

She flipped on the light.

"Well, well, young lady. It's about time you got home," John said from his seat in the chair by the window.

Jane blinked, then frowned. "You scared me. Why were you sitting here in the dark?"

"I was thinking," he said, standing up. He was still dressed in his new slacks, his white shirt open at the collar and with the sleeves rolled up over those impressive forearms. "I think better in the dark."

"Okay," Jane said, shrugging. If he wanted to be a jerk, he could be a jerk. *She,* on the other hand, had spent a marvelous evening, walking the beach with Dillon, sharing drinks and a really interesting conversation in the hotel's pub, the Blue Pig Tavern.

"So? Where were you?"

Jane counted to ten as she opened the closet and put her shoes inside.

"At the Blue Pig."

"No, you weren't. I was at the Blue Pig."

"Which room?"

"What do you mean, which room? *The* room."

"John," Jane said, pushing both hands through her hair as she looked at him. "There are *two* rooms in the tavern. Let me see, how did the brochure describe it? Oh. There are two dining rooms, each with its own mood. One has an open, airy garden motif, and the other is reminiscent of a cozy tavern. Dark walls, a huge fireplace, dim lights . . ."

"So what you're telling me is that you and Holmes were sitting in the dark, drinking in the dark."

"Yes, I am. While you, obviously, were in the other room. Alone?"

"No, not alone. I was with Henry Brewster."

Jane couldn't resist. "You two could have been cozier in the back dining room."

John brushed past her, heading toward his bed. "I liked you better cute, and *nice.*"

"And I've never said I liked you at all, *pal,*" Jane shot back, stung. Then she sat down on her bed and shook her head. "We're fighting again. Why are we fighting? This is ridiculous. We don't know each other well enough to fight."

"That's right, and we're not fighting. I'm just reminding you that you're my . . . my employee, and I want you to account for your time."

Jane glared at him. He glared back.

"Oh, all right, so I'm being an ass," he said at last. "I'm sorry. Did you have a good time?"

"I had a wonderful time," she told him, lifting her chin. "The beach was lovely, and then we went to the Blue Pig, and I had two drinks with umbrellas in them." She smiled, then rubbed at the tip of her nose with the palm of her hand.

"Really. What was in the drinks?"

"I don't have the faintest idea; but I asked for something

with an umbrella in it, and the bartender brought me this lovely big, curvy glass with pink stuff and an umbrella in it. It was sweet, almost like strawberry milk.'' She smiled, sighed. ''I haven't had strawberry milk since I was a little girl.''

John stripped off his shirt, and Jane looked away, because in the dimness of the single overhead light, his muscles were cast in light and shadow, and she had this almost irresistible urge to run her hands over him and . . .

''You don't drink, do you, Jane?''

''Huh?'' she asked, shaking her head to clear it. ''I don't—well, of course I do. I have a glass of wine with dinner sometimes, and I—no, that's about it. But I *do* drink. I'm not a teetotaler.''

''A *tee*totaler. Man, I haven't heard that one in a while.''

''My grandmother used to say that word. *Tee*totaler. I have no idea where that came from, do you? Is it tea, do you think? You know, like oolong? Or tee? Like in . . . like in, tee-hee?''

''Oy-jeez,'' John said, picking up his open suitcase and tossing it on the floor. ''I wouldn't say you're hammered, Jane, but you are a little tipsy. You do know that, right?''

She sat up very straight. ''Don't be ridiculous. I am not tipsy. I'm . . . I'm mellow. Yes, that's it. I'm mellow. And what else did you expect? You lock me in a yellow deathtrap and let it rain on me, you lose our reservations, and you stand there half naked, and your side of the room is a pigsty—all while I know we're both going to be sleeping in the same room. I should have had *three* umbrella drinks.''

''Not quite a pigsty. Not yet. Give me a couple of days.'' The overnight case and the suit bag joined the large suitcase on the floor. ''And I'm not saying you've had an easy time of it so far, Jane. Neither have I. But if you're going to be of any help to me, you can't go getting looped every time something doesn't go your way.''

''Now I'm looped? Oh, wonderful. That's just so . . . so

darn *nice* of you, John Romanowski. And after all I did for you tonight, too."

She stomped over to the dresser and opened the third drawer, the one with her pajamas in it. A part of her brain blessed Molly's oversight in not picking out new nightwear for her—Molly slept in the nude, so it probably would not have occurred to her. She pulled out a pair of pajamas, sky blue ones, with little clouds all over them, and headed for the bathroom.

"Be in your pajamas by the time I get back, John, or I'm leaving here tonight."

"I don't wear—oh, hell, at least I bought some shorts. I'll wear those."

"Sounds like a plan. Just shovel through that mess you've made. I'm sure you'll find them."

"Wait a minute. You said after all you did for me tonight? What did you do?"

Jane concentrated on walking a straight line to the bathroom. She'd walked straight enough on her way to the room, but suddenly she was feeling just a little bit off balance. A little tipsy. A little. . . . Damn, she really didn't want him to be right.

"What did I do?" she asked, surreptitiously leaning against the doorjamb, so that she wouldn't sway. "What did I do, the man asked. Well, I'll tell the man what I did. What I did was I got us invited to a small party . . . an *intimate* party . . . the seno-*ter*—I mean, the sen-*ator*—is hosting tomorrow night in his suite. Our suite. Used to be our suite. Betcha."

And then, while John stood there, showing off his chest, darn him, Jane turned and disappeared into the bathroom, where she stood with her hands braced against the edge of the sink and stared at herself for long seconds, trying to get her eyes to focus.

She had to calm down, she decided as she creamed off her makeup, then washed out her pantyhose and defiantly hung them over the shower rod.

Calm down? How was she going to do that?

She had a dangerous, barely civilized *hunk* in her bedroom—or she was in his. Either way, it wasn't a good thing. She had experienced the man of her dreams walking her to the elevator and giving her a chaste kiss on the cheek. She had a brewing adventure, trying to discover what Senator Harrison was up to . . . and please God, don't let it be Brandy Hythe, because that would just be disgusting.

And, just to top it all off, she was here under false pretenses, on a Mission From Molly, and if John ever found out, she was dead meat.

Calm down? Sure . . . right after her *break*down.

Jane buttoned her pajama top all the way to the neck, then gave herself a last look while holding her arms out at her sides, just to be sure light wouldn't make the material transparent. Not too bad. She loved these pajamas. They were just enough too long in the pant legs and the sleeves to make her feel small, comfy—sort of Meg Ryanish. The cotton was thin thanks to its age, but not really transparent. Not unless she stood in front of a spotlight.

She gathered up her clothing, took a deep breath, and opened the door to the bedroom . . . and stepped into a spotlight.

The man had turned on every light in the room. Jane had to blink and shade her eyes with her hands, although she really wanted to strike that *September Morn* pose, one arm across her breasts, one placed strategically lower.

"Are you planning on landing a 747 in here?" she asked, blinking. "I don't see a runway."

"Just stand still, don't move. I'm looking for my contact, damn it," John said, and she noticed that the reason she hadn't seen him was that he was on his hands and knees between the two beds.

"You wear contacts?" Jane said, standing very still. "I didn't know. Are they . . . colored ones?"

His head came up. "Colored ones? Oh, you mean tinted ones? No."

No. Of course not. Because his eyes were still that wonderful blue-green, or green-blue, or whatever they were, except now they were slightly unfocused, and softer. What they also were was wonderful, and sexy, and. . . . Maybe she should go back into the bathroom and regroup.

"Damn it," John said as he advanced slowly, on his knees, lightly running his fingers over the carpet. Then he looked up at her again. "You could help, you know."

"But you told me to . . . oh, never mind," she said, getting on her hands and knees and mimicking his careful hand swiping. "You don't wear disposables?"

"If I did, would I be down here, doing this?"

"Good point," Jane said, continuing her search. "You might want to consider the disposable ones, you know. They have a kind you can wear and clean for a few days, then throw away. I think they even have a type that you wear just one day, then throw away. Besides, they're probably more sterile, when you think about it, and if you drop yours a lot, you might want to think about having an extra—found it!"

She went back on her haunches, the contact neatly stuck to her index finger, to see that he was also sitting back, looking at her strangely.

"Gimme that," he said, just about grabbing the small lense from her, certainly not acting at all appreciative.

"And you're welcome, John. Now don't just spit on it and put it back in, because—"

"Would you cut me a freaking break, teach?" John said, getting to his feet. "Next thing, you'll be telling me to be sure to brush my teeth before I go to bed."

Jane rolled her eyes. "Don't be silly. You're a grown-up, John. Of course you brush your teeth before you go to bed."

"No, I don't. Not if I don't want to. *Because* I'm a grown-up."

"That's ridiculous. You're being ridiculous," Jane told him as she turned down her covers, carefully folding the bedspread at the bottom of the bed. Before she left home her mother had told her that hotels may wash their sheets every day, but bedspreads were probably another matter; so whoever had occupied the room last had probably used the same bedspread.

Her father had then chimed in, telling her about a television special he'd seen that showed how many germs there were on the carpets, the telephones, even the lamps . . . and where a lot of those germs came from.

Which explained the can of Lysol she had found zipped into the front pocket of her suitcase.

"Oh, my God!"

John, who had been in the process of dropping the contact lense into its small plastic case, dropped the thing onto the carpet once more. "Son of a—what's wrong?"

"My parents," Jane said, plopping down onto her back on the bed. "I never called my parents to tell them I got here safely." She lifted her chin and tried to see the clock on the table between the beds. "What time is it?"

"You're asking a man who just took out his contacts? A little past midnight, I think," John told her, lifting his own head, because he was on the floor once more, looking for his lense. "But don't tell me you actually call your parents to tell them you—wait a minute," he said, locating the lense and quickly securing it in its case. "How old are you, anyway? I mean, am I going to be arrested here?"

Jane jackknifed into a sitting position. "I'm twenty-seven years old, John, but that doesn't mean my parents don't worry about me when I'm away from home. They're probably getting ready to notify the police right now. I should call them. Do you think it's too late to call them?"

He sat down on the other bed, facing her, and she couldn't help noticing that with them both sitting like this, their knees nearly touched. Why had she thought the room was bigger?

"I think I'm getting this now," John said, shaking his head. "You run a day care."

"And nursery school, yes. You know that," Jane said

absently, scooting down to the end of the bed, to get her knees out of the way. She looked for her purse and the cell phone inside it.

"And nursery school, yes, how could I forget? You're a *nice* girl. You're cute and always a bridesmaid, and all of that good stuff. There's only one thing that could top off all of that, and I think I just figured it out. You *live* with your parents, don't you?"

"That's a crime?" Jane held onto the cell phone, wanting to dial, but suddenly feeling as though he would just laugh at her again.

"If it's not, it should be. What are you doing here, Jane? I mean it. What *are* you doing here?"

"What am I . . . I mean, why shouldn't I . . . that is . . . oh, I can't do this. Molly could do this, but I can't do this."

She lifted her shoulders, let them droop, and put the cell phone back in her purse. She would call her parents tomorrow morning, first thing, and apologize. Heck, she'd probably be home tomorrow.

"Jane? Are you all right?"

"Sure. I'm just having a momentary mental aberration, that's all. At least I think that's what it is." She looked at him hopefully. "I've got to tell you something. Do you have an hour? I mean, I could probably explain it all if you gave me an hour, because I think I really should start with second grade, so that you'd understand how it is between Molly and me. Except that would take all night, and I really, *really* don't want to go through all of that."

John looked at her for long moments, then reached for the box of taffy. "Cinnamon or licorice?" he asked, offering her the box.

"I already brushed my teeth and—oh, all right." She rooted through the box, located the last of the licorice taffy, and then crawled beneath the covers, propping herself against the pillows.

"You're going to hate me," she said as she unwrapped the taffy. "And then you're going to kick me out, and I won't have my adventure, and that really stinks. Because I was going to be a great help to you, honestly I was. I'd already decided that I wouldn't have told Molly anything.''

"Molly. Why does that name keep coming up? That would be Molly Applegate, the one who works in the Senate?''

Jane chewed on the taffy for a while, then stuck it against the inside of her cheek, to let the rest of it melt there. She'd have to brush her teeth again, but that was all right. The licorice was worth it.

"Molly . . . Molly doesn't work in the Senate, John. She used to, when she first graduated from college, but she's had a lot of jobs since then." Jane rolled her eyes. "I mean, a *lot* of jobs."

John, who hadn't bothered to turn down his own bed, leaned forward, his bare legs crossed Indian-style, and asked, "Just tell me this. What does Molly have to do with *you* being here?''

Jane had folded the taffy wrapping paper into a neat little square, and now didn't know what to do with it. "She blackmailed me," she said, then turned to look at John, gauge his reaction.

"For what? Feeding the kiddies fake cheese for their snacks or something?''

"I'd *never* give the children anything other than real cheese." Jane flipped the little square into the air and watched it fall to the floor at the bottom of her bed. She beat down the urge to get up, pick it up, and find a wastebasket . . . and then clean up John's side of the room. "Let me start at the beginning, okay?''

"All right, just make it fast. I'm getting nervous here.''

"Oh, you are not," Jane told him, and then looked at him again. He did not look nervous. He looked hairy and unfocused and sexy as sin. She'd take the sight of him, clad in nothing but a pair of blue nylon gym shorts, sitting on top of the bedspread, his hairy legs crossed, and his hair all mussed, with her to the grave.

130 *Kasey Michaels*

Also beating down that thought, Jane sighed, ignored the taffy paper, and began her story.

She told John all about Molly, who came to visit in Fairfax every summer between stints at different boarding schools— schools Molly got herself tossed out of with astonishing regularity. She told him how Molly's parents liked to travel and how they never thought to take Molly with them. She told him about what a live wire Molly was, what a mischief maker she was . . . and how Jane had always loved her cousin, even while envying her cousin's spirit.

She did not tell him about Sean Gentry. He didn't need to hear about her bad boy . . . not when he had all the makings of yet another bad boy.

"I think Molly misbehaved to get her parents' attention," she said after describing the time her cousin had locked herself in the freezer at Hartzell's Meats, refusing to come out until someone located her parents in Bali and got them on the phone so she could tell them to come get her. She had been seven at the time.

John shook his head. "That's sad, you do know that."

"Oh, I know that. And my parents knew that, which was why we kept taking her in, every summer, and then for our final two years of high school, when she'd run through every boarding school within a thousand miles."

"Now explain the blackmail."

"Well, not precisely blackmail. Molly . . . Well, Molly has this way of making everything an adventure. With her parents gone now, and a trust fund that goes on forever, she's been living the good life. I . . . I might envy that, a little. The good life part of it. But her parents put a string on the trust fund. Until Molly marries, she has to stay gainfully employed at least ten months a year in order to collect the income. They thought she should learn responsibility."

John was listening intently, so Jane went on to explain that Molly was on probation at her latest job and had gotten this great idea to . . .

"*Harrison?*" John was on his feet so quickly at the end

of her story that Jane didn't even see him move. "She wants you to get a scoop on *Harrison?*"

The licorice had collided with the pink strawberry-tasting drink in her stomach, and suddenly Jane wasn't feeling too well. "I'll leave in the morning."

"Shut up," John said, but he said it quietly, as he paced the carpet. "Molly works for the largest newspaper in Washington, one that isn't all that sympathetic to Harrison. Information you give her—information I give you—could end up printed in that newspaper. Yes, I like this."

"You *like* this? You like *what?* I thought you wanted to write a book?" Jane asked him, finally giving in and picking up the taffy paper, walking it over to the waste can ... and giving a lot of thought to returning to the bathroom, supposedly to brush her teeth again but more probably to hug the porcelain bowl. Instead, she retreated to the bed, crawled under the covers once more, and pretended she was fine, just fine.

He waved his hand at her, as if giving permission for her to lie down, and kept pacing. Like a caged lion, or panther, or great big sexy man. Finally, and with a smile on his face that made her want to twitch her nose and disappear, he turned to face her.

"I'm a lousy writer," he said, his grin growing wider.

"Oh, don't say that, John. You had one bad idea," Jane told him gently, forcing herself to sit up once more.

"No, no. I'm a lousy writer. I am. But I've got a great lead on Harrison. I think I can dig deeper, blow the cover off the man. But I'd never sell the book. Besides, it would take too long to get the book into print, and Harrison could already be nominated, even elected. But if we were to feed your cousin Molly what we can find out, together, and she was to feed her bosses at the newspaper? Yes. Yes, Jane, it could work."

"You'd give up your hopes of a book, just like that?"

"In a heartbeat. I told you, I don't like Harrison. There's something ... something ..."

"Something slippery about him?" Jane offered, nodding her head. Bad move. Nodding her head made her stomach nod as well, then do a half-gainer inside her.

"You think so, too?"

"I'll tell you what I think, John. I think it's quite a coincidence that you and I are both here to try to investigate Senator Harrison. I mean, what are the odds?"

John sat down on his bed once more. "Jane, there are, at my count, six journalists here for the retreat. Do you really think they're here to discuss global warming or political ethics? No. They're here because the incumbent can't run again, but the vice president already said no because of his health; so Harrison is a sure lock—if he chooses to run."

"What about the other party?"

He shook his head. "The opposition is in disarray, with eight guys already announced, all unknowns, so there's no story there for months, until one or two guys emerge from the pack. Harrison's not only the biggest story in town this summer, Jane, he's the only one. That you and I are here on pretty much the same mission is a coincidence, but not that big of one. Half the people here, conservatively, are here to do some Senator Aubrey Harrison-watching."

"Even Brandy Hythe?"

John shrugged. "Could be. She wouldn't be the only actress with aspirations to higher office. Look at Marilyn Monroe. Grace Kelly. Barbra Streisand. Liz Taylor. Marry it or finance it, ride it as long as you agree with the politics, one hand washing the other. Maybe Brandy Hythe is thinking about being First Lady. Fame, or a real political agenda. There are a lot of women out there who long to be the next Jackie Kennedy or the next Hillary Clinton."

Jane pressed her fingers to her temples. She almost welcomed the headache. It took her mind off her roiling stomach. "I'm not cut out for all this intrigue. Is politics really so convoluted?"

"Nope. Just follow the power, follow the money. And, right now, follow Aubrey Harrison and see where he leads.

Out of two hundred attendees, I'm betting at least three-fourths of them are here only to see if they can find out what Harrison's up to. The rest already know, and I want to know what they know.''

"And then you want me to feed it all to Molly. I thought you'd want to kill me."

"Nope. We're a team, Jane. Just as long as you don't go ape-shit over Dillon Holmes."

"I don't go—and that's crude."

"Sorry. All I'm saying is have your adventure, Jane. Have a ball, let it all hang out. Play at being your cousin Molly for a week. But remember one thing—Dillon Holmes is in love with Dillon Holmes. You'd be better off looking anywhere else but there."

"I didn't want *that* kind of adventure. You make it all sound so sordid, as if I'm looking to jump into bed with the first man I see."

"Don't look now, Janie Preston, but you're already sleeping with one man."

Jane glared at him, then turned over on her side. "I think I need some sleep."

John walked around the room, turning off all the lights. "Don't forget to brush your teeth," he said as he climbed back into bed, and Jane pulled the covers up over her head.

"You're looking smug," Aubrey Harrison said, turning away from the makeshift bar, a glass of scotch, neat, in his hand.

Dillon Holmes walked across the living room of the small suite, loosening his tie, and took the glass from the senator. "Thank you, I would like a drink. How did you know?"

Harrison puffed out his cheeks a time or two, then turned and poured himself another glass, this time a double.

"I just saw Toby Patterson," Dillon said, sitting himself down neatly, pulling up his slacks just a tad, so that the knees wouldn't wrinkle. "He's getting nervous."

"Why? What crawled up his ass?"

Dillon shrugged, elegantly. Everything he did was elegant. "He wants you to commit, now. This week. Yesterday, if possible. I'd tell him when, but I like him where he is, out of the loop. Still, some of his contributors are starting to make noises about Claxton, about backing him, getting Patterson to endorse him. After all, Claxton is the very popular governor of Patterson's state."

"Governor of Pennsylvania? Quick, Dillon, give me the names of all the presidents from Pennsylvania. I can give you one, because there's only ever been one. Buchanan. Old Jimmy couldn't even keep South Carolina from seceding, and we all know what happened next."

"Still, Claxton is squeaky clean, and a lot of people like him. I'd say tap him for your vice president, except nobody would buy a president from New Jersey and a veep from Pennsylvania. You still need California."

The senator pulled a straight-back chair away from the small table in the suite and straddled it. "You're so sure I'm going to run?"

"Everyone's sure you're going to run, Aubrey. You should have heard our little Miss Preston warbling your praises tonight. According to her, you're a hit with everyone, including Romanowski, which we both know is crap. He still worries me, but not as much as he did before I met him. I think he just wanted to see you, see if you remembered him. Oh, and I'd back off a little with Brandy if I were you. We want California, sure, but Orange County, not Hollywood. I don't like any hint of a Hollywood connection."

"Maybe I don't care what you like," the senator said, leaning his forearms on the back of the chair.

"And maybe I don't care if you like it, or me. Maybe you'd better start remembering who's calling the shots here, Aubrey."

"You never let go, do you? You know I didn't mean anything I said that night, damn it. I was only blowing off some steam."

"I'm sure the media will believe you . . . if you want to call a press conference, explain what you said, see what happens," Dillon supplied smoothly. "Excuse me while I just go get the printout."

"Oh, sit down. You still carry that with you wherever you go?"

Dillon was back in five seconds, waving two stapled pages. "Here it is, as always, just a reminder, so you don't forget. But not the tape, Uncle. But we both know that, too." And then he smiled. "Now, I've decided to arrange a small cocktail party here tomorrow night. We'll set it up as a simple meet and greet. We'll have the usual group, plus a few red herrings, just in case anyone is too interested, taking names. And I want you to pay more attention to this Preston woman, as we've already planned. She's perfect, Aubrey, even better than advertised. Young, and cute, and wonderfully naive. She's a gift from the gods."

The senator rubbed at the back of his neck. "Okay, okay. Do we want photographers?"

"Sure. You and the little lady smiling for the cameras. She's going to be a big help with the soccer moms, remember? But don't be adoring, Aubrey. She's too young. Smile at her, but be avuncular. You do know what avuncular means, don't you? That means you stay the hell out of her pants."

"You're such a shit, Dillon. My sister's child. I should have known. She's a shit, too."

"Yeah, yeah, sure." Dillon took another sip of scotch. "Photos. Maybe some local TV. That would be good. We can rent a couple of kids . . ."

Chapter Eight

Sunday morning in Cape May dawned sunny and already warm, although the breeze that blew off the ocean and across the balcony of John's room promised that the day, if warm, would be comfortable.

Probably a lot more comfortable than he was, sitting on the wicker rocker on the balcony, tossed out of his own room by the unlikeliest roommate a man ever had.

A roommate who looked entirely too neat, even as she slept; lying on her side, none of her covers mussed, one hand tucked under her cheek. When he had awakened at six, he'd had to tell himself his mission in life was *not* to climb into her bed and see how she would look tangled in the sheets . . . tangled in his arms.

"You done yet?" he called through the open door. "I've had enough nature, and there's a seagull out here who's looking at me like I either give him breakfast, or become breakfast."

"Don't be silly," Jane said, stepping out onto the balcony. "Seagulls don't attack."

"Oh, yeah? Ever try walking a boardwalk with a paper

cup of French fries in your hand?'' He pushed himself up from the rocking chair. ''So? You're done? Will I ever find anything again?''

Jane rolled her eyes. ''Stop complaining. And believe me, I didn't want to clean up your mess. I just knew that given one more day, we'd need to *crawl* across the floor, climbing over your clothing. And may I remind you that it was *you* who said you couldn't bear to watch as I hung up your clothing.''

''I was once badly frightened by a wire hanger. Either that, or Joan Crawford's eyebrows, I forget which,'' he told her, reentering the room, which looked as if no one was in residence. ''Where the hell did you put everything?''

She brushed past him, going over to the dresser, pulling out drawers. ''Top two are yours, bottom two are mine. You're taller, so that seemed fairest.''

''Fairer. More fair. I think you need three to be fair*est*. Where's my computer?''

''Right there, on the desk beside you. Along with some books, a few folders of notes, and a pen and scratch pad. Oh, and I found your modem cord and plugged that into the phone. Your toiletries are all arranged in the bathroom, the tags are off your clothing, and your suitcases nested quite nicely inside each other. They're in the closet.''

John rubbed at his arms. She'd done all that in fifteen minutes? ''You're creeping me out, you know that, right? I don't think I can live like this. I need . . . I need sprawl.''

''And I need neat. Neat wins, because neat can always become sprawl, but it's very difficult to make sprawl neat once it's . . . sprawled.''

John pinched the bridge of his nose, made a face. ''And all of this before my first cup of coffee. Come on, little Miss Prim, let's go find some food.''

Jane gathered up her purse and the retreat folders they'd picked up last night. ''I already checked, and breakfast is served in the banquet room, which will then be separated by folding doors into three separate meeting rooms. There are three sessions every ninety minutes, from nine until five. Oh, and I think you'll want to check out the seminar on government: *Reducing the power of the federal government. Good idea, or an invitation to corporate corruption?* Harrison's sure to attend, don't you think? Unless you really think the senator is interested in acid rain or copyright issues.''

"Definitely not the one on acid rain. He doesn't believe in anything his backers think might cut into their bottom line, although I'd be interested in the one on copyrights,'' John said as they stepped into the hall, the door swinging closed and locking behind them. "Damn. I forgot my key card."

Jane held it out to him, along with another sticky-backed badge on which was printed Professor John Romanow$_{ski}$.

He slapped it on his chest, because he had already figured out that arguing with his "pal" and roomie was sort of like trying to stack marbles. "You're starting to really annoy me, Jane. Stop being so damn perfect."

Jane stabbed the button for the elevator. "I'm not perfect. I got nervous and had too much to drink last night, and I've already swallowed three aspirin this morning to make just a small dent in my headache. I'm rooming with a grouchy slob who obviously doesn't like mornings, even beautiful ones, and I have the distinct feeling that big and hairy and manly as you look, unless kept on a strong leash, you'd self-destruct in ten minutes."

"Oh, good. I'm rooming with Aunt Marion. All that's missing is the apron," John muttered, turning the corner, to see Senator Harrison and his faithful companion Tonto—er, Dillon Holmes—already waiting for the elevator.

"Good morning, Janie dear, and well met. You, too, John. Lovely day, lovely day." Senator Harrison obviously liked mornings, because he was combed and polished and smelled as if someone had dumped half a bottle of expensive cologne over him. "Will you be joining us for breakfast?"

"Oh, Senator, thank you. But it says in the registration

packet that breakfast is served buffet style and there are no table assignments, so there's really no need for you to think that you have to—''

She shut up when John surreptitiously pressed down on her toes with the edge of his left loafer, so that he could say, "We'd be delighted, Senator. Ah, here's the elevator. Dillon? Will you be joining us, too, or are you just coming along for the ride?"

"Very funny, John," Dillon said with a tight smile.

John gave the man a small, irreverent salute and waited for Dillon to precede him into the elevator. Shame on him. Every time he saw Dillon Holmes, he couldn't help himself; he made a crack. No, he never would have been able to pull off the nerdy professor act.

They rode down the single floor in silence.

Everyone stood back as Jane exited the elevator first, and John hastened after her, the two of them walking ahead of Harrison and Holmes.

"Hey, slow down, where's the fire?"

"You're obnoxious, do you know that? Sucking up to Harrison, making snide remarks to Dillon, who has been nothing but a gentleman to me—and to you. And what makes you think I want to have breakfast with them, anyway? Isn't it enough that we're assigned to the same table for lunch and dinner all week? It's Sunday, and I think Sunday should be my day off. Can't I have at least a little fun?"

"I thought you had fun alphabetizing my toiletries, or did you do that by size, or function?"

She turned her head to glare at him, but kept walking toward the ballroom. "You're not funny. And I'm not having fun. I spoke with my parents this morning, you know, while you were taking that twenty-minute shower. Lucky for you they called Molly when I didn't call them, or else they would have been here this morning, just in time to hear you doing your very bad Springsteen imitation. Wouldn't that have been wonderful? And, just in case you're wondering if the acoustics in the shower make even a bad voice sound good? They don't.''

"So this is about your parents, huh?" John said, trying to ignore her swipe at his singing talent, or the lack of it. Besides, it sounded as if little Janie Preston was coming out of her "I'm a good girl" shell a little. If he pushed her far enough, she might even cuss at him . . . or figure out that, no, sweetie, they were *not* pals. "Did they give their little girl a hard time?"

"No. They were very understanding when Molly told them that there'd been a freak thunderstorm in Cape May and that all electricity and phone service had gone out yesterday afternoon, right as I was talking to her, as a matter of fact.''

"Thinks fast on her feet, your cousin," John said as they joined the line at the buffet table.

"Fast, yes, but not far. Her lie only worked until my dad checked the weather on the Internet this morning, and there was no mention of a freak storm in Cape May. So I told him the truth. Sort of."

"Sort of?" John asked, handing her a still warm plate and watching while she began loading it with several kinds of fruit, even copped a fat sprig of ornamental parsley or some other curly green thing he wouldn't eat if he was starving, and placed it on top, just so.

"I told him my car broke down, and by the time I got here, I was so tired I just fell into bed until this morning. Cantaloupe?''

"No, thanks. Are you building a pyramid, or are you really going to eat all of that?"

"Eat all of this? No, of course not. I just thought it would be nice to make up a fruit plate for our table. For everyone to share."

"I'll say it again, Jane. You're scary," John said, ladling scrambled eggs onto his plate. "You could organize anything, couldn't you? I'll bet you could herd cats."

She finally grinned up at him. "Have you ever seen a gang of four-year-olds holding on to a towline as they go for a walk? It's great in theory. One long piece of rope, with straps on it for the kids to hold on to as the leader leads the way. But if just one child decides to let go, they all let go, and then, yes, I herd cats, or I did, until I got a rope with little bracelets on it.''

"Your own toddler chain gang. Nice—if you'll pardon the expression. And now you're herding me, and from the looks of that fruit plate, the senator and Holmes as well. Try to remember that you're having an adventure, Jane. Nobody said you have to hang on to the strap all the time. You can throw your clothes on the floor. You can leave the cap off the toothpaste. You can eat good, not just healthy. I mean it. Try it.''

She looked at him, looked at the plate, looked at him again. And then she set down the plate and picked up a new one from the stack next to the hot food. "I'm going to have eggs, and bacon, and maybe some ham, and two pieces of white bread toast, not wheat, and then I'm coming back for pancakes.''

"That's it, Jane, go wild. With strawberry syrup for the pancakes?'' John asked, grinning at her.

She gave him a horrified look. "God, no. I'll never eat strawberries again.''

"Okay. We'll start small. Later, you can cut loose some more, maybe not write out all those postcards, maybe stand on the beach without sunscreen or a hat and sing a few choruses of 'Born Free.' ''

"You make me sound like some sort of uptight nut case,'' she said, carrying her fully loaded plate as he led them to their assigned table, because too much deviation from routine and he was afraid she might just implode.

"Not uptight. Repressed. Suppressed. *Way* too conscious of the rules. A *good* girl. I'm still trying to figure out how your cousin got you to agree to come here.''

She put her head down. "I wanted to, that's why. Do you really think Molly could blackmail me into anything? I've never *done* anything.''

"Until today. Yesterday actually. And definitely last night. I think you're going to be fine. Just lay off the booze."

"I thought it would loosen me up. Instead, I only felt sick, and then told you everything." She sighed, placed her napkin on her lap. "I still can't believe you're actually happy about Molly working for—"

"Senator! I see you found Janie's plate of fruit," John said quickly. "We were talking, and she was piling, and piling, and finally realized that she'd never have room for her eggs."

"You did this?" Harrison asked, pointing to the plate of fruit before placing it in the center of the table. "Very artistic."

"Isn't it?" John said. "It's almost frightening to think about what she could do with Lego blocks."

"Senator," Dillon said, pulling out his own chair, "we really must hurry if you're going to make your meeting with Congressman Patterson."

"Yes, yes, I remember," Harrison said, then leaned closer to Jane. "He's so damn organized. Drives me crazy. Don't you prefer to be spontaneous, Janie? I know I do."

John bit his bottom lip as Jane's cheeks flushed, and she struggled to answer the man.

"Oh, Janie's spontaneous. Aren't you, Janie? In fact, she was just telling me that she'd rather I blew off the morning seminars and we went down to the beach. I think we're going to build a castle in the sand."

"We are?" Jane asked, her lovely hazel eyes gone wide.

"We are," John answered, surprised at how delighted he was that she seemed delighted. "Oh, yeah. Definitely."

"I envy you, John," Harrison said, sighing. "I don't remember the last time I was able to do something just because I wanted to do it. I'd join you, but I have to take this meeting. Dillon? Why not go with them? I don't need you around to talk to the congressman."

John hid his surprise as Dillon Holmes's face first showed

shock, then quickly suppressed anger. "Really, Senator, I don't mind. And I've made a few notes . . ."

"No, no, go—I mean it. Go! Politics, building castles in the sand. Pretty much the same thing, don't you think? Except," he added, winking at Jane, "the sand doesn't shift as much."

"Excuse me, Senator Harrison," John said as he put down his coffee cup, "but that doesn't sound like a man who plans to run for the presidency. In fact, if I may be very blunt, that sounds like a man who's pretty disenchanted with the entire political process."

"No, John," Harrison said, buttering a piece of rye toast, "that sounds like a man who *knows* the political process. It's a nasty business, but when your country calls, you have to answer." He looked at Dillon, just for a second. "At the end of the day, you have no choice."

The rest of the meal was fairly quiet, until Jane stepped up, turning the conversation to that evening's cocktail party, asking that age-old female question: "What should I wear?"

"Something a little colorful, Jane, please. Something that photographs well," Dillon told her. "We've invited the press."

John felt he should be making some notes of his own. "The press? I thought these retreats were meant to be more private, more off the record."

"And you teach political science?" Dillon said condescendingly, so that John wanted to smack him. "The presidential election is less than two years away, *Professor*. Nothing a potential candidate does is private."

Jane said quickly, "And you said you didn't know if you were going to run, Senator. But you are going to run, aren't you?"

Dillon laughed. "Everyone asks that same question. If it were up to me, my uncle would announce his candidacy today. But we're still looking at informal polls, considering the issues. That all takes time, Jane."

"And money," John added, shoveling eggs into his mouth. "Let's not forget the money."

"Good morning, all," Henry Brewster said, pulling out the chair next to John. "Lovely day, isn't it? I've already had breakfast and a walk on the beach."

John looked at Henry's loaded plate. "Worked up another appetite?"

"I know, I shouldn't, really, but who can resist?" the publisher asked, slathering cream cheese on a toasted raisin and cinnamon bagel.

He had placed a book on the table beside him, and Jane peered across John to read the title. "*Shallow Ground?* And it's J. P. Roman? I thought I had all his books."

Visions of Henry hanging from the nearest flagpole danced in John's head as he quickly loosened his grip on his coffee cup, before the handle snapped.

"Oh, this? This is an ARC, Janie. An advance readers' copy. The hardback won't be out for another two months. I've already read it several times, in all its incarnations, but now I'm reading the finished product purely for pleasure. You read J. P.?"

John shifted his gaze to his left, in time to see Jane nod her head. "Oh, yes. He's quite good. But I read him in paperback, which means I'm always a year behind, doesn't it? I've got his latest release upstairs, as a matter of fact."

Not for long, John decided, even though the photograph on the back cover could have been any man with a head and two shoulders.

"Well, that's enough cholesterol," he said, getting to his feet. "Henry? Would you care to build a sand castle?"

Henry looked down at his designer slacks. "I don't think so. I'm going to sit in on the discussion of copyright. Fool that I am, I'm going to listen to all the reasons why Congress hasn't passed any new legislation protecting copyrights, while they've got plenty of time to declare national turnip day."

"Lots of luck," John said, patting his friend on the shoul-

der, then held out Jane's chair for her. "Dillon? You coming?
It doesn't have to be a castle. We could try building our
own version of the White House, if you want. God knows
everyone else has."

"Thank you, John, but I really do need to brief the senator
about his meeting. Another time, perhaps?"

"You bet," John told him cheerfully, already ripping off
his badge as he took Jane's arm.

Jane walked up from the shore, carrying two large plastic
pails full of sodden sand, and John dumped them in the
courtyard of the castle. "Tide's coming in," she said, looking worriedly back toward the water. "I think we should
have done this farther up the beach."

She watched John's back muscles ripple as he spread the
sand, forming some of it into a low wall. "And I told you,
we needed a base of hard, wet sand to build on. You didn't
expect this to last forever, did you?"

"No," she said, looking at the work of nearly six hours,
as they had stopped several times to swim, to eat hot dogs,
to rest. The castle wasn't huge, but it had turrets, and ramparts—whatever those were—and an arched entryway, and
even a moat, although they couldn't seem to keep the water
from draining out of it.

She sat down on the towel she had brought from the room
and dusted at her sandy fingers.

This was fun. This was more than fun. And it would be
comfortable fun, too, if she could stop looking at John's
body as if she'd never seen a man before. But, then, he was
so *much* man.

She had always been drawn to types like Dillon. Smaller,
leaner, blond, more civilized looking, definitely. All right, all
right, so Molly had hit it—less threatening. Jane knew, given
her options, she would never have given someone like John
a second look. Overpowering. Too big. Too hairy. Too scary.

Now she wondered how she would feel if he took her in his arms. Scared? Or safe?

Oh, well, back to the castle. . . .

John had gone into the gift shop and bought the pails, a rake, two large red plastic shovels, and even some sand molds he'd used to press sea horse and sunburst designs into the walls of their creation.

The man took his sand-castle building very seriously.

And he looked so adorable as he worked. His long black hair blowing across his forehead. The frown of concentration as he had fashioned the highest turret, anchoring it with the sticks from the popsicles he'd bought for them at a nearby snack bar. His long, muscular body, already so tan, the hair on his legs actually glinting golden in the sun.

He'd even been very appreciative of her pink bikini, once she had finally dared to remove the white bathrobe she had taken from his closet and claimed as her own.

Even his bathrobe had made her feel good. Sleeves six inches too long, at the least, the hem nearly dragging on the ground. She'd felt so small, and so wonderfully comfortable with it wrapped around her. And it smelled like John . . . which also wasn't a bad thing.

Stop it, stop it! He isn't anything you want!

"We should name it," John said, sitting back on his haunches to admire their work.

"Huh?" The bathrobe? Oh. No, no. He meant the castle. "How about Romanowski's Keep?"

"Not grand enough. We're bigger than a keep. We've got ramparts and a moat. And we Romanowskis lived in wagons anyway, traveling all over Europe. We wouldn't know what to do with a castle. How about Preston's Play Yard?"

She relaxed and joined in the fun. "I couldn't let the children near the moat."

He smiled at her. "You know, that's what missing here. Children. I feel a little silly, building this thing, without some kid running around, knocking down the walls as he tries to help.''

Jane leaned back on her elbows. "You like children?"

"For the main course, or just as an appetizer?" he asked her, then winked.

"Idiot," she said, but she smiled. She was content. Warm from the sun, sandy all over thanks to a reapplication of sun screen that seemed to attract sand like a magnet, her hair all blowing in the breeze as gulls wheeled and laughed overhead.

She looked out over the water, to see a large sailboat showing stark white against the blue horizon, then shifted her gaze nearer the shore, to where a rather corpulent gentleman, a huge cigar in his mouth, was trying to jump the waves.

The waves.

Jane got to her feet. "Quick, the tide's really coming in."

"Quick? Quick what?" John asked, but Jane was already running toward the shore, the empty buckets in her hands.

She came back and dumped the buckets of wet sand on the front of the low wall that surrounded the castle. "If we can just build up the wall high enough . . ."

"You're planning on keeping back the Atlantic Ocean?"

Jane glared at him. "You have a problem with that?"

"Me? No, I don't have a problem with that. I like our castle. I'm even fond of it. Except you'll probably want me to help."

"Very funny." She tossed the two buckets at him, then went to work, smoothing the now higher wall.

Jane knew what she was doing was the ultimate exercise in futility. But this castle was the first totally foolish and frivolous thing she'd done in so long—the pink bikini didn't count—that she really, really hated to see it destroyed. She hadn't even gotten a photograph of it.

"John! Get my camera out of my bag, please," she said as she took the two buckets from him and continued building her wall.

"Guess now we know whose castle this is," John grumbled, obeying her latest order. He was back a few moments later, after moving their towels and Jane's beach bag higher up on the beach. "I'll take one of you posing with the castle, and then you can take one of me, okay?"

The waves were beginning to creep up the beach, the last one trickling across the sand to greedily lap at Jane's feet. "All right, but we have to hurry, because the castle can't stand much longer. We need more sand."

"We need a backhoe bucket of sand," he said, then snapped three quick pictures of Jane as she worked. "Now me. Aunt Marion will get a kick out of this. She always says I fight any tide."

"Can I help?"

Jane looked up to see the bum—no, not a bum, just because John said he was a bum—standing over her.

The guy still wore his trench coat and combat boots, even in the heat of mid-afternoon, and he had a good five days' growth of beard on his narrow face. But his eyes were very blue, and seemed kind. "Sure, and thank you. John, give this man my camera."

"Jane, I—"

"Oh, here comes another wave! Hurry up, give him the camera. That way we can have a picture of both of us with the castle."

"Oh, what the hell . . ." John said, tossing the camera to the bum before pulling Jane to her feet, posing with his arm around her waist. "Speaking of waves? Wave good-bye to your camera, Janie."

She smiled, and spoke through gritted teeth. "Cynic. But maybe you could give him five dollars? I think that would be nice. He looks hungry."

John also smiled as he spoke quietly. "What are you, the poster child for 'there's one born every minute'? If I give him money, he'll just buy a bottle with it, or hop the next bus to Atlantic City to play the nickel machines. Oh, shit— look out, here comes the tide."

Jane knew she would have to find a store that developed film overnight, because the picture the bum got of John throwing himself prone in front of the crumbling wall, as a wave crashed over him and took out the castle, had to be a real winner. . . .

"I'm still digging sand out of my ears. And my teeth," John said as he walked into the room, using a washcloth to rub at his left ear.

"Uh-huh," Jane said, looking up from her book. "But I thought you were very brave."

"I was stupid. I still can't figure out what possessed me to do that swan dive in front of the castle, just so we could get one more picture."

"Sir Walter Raleigh would have been proud."

"Maybe. But Queen Elizabeth wouldn't have laughed until she had to sit down on the sand, because her legs wouldn't hold her anymore."

"Sure she would have. She probably would have chopped off your head later, though. If that's any compensation. And wasn't it nice of Kevin to help us gather up our stuff? He even took away all our garbage, our cups and stuff."

"Yeah, Kevin. Your bum. I'm still trying to figure out what's missing. Because something has to be missing. Do you have your key card?"

"Yes, John, I have my key card. Stop being such a cynic," she said, and went back to reading her book.

The book.

"What are you reading?"

"The excerpt from J. P. Roman's *Shallow Ground*. It's at the back of this book. I wonder if Henry would be willing to let me read his copy when he's done. It sounds very interesting. A murder, right in the Senate cloakroom."

"Sounds sort of lame to me," John said, looking at Jane's frown of concentration.

Damn, but she looked good. Those interesting blond

streaks—he wouldn't say tantalizing, because that would just get him and his traitorous libido in more trouble—seemed even lighter now, against the faint color she had picked up on the beach. She'd covered her new crop of freckles with makeup, but he knew they were there.

Freckles as an aphrodisiac? Who knew. . . .

She looked younger tonight, in an ankle-length, sleeveless cotton dress of pink flowers on a light blue background. She had touches of sun on her bare shoulders, and there were freckles visible in the scoop of the neckline.

Did he dare tell her he liked her better this way, looking less sophisticated, and definitely more touchable. Or that he liked her even better with her hair mussed, sand stuck to her knees, and smelling of the sea, the sun, and really great-smelling sun screen?

Not to mention how her petite yet rounded body looked in that pink bikini.

She put down the book and got to her feet, looked at him. "Your nose is red," she told him. "I told you to put on the sun screen."

"I'll live," he answered, picking up his wallet and room key and shoving them into his pants pocket. "Are you ready for the cocktail party?"

"I'm not wearing a wire, like characters in J. P. Roman's books do sometimes, but yes, I'm ready. Except that I don't know exactly what I'm supposed to do once we're there."

"Mingle. Smile. Keep your ears open. What I'm looking for is who Harrison talks to, who cozies up to him, and see if that jives with the information I already have—except I'm losing my affection for that idea. So get chummy with Brandy Hythe, if you can. Find out just how close she is to the great man."

"And what will you do, other than look? You certainly can't go up to the senator and say, 'Hi, so, what scandal are you hiding?' If there even is a scandal."

Again with the questions. Good questions. He was here, and he had damn well use some of his time to check out the other guests, possibly gain something useful for his next book, or the book after that. But what he really wanted was a good, juicy sex scandal, with Aubrey Harrison—always the first to condemn any other politician as immoral or lacking character—with his pants down at the wrong time, and in the wrong place

So John did a little tap dance with the truth. Again. He felt bad about it, but he did it. He just didn't know how long he could look into Jane's trusting, honest eyes and keep on doing it.

"I've pretty much given up on the idea of a political scandal. Kickbacks, bribes, whatever. I mean, I have ammunition, from my student, from my own digging, but I've realized that it would take too long to document it all, bring all that out. I mean, think of Watergate. That took years. So it's his associations with women that I'm most interested in now. A pattern of behavior, a moral flaw that I can pry open, so that everyone sees the crack; that's more what I'm looking for."

"Like Brandy Hythe? So what if she's his girlfriend?"

"Trust me, it's not just Brandy Hythe. It's the *pattern,* the way he *treats* women."

"He seems to like women."

"Does he? Does he really? I can't get Harrison for getting into bed with corporate sharks willing to pay for targeted tax breaks or favorable legislation. I can't get him for taking what could only realistically be called bribes, in order to get himself elected. I can't, because nobody cares, or it's all too complicated and they don't understand. But I can get him for getting into bed with the fairer sex, the way he treats women, how he thinks about women. The public eats that up—and down, down goes the politician who's been spouting *character* and *moral behavior* and *holier than thou* for thirty years."

"But, again, John, the senator isn't married. Who cares who he sleeps with?"

"You'd be surprised," John said, feeling a tick beginning

to work in his cheek as a mental picture of Maryjo, in her last, sad years, flashed inside his mind. "What?" he asked, when he realized Jane was looking at him strangely.

"I don't know. I was just wondering. You really, really dislike him, don't you? Not just his politics, but him. And yet, who's the dirty old man here, John, the senator . . . or you and the general public?"

Yeah. Good questions. Good questions he was going to ignore, for now.

"Come on, let's go. I told Henry we'd be there by five. He doesn't like being alone in social situations."

"He told you that? When?"

Damn.

"Earlier. When you were in the shower. He phoned."

"Oh. Maybe he should have hired a companion, too. Someone to keep him company."

"I don't think they allow beagles at the retreat," John said, opening the door for her. She gave him a quick backhand in the gut as she passed by him, into the hallway.

Funny girl.

Maybe this being pals business wasn't all that bad. He was hacking it okay, and it had already been more than twenty-four hours.

Of course, the shower he had taken after getting back from the beach—and the sight of that pink bikini on his "pal"—had been a very *cold* shower.

And he would need another one if he didn't soon quit standing here like some construction worker goggling at women on a city street, watching her walk down the hall, rather than catching up with her. . . .

Chapter Nine

Jane had never thought the brainy and powerful could be so boring, but if this cocktail party didn't break up soon, she was going to fall asleep, her nose in the clam dip.

She popped another cracker into her mouth as she tried to tell herself that her problem wasn't that there were only two females in the room—not counting the female servers—and that all the men were flocked around the other one, Brandy Hythe.

What was she anyway, chopped liver?

What was on her cracker? Chopped liver?

Eeeeuuuwww!

She looked around for a napkin and a corner to hide in while she spit out the half-chewed cracker.

How very sophisticated of her.

"I've got to get out of here," she told herself as she watched John doing his mingle thing with Artemis Slade, the CEO of some oil company. He'd already done his thing with Congressman Toby Patterson, and then threaded through the crowd to zero in on a Sunday morning newscaster, Donald Sampson.

He'd said he had given up on the political scandal thing, but he sure looked like a man still doing research for something. It was as though he had an attack plan, and those three men were his targets.

What did he know that she didn't know? He was supposed to be looking into the senator's love life, right?

He had been welcomed by each of the three men, probably because he was very good at schmoozing, or whatever he wanted to call it, and she really couldn't watch anymore because she was sure that for all his smiles and small talk, John didn't like any of these people, not one bit.

Jane fought the thought that this didn't make John any better than the rest of the people in this suite.

About the suite . . . it was really nice. Spacious, well decorated, with two bedrooms, a large balcony overlooking the pool and the ocean. She would have enjoyed this suite.

Except then she wouldn't have gotten to see John wrapped only in a towel . . . and that was a memory that would keep her warm into her dotage.

She checked her watch, saw that there was still another forty-five minutes before dinner, and wondered if one drink, just one small glass of wine, wouldn't be bending her new teetotaler rule too far.

And then her cell phone rang.

She didn't realize it was hers for a moment, because cell phones seemed to be ringing every few seconds in this room, but after four rings, and a few people sort of glaring at her, Jane got the idea.

"Whoops, sorry," she said, grabbing the phone out of her purse and heading out onto the balcony. "Hello? Molly?"

"No, it's Mel Gibson's personal assistant. He says he can't take it any longer, Miz Preston; he's just got to have you. There will be a helicopter waiting on the beach in ten minutes. Be there."

Jane grinned. "Yes, I can see the helicopter approaching now. Gotta go. Thank you, bye."

"JanePrestondonothanguponme!"

"Molly? Oh, goodness, is that you? Well, why didn't you say so? I guess this means Mel won't be by until later? Bummer."

She could hear her cousin's low growl. "I hate when you're in a good mood. No. Wait a minute. Why are you in a good mood? Do you have anything for me?"

Oh, she could say that. She sure could, if she was about to tell Molly that she'd spilled the beans to John, that John had been going to write a book on Harrison but now just wanted to bring the man down, and if Molly was the way to that, so be it.

Sure. She could tell Molly that.

She could also tell her about the mixup with the rooms, the fact that she and John were sleeping together—scratch that—sleeping in the same room. She could tell her cousin that against all that she'd ever thought about herself, and men in general, she was somehow finding herself very attracted to the Incredible Hunk.

Or she could fake it.

Faking it was good.

"Nope. Sorry, Molly, nothing yet. But I will tell you that besides snagging a seat at the senator's table, I am, even as we speak, in the senator's suite, attending a very select cocktail party. He and Dillon share a lovely suite, and right now I'm on the balcony that overlooks the ocean. The sky is blue, the ocean is bluer, and I built a sand castle on the beach today. Are you eating your heart out yet?"

There was a slight pause. "How much have you had to drink?"

Jane took the phone away from her ear and glared at it for a moment. "I have *not* had anything to drink. I don't drink. I never drink."

"Oh, so you're high on life, huh? I think maybe it's time I heard more about this John character. I thought you were pulling my leg yesterday, but now I'm not so sure. Is he really hot?"

Jane looked through the open door, into the suite. John

had now made it as far as Brandy Hythe, and the woman had her hand on his arm, was smiling into his face. The actor hadn't paid that much attention to him on Saturday, but she probably wouldn't feel her week was a success unless she had every man at the retreat licking her shoes.

"Hot? Some might think so," Jane said, wishing she hadn't also felt a brief urge to go pull Brandy Hythe's hair straight out of her head.

"Are you going to have a fling with him, Janie? I mean, these cell phones are good. I can almost hear the Janie's-out-of-her-box-so-everyone-look-out voice. Haven't heard it in years, but I hear it now. I always said you had the makings of a party girl. You just never met the right parties."

Jane frowned, turning away from the sight of John cozying up to Brandy, and faced the ocean. That lasted two seconds. If he was with Brandy, she wanted to see what he was doing with Brandy. "You make me sound so darn dull."

"Except for the sharp points on that cube life you live, you are," her cousin told her, laughing. "But I know there's another Janie in there somewhere. I've seen her a time or two. Cut her loose, Janie. Do it if you want to. Boff the prof."

Jane closed her eyes. "That's vulgar."

"Possibly. Sorry about that. But if I'm going to be playing nursemaid to a bunch of sniveling toddlers for two days, I could at least take some solace in believing that my dearest and only cousin is having herself a ball. And I do mean that literally. Whoops, vulgar again, right? Must be this third glass of wine. I needed it, after reading that ten-page memo you typed up about the dear kiddies. Or blame it on my all-girls-school education. It was either geometry, or talking about boys. Guess which won."

Jane was barely listening. Dillon had joined John and Brandy, and Jane was comparing the two men, the one she should be attracted to, and the one who was driving her crazy.

Dillon looked very handsome in a light gray suit, white

shirt, and navy blue tie. Every blond hair on his head was in place—and would probably stay in place, even if a hurricane blew through the suite. He held his wineglass gracefully, a paper napkin tucked around the stem. He was so ... sophisticated. So ... unthreatening.

And then there was John. He had shaved again—she had heard the electric razor through the bathroom door—but already a dark shadow showed on his cheeks. He had this habit of shoving his fingers through his hair, and now a few locks of the thick black mop had fallen forward on his forehead. There! He pushed at his hair again.

When he did that, he also had this way of dipping his head slightly, so that if he was looking at you at the time, his blue-green eyes appeared to be just below his winged black brows. Sort of like Tom Cruise ... but with more intensity, and an extra shot of testosterone.

He wore his sport coat and slacks well, but he didn't seem to notice that he was wearing either. They covered him, but they didn't *make* him. He made himself. All six and a half feet of him: his broad shoulders, his narrow waist, his long straight legs.

"Oh, boy," Jane said, sighing.

"Oh, boy?" Molly said. "What do you mean, *oh, boy?* I said I found the keys to the place again. I don't know how they got in the pizza box, or in the refrigerator for that matter, but sometimes things like that happen to people, you know. So no more *oh, boy,* okay? I'm getting it together, and the place will open on time tomorrow. Honest."

"Huh?" Jane said, dragging her attention away from John's hands, which dwarfed the glass he was holding. Such large hands. Such long, straight fingers. "I'm sorry, Molly. Look, there's a party going on here. I told you that, right? I'll call you later, if there's anything to report."

"All right, but what about the reason I called?"

Jane shook her head. Molly had a reason? Man, she really hadn't been listening. "I said, I don't know anything about the senator's plans yet."

"Not that reason. Pay attention, Janie. It is your place, remember? I just wanted to tell you that if you don't answer your cell, I'll leave a message for you on your room phone. Just in case I have a problem, although I'm not going to have a problem, why would I have a problem?"

"No!" Jane had a flash of herself being in the shower and John answering the phone and saying she was in the shower. "Don't call my room, Molly, okay? I'll keep the cell on, honest."

"Yes, but will you answer it? This is the fourth time I've tried to call you, Janie. Have you even checked the messages on your cell?"

"Messages? I can do that?"

"Obviously not," Molly said, and Jane could imagine her cousin shaking her head, rolling her eyes. "Look, just call me later, after dinner, before bed, whatever. I get nervous when I don't hear from you at least twice a day. I mean, when your dad called, I thought about telling him about Romanowski, the escort thing, and then I thought—are you out of your mind? How could you have sent little innocent Janie off with a stranger for a week?"

"I'm not innocent, Molly," Jane said, watching John walk away from Brandy and toward her. "Molly?" she added quickly. "Do you really think I need another bad boy in my life?"

"One to cry over, one to marry. Why?"

"Marry? Not just . . . just have a fling with? Quick, Molly, answer me."

"I can't answer that. Janie? What are you doing, planning on doing, going to—Janie! You mean Dillon? God, you would think that dull stick is a bad boy, wouldn't you? Janie Preston, don't you dare!"

"I wouldn't think of it," Jane said.

"Oh, good. I just can't see you with another white bread guy, not that Dillon didn't have his moments. But, mostly, he's really pretty boring. If you want a fling, fine. Go fling.

You have my permission and my blessing. But not with Dillon. Anyone else. Not another white bread *safe* guy.''

"It's a deal," Jane said, smiling at John as he joined her on the balcony. "Bye, Molly, and thanks."

She pressed the End button, then the Power button, and dropped the cell phone back into her purse.

"Checking in with Mom and Dad again?" John asked her, holding out a small plate of breaded mozzarella sticks.

Jane took one, took a bite, then fought with the warm, stringy cheese for a moment before sort of wrapping her tongue around it, biting down to break the string, and then pulling it into her mouth.

"Jeez," John said, shaking his head. "Don't do that again, Jane, okay?"

"Sorry," she told him, licking at her fingers, one by one.

"And don't do that again, either," he told her. "Or are you going to tell me you didn't know what you were doing?"

Jane licked one last finger. "Doing? I'm not doing anything. These are sort of greasy, that's all." Her eyes went wide. "Oh."

"Yes," John said, grinning. "Oh."

"Oh. Oh, *no*. I wasn't . . . That is, I certainly didn't mean to turn you . . . I mean, it wasn't as if I was doing it on . . . Oh, stop laughing at me!"

"It's either that, Janie, or I'd have to be insulted. So, you weren't trying to—let's see, what do I think you were going to say? Oh, yeah. You weren't trying to *turn me on?*''

"No, of course not! Why would I do that?"

He took a step closer. "I don't know why you'd do that, but you do *do* that. Often. Without even trying."

"Well . . . Well, that's your problem, isn't it?" Jane said breathlessly, wishing his eyes weren't so gorgeous. She stepped back a little, feeling overpowered, by his sheer size, by his intense gaze, by the hot, squishy feeling that was growing low in her belly.

He smiled a lopsided smile. So cute, for such a big man. Almost adorable, if she wasn't wishing she could find a stepladder somewhere, prop it against his broad chest, climb it, and punch him square in the nose. *"My* problem?" he continued, just as maddeningly happy. "We sleep together, Janie, remember? Maybe it's your problem, too."

Okay, here it was. Twenty-four hours into a week of being a good girl out for a semigood time, and she was somehow at a crossroads. Good girl, bad boy. Not so good girl, maybe even better boy?

"What . . ." She stopped, licked her lips. "What if I were to say okay?"

"Okay?" John's smile faded. "Okay what?"

She rolled her eyes. Molly would handle this *so* much better. "Okay to . . . to . . . to you know. *What."*

"Oh, Christ," John said, stabbing his right hand into his hair. "I've created a monster. Jane, I was kidding, okay? I was just kidding."

She didn't know where the smile came from, and it sure hurt to produce it, but she did. "Me, too. Gotcha!"

Jane took another mozzarella stick from the plate he was still holding, bit down on it just enough that she could pull on the other half, leaving a string of cheese hanging in midair. She wrapped her tongue around it, slowly pulled it into her mouth. "Ummm . . . That's *so* good. See you later, John-boy," she then said, thinking *suffer,* and brushed past him, on the hunt for the bathroom and a little privacy.

What she got was Dillon Holmes, who snagged her just as she rounded the fat man from the beach—still with a cigar in his mouth.

"There you are, Jane," Dillon said, deftly slipping an arm around her waist and guiding her toward the senator, who had taken up a position in front of the portable bar, a glass of lemonade in his hand.

Lemonade? She'd seen him earlier carrying a scotch on the rocks.

Jane looked around, saw the television cameras, and understood.

Of course. Lemonade.

INTRODUCING

Zebra Contemporary —

To start your membership, simply complete and return the Free Book Certificate. You'll receive your Introductory Shipment of FREE Zebra Contemporary Romances. Then, each month as long as your account is in good standing, you will receive the 3 newest Zebra Contemporary Romances. Each shipment will be yours to examine for 10 days. If you decide to keep the books, you'll pay the preferred book club member price of $15.95 – a savings of up to 20% off the cover price! (plus $1.99 to offset the cost of shipping and handling.) If you want us to stop sending books, just say the word… it's that simple.

BOOK CERTIFICATE

Yes! Please send me FREE Zebra Contemporary romance novels. I only pay for shipping and handling. I understand I am under no obligation to purchase any books, as explained on this card.

Name _____

Address _____ Apt. _____

City _____ State _____ Zip _____

Telephone (___) _____

Signature _____
(If under 18, parent or guardian must sign)

Offer limited to one per household and not valid to current subscribers.
All orders subject to approval. Terms, offer, and price subject to change. Offer valid only in the U.S.

Thank You!

CN023A

llI..l..ulll....ll.l.l..ll.l.l..ll..l.l..ll.l..lll..l

Zebra Contemporary Romance Book Club
Zebra Home Subscription Service, Inc.
P.O. Box 5214
Clifton , NJ 07015-5214

PLACE
STAMP
HERE

"I found her, Senator," Dillon chirped happily, doing everything but picking Jane up and depositing her at the great man's right side.

"Senator," Jane said, dredging up every rule of etiquette her mother had drummed into her head over the years, "I want to thank you for including the professor and me this evening. It's a lovely party."

"My pleasure, Janie," the senator told her, slipping one arm around her waist. Low on her waist. "But now it's time to sing for your supper, or at least your canapés. Dillon? We're ready here."

The senator's hand slipped lower. Jane wanted to step away from him, but now there was a camera stuck in front of her, and a microphone. There were lights suddenly switched on, and a man was looking into the camera and saying things about how Senator Aubrey Harrison, his party's front-runner for next year's presidential election, was here in Cape May to talk to the world's greatest minds, leaders of industry, and, yes, "everyman."

Jane shifted her eyes to the left, desperately hunting for John, and thinking, *Guess who you are in that mix, Janie. Oh, go ahead, guess.*

The man turned now, still keeping his profile in camera range, and said, "Good evening, Senator Harrison. May I say how honored New Jersey is to have its own favorite son with us this evening."

The senator said, "Thank you, Jim. There's nowhere I'd rather be than in the great state of New Jersey," and they were off.

Jane thought that since "Jim" was standing in front of her, maybe she could just sort of sneak out of camera range, but when she tried, Harrison tightened his grip on her waist. No, not her waist. His hand was way lower than her waist.

She tried to listen to the interview.

"I've spoken to many experts over the years, Jim, on many subjects, but I know that the best way to learn what's really going on out there, in the trenches so to speak, is to talk with the people who are in those trenches every day. Like Janie Preston here.''

Gulp.

''Janie lives in Fairfax, Virginia. Lives with her parents as a matter of fact, a single woman tending to these elderly people even as she owns and operates Preston Kiddie Kare, her own small business. Was that financed with a loan from the Small Business Bureau, Janie?''

''Uh, no, I—and my parents really aren't—''

''We all know about the problems in day care today,'' the senator pushed on, ''but we know only in the abstract, unless we've got kiddies of our own in need of that care. Now, since obviously *I* don't have any toddlers of my own . . .'' Pause. Wait for polite laughter. ''I've got Janie Preston here this week with me, to explain to me just where the shoe worn by parents needing quality and affordable day care for their children pinches. Right, Janie?''

''Well,'' Jane said, conscious of both the camera and John, who was standing to her right, grinning like a loon, ''since you asked, I do have some very definite ideas on—''

''Wonderful!'' the senator said, dropping his hand another inch—and pinching her. Pinching her! ''Jim, Janie here is only one of the people I've been talking to across this great land as I consider the goals of my possible campaign, the planks I'd want to see in the strong platform my party builds next year.''

''Thank you, Senator,'' Jim said, turning fully to the camera, and stepping right in front of Jane once more. ''This is Jim Waters in Cape May with Senator Aubrey Harrison. We'll be broadcasting nightly from the retreat for Live At Six, for the remainder of the week. Back to you, Suzanne.''

The lights went out, and Jane pulled away from the senator. ''You *pinched* me,'' she whispered quietly, glaring at him as he turned away from her. ''How dare you pinch me? And how dare you *use* me like that? And how did you know about my parents? I didn't say anything about my parents.''

''He doesn't hear you, Janie; he's already on to the next

thing on his agenda." Dillon took her arm and led her back out onto the balcony as the senator nodded his appreciation to everyone who had come up to him like lemmings rushing to the sea, to congratulate him on his performance.

"He pinched me," Jane repeated to Dillon. "And how did he know I live with my parents?"

"Sweetheart, we know your bra size."

Okay. That stopped her.

Dillon smiled. "Jane. You're at a gathering of very important people, from government, from industry. Academics. The President will attend one day this week. Did you really think there wouldn't be background checks on you? As a senior senator, my uncle of course has access to these reports."

"On me," Jane said, her mind whirling. She must have passed. Otherwise, she wouldn't be here, now would she? She would have been politely shown the door the moment she'd shown up at Congress Hall . . . or before she'd even left Fairfax. "You . . . Then, you've seen this report?"

"I have, yes. You're squeaky clean, Jane, you and your family both. Except for one small flaw."

My bra size, Jane thought, nearing hysteria, because she didn't want to think about what Dillon might consider her other flaw.

"Molly Applegate."

And there it was.

"My cousin?" Jane asked, her voice coming out as little more than a squeak. "What's wrong with my cousin?"

"She has a police record, for starters."

Jane rolled her eyes. "It was a college sit-in," she told him. "I can't even remember what it was about, but Molly wasn't the only one to get hauled off to jail."

"She's the only one who served fifteen days rather than pay the fine."

"Molly has principles." *They shift from time to time,* Jane reminded herself silently, *but Molly has always had principles.* Her parents had also refused to either bail her out or pay her fine. There was also that.

Dillon smiled. Sweetly. In a nonthreatening, trust me, sort of way.

Jane was surprised by her reaction. She longed to smack him.

"Your cousin to one side, Jane," he continued, "you came up squeaky clean in the security investigation, and came to our attention. The senator is very serious in wanting to speak with you in more depth about day care in this country."

"Uh-huh," Jane said distractedly as she saw John pass by the open French doors. "You said the Secret Service, or whatever it was, investigated *everyone?*"

Dillon turned slightly, looking into the room, then smiled at Jane. "Ah, the stranger who hired you. The stranger you're sharing a hotel room with all week—although we've had the hotel register amended to show you are in your own private room, just in case anyone should ever check. Now, what do you want to know?"

She had no idea. "I have no idea," she said, blinking. "Is there anything I should know?"

"You should know better than to spend a week in a man's hotel room, I suppose. But," he added, his sigh theatrical, "there are no rules today, are there? You're both single and of legal age."

"There's nothing going on between us," Jane told him, feeling her cheeks flush. "Nothing."

"Good, you stick to that. Now, excuse me. I've got to make sure the senator isn't giving another speech with no one there to take notes or photos."

Jane followed Dillon into the suite, watching his back, wondering why she had ever thought the man harmless, or even vaguely appealing, and went off to find John.

"The Secret Service or the FBI—somebody—has investigated all of us, John," she told him when she found him, standing alone in a corner of the room, "observing."

"The President will be here, Jane. Of course we were all given thorough background checks. Luckily, you signed on a good three weeks ago, giving them time to run a check, or you wouldn't have been allowed to attend."

Jane shifted her eyes from left to right, then looked up at him. "You don't sound upset. Aren't you upset?"

"Not really, no. The files are kept secret."

"Oh, yeah? Then how did I find out about them?"

He looked down at her, one eyebrow raised. "Good point. I thought you guessed."

"No. Dillon Holmes *told* me about them. He knows all about me. About my parents. Molly. Everything."

Like my bra size. Although the man had to be kidding about that, right?

John took her by the elbow and ushered her through the suite, out into the hallway. "What did Holmes say about Molly?"

"Nothing. Well, nothing except that she has a police record."

"Oh, good. That's just wonderful. Your cousin the felon. He didn't mention that he knew her?"

"No. I don't think he had to. I could tell from the smug look on his face that he knows that I know that he knows her. He probably just thinks she's a kook, and harmless. That's insulting."

"Is she a kook?"

"Well, *yes,* but who is Dillon Holmes to say so?"

John applied a bent knuckle to his left ear and gave the knuckle a shake. "Sometimes, Jane, when you talk, I think my hearing has gone wacko."

Jane stood there, clasping and unclasping the magnetic fastener on her purse. "He knows we're sleeping in the same room."

"Does he now. Did you fib and tell him it's a suite, with two bedrooms?"

"No. He told me that the hotel register has been changed

to show me with my own room. Because the senator wants to use me for publicity.''

''Hmmm. Sounds to me like the man is running. Doesn't it?''

''I hadn't thought about that. I was too busy thinking about how violated I felt.'' She brightened. ''Does this mean we can call Molly and tell her? I don't think I can stand too much more intrigue.''

''Sorry, babe, but that's not enough. And we can't count on Brandy. According to her, Harrison's just *the sweetest old man.*''

''Oh, yeah? That sweet old man *pinched* me, John.''

''Pinched you? Where?''

Jane gave one sharp inclination of her head. ''Right in front of the television camera.'' Then, as John grinned, she frowned. ''Oh. That wasn't what you asked, was it? You know where he pinched me.''

''Maybe it got on camera?''

She shook her head. ''No, the reporter was standing right in front of me at the time, and we were backed up against the bar. But it was no accident. The senator isn't a sweet old man. He's a dirty old man.''

Jane closed her mouth with a snap, then opened it again. ''You know what? I want him. I want to take him down. So we don't call Molly.''

''I already said that.''

''Don't interrupt,'' Jane said, wagging a finger at him. ''You were right, John. Your student was right. The man doesn't deserve to be president. Not just because of the pinch, although that was bad enough. But not bad enough not to vote for him. I mean, my friend Mary's Uncle Arnold is always pinching the girls, and he's a very good bank president. Mary calls him Arnie the Ass Man.''

''You lead such a varied life, Jane,'' John said, grinning as he pushed the button for the elevator.

''No, I don't. I lead a very boring life, or I wouldn't be here. And you're not really listening, John. A pinch is one thing. But the senator's different. It wasn't the pinch that really upset me. He was *using* me tonight, to make himself look good to the voters. How much do you want to bet that he never asks me to sit down and *really* talk about day care?''

"I don't take sucker bets, Jane," John told her as the elevator doors opened.

Jane stepped forward, then jumped back. "Oh, nuts. I forgot my registration packet. Stay here, I'll be right back."

"Leave it. I've got one you can use."

"No, no. I've got my postcards in it."

She half ran back down the hallway and into the suite, looking around on the small table beside the couch for her blue registration folder.

"May I help you, miss?"

Jane smiled at the uniformed server who had approached, holding a tray filled with empty glasses. Clearly the party was breaking up, and the servers were doing some cleaning up.

Even as she stood there, at least six other people left the suite.

"Thank you. I was looking for my registration folder. I know I put my purse down here, on top of it, but now it's gone."

"Was it blue?"

"Yes," Jane said, nodding. "Do you know where it is?"

"I'm afraid someone spilled a drink on it, miss. I put it in the other room, to dry out. I thought it belonged here, to one of the gentlemen in the suite. But be careful. It's a jungle in there."

Jane looked where the young woman pointed, then headed for the bedroom to the left of the living room. She knocked on the door, which was partially open, and then stepped into the room.

There were papers everywhere. Stacks of them. On a desk, on the floor, on top of the television set that was on and tuned to CNN. Manila folders were piled haphazardly. Computer spreadsheets tumbled all over the unmade bed. A paper shredder positioned over a large waste can was full to overflowing.

There were no dirty socks on the floor, no empty shoes scattered about, no clothing lying rumpled on chairs . . . but in it's own way, this bedroom was as messy as John's had been.

Amid the clutter, Jane saw a sticky-backed name tag stuck to the edge of the night table, and she could see Dillon's name on it.

And then, just as she was about to back out of the room, ask Dillon for help, she saw it. Her registration folder. The server had opened it and placed it, facedown, on one of the stacks of papers on the desk.

"Oh, good. I don't want to have to lie again on a whole new stack of postcards," she said as she grabbed at the packet with both hands, sort of pushing it shut . . . and the whole tower of papers came tumbling down.

"Darn it, darn it, darn it," Jane grumbled, dropping to her knees, to pick up the mess. She grabbed papers, all of varying sizes, and stacked them back on top of the desk, gathered up her packet once more, and headed out of the room.

"Looking for something, Jane?" Dillon asked, just walking into the bedroom.

"Dillon. Hi." Jane summoned a smile, irritated to realize that she felt guilty, as if she had invaded the man's private space. "It's all right, I found it." She held up her folder. "Someone spilled a drink on it, and one of the waitresses put it in your room, to dry out."

"Servers. One of the servers. We don't say waitress anymore, Jane. It's not PC."

"Right," Jane said, giving him another smile. "Well, gotta go."

He put his hand on her forearm, so that she couldn't walk away without first yanking herself free. His smile was warm, intimate. How did he do that—turn it off, turn it on, and still look so darn sincere? "Are you sure you can't stay? We never did get much time to talk . . . alone."

"I know," Jane said, tipping her head to one side, trying to look disappointed. "But John is waiting for me at the elevator."

"We'll see you at dinner in a few minutes, then," Dillon called after her. "And then, if you don't mind, we'd like some photographs of you and the senator out on the verandah behind the hotel. I asked a few of the hotel employees to bring their children for the photos. Got a couple of balls, some dolls, some tennis rackets. It should be great."

That was when she noticed that his smile didn't quite reach his eyes.

"Sure," Jane said, fighting the feeling that this man, this smiling man, this totally safe, unthreatening man, was really quite angry with her for some reason. Molly? Could it be that he had found out about Molly's idea? "Good-bye for now," she chirped, and took off toward the elevators once more.

Chapter Ten

"Hey, Janie! Where's the fire, sweetheart? Dining room's that way."

John prided himself as being pretty quick on the uptake. He noticed right off that Jane wasn't listening to him. His first hint was that she had bolted out of the elevator, made a left, and kept heading in the direction of the doors leading out onto the verandah overlooking the beach.

His second clue was that upon reflection, she didn't even seem to notice that he was with her, had ridden down the single floor with her in the elevator.

So he went after her, catching the door as it started to close behind her, and caught up with her as she stood on the verandah, taking in huge gulps of sea air. Her arms were stiff at her sides, her hands bunched into fists, and he didn't know if she was angry, ready to burst into tears, or had just eaten something that hadn't agreed with her.

Except the senator had pinched her. He half turned to go back into the hotel, then looked at Jane again. If that no good bastard had—

"What happened? Did that swarmy son of a bitch pinch you again?"

Jane closed her eyes, took a deep breath, then let it out slowly. "No. I didn't even see the senator when I went back to the suite. Which was a good thing, because I certainly do want to tell that man never to touch me again. I really, really need to give that lech a piece of my mind!"

John smiled at her fierceness, but mostly at her use of the word *lech*. "Just let me know when you want to go after him, because I want to listen in, maybe act as referee." Then he got serious again. "So? What? You seemed all right in the elevator, but now I can see you're shaking like a leaf. What happened?"

"Nothing," she said, shaking her head. "Nothing happened. I just needed some fresh air."

Right. And he was the queen of England. "Okay, now you've had some air." He took hold of her elbow. "Let's go in to dinner."

"No!" She seemed panicked, but she didn't turn to him, just kept looking out toward the ocean, as if the sight might calm her. "I mean . . . Can't we skip dinner tonight? I had so much to eat at the party, I'm not even hungry. Especially after the chopped liver. They ought to label those canapés. I *hate* liver. Do you hate liver?"

She kept trying to change the subject. John knew he could fight her on this, badger her until she told him what the hell was going on. He also knew she could cut and run, lock herself in the bathroom of their room—just like a woman—and he would still not know anything.

"I like liver, sorry. And I'm hungry. There's a hot dog stand down near the beach. Mustard and onions?"

She closed her eyes once more, nodded. "And relish."

Okay, he could read clues. She *was* hungry. She just wanted to get as far from the hotel as she could.

Why?

He'd just have to wait her out.

She lasted as long as it took to walk to the small shop,

purchase five hot dogs and two sodas, and take them to a small table on the side of the shop.

"I was in Dillon's bedroom," she said, just as John took his first healthy bite of hot dog—which meant he had damn near a third of it in his mouth at the time. He was still half wondering if he should have gotten himself four hot dogs, not just three. Maybe that was why Jane's statement startled him so much.

Jane jumped up and went to him, pounding him on the back until he could breathe again.

"I'm sorry. I didn't mean it to sound like that."

Wiping at his eyes with a small paper napkin, John said, "Too bad, because it sounded *just* like that."

"I know, sorry again," she said, balancing her elbows on the tabletop, holding her hot dog with both hands. "What I meant to say was that someone spilled a drink on my folder, and then someone thought the folder belonged in the suite, and then that someone put the folder in one of the bedrooms, and then I went in there after it—what a mess in there!—and when I tried to scoop it up, it fell, and all the papers on the desk fell, and I had to quickly pick everything up, and then Dillon was standing in the doorway when I went to leave the room."

She took a bite of hot dog and spoke around it. "I think he was angry. I mean, I think he was *really* angry."

"You invaded his privacy?"

"Probably. Sure. Yes, I did. It was his room, I know that, because I saw an old name tag. Let me tell you something, John, the man definitely isn't here to enjoy himself. He's got about five file cabinets of papers in his room—minus the cabinets. There are just papers, and folders, and printouts, all over the place."

"Doing a little business, huh? Sure does sound more and more like Harrison's going to announce this week, so we'd better hurry up if we're going to do anything," John said, finishing his third hot dog and eyeing Jane's second one. He'd ask for it; but then he couldn't watch her eat it, and watching Jane eat a hot dog was even better than watching her eat a mozzarella stick. "You didn't by chance happen to see any prototypes of Harrison For President posters lying around Holmes's room?"

She shook her head, looked at her second hot dog, and pushed it toward him. "I really didn't see anything. You know that saying? Couldn't see the forest for the trees? Even if I had gone in there to search for anything special in those papers, it would have taken me months to find it. I was just lucky to see my folder, and I only could do that because it's blue."

John looked at the still-damp folder as he sucked on his straw, wincing when he hit bottom and the straw made a noise. "Sorry. So you think Dillon's ticked? Really?"

Jane shrugged, getting up from the table as she gathered up all the hot dog papers and looked around for the nearest trash can.

"I can throw away my own garbage, you know," John told her, holding the lid of the waste can for her.

She nodded again. He really didn't like this. She was not happy. Definitely not happy. And, being an observant sort, he had noticed that the more unhappy she was, the neater she got. It must be some sort of sickness, one he knew he didn't suffer from.

"Dillon didn't say anything, except that he wanted me to stick around after dinner for some sort of photo-op with the senator. He's even lined up some children for the photographs. Which," she said, looking up at him as they crossed the street and headed for the beach, "I think is really tacky. Don't you think that's tacky?"

"Welcome to the not so wonderful world of politics, Jane," he said, content to act as a tree, or whatever, as Jane leaned against him and took off her shoes.

"Don't look," she said then, and sort of squatted down nearer the sand. "I mean it, don't look." Her hands disappeared under the long, full skirt of her dress.

"Okay," he said, turning away. Then he turned back, and

looked, just in time to see her slowly standing up as she neatly pushed her pantyhose down past her knees.

He did his tree impersonation once more as she stepped out of the pantyhose, rolled them up, and shoved them in her purse.

"I didn't want to ruin them," she told him, taking back her folder. "Can we just walk?"

"Sure," he said, getting rid of his own shoes and socks, then rolling up his pant legs. He reached into his pants pocket and took out his wallet and key card, putting both in his inside jacket pocket. He loosened his tie and opened the top button of his shirt, then shrugged out of his sports jacket and threw it on the sand, next to their shoes.

"John!" Jane said, picking up the jacket and shaking it, then turning it inside out, folding it into an incredibly neat package, before placing it on top of her folder and purse. "There. That's better. It will need to be pressed, but at least you won't have to send it out to be cleaned."

"Lucky me," John said, taking her hand and walking toward the shore. "Why do I get the feeling I'm in some male cologne television commercial?"

She grinned up at him. "The sand, the sea, the obligatory flowing skirts on the woman, the white-white shirt on the man. All we need is a palomino. Do you ride?"

He shook his head. "I never found a horse big enough that I didn't feel like I was punishing it, and a Clydesdale would have been pushing it. I've got a motorcycle, but I don't ride that, either. It's hard to look cool with your knees stuck up around your ears."

"I . . . I think you're a nice size," Jane told him, just as if she hadn't noticed that she actually had to reach up a little bit to hold hands with him, all five feet and about three inches of her.

"You don't mean that. You just want to paint me green and send me out for candy on Halloween."

"I do not," she answered, laughing. "Although, if you'd

want to do that, and stop in at Kiddie Kare, I could promise you a caramel apple.''

John grinned down at her. "So much for you still being afraid of me."

"Afraid of you? I'm not afraid of you," Jane said, almost dancing toward the sea water that ran up the beach from the last breaking wave.

"Then, that wasn't a look of pure panic on your face Saturday, outside the escort service?"

"No, of course it—yes, it was. You are very big, John." She grinned. "Big Bad John. Wasn't there a song with that title, eons ago?" Then her smile sort of slipped. "Maybe it was only Big John, not Big Bad John?"

"No, it was Big Bad John," he told her. "I know, because I got to hear it often enough, growing up. But I'm really not that tall. Tall for high school basketball, tall for the football team—which made me a great quarterback, by the way. But not tall enough to make a career out of any of it. I'm just big."

"Very big," Jane said, and he could see her point, now that her high heels were sitting back there on the sand, and she was in her bare feet. "And hairy."

He stopped walking. "I beg your pardon?"

"Hairy," she repeated, then giggled as she dropped his hand and went dancing into the ankle-deep water. "Don't tell me you never noticed. You must wear out three electric shavers a month."

"Two a year," he said, "and I'm going to get you for that." He walked into the foaming surf and gave a kick of his right foot, sending a shower of water in Jane's direction.

The result was a little more *drenching* than he expected.

She wiped her face, pushed back her damp hair, tucking it behind her ears, and shook out her skirt. "You do know, Professor, that this means war?"

"Gee, I'm so scared."

"Good. Be scared. Be very, very scared," Jane said, walking farther into the water.

"You talk a good game," he said, following after her, watching her back—and her hips—"but so far I'm not seeing anything. Don't talk the talk, Janie, unless you're ready to walk the walk."

The last thing he saw was her stopping, then turning to face him, an unholy smile on her face. He did see again, once he'd wiped the water from his eyes. He shook his hands at his sides and grinned at her. "Okay, you got me. But that doesn't mean we're done. All's fair?"

"All's fair," she agreed, standing partially bent forward, her hands aimed toward the water, her eyes sparkling with mischief.

The tide was out, so there was lots of room to run through the water, ankle deep, calf deep, finally thigh deep—on Jane, definitely not on John.

They played in the surf for a good thirty minutes, John getting the better of their duel for the most part.

He could move faster, kick harder—and had much bigger feet—but Jane held her own, splashing him, then running away, circling him, getting him from behind, then running away again, her entire dress soaked.

But she didn't seem to care. He knew he didn't care. She was laughing, she was happy, and the white, pinched-face look she'd had telling him about getting caught in Dillon Holmes's room was gone. The sadness that had been in her eyes, the disillusionment when she had talked about her disappointment in Harrison, in politics in general, had vanished behind a mischievous sparkle and playfulness that made John want to pick her up, twirl her around, and plant a great big, wet kiss smack on her mouth.

So he did.

"What was that for?" she asked him, her head actually higher than his as he held her tightly, as she rested her hands on his shoulders, her forehead against his.

"I don't know," he told her honestly, realizing that she weighed no more than a feather, even soaking wet. He could crush her ribs without even trying, and the thought frightened him, because the last thing, the very last thing in the world he would ever want to do would be to hurt her. In any way.

"I liked it," she said as he moved deeper into the water, so that the low waves broke around his thighs, around Jane's feet as they hung there, a good foot off the ground.

"Me, too," he said, and then he kissed her again.

Her mouth opened against his, and he took advantage of the invitation. She tasted of hot dogs, and onions, and relish, and salty sea water, and he thought he had never tasted anything so good.

Her arms were linked tightly behind his neck as he walked deeper into the ocean, because she'd wrapped her legs around him now, and he had enough common sense left somewhere in his brain to know that someone could be on the beach, watching them.

Damn the sun, for shining. Damn the beach, for being public. He wanted night, he wanted moonlight. . . . He wanted privacy. He wanted Jane. Here. Now.

"Hey! Hey, you out there! No swimming allowed after six!"

"Did you hear something," Jane breathed against his ear.

"Did you hear me? No lifeguard on duty! You have to come in!"

"Nope," John said. "Didn't hear a thing. Would you like to go to Paris? Maybe we can wade out, catch a ride on a cruise ship."

"Sounds like a plan," Jane said, just as a spoilsport of a wave caught them both, sending them under the water. They came up, sputtering, just in time to hear the killjoy on the beach yelling, *"Told* you so! Tide's coming in!"

Jane clung to John as he walked back to the beach, smiling as the killjoy goggled at them, looking at their drenched clothing.

"You . . . You aren't even wearing bathing suits," the guy said, sneering. "This is Cape May, bucko, not the Riviera."

"Thanks. We'll remember that," John said as he and Jane walked past the man and headed back up the beach. "Hey!

Get away from there!'' he called out as he saw the bum bending over his jacket.

"Don't yell, John. It's only Kevin."

"Yeah? And that's only your purse, under my jacket, remember?"

Kevin, hearing John's yell, straightened, gave them both a wave and a smile, and trotted off toward the road, his trench coat flapping around his knees, his combat boots making deep impressions in the soft, dry sand. John could chase him, but what would be the point? He could already give a great description to the local police. "Check your purse," he said to Jane as they got to their pile of belongings.

"I don't have to," Jane said, sounding a little miffed. "I trust Kevin."

"Kevin. What a name for a bum. I'll bet his mother said, 'Oh, I know, we'll name him Kevin—can't end up a bum, not with a sweet name like Kevin.' "

"I hate when you do that," Jane said, pulling her sodden skirt away from her legs. "There's good in everybody, you know."

"Prove it. Check your purse. Because, in case you haven't noticed, your neat, military folding has been shot to hell by our bummy Boy Scout. Or do you think he was just looking for a match? Damn, you'd think that jackass back there would have been yelling at Kevin, not us."

"Everything's here," Jane said, closing her purse. "Wallet, money, lipstick, pantyhose on top. Even my penny, the one you made for me. Are you satisfied?"

Was he satisfied? "I'd had hopes . . ." John muttered, and he wasn't talking about her purse. "Come on, let's get back. We look like two drowned rats."

"Can we go into the lobby this way?" Jane asked him. "I'm still dripping."

John took her hand in his. "To quote my Aunt Marion, who was probably quoting somebody else, if they can't line you up against the wall and shoot you for what you did, then it's not so bad. I think we're safe."

''My grandmother used to say the same thing. Isn't that a coincidence! And that's good, too, because I think I've got five pounds of sand down this dress, and I'm starting to itch. Oh, darn, there's Dillon.''

John looked over at the small crowd on the verandah. Dillon. Harrison. Cameras. A bunch of kids who were definitely not on their best behavior. ''The photo-op.''

He could see damn near all of Jane's teeth, her smile was that wide. And wicked. The little teacher had a wicked streak. Who knew? ''Obviously neither of them know how to communicate with children. Do you think he'll still want me?''

''I don't know. Wanna ask him?''

''No, I'm not that brave. But I wish I were. Come on, let's run.''

Still holding his hand, Jane broke into a trot, and he followed her at a brisk walk, pausing only to give a slack-jawed Dillon Holmes a friendly wave as they passed by, into the hotel.

They all but fell, chortling, into the elevator, and Jane bent double with laughter as an older couple who had been in the elevator when they got there, stepped out before the doors closed, saying, ''We'll take the next one.''

It was only when they got to their room that the laughter stopped.

''Let me get my key card,'' Jane said, pulling her panty-hose out of her purse. ''Oh, God, I'm shaking, and my teeth are chattering. I guess it's the air-conditioning; it's freezing in here. Hang on, I'll find it.''

''That's okay, I've got mine in my jacket pocket.'' John held up the jacket by the collar and reached into the inside pocket . . . and came up empty.

Jane wrapped her arms around herself, her hem dripping on the carpet. ''Maybe you put it in another pocket?''

''No, I distinctly remember putting it in my inside pocket. The key card, and my wallet.'' Still, Jane was shivering, so he checked his outside pockets and found both in the left one. "Damn."

"See? And you were about to blame Kevin. Which would be silly, because our room number isn't even on the card. Shame on you—and open this door!"

While Jane was in the shower, probably using up all the hot water in the building, John mentally retraced his steps. After Jane had handed him his card that first night, he'd been very careful to know where it was at all times. Made neat by embarrassment—what a concept.

Anyway, he had put the card in his inside pocket. He was sure of it. Had they come back up the beach in time to disturb Kevin, who had been stealing the key card and wallet. . . ? Or had they disturbed him as he tried to put them *back?*

Was Kevin a bum? A garden variety thief?

Or was he privately hired talent? Was someone checking up on him?

Had he written too many thrillers, and his imagination had turned to paranoia?

The computer!

All his notes on Harrison, on Dillon Holmes, and on the main money players he had singled out in Harrison's possible campaign were in that computer. Not to mention his manuscript in progress, and the fact that he'd stupidly named his word processing program "J. P. Roman, Superstar."

That would teach him to have such a big head.

Cursing under his breath, John went over to the desk and opened the case of his laptop. He turned it on, and the security program kicked in, asking him for his password.

That was normal. But how would he know if Kevin had broken the password, or bypassed it somehow? John wasn't too deep into techno-type plots, so he really wasn't sure what could and could not be done with a two-hundred-dollar laptop security program and a talented computer hacker.

"Probably about as much as a burglar could do with a cheap lock and a credit card," he said, running down the list of files to see their last reported "Date Modified."

And there it was. Three files had been breached; just the three he had worried about.

Sure. Like someone was going to break into his computer to play solitaire.

Why would the guy be able to break into the computer and not be able to cover his tracks?

Or was this some sort of message? Was the key card being in the wrong pocket the first message? Had Kevin *wanted* him to know he had copped the key card?

"Shit. Shit, damn, fu—"

"John? What's wrong?"

He turned off the computer and shut the lid. "Wrong? Nothing. I was checking my e-mail, looking for a confirmation of my latest book club order, and all I had waiting for me were seven messages about how to increase the size of my—never mind."

He looked at her, all warm and rosy from her shower, dressed in those same blue and white, too big, cloud pajamas, and looking so damn seductive that the thoughts leaping into his mind were probably illegal in at least five states.

"I was really worried about my new watch, but it seems okay," she told him, holding up the watch by its gold band. "How is yours?"

"Good at fifty feet below sea level, and probably on the moon," he said, not even looking at his wrist.

A watch? Who cared about a watch? Somebody had been in his computer, in this room. He stood there, looking around, wondering what to check next. What else had been touched? And what did he tell Jane when she asked him why he was tearing the room apart, looking for an electronic bug? A bug—man, he really was going overboard.

"Don't you want to get out of those wet clothes?" she asked him as she stood in front of the mirror, combing through her damp hair. Acting as if they were just two ordinary people doing ordinary things . . . when she had to know that there was nothing ordinary about what had happened between them on the beach, and what might, could, damn well should, happen to them here, in this room. Tonight.

Screw the bug, if it existed. He and Jane had started something down there on the beach, and he wanted to finish it. Also tonight.

"I'm on it," he said, grabbing clean underwear and his nylon shorts from the top drawer of the dresser—quickly checking the drawer to see if anything was missing before realizing he wouldn't know it if it was—and heading into the bathroom.

He should take a cold shower. He should take six cold showers.

Why? Hadn't she suggested earlier that she wanted him to come on to her, wanted to have a fling this week with him? Not Holmes. That guy had thoroughly screwed his chances, bless him.

No, she'd said him.

But then she'd said she was only kidding.

Because he'd said he was only kidding.

"You have one damn big mouth, John Patrick," he grumbled as he turned on the shower and ducked his head beneath its needle-fine spray.

But he couldn't take advantage of Jane.

Why not?

She hadn't planned on sharing a room with him. She was a good girl, a *nice* girl.

So? Nice girl? What does that mean? She's an adult, isn't she? We're both adults. And we're both in this room.

Proximity?

No, that couldn't be all of it. He wasn't some damn rutting animal who would bed anything convenient.

So what was he? He shut off the shower, quickly and not very thoroughly toweled off, pulled on his briefs and shorts.

"Jane?" he asked, storming back into the room, still rubbing at his hair with a hand towel.

She was hanging up his sports jacket. She was so damn domestic. So damn neat.

Playing house?

Nah. Jane didn't live in some dream world. She had her own business, was wonderfully intelligent, mature. She might talk about a fling, mutter about her lack of an exciting life, but she wouldn't hop into bed with him just because he was handy, just to put a little excitement in her life.

No. She would want commitment. She would want words of love. She would want marriage.

And he would understand, because you didn't have sex with women like Jane Preston unless you were willing to take everything else that came with it.

John suddenly realized that, damn, maybe he didn't need a cold shower after all.

"John? You were going to ask me something?" Jane said as she brushed past him, into the bathroom, and began picking up their sodden clothing, hanging it over the shower rod.

"Not really. I was just a little hungry after all that exercise and wondered if you wanted me to call down for something."

She looked at him over her shoulder as she held his wet, sandy, black briefs in her hands.

Oh, God. Now there was an image.

"Do you think they have pizza?"

"I'll ... I'll go find out," he said, backing away from the bathroom doorway, tripping over his shoes, and all but crashing to the floor. He had to start picking up after himself, before he killed himself. Or before having Jane meddling around in his underwear driving him completely nuts.

Forty minutes later, Jane—after phoning Molly and saying a whole lot of nothing to her cousin—was lying propped in bed under the covers, reading his book, and John was channel surfing, looking for ESPN and the Sunday night ball game.

He itched to tear the room apart, see if anything else had been disturbed. Jane, in her neatness and meticulous folding, stacking, and hanging up, made it easy to see if anything was out of place. On his own, this room would have already looked as if a bomb had gone off, and he wouldn't know someone had been in his stuff unless they left him a note taped to his mirror.

Tomorrow. He would shake down the room tomorrow, because Jane had already told him that she planned to attend one of the first sessions, one on public school lunch programs, and he had already told her that he was going to skip the first session to go over some notes.

So here they were, each in their own bed. One going nuts, one totally oblivious . . . or really, really good at acting as if she didn't know the man in the room with her was fighting a mind filled with distinctly lascivious thoughts.

The pizza arrived, the one he'd ordered from a local shop, along with two sodas.

Jane got to her knees and motioned for him to put the box on her bed, then join her. She lifted the lid and grinned, breathing in deep through her nose. "Oh, heaven! Smell this, John. Doesn't it smell good?"

John looked at the pizza in what he might describe in one of his books as *growing horror*. "Sure. Great."

He'd just realized that, hey, pizza had cheese on it. The kind of cheese that sort of strung itself out when you bit into it, so that Jane would probably do a reprise of that wrap her tongue around it thing and . . . and he was a dead man. Face it. A dead man.

How the mighty has fallen. . . .

Jane took charge of doling out the pizza, separating a slice for him and placing it on a napkin. "Be careful, it's still pretty hot."

"I like hot," he said, then took a bite. Great. Cheese burn. Right on the roof of his mouth. Not that he'd tell Jane she was right. "Hmmm . . . good pizza," he said, quickly reaching for his drink.

"Not too hot?"

John tongued at the roof of his mouth, wondering if it was a second or third degree burn. Who was he? He used to be relatively sane, mature, even urbane. Well, maybe not urbane. But he hadn't always been the village idiot, had he?

"Nope," he said, sucking on some ice. "Just right. Although you might want to wait a few minutes."

"Oh, but I'm so hungry. I wasn't until I smelled it, but now I'm ravenous."

Ravenous. Good word. He was ravenous.

But not for pizza.

He caught his groan before it could escape as Jane, obviously in a hurry to cool her slice, held it close to her mouth and began blowing on it. Lips sort of pursed. Moist. Eyeing the pizza in a way that if she had turned that gaze on him, he would take it as an open invitation to grab her, throw her down, and have his wicked way with her. Repeatedly.

But he couldn't do that, because she was a *nice* girl, and she trusted him. . . . And she wouldn't say anything about commitment or marriage; but she would think it, and he would know she was thinking it. She would think she was having a fling, one wild week of excitement, but later, when she was home again, she would be ashamed of herself.

He couldn't let that happen.

Finally, Jane took a bite of the pizza, and damn if the cheese didn't do that string thing, so that John, in a last act of self-preservation, quickly removed himself to his own bed and stared at the television screen.

"Who's playing tonight?" Jane asked from her bed.

"Not me," he said, thumbing the channel changer with some force as he switched the channel, taking out his anger on the changer, because she would ask why if he stood up, then kicked himself.

It was going to be another damn long night. . . .

Chapter Eleven

Jane finished putting on her makeup—having decided that lipstick, some mascara, and a little blusher and powder were about as intricate as she really wanted to get on an everyday basis—then picked up all the still-damp clothes on the bathroom floor and arranged them over the shower rod once more.

She had rinsed everything last night in the bathtub, but she knew sand still clung to the material, in the seams at least, but it had been the best she could do.

Once the clothes were completely dried, she would fold everything and put it all in the two plastic laundry bags provided by the hotel, stick them in the bottom of the closet, and hope very, very hard that they wouldn't start to smell like five-days-dead clams before the week was up.

Or she could wash everything out by hand in the bathroom sink.

No. She was on vacation. Nobody did laundry while on vacation.

She stood there another two minutes, until her neat-nik

side won the battle, then compromised. She would wash out
the underwear with some of the courtesy shampoo.

She washed her underwear, pants and bra, and her pantyhose, then followed that by a quick washing of John's white
shirt, then emptied the sink.

"You done in there?" she heard John ask as she was
filling the sink a second time, after pouring in the rest of
the shampoo, swirling one hand in the water to make bubbles.

"You can come in," she said, "door's unlocked." She
turned off the water, then grabbed his black briefs from the
shower rod.

"Gimme those," John said, yanking them out of her hand.
"What the hell do you think you're doing?"

She rolled her eyes. "John, don't be embarrassed. I've
been washing, drying, and folding my father's underwear
for years. It's just some cotton and elastic."

"Yeah," he said, balling up the briefs and looking around
for someplace to put them, "but it's *my* cotton and elastic."
He looked at the shower rod, at his white shirt that she had
left to drip dry with a towel under it to catch the drips, and
he pulled the shirt down, then grabbed at his slacks. His
socks followed, one by one. "Mine," he said, saying the
word very slowly and distinctly. "Yours," he added, pointing to her bra and panties. "Stay here."

She shook her head, trying not to smile, and waited for
him to return to the bathroom, which he did, carrying one
of the plastic laundry bags, his clothing already inside it.
"Here, put your stuff in here, right in here, and we'll call
to have someone pick it all up. You know why, Jane?
Because this is a *laundry bag,* and what we have in it is
laundry."

"Oh, but they probably charge an arm and a leg to—"

"I'll pay it!" he interrupted, pulling her dress from the
shower rod and stuffing it in the bag, then reaching up again
for her bra, then quickly pulling his arm down again. "Do
it!" he said, tossing the laundry bag at her and leaving the
room once more.

Jane stood there again, biting her lips together, trying not to laugh. Big Bad John? Easily Embarrassed John, that was more like it.

He was *so* sweet.

And considerate. He knew she had enjoyed their kisses, but he hadn't pushed, hadn't tried to get her into bed once they had gotten back to the room.

He was going slow, being a gentleman, and she thought that was just about the sweetest thing. . . .

Jane frowned. So what was the matter with her anyway? Hadn't she excited him, turned him on? Had he tried a couple of kisses, they had left him cold, and he had decided to just leave it at that?

He could have ordered something from Room Service, strawberries in cream for instance, and a bottle of wine. But, no, he had called out for pizza.

Not very romantic.

Jane opened the drain in the sink, then stood there, looking at her reflection in the mirror. The great chunks were still there, helped along a little by the bright summer sun. She had some freckles on her nose and cheeks, but they weren't so bad. Her eyes were bright; she had natural color in her cheeks. She had on the skirt from the pink suit and had worn a white shell with it instead of the black because, after all, it was still morning. No white before Memorial Day or after Labor Day, and no black before noon, unless you were going to a funeral. Those had been her grandmother's rules.

She looked young, and fresh. Well groomed. Pretty in pink, as Angel had said. She looked . . . she looked. . . . Oh, God, she looked *virginal!*

She looked like just what she was, a good girl, a nice girl.

And John was a gentleman. That was the problem. John was a gentleman.

And it was Monday. And they'd be leaving here on Saturday, after sharing a hotel room every night.

If the man wasn't a saint, and she was pretty sure he

wasn't, then he wasn't attracted to her. . . . Or he was a gentleman.

She should call Molly. Molly would know how to read the "signs." She would be able to tell her if John's kisses last night had meant anything. But Molly was at Kiddie Kare and probably up to her elbows in the usual Monday morning madness.

She'd call her later.

"I repeat, although it has been some time now—are you done in there?"

"Oops, sorry, John," Jane said, quickly stuffing her clothing in the laundry bag and leaving the bathroom. "You can go in now."

"I don't want to go in," John said, then sighed. "I just didn't want to yell at you through the door. Sit down, Jane. It's time for some strategic planning."

She glanced at her watch, told him she would have to hurry, as it was already quarter to nine, then began cleaning up their breakfast dishes, replacing the metal covers they had laid on the bed, folding the cloth napkins—

"Stop that!" John said, grabbing the napkin from her the same way he'd grabbed the briefs. "I'll do it later, promise."

She linked her hands together, so she wouldn't be tempted to move his empty orange juice glass from the desk to the portable table brought in by Room Service. "I'm sorry. I get neat when I get nervous."

"I know, I've already figured that out. Why are you nervous?"

She shifted her eyes from left to right, then looked down at her brand-new bone-colored heels, the ones with the little strap across the instep. She loved these shoes. She'd think about the shoes.

"Jane? Is this about last night? The on the beach part of last night?"

She blew out her breath through her mouth, drew in another one, and lifted her eyes to him. It was such a long way up, and he was so big, and she had never felt so safe, so protected, as when he had held those big arms around her. He was like a whole brand-new continent, one she would love to explore, inch by inch.

She nodded.

"I thought so," he said, and he sounded so incredibly sad. "I shouldn't have done that. We were having fun, and I went and ruined it."

"You did?" How did he ruin it?

He pushed his fingers through his hair, and she wondered if he was upset, or nervous. She decided to settle for nervous. Nervous was good. At least then they'd both be on the same page.

"I shouldn't have taken advantage of you. You're here because your cousin bailed, and you're in this room because I screwed up with that nerd thing, with the Rabbit. You want an adventure; you as good as told me that. You're damn attractive, and I'm damn attracted. But—"

"But you won't be used?" Jane interrupted, feeling her cheeks go hot. "Is that what it is? You think I'm using you to have myself an *adventure?*"

He scratched at his left ear. "That doesn't sound right, does it?"

"No, John, it most definitely doesn't sound right. Want to try again?"

"Maybe later, when I can figure out what the hell is going on here, because something is sure as hell going on here," he said, his smile almost sheepish.

Hah! She didn't have to call Molly. She wasn't stupid. The man wanted her! Well, Big *Bad* John, tonight would be time to come to Mama, and if the mountain didn't come to her, she would go to the mountain.

Then she felt her blush deepen. Come to Mama? Maybe she'd had too much sun or swallowed too much sea water. Because she was actually thinking about *seducing* the man.

"What I'd like to talk about now is difficult, I know, but I'd like you to try to cozy up to Dillon Holmes some more."

Well, that brought Jane back to reality!

"You . . . You want me to *what?*"

Now he started fooling with the breakfast dishes, actually making them look messier than they were. It must be a talent. "It's why we're here, Jane, remember? To find out if Harrison's running or not—that's you—and to expose him for the bastard he is so he can't—that's me."

"I don't believe this," Jane said, grabbing her purse and her blue folder. "You actually want me to go hit on Dillon? After I told you that he looked so angry with me last night? Besides . . ." She stopped herself before she could say something dumb like, *Besides, I don't want him. I want you.*

"I'll throw in an extra thousand, Jane. You can use it for playground equipment or something."

Jane felt her eyes growing wide in anger. He could probably see the whites all around her eyes. She blinked, quickly, so that her eyes wouldn't pop straight out of her head.

"Oh, cripes, Janie, don't look at me like that. I'm not asking you to go to bed with the man. I just want you to stay on his good side."

"Fine," Jane said, clutching the folder close to her chest. "I'll do that. I'll cozy up to the man. I'll be nice. I'll get us invited everywhere. I'll get Dillon to tell me all his deepest secrets. Hah! Like he'd do that. And while I'm being nice, you can be downstairs finding another room for you and your big, fat dumb . . . dumb . . . *dumbness!*"

"You're pissed," John said, taking a step toward her. "I should have known you'd be pissed. I'm sorry, Jane. I'm usually pretty good with women."

"Is that so? You could have fooled me," she said, then slammed out of the room as he called to her to wait, that he still needed to tell her something else.

She didn't want to hear it.

"Dillon," the senator remarked, looking up from his newspaper. He was still clad in his pajamas, burgundy silk affairs with gold piping on the seams, and a matching bathrobe. His legs were crossed as he sat at the suite's fairly large dining table, one slipper dangling from his toes. "You're looking particularly harassed this morning."

"We've got a problem," Dillon said, pouring himself a cup of coffee.

"Yes, but she'll be gone in another few minutes," Harrison said smoothly, then put a finger to his lips as the redheaded hostess from the club they had visited last night exited the senator's bedroom, still buttoning her blouse. "Good morning, my dear."

"Aubrey, that bathroom is amazing. So wonderfully retro," the tall, fairly heavily made-up young woman said, putting a little extra hip into her steps as she came over to the table and dropped a kiss on the great man's snow-white head. She pointed to the metal cover still on one of the dishes brought up by Room Service. "For me?"

"Oh, so sorry, my dear," the senator said, his aging but still handsome face going all sad and hangdog. "I'm afraid not. I have a meeting with Dillon here, and a few others in just a few minutes. Dillon, hurry and eat before they get here, if you please."

The woman pouted, but then Harrison stood up and put his arm around her, deftly snagging her purse from the chair as he walked her to the door of the suite. "Let me give you money for a cab. And I am so sorry. We'll make up for it tonight, my dear, I promise you. Say elevenish, outside your place of business?"

"Really, Aubrey?" the young woman said, sounding faintly pathetic as she took the fifty he handed her and shoved it down her bra. "I'll be there."

"Good. Very, very good. And remember, this is all our secret." Then he kissed her forehead, placed her purse strap on her shoulder, ran his hands down her arms, and neatly got her out the door.

Dillon threw down the folded newspaper he had been reading. "You're going back for more? Once was more than enough. What is she? Twenty-two, twenty-three? If anyone we don't control in the press got wind of this—oh, hell, I'll call her later and give her your regrets. What's her name?''

"I haven't the faintest idea, nephew. It's why I call them all *my dear*. Much simpler that way.'' The senator sat down once more, spread the ivory linen napkin in his lap, and looked across the table at Dillon, who had finally sat himself down. "Now, what's the problem?''

"Other than the surety that one of these days our friends in the media aren't going to be able to keep the lid on the fact that you're screwing everything in a skirt, you mean? Was she even twenty-one? She didn't look it this morning, even with all that makeup. All you need, Uncle, is an under-age bimbo. Besides, you already owe our friends in the media too much in exchange for their silence. What are you going to give them next, the keys to the Oval Office?''

"They all seem to believe that, don't they? They don't know that I've already handed them over to you. President Holmes. All the power, but never the title. Does that rankle, nephew? I do hope so. Again, what else has your knickers in such a twist, hmm?''

Dillon added a spoonful of sugar to his coffee, his hand noticeably shaking. "Don't bullshit me, Uncle. What are you planning to do with it? Because it won't work, whatever it is. It's just a copy.''

Senator Harrison placed his elbows on the table and folded his hands together, resting his chin against them. "I'm certain you know just what you're whining about, Dillon. Now, perhaps, you'll tell me?''

"The printout, damn it,'' Dillon said, pushing back his chair so hard that it tipped over. He stood there, his palms on the tabletop, and glared across at his uncle. "I had it on top of the desk in there. I put it there right after I showed it to you. What did you do with it?''

Aubrey Harrison sat very quietly, the only animation being the way his Adam's apple went up and down as he swallowed . . . hard. "What printout?''

"*The* printout, Aubrey. *The* printout. It's gone.''

Harrison got to his feet, already heading into Dillon's bedroom, his bathrobe flapping as he went. "Are you sure? How could you know? There's crap everywhere. It looks like someone turned on a fan in here. You said the desk. You looked through everything on the desk? Where else did you look?"

He turned to his nephew, his face white. "Damn you, where is it?"

Dillon stomped over to the desk. "It should be here, right on top," he said, jabbing at a towering pile of papers. His jab set gravity in motion, and the whole stack slid to the floor. "Oh, hell! Never mind, it's not there. I looked, twice."

"Son of a—" The senator spied the overflowing waste can with the shredder sitting on top. "Did you shred it?"

Dillon began to massage the back of his neck with both hands. "I . . . I don't think so. No, I didn't shred it. Why would I shred it?"

"True. You'd rather wave the thing under my nose every time you want something else from me. You pompous, arrogant, sadistic *ass.*"

"Save it, that won't do us any good. We had a million people in here last night. Did someone see it? Did someone take it? We have to find that printout."

The senator looked around the cluttered room. "You expect me to search this pigsty?"

"I already did. Damn it, I've been up all night, or haven't you noticed that I haven't even undressed yet, or showered, or shaved?"

"I've never been interested enough in you, Dillon, to pay much attention, to tell you the truth. So you've looked everywhere?"

"Everywhere. But I have an idea . . ."

"Slitting your throat? Splendid, Dillon."

"No, no. It's that Janie Preston woman. She was in here, last night. She said she came in to find her conference folder, but how can I be sure? She looked guilty as hell when I found her."

Walking back into the main area of the suite, the senator asked, "I thought we'd decided Romanowski wasn't a threat. You think he put her up to it?"

Dillon flopped down on the couch, rubbed at his morning beard, which was very light. "Do I think they're working together now, you mean? Yes, I do, now. He talks a good game, but I watched him that first night. He half expected you to recognize him. Maybe you should have, told him you knew who he was, apologized, even groveled a little. Something. We probably should have done something. I dismissed him as just another wimp factor, but maybe we were wrong."

"Hummph. Maryjo's brat. Dangerous? He sent me a letter once, you know, years ago, when he was still a teenager. Telling me Maryjo was dead. I sent lilies, a whole basket, I think. Who would have thought that tall, gawky kid could grow up to be J. P. Roman?"

"I know. You really have to watch out who you're stepping on, Uncle, because sometimes they grow up and step back."

"Meaning you?"

"Meaning everybody. I've thought about this J. P. Roman crap ever since we got his background report last month and put two and two together. He's been writing about you for years, you know," Dillon said, stripping off his tie, which had been hanging loose under his collar all night. "Not enough for a slander case, but we both know what he's been doing. And now, if I'm right, he's finally got ammunition. You could go to jail, Uncle. You could—"

"You know I didn't—"

"I do? How do I know that?"

"You know because it was *you* who—"

"Oh, save it for the courtroom, Uncle. We're finished if this comes out, both of us. I can only hope she doesn't know what she's got."

"No names on the printout?"

Dillon's complexion went very pale. "Anyone can write

down names. It could be anything. A scene from a movie, dialogue from a book—hey, we could say Romanowski wrote it and tried to pass it off as ours. I don't know. I've got to think. The best I can hope for is that the bitch picked up the printout by accident and doesn't even know she has it. I need that folder of hers. She always carries it with her.''

Harrison rallied. ''You're right, Dillon. Cancel the woman for tonight. I'll be busy, romancing our dear young Miss Preston.''

''After that pinch last night? She wouldn't let you within fifteen feet. No, this one's mine. If I hurry, I can be downstairs just as the first sessions let out. Besides, I've got to meet with our man. I had him check out Romanowski's room last night. Maybe he's already got it.''

''Dillon?'' the senator called after him as he headed into his bedroom, already stripping out of his shirt.

''What now?''

''Don't screw this up, Dillon,'' the senator said, ''or I swear, I'll feed you to the dogs.''

''Me? They'll be too full to take more than a small bite after chewing on you.''

Harrison sat back against the dining chair and closed his eyes. No matter how this turned out, he had to rid himself of Dillon Holmes. He couldn't be the most powerful man in the world and have Dillon hanging that damn tape over his head. . . .

The phone rang just as John had finished one last inspection of the room, making sure everything was back in place, as neat as Jane had left it.

He had found nothing. Nothing extra, nothing missing.

He had checked his computer three times, just to prove to himself that he wasn't crazy, that the files had been ''modified'' at the same time he and Jane had been kissing on the beach.

He had come to a few conclusions while he searched, the

biggest being that he had behaved like a jerk this morning with Jane, and the second being that it was time he told her the complete truth.

Who he was.

That would be for starters.

How he felt about her.

That was more difficult. Horny didn't cut it, he knew that much. He had figured that out in high school. He just didn't have what it took to be a love-'em-and-leave-'em type, so he had stayed away from women for the most part, and only dated those who knew the score, that he wasn't the settle-down-and-raise-two-point-four-kids type.

Being attracted to Jane broke all his self-imposed rules.

But he wanted her. Oh, how he wanted her.

He wanted her enough that he had gone downstairs and done everything but get down on his knees and beg for another room, just so that Jane didn't come back after her morning seminar, pack up her clothing, and head for the bus station.

And he had gotten one. He'd already checked it out, and it wasn't a bad room, overlooking the street rather than the ocean. No balcony, smaller bathroom, but a good room. He had decided to move, leave Jane with the view. Hey, he'd score points wherever he could.

All he had to do was pack his bags, and he would be ready to move down the hall to 227.

John picked up the phone and said hello, his mind still on Jane and whoever had been in their room.

"Well, hello, yourself. Who are you?"

Oops.

"This is John Romanowski," he said, sitting down on the side of the bed. "Let me guess. You must be Molly Applegate, the woman who backed out on being my companion this week."

A rather delightful laugh came over the wires to him, followed by, "And aren't you glad, huh, John? I know Jane is. Whoops! Forget I said that. But you *are* in her room, aren't you?''

"I just stopped by to pick up a sweater for Jane, who's still in one of the seminars. Air-conditioning, you know,'' he improvised quickly. This being a good liar thing was really paying off. "I'll have your cousin call you.''

"No, no, wait,'' Molly said quickly. "I do need to talk to Jane, but I'd also like to talk to you, tell you I'm sorry I had to bail. That, and that if you hurt my cousin, I'm going to have to hurt you, bad.'' She laughed again. "Did that sound fierce enough?''

"I'm sitting here shaking in my shoes. Really. It's embarrassing,'' John told her, relaxing a little. She had said nothing about Jane reporting back to her about Harrison. Had she told her cousin about her change in plans? Apparently not. It was getting hard to tell the players around here without a scorecard, and he would have to fix that . . . soon.

"Good. That said, John, I hope you're romancing the girl, just a little. She could use a summer fling. Poor girl doesn't get out much, and let me tell you, one morning here with these little darlings of hers, and I'm surprised she can still string words together into a coherent sentence. In other words, since Jane seems to like you, you have my permission to . . . Well, I imagine you can figure that out for yourself.''

He had no snappy comeback for any of that, so he changed the subject. "It's a nice place, Preston Kiddie Kare?''

"Lovely, if you're into kids, which I'm not. And that's why I called, John. It seems like I've got just one itty bitty little . . . problem. Well, two, but we won't count the kid who keeps dropping his drawers.''

John laughed.

"Sure, laugh,'' Molly groused. "I did, too, the first time. But it gets old real fast, trust me. Anyway, I've got this other problem. A sort of mixup with her newest client. The person who did the interview for Jane thought the guy was hiring the place for August, not July.''

"Big mistake, huh?''

"Too true. And not my mistake, I wasn't even here, which I'll remind Jane of when I talk to her, except then she'll remind me that I took her shopping the day of the guy's interview and it's all my fault. Anyway, it seems this guy also thought the place was open all this week, and next, which it isn't. Jane closes up for the Fourth of July and stays closed for almost two weeks. The man is incensed, I tell you. *In-censed.* He slammed the phone down on me and is supposedly on his way over here right now. I'm thinking about barring the doors."

"And how is Jane supposed to handle this?" John asked, once more getting a mental picture of Jane packing up, heading home to Fairfax.

"Hmmm," Molly said after a moment, "I don't know. Good question, John. I mean, she's way up there."

"So, since you're way down there, you'll handle it, right? I know Jane worries that you won't be able to do her job, but that's ridiculous. I mean, they're just little kids, right?"

"Uh-huh," Molly said, her voice sounding very small. "Oh, damn. She'll never let me live it down if I screw this up. I mean, I promised her I could handle things, didn't I? And this guy is only a man. I can handle a man, for pity's sake. Okay, okay, tell you what. Pretend I didn't call. Can you do that, John?"

"Done," he agreed, relaxing. He heard Jane's key card in the door. "Here she comes. Good luck, Molly," he said, and then quickly hung up the phone and moved away from it before Jane could open the door.

"Hi," he said, ready to tell her about the hotel room.

"Whatever," Jane said, brushing past him on her way to the dresser. He could feel the chill in the air as she walked by.

"Let's see if I'm reading this right. Still mad, huh?" he asked as she opened the third drawer, slammed it shut, then opened the bottom one.

"Not at all, John," she said, closing that drawer, too. "I threw myself at you, and you threw me back. Too small a fish, huh? But you'll be happy to know that I've earned my keep this morning. Dillon seems to have totally forgiven me, and we're going to skip lunch here and go to one of the restaurants along the beach. After that, we're going swimming.''

''Oh,'' John said, sitting down on the edge of the bed, having realized that the last damn thing he wanted was Jane in Dillon's company if that meant she was also out of his, John's, sight. He had seen her reaction to her first look at the man on Saturday night. He was ''her type,'' she had made that clear. While he, big and hairy, was not.

Jane opened the closet doors and pulled out a hanger with the two scraps of pink bikini clipped to it.

''Hold it,'' John said, getting up. ''You don't think you're going to wear that, do you?''

Jane unclipped the two pieces. ''This?'' she asked, holding it up. ''With the cover-up overtop it until we get to the beach? Of course I am.''

''The hell you are,'' he said, grabbing the two pieces and throwing them behind him, on the bed. ''Don't you have something else? Something that covers you, for God's sake?''

Jane brushed past him and picked up the suit. ''Now you're being ridiculous. Excuse me,'' she said as he tried to block her way, and he stepped to one side, allowing her to go into the bathroom. He heard the lock turn.

Like he was going to open the door, knowing she was in there, changing into the bikini?

That was insulting. He wasn't an animal. He could live in this same room with her every day, every night, and never be reduced to something like that.

He could.

And, he decided, drawing himself up to his full, impressive height, that was just what he was going to do. Another room? Hell, no. He fished the new key card out of his pocket and shoved it in the back of his wallet, where it could stay until they checked out.

And in the meantime, he would keep a close eye on Jane, so that she didn't get too wrapped up in that blond god, Dillon Holmes, all in the name of having herself some excitement, a summer fling.

Somebody had to protect the woman from herself. It was the least he could do.

"Okay," he muttered out loud, "so now you're full of crap. Just as long as you *know* you're full of crap . . ."

Chapter Twelve

As a girl's teenage dreams actually becoming reality went, this one had turned out to be pretty much of a bust.

Lunch hadn't been bad, as Dillon had asked Jane all about Preston Kiddie Kare and seemed to be truly interested in her answers. He had smiled at her over their turkey club sandwiches and flirted lightly with her about the freckles on her nose. He was smooth, and urbane, and she couldn't help thinking he was doing and saying everything she wanted to hear . . . except not from him.

Jane would have enjoyed walking around the shops for a while, but she'd been dressed in her bathing suit and cover-up, which was all right for the casual beachside restaurant Dillon had chosen, but not dressed enough to go shopping.

So they went to the beach.

Dillon looked good in his bathing suit, a nice dark blue that reached halfway to his knees, but wasn't too tight or too loose. He wore a light gray T-shirt with a small white Nike swoosch on it, a blue-and-gray-plaid shirt he wore open over the T-shirt, and Docksiders without socks. He looked almost ''preppy,'' if a person could look preppy in a bathing suit, and blond, and still as drop-dead gorgeous as she'd thought him to be that first night.

Polished, sophisticated, soft spoken, excruciatingly polite.

Nonthreatening? Oh, all right, so Molly had been right—nonthreatening.

This was the prince of her dreams, come to life right in front of her. Everything she'd always thought she wanted.

Funny. He looked sort of puny.

She watched as Dillon spread out two large white towels he'd brought along, then stripped off both his shirts.

Tsk, tsk, tsk.

Oh, he was built just fine. Nearly six feet tall, there was no flab on this man. Unremarkable shoulders, a fairly narrow waist. He had the body of a jogger, and his legs were good, sprinkled with golden hair. If he turned around, she probably should take a look at his butt.

Dillon Holmes was a handsome man. No question about that. And he was paying her very devoted attention. If she was going to go full out, have herself a fling while here in Cape May, this was the guy she should choose. Definitely.

Boy, he was puny. . . .

"Those waves definitely look inviting," Dillon said, standing with his back to her, his hands on his hips, looking out over the ocean.

So they'd gone into the water. Not too far, because Dillon didn't think that was safe. They held hands and jumped the waves, and Jane was amazed at how boring it was being in the water with Dillon after being in the water with John.

So she splashed him.

She splashed him, and the look was back, that same angry flash she'd seen in his eyes the previous night when he'd seen her coming out of his room.

"I'm sorry, Dillon," she said, following him back to the towels and watching as he wiped at his dripping face. "You don't like water battles?"

He pulled the towel down so that his eyes and the top of his nose showed. "No," he said succinctly. And then he lowered the towel some more and smiled, a really false, I'm-mad-as-hell-but-I'm-pretending-not-to-be smile. "Sorry. I guess I'm not as big a fan of the beach as I thought I was. Salty water, shells underfoot, all this sand, waiting for a gull to dump on you? What do you say we go back to the hotel, get out of these suits, and go shopping? I should have suggested that in the first place."

Jane gathered up her belongings and walked across the beach with him. "Why did you? Suggest the beach, that is. If you don't like the water?"

He shrugged. Eloquently. "I don't know. You seemed to like it. I mean, last night you came back looking like a drowned—that is, I thought you liked the beach."

"Well, I do, but it's not *all* I like."

"But you like physical activities, don't you? The rough-and-tumble sort? I'll bet you enjoy rolling around with the kids at that day care of yours. I play golf, and I jog at an indoor track three days a week. Oh, and I ski."

And bully for you, Jane thought, but she didn't speak the thought out loud. "Well, it was very nice, very thoughtful of you, to go out of your way to please me. But please don't do it again."

Dillon stopped on the verandah and looked at her. He cupped her cheek with his free hand. "I'm sorry, Jane. If you weren't so important to me, I probably would have handled this better."

"I'm . . . important to you? Oh, I get it," she said, definitely not the same girl who had looked at him Saturday night and gone all ga-ga over the man. "I'm important to the *senator.* I really don't see how."

He looked at her intensely, then motioned for her to sit down in one of the ladder-back rockers and sat down beside her. "Truth, Jane?"

She lifted her chin. "I think that would be a good idea, yes."

"Okay," he said, sighing. "Your name has already gone out to the press. You know that. You were seen on local television with the senator, and the networks picked up the feed. That was last night. By this morning, the clip was on all the morning talk shows, and the spin so far is that the senator will make child care—affordability, availability, children's health, and of course early childhood education—in America the linchpin of his presidential campaign if he chooses to run.''

Molly, I may just be getting you your scoop in the next few minutes, Jane thought, trying to keep her expression neutral.

''Except,'' Dillon went on, ''one of the networks commented that you didn't show up as advertised last night, for the photo-op. You'll be getting calls, Jane, asking you if you and the senator had a falling out, if you're not as happy with his plans as we've said you are. Whether you like it or not, just the fact that you're attending this retreat makes you a bona fide expert, at least with the people who count.'' He smiled at her. ''That would be the public, Jane.''

''And all coincidental. All because I overturned my ankle and the senator asked me to join his table?''

Dillon's smile was sympathetic. ''It would look that way, wouldn't it, at least at first glance. Except that we knew you were coming and had already planned to use . . . to confer with you about child care issues, as our private polls have shown child care, children in general, to be one of the hot buttons for this election.''

''Oh, right. The senator saw reports on every person here, for security purposes. Heaven knows I can't forget that particular invasion of my privacy. You're saying that he saw my name, weeks ago, and decided to *confer* with me. And I thought my cousin was the master at using me.''

''Molly Applegate? Lovely girl, but not the steadiest person, is she?''

Jane slid her gaze away from his.

''Oh, come on, Jane. I already told you I know about your cousin, and I'm sure she already told you about me; so you know my information is both of a security nature

and on a more personal level. That's why she isn't here and
you replaced her at the last minute, right? Because she'd
decided I wouldn't let her close to the senator once it was
known that I was going to attend the retreat with him? That
was the reason for the switch three weeks ago, wasn't it?''

''I refuse to answer on the grounds that it might make me
look really, really dumb,'' Jane said, realizing that nothing,
absolutely nothing a person did, remained secret when the
President was coming to town and that person was going
to be there when he did.

Dillon laughed, definitely in real amusement. Then, just
as quickly, he became serious once more. ''Jane, I'm going
to tell you something now, something very secret, very
important.''

''No, don't do that,'' she said, panicking. ''Please don't
do that.''

''But I trust you, Jane. You're a good person. You pay
your taxes; you vote in every election—although you could
try voting for the right party. You're good to your parents,
you have your own business, and your credit history is top
rate. You even volunteer in the children's ward at the hospital
twice a month. You're squeaky clean. Much as I don't like
to admit this, I have to hand it to Molly. I couldn't have
done much better if I'd handpicked you myself. We regret
that she's not here, but you're actually even more perfect.''

Jane felt as though she needed a shower, and not just to
get the sand off her body. ''Is there a point to this, Dillon?
Because I really don't want to listen to anything else. You
may know everything about me, but believe me, I don't
want to know any more about you.''

''Not me, Jane. The senator. I'm about to give you what
you came for, what Molly sent you here for.''

Jane, who had been in the process of getting to her feet,
sat down once more. ''I beg your pardon?''

He leaned closer. ''Words of the fewest syllables, Jane.
Molly Applegate needs to go to an escort service for a social

life like your friend Romanowski needs to grow another inch.''

Jane just shrugged. She couldn't disagree with that one.

"More, Jane. I know where Molly is playing at working right now. And, knowing Molly, she decided she'd be one of the horde of newshounds who are hanging around here this week, waiting to see if my uncle announces or not, hoping to parade her big baby blues by him—not to mention those long legs of hers—and convince him to tell her first, give her the scoop.''

Jane sort of waved her hands, then let them settle in her lap. There really wasn't anything she could say, was there?

"Good move, Jane, you needn't bother lying to me, because I'm right, and I know I'm right. We're knee-deep in reporters expecting an announcement. That's partially because we've been dropping some heavy off-the-record hints about a major announcement being in the works for this week. Although, to be truthful, we hadn't expected your part in this to get as big as it has. Are you with me so far?''

"Why don't you like Molly?'' Jane asked, for no particular reason. It was just something to say.

"She's a kook,'' Dillon said in some disgust. "But that's not all of it. She's a sloth. She lives off her trust fund and doesn't know the meaning of a good day's work. She *plays* at life.''

Well, she had asked. Jane sort of nodded, sort of agreed. She would point out that Molly hadn't exactly had the greatest childhood, and that she had a heart as big as all outdoors, but she was pretty sure Dillon could not care less.

"The funny thing is, we would have handed her the story. We'd begun to plan on it. Nothing like a beautiful redhead standing next to you when you make a big announcement. Anyone can stand beside Peter Jennings. But then she backed out and sent you in her place. As I believe I've already said, it turned out that you were even better for us than Molly.''

"The senator pinched me, you know. I wouldn't pose with him again for all the tea in China.''

"But you will stick around to get your cousin the chance at the big exclusive she sent you here to hopefully get. I've already left instructions for her to get a press pass on Friday," Dillon said, sitting back in his chair, crossing his legs. "In return, name one thing you really want changed in the way the federal government handles day care."

"You don't mean that."

"Oh, but I do, Jane. That's how it works. One hand washes the other. Give us a few good photo-ops, play nice with the senator this week, and in return we'll give Molly her exclusive . . . *and* make a formal announcement of whatever the hell it is you want, saying it will be the first legislation President Harrison will introduce to Congress at twelve-o-one on January twentieth. Within reason, of course."

Her mind was spinning, but one thing was clear. Still, she needed to hear Dillon say it. "So he's definitely going to run."

"Like a rabbit," Dillon said, getting to his feet and holding out a hand to her. "Not that you'll spill the beans before time, Jane. Not when we've got these," he said, pulling some photographs out of his shirt pocket. "In baseball, although I'm not really a fan, I believe these would be called covering all your bases."

She looked at them for a few moments, and they became indelibly impressed upon her mind. She and John, kissing in the surf. She and John, her with her legs wrapped around his hips, the long skirt of her dress hiked halfway up her thighs. She and John, walking hand-in-hand up the beach, her sopping wet dress riding low on her breasts and clinging to her in ways she hadn't imagined. She was looking at John as if she wanted to eat him. . . . And his expression wasn't exactly platonic.

"I'll take those," Dillon said, and Jane didn't think quickly enough to hide the photographs behind her back, then rip them up. Not that it mattered. They couldn't be all of the photographs that had been taken. Taken by whom? And did that matter?

"So. Beauty, the Beast, and the Frolic on the Beach. And they're sharing an illicit love nest, too, right here at the retreat? A hired escort, boinking her john—that's john with a lowercase *J*, Janie—the two of them sullying the high moral content of this august gathering? Oh, my, and everyone thinks you're such a good girl. Your parents get a photo, Jane. The local newspaper in Fairfax gets a full set, along with all the major networks. The parents of all the little kiddies see the photo in the newspaper. Life lesson, Jane. Never, never ever, do anything compromising in public, not if you don't want it *made* public."

Jane struck blindly. "The senator pinched me, remember. I could tell the reporters that one, say that's why I didn't show up for the photo session."

"Tabloid reporters, I'm sure. They love a good scandal. Of course, they'd want photos of Preston Kiddie Kare for their pages. And most of the world would say your accusations were nothing but sour grapes."

"The tabloids. Oh, God, no. I hate those things. I read all the headlines while I'm in line at the checkout, but I really hate those things."

Dillon patted her cheek. "I'm sorry, Jane, it would have been easier, I suppose, just to romance you, get what I want that way; but you didn't seem to be playing, and I don't have a lot of time. So." He leaned closer and kissed her cheek. "You like the water, Jane? Now you're swimming with the big fish. See you at dinner, my dear. Wear the pink again, it will look good on television."

And then he turned on his heel to walk away, but Jane grabbed his arm. "Wait. I want something else."

Dillon shook his head. "They always do."

"I'll ignore that, because you're slime, Dillon. I want to know everything you know about John Romanowski. Everyone was investigated for possible security problems; you said so yourself. So tell me about John."

"What do you know about him?"

Jane shrugged. She wasn't even sure why she'd asked the

question. "He teaches political science. What else should I
know?"

Dillon hesitated only a moment. "What else is there to
tell? College professor. Single, lives with his aunt, parents
dead, likes fast cars, and he can always double as Underdog
in the Macy's Thanksgiving Parade, if they need another
oversize hot-air balloon. You're the one who'd have to tell
me if he's good in bed, not that I give a rat's ass."

Jane dropped her hand and turned away from him, because
that fat man who always had a cigar stuck in his mouth
was approaching, having already called out Dillon's name,
asking something about a meeting scheduled for later that
afternoon.

She wanted to go upstairs, tell John everything that had
happened. But she was mad at John. She'd left their hotel
room in a huff, so how could she crawl back there on her
hands and knees, telling him how *used* she felt, how horrible
Dillon and the senator were?

Wait a minute. John was the guy who'd sent her off to
make nice-nice with Dillon. Anything that had happened to
her had happened because of John.

Not really. Some of it was Molly's fault, and some of it
was her own fault—but a whole big bunch of it was John's
fault, darn it. At least, if she closed her eyes to most of the
facts, she could see it that way.

She took several steps toward the door to the hotel, and
then another thought struck her. *Molly.* That was it, she
could call Molly.

Jane walked to the end of the verandah as she dug in her
purse for the cell phone, then ducked around the corner, out
of sight, out of earshot. As Dillon had said, don't do it in
public unless you want it made public. Although he'd talked
to her in public, hadn't he? Was arrogance one of the seven
deadly sins?

She realized she was counting rings at Kiddie Kare and
had already gotten to five. When she was there, all phones
were answered by the third ring, tops.

"Preston Kid Kare," Molly said at last, and sounding fairly breathless.

"That's *Kiddie* Kare, Molly," Jane said, shaking her head. "Where were you? I thought you'd be hiding in the office all day."

"Yeah, well, sure, that's what I thought, too. But some knucklehead sliced through a power line a couple of blocks from here, and we have no electricity. No air-conditioning, Janie. No videos to play for these screaming kids. I was just entertaining them by trying to teach them my tap dance. You remember that one, Janie? The one I did in second grade, to 'Good Ship Lollipop'? I brought the house down at Miss Chandler's School for Girls. But I have to tell you, these kids are a tough audience."

Jane tried to form a mental picture of her cousin standing in front of a bunch of four-year-olds, saying, "Tap, step, tap." "But at least you're trying, Molly. I think that's wonderful. Have you activated the chain?"

"What chain? I was just kidding about the whips and chains, Janie. Jeez. The kids aren't *that* bad."

"No, no, Molly. If you've called the utility company, and I'm sure you have, and if the power is to be off for more than an hour or so, you start the telephone-calling chain, where we contact several mothers, and then they contact other mothers, until everyone knows what's going on. We stay open until the last child is gone, but many parents would rather take their children home."

"Fascinating. I mean it, Janie, truly riveting," Molly said flatly. "Why didn't anyone tell *me* this?"

"I wrote it all down for you, Molly. I thought you said you read my notes."

"No. I said I got a headache reading your notes. I never got past page two of that opus. So where do you keep that list of—hey, never mind. The power just came back on. See that? If I'd read your instructions, this place would be a madhouse of mothers and telephone calls and—who said I couldn't handle this place?"

"It sounds as if you're doing a great job, Molly," Jane said, relieved. "Do you have a few minutes to talk about something?"

"Sure," Molly answered. "But first—congratulations, Miss Television Star."

"Huh?" Jane winced. "You saw that?"

"Saw it? Your parents taped it the second time it came on—it was on every station. Let me tell you, the parental units are busting their buttons, late last night and again this morning. Their little girl, confidante to the next president, yadda yadda. Small-town all-American girl makes good. You're a hit, Janie, a real hit. And the dress looked good, too."

"It wasn't my idea," she said, leaning against the yellow-painted brick. "We're being blackmailed, Molly."

There were three seconds of silence—Jane counted in her head—and then Molly exploded: *"What!"*

It took several minutes, some of them spent calming down Molly as she called Dillon every name in the book—and some Jane was pretty sure her cousin had just invented—to relay everything that had happened. But, in the end, Molly being Molly, her last comment was "So the prof is hot, huh?"

"Oh, for crying out loud, Molly! I'm being *used* here. *You* are being used here. Politics is a cesspool. Don't you care about any of that?"

"Janie, Janie, Janie-girl. I live in Washington, remember? Welcome to the real world. And remember, this washes both ways. Dillon means it when he says he'd throw you a fish for helping, although he can't promise to get Harrison's law through Congress. He can only promise it will be presented—just make sure that's part of the announcement this week, so it's on the record and Harrison can't renege without coming off looking like a schmuck. And, on top of that, I get my story, save my job. And *you*—well, I think we both know what you'll be getting out of this, if you haven't already. You didn't happen to grab one of the photos, did you? I'd love to see your Professor Romeo.''

"That's Romanowski, and you aren't funny. Good-bye, Molly, you've been a big help—not,'' Jane said.

Molly's clear laugh had Jane pulling the phone slightly away from her ear. ''No, no, don't go away mad. Just calm down, Janie. This isn't all a bad thing; it really isn't.''

"Sez you,'' Jane groused. ''You're handling your end just fine. It's me that's in a mess.''

"Yeah. Sure,'' Molly said quickly, very quickly, which might have alerted Jane to trouble, except she was too busy concentrating on her own problems. ''I am doing wonderfully well, aren't I, while you're in it up to your knees? What a switch! Now, here's what *you* do. You go tell the prof everything you just told me. And tell him about me while you're at it. I give you permission, considering Dopey Dillon already figured it out. Lay it all out to the prof. My bet is he goes along, even helps you, because you told me he's got his own axe to grind, right?''

It was at that point that Jane belatedly remembered Molly didn't quite know *everything*. She had given her cousin an edited version. She didn't know that Jane and John were sharing a hotel room. She didn't know that John already knew about Molly's plan and had already agreed to help her get a story on Harrison. An exposé, actually. A bring-him-to-his-knees blockbuster.

"Oh, this is all getting way too confusing,'' Jane muttered, and her cousin heard her.

"Such is life, Janie. It can't all be story hour and nap time. You just have to roll with the punches. You did want an adventure, remember?''

"I did not! You tricked me into helping you. I never wanted to come here.''

"Lie to yourself, sweetcakes, but not to me. You were itching to bust loose. A woman doesn't buy that much new underwear without a reason, and you bought a *bunch*. Well, anyway, it doesn't get much looser or wilder than what you've got going now, does it? Oh, damn, I just heard a crash and . . . yup, there it is—the wail. I tell you, a woman's work is never done. Gotta go, Janie. But first, some advice from your worldly cousin Molly. Lock your conscience in a drawer somewhere, toss your goody-two-shoes in the ocean, and go wild. You deserve it! Bye."

Jane stared at the cell phone, dumbfounded. Great. Just what she'd needed. Permission from Molly to have a fling, an affair.

"Thanks, Molly," she said after a moment, and actually smiled as she headed into the hotel.

John met Jane at the door of the hotel room and told her the damn phone had been ringing off the damn hook with damn people wanting to talk to her, until he had called downstairs and told the damn switchboard operator to hold all the damn calls.

"Yes, I already know," Jane said, stripping off the cover-up, so that she stood there in just the pink bikini.

Funny thing about that. A bikini on the beach was a bikini on a beach. Sexy, fun, and okay.

But a bikini in a hotel room looked a whole hell of a lot like a bra and panties and a whole lot of skin. . . . And John, who had been shocking himself more and more with his Victorian attitude toward Jane, turned his head away from the sight that had him thinking about a lot of things, none of them being *nice,* or *pal.*

"John? Are you blushing? No, you couldn't be. You're just angry again, aren't you? I can explain everything. I'll just be a minute," Jane said, grabbing fresh clothes and heading for the bathroom. "You stay right there, because we have to talk."

"And the phone calls—?" he yelled after her.

"I told you, I already know about those. I'll explain everything after I get out of the shower, all right?" The bathroom door closed, but did not lock.

Left with no choice, John contented himself with pacing the carpet until she reentered the room, her hair still wet, with no makeup on her freckled face, wearing white short-shorts and a short-sleeved kelly green summer sweater that didn't quite cover her flat belly. She smelled of soap and shampoo and mint toothpaste.

Did this woman *know* what she did to him? Cripes!

"Okay," she said quietly, and he finally noticed that she looked upset. "Sit down, John, and let's talk. Me first."

So John sat down quietly and let Jane talk. It wasn't as if he had many options.

He watched her pace the hotel room after putting on her little white satin slippers—she was never barefoot in the room, he'd noticed—occasionally stopping to pick up and fold his same sports jacket, over and over. He saw the quick flash of tears in her eyes when she talked about Dillon threatening her with sending the photographs to her parents.

That was it. He couldn't sit there another moment, doing nothing, saying nothing.

So then Jane, bless her, sat quietly and let him talk. Let him rant. She watched as he picked up his sports jacket, wadded it into a ball, and slam-dunked it into a corner. He did his best to hide the homicidal glint in his eyes as he spat Dillon's name.

"Feel better now?" she asked quietly when, at last, he pulled out the desk chair and plopped himself down in it.

"No, not particularly, but thanks for letting me go nuts," he said, trying to smile at her. She'd probably lived through a million tantrums and learned that the best thing to do was just stand back and let the tantrum thrower have at it. "Let's recap, all right?"

She nodded, then sent a quick glance toward the corner of the room, and he got up, retrieved his jacket, not just shaking it out, but actually hanging it up in the closet.

"Thank you," she said, at last summoning a small smile of her own.

"Don't thank me. I've got a feeling that if I dumped all

these dresser drawers all over the place, you'd be in pig heaven, because then you'd have something to do.''

"Something *constructive* to do, John," she corrected. "Although my mother says I'm just naturally neat, because I'm a Virgo. That was fine with me, until Molly told me that many call Virgos the virgins of the zodiac. Well," she added, quickly averting her eyes, "we don't need to talk about that, do we? You were saying? A recap, was it?"

"Right," John said, heading back to the desk and sitting down once more. "From the beginning." He frowned. "Where the hell's the beginning?"

"For me, or for you?" Jane asked. "For me, it was Molly, bursting into my life yet again, begging a favor. For you, I suppose it was your student telling you things about Harrison, and then the book."

"The book? Oh, yeah, right." He frowned. She sure did have a real steel-trap memory for all of his stupid lies. "The book. That never was a good idea."

"No, probably not," she said, nodding. "Oops, I'm sorry. I'm sure you're a very good writer, John. You just picked a bad subject, trying to bring the senator down via either something illegal or his . . . his amorous adventures. That last was probably a leftover from that love story you tried to write. Either way, it was a good effort. I'm sure you'll publish something, someday."

John rolled his eyes. "Gee, thanks, teach. What next?"

"You dropped the nerd act and told me you've come here to dig dirt on Harrison and wanted my help. And then I told you why I came here and—no, I didn't tell you that right away, did I?" Jane sighed. "Maybe we should be writing this down."

"We don't need that exact a timeline, Janie. It has only been three days. You told me eventually, and we agreed to join forces," he reminded her. "So let's skip ahead. While we were merrily doing all this heavy-duty planning, Dillon and Harrison were about six steps ahead of us, maybe a dozen, having already figured out ways to use you weeks ago, along with your cousin Molly, and probably sixty percent of the other people here this week. I don't even figure in their plans.''

That brought him up short, and he busied himself getting paper and a pen out of the desk drawer, pretending to write down what they'd learned, as Jane suggested. But what he was thinking was quite another thing.

First of all, he was thinking he had really screwed up. He'd known there would be government background checks of attendees because the President might show up at the retreat. He and Jane had even talked about those background checks last night, at the cocktail party.

But he hadn't taken that knowledge far enough. He, the cynic, the guy who believed everybody had an angle, had been naive. Badly naive. He hadn't considered Harrison bending the rules and getting his hands on copies of those reports for his own use.

The senator had to have known John was Maryjo's son going in—he had figured that out the second Jane had told him that Harrison had gotten copies of the government background reports—and the bastard had decided to pretend he hadn't connected the name with Maryjo's.

Okay, John had accepted that; the guy was a gutless weasel. But had Harrison also known that he was J. P. Roman *before* Kevin the Bum had broken into the computer? Of course he had. That was *why* Kevin had lifted his key card, broken into this room. Kevin the Bum worked for Harrison, and Harrison wanted to see if J. P. Roman had written anything about him in his computer. Absolutely. Well, maybe. It was one explanation anyway.

"John? Is something wrong?"

He shook his head. "No. I was just thinking. I must be pretty boring if Harrison hasn't figured out any way to use me. He's probably putting pressure on almost everyone here, one way or another, doling out promises in exchange for support, financial and otherwise. But not me. I guess the background check didn't reveal anything interesting about me.''

''According to Dillon, you're right,'' Jane told him, gaining his full attention. ''Oh, don't look so shocked. I asked, and he told me. Single, orphaned, living with your aunt, a professor at a local college. That was about it.''

''Well, I'm insulted. They didn't even find out that I got caught in a panty raid while I was in college? Excuse me, Jane, I want to go down the hall and get us some sodas. I'll be right back.''

John had a conversation with himself as he fed dollar bills into the soda machine.

That was about it, Jane had said? No, it wasn't. Even a cursory background check would have come up with his parents' names. James and Maryjo Romanowski. So it had all been an act that first night. Harrison *knew*, he had to know. His initial conclusions had to be correct, and Dillon had lied to Jane.

Still, Harrison had to be worrying that John was going to confront him, publicly, about Maryjo.

And, if he had found out who John really was, both personally and professionally—knew anything at all about John's novels—then the guy also had to think he was here to do research—and be scared out of his wits about what J. P. Roman might be planning to write about next.

Which would explain why someone broke into his computer.

Okay. He had thought about it, thought about it again, and he was confident now in his conclusions.

Unless the senator and his lapdog had figured out a way to use *him*, too. But how?

''Sonofabitch,'' John grumbled on his way back down the hallway with the icy cans. ''And I can't do anything about it. Confront him, accuse him of breaking and entering. Nothing.'' Because those photos might have been shown to Jane, but he knew they were meant for him, too. If he made waves, the photos would be sent out, and Jane would be devastated, and it would all be his fault. "Son of a *bitch*."

Then he thought of something else. Jane had been honest with him. But he hadn't been honest with her.

What if he were to tell her the whole truth now? Who he was, why he was really here to bring down Harrison. What he already knew about Harrison, which still wasn't quite enough to go public with, damn it. How it wasn't her cousin Molly who had gotten her into all this trouble, but him. How their room had been broken into, his computer broken into.

John stood at the door of 217 for a few moments, considering scenarios, the way he would in one of his books.

He tells Jane, and she smacks him square in the chops.

No. Jane wouldn't do that. She was every inch the lady. She would leave.

No. She couldn't do that. Harrison had her just where he wanted her.

She would find out he was J. P. Roman and throw herself into his arms, and they would make mad, crazy love?

Hmmm. . . .

Naw. That only happened in fiction.

Besides, there was already too much information in front of them right now. J. P. Roman could wait.

John held both soda cans in one of his large hands and opened the door to 217, stepped inside. "Okay, here's the drill," he said, handing one of the cans to Jane. "They've got us, Jane. They've really, really got us. It goes without saying that if those photographs could be sent to your parents, they could also be sent to my dean, along with proof that we're sharing a room. I got this invitation through the university, and I don't think Dean Hennessy would be real keen on having the school's reputation dragged through the tabloids."

Jane pushed out her bottom lip. "It isn't as if those photos are *that* bad."

"Bad enough, I'm afraid, when coupled with the fact that we're sharing a room. Reporters are beginning to show up in droves, for the President's visit, and they'll be looking for all the stories and air time they can squeeze out of this place—and we all know, sex sells. Hell, we're talking about a breed of lowlifes still trying to dig up dirt on JFK's sex life, and he's been dead for forty years. But enough of that. What we've got to do is turn the tables on these bastards. Figure out a way to reveal Harrison and his faithful dog Dillon for the slime they are, to the press, to all the media and, most important of all, to the voters.''

Jane nodded. "It's what you seem to have wanted all along, yes. But how are we going to do that? I didn't come here to uncover any scandal. I came here to find out if he's going to run for president, remember? And all you have are rumors from some student whose uncle or cousin or somebody said something to him.''

Again with the imaginary student. He really, really should tell her the truth.

But not yet.

"Jane, I have some pretty good information. I know that at least three of the men here this week are already in bed with Harrison and a little nonprofit *fund* he and Dillon have set up, and not quite legally, either, not if someone looks really hard. It's good information, and I can document most of it.''

But he would much rather bring Harrison down for his sins of the flesh, for having broken Maryjo so badly, so thoroughly—and definitely without bringing his mother's name into it. Except that now, with Jane involved, he would do it any way he could, just to get her clear of any trouble.

Jane shrugged. "So? What do we do with this information if it can't all be documented?''

"Hey, give me a break here. I'm only beginning to come up with an idea. There's an evening seminar tonight, right? Does it sound like anything Harrison would attend?''

"I don't know." She stood up, went over to the night table, and picked up her folder. It was sort of bent now from the liquid that had spilled on it. She walked toward the desk, toward him, as she opened the folder and began looking through the pages. "Okay, where is that schedule? I really made a mess when I dropped this. Oh, and the ink on some of the postcards is all smudged. Darn it."

John was barely paying attention. How could he get Harrison? He had to find a way to get him in some compromising position when the media was around and take him down fast, take him down hard. Preferably before Harrison announced his candidacy, which he would probably do Friday night, before the retreat was over.

As he had said to Jane, there were already a couple of network news vans parked in the lot at Congress Hall to cover the President's visit. But the vans would stick around, thinking Friday, because Dillon would leak it, that Friday was the big day.

Today was Monday. He had five days. Five days to come up with something new or go with what he had—either on Harrison's backroom deals or the still-sketchy proof that he had driven his second wife to drink—and eventually her fall down the stairs—with his affairs.

Would it be enough? He really needed a few more months of research, confirmation of what he had learned, on both fronts. Henry had made that very clear to him. He'd been so close. If only this damn retreat had been planned for September instead of July.

"John?"

He looked up, and saw that Jane was frowning. "What's the matter? No seminar tonight?"

"I didn't look. I don't know," she said, still looking at the stapled papers she held. She handed the papers to him. "John? What's this?"

Chapter Thirteen

Jane fought down the urge to slip behind one of the potted palms lining the verandah, pull up the collar of her nonexistent trench coat, and whip out a miniature spyglass to survey the scene.

Which was ridiculous. . . . But for a girl who wanted a little adventure in her life, she was suddenly getting it. In spades.

And, shame, shame on her, she was having fun. She was nervous, not sure she could pull it off, but she was still having fun.

Her mission this Tuesday afternoon, if she chose to accept it—and she had—was to locate one Brandy Hythe, and "get chummy with her. You know, girl talk."

Sure, that was easy for John to say—although she had been somewhat surprised to hear him use the word *chummy*. But, then, he was a college professor.

The man had no idea how difficult it could be to have girl talk with the reigning queen of Hollywood. What did they have in common? Okay, so they were both women. They both came with the same standard equipment. But

Brandy Hythe had much better options. Put another way, Brandy was a top-of-the-line Jaguar ... and Jane was a bargain-basement Neon.

But she wouldn't think about that ... much.

All she needed was a way in, an opening. She could play supplicant ... fan ... simpering sycophant. *Sycophant.* Now there was a word! Jane silently blessed her grandmother, yet again, for the woman's wonderful vocabulary.

Except that Brandy Hythe must be hip-deep in sycophants and certainly didn't need another one.

"Now, here's an idea," Jane said as she spied Brandy climbing out of the pool—the woman even did that gracefully. Sure, her suit wouldn't ride up; it wouldn't dare. She probably never got razor burn, either. "Stop it, Jane, concentrate. You just had an idea. You'll be up front. You'll be honest. Direct. John may not recognize the concept, but you do."

So thinking, Jane squared her shoulders and headed toward the chaise lounges set up around the pool, zeroing in on the empty one beside Brandy.

"Hi, how's the water?" Jane asked as she she sat down, pushing herself back so that she was sitting at her ease, her legs straight out in front of her. She couldn't help noticing that Brandy's feet rested near the bottom of her chaise ... while Jane's own were about six to eight inches shorter, yet were heavier. Jane even had dimples on her knees, which would have been cute were she still six years old.

The gods did not bestow their gifts fairly; that was all there was to it.

"Hello, Janie. And the water's wonderful," Brandy said in her faintly husky voice, a sort of Lauren Bacall voice. Another gift from the gods. Lauren Bacall could even seduce people into buying cat food on TV ads, and did. Brandy Hythe, with her youth and great looks, and that voice, could probably sell bubble gum cigars to Fidel Castro.

Okay, one subject down. Pick another one. "I saw you

in this morning's seminar on global warming. What did you think?''

And they were off! Jane couldn't believe it. Yes, she knew she had one of ''those'' faces, or whatever it was that seemed to draw people to her, to tell her their secrets, their troubles, their worries and dreams. But she hadn't expected Brandy Hythe to notice that.

The woman sat up, put her feet on the cement, leaned her elbows on her knees, and launched into a twenty minute tirade on global warming being one of the most important problems facing the nation, nay, the world, today. She lived in California, on one coast, and had been raised in New Jersey, on another coast, and she was about as well informed as any one person could be without having a degree in the subject.

Jane barely got a word in edgewise, as a matter of fact, and finally contented herself with frowning or nodding at what seemed like appropriate times. She even slipped a sincere *tsk-tsk* in there at some point.

''. . . and Senator Harrison doesn't see it, Janie,'' Brandy said, winding down a little at last. She sat back against the chaise lounge once more. ''The man just refuses to see any of it. Probably because global warming doesn't wear short skirts and walk with a wiggle, or contribute to his campaigns. Sure, he talks big, makes all the right noises, but does he *do* anything? No. No, he doesn't. A word of warning, Janie. Never trust a person who smiles when he talks. Oh, he makes me so *mad.*''

She shifted her gaze to Jane, looking faintly surprised. ''Why am I telling you all this?''

Jane remained silent, letting Brandy's words hang out there for a few moments as she digested them. John had been more right than he knew; Brandy Hythe did not like Senator Harrison. Not even a little bit. ''The senator wants me to give him some of my ideas on government-sponsored child care in America,'' she said at last.

Brandy snorted—just like a real person. ''Oh, I'll bet he

does. Just wear your running shoes if he invites you up to his suite. And maybe carry a stun gun.''

There was a limit to how long Jane could play dumb. Besides, this was why she was here, to find out all Brandy might know about her fellow New Jerseyite. She had thought the woman liked him, John thought he had sensed a certain distance between them—but neither of them had expected this.

Or maybe John had. She would have to think about that, later.

Now Jane pushed it a little, gave the woman a nudge to hopefully move the conversation deeper into personalities. ''He pinched me, you know. Right in front of the television cameras. He's a lech.''

''Good word, lech.'' Brandy sat up once more, swung her feet back to the cement again. She looked around, to see that there was no one within twenty feet of them, and motioned for Jane to lean closer. ''Janie, I could tell you *stories* . . .''

Drooling in anticipation probably wouldn't be very cool. Neither would groping in her purse for a pen and paper. So Jane contented herself with her own look around, followed by a raised eyebrow and a whispered, ''Really?''

''Really. And I'm just angry enough to tell you a few. I'm angry enough right now to tell the whole world a few. As a matter of fact, I made up my mind this morning to do just that. The no-good, back-stabbing—do you know why I'm here?''

Jane shook her head. She was already fairly certain that her answer would be ridiculous, but offered it anyway: ''For the seminars?''

''Yeah, right, like this particular collection of jackasses cares about anyone else's opinion. Oh, they've got a couple of regular guys sprinkled around, to make it look good. Your Professor Romanowski, for one, you for another. A couple of scientists they've only semicorrupted with promises of funding, that sort of thing. But do you know what this week really is, Janie? It's the kick-off of Harrison's presidential campaign, that's what it is. He's lining up money, doling out empty promises, gathering paybacks, blackmailing others into throwing their support his way. There's a whole other world going on here, Janie, beneath the surface.''

"And you?" Jane asked, too inexperienced at intrigue to do anything more than simply ask the first question that came to her mind.

"Me? I'm window dressing. New Jersey girl makes good. Scholarship student at Princeton, big star in Hollywood, all of that crap. It was the Mirabelle Flanders Harrison scholarship, by the way. Named after Harrison's first wife. I was so grateful, Janie. I volunteered for his campaign, made stump speeches once my name became known. But when I began to figure out that the man didn't match his image and wanted to get away from him? Oh, he wasn't going to let that happen, let me tell you. Damn it, I don't care anymore, Janie. Let him publish the pictures. I'm through being his showpiece!''

Jane laid a hand on Brandy's arm. John had told her he already had two reasons, two possible ways to go, to bring Harrison down and had yet to pick one of them as the best way. Now it sounded like maybe there was a third option. Senator Aubrey Harrison. What a pile of pond scum! "Maybe we should take a walk, go somewhere private, get you something cool to drink?"

"Henry," John said, sitting down across from his friend and editor in the Blue Pig.

"John," Henry answered, not looking up from the manuscript he was reading, red pen in hand.

"The hotel's on fire."

"Uh-huh," Henry answered absently, then laid down the pen and folded his hands together on top of the manuscript pages. "Would you read a book about hair loss and replacement?" He held up his hands, smiled sheepishly. "Scratch that. Stupid question. Not you, the rest of the world. Do you think the world needs another book on hair loss and replacement?''

"Does it say anything that hasn't been said before?" John asked. He had gotten the attention of the bartender and signaled for two frosted mugs of beer.

"Possibly. It concentrates on female hair loss, which is different just for starters. It's sort of interesting, actually. And there's a lot of psychology and support, of course, as women aren't supposed to lose their hair the way men do—not in our society. But they do. This gal's agent quoted me numbers, and if a third of these women with hair loss buy the book, I'll have a nice seller.''

John took a healthy swallow of ice-cold beer, then picked up one typewritten page. " '. . . Take a look, a good look, at your favorite female newscaster on television. See all that hair? Chances are, it's not all hers.' '' He looked at Henry. "Really?"

"Really. The author actually got about fifteen female newscasters to talk on the record about it. I think I'm going to buy this.''

"Henry, you're already writing copious notes in the margins. You know you're buying it. I'll bet you brought a trunk full of manuscripts with you. Have you been to any of the seminars?''

"Me? Only the first one, on copyrights. Everybody talked, nobody listened. Save your pennies, John-boy. If something isn't done, and done soon, to protect copyrights, there won't be anything new to copyright, because I'll be out of business and so will everyone else. You know, for a society so hellbent on making money, you'd think people would understand that publishers and authors, recording artists, scriptwriters, movie studios also have to make money or the product will disappear. We'll all be reading the backs of breakfast cereal boxes for entertainment.''

"Damn, Henry, you're really incensed. I thought I saw your nostrils flare there for a moment," John said, grinning.

"Seriously, why don't you run all of this past Harrison at dinner tonight, since he's running around doling out campaign promises this week? We are sharing a table, you know, or you would if you ever took your head out of a book to see who you're sitting with, old buddy."

Henry shook his head. "Been there, done that. Yesterday. Didn't work. It's not high profile enough for our man Harrison and steps on too many voter's toes. You know, those people who think it's their God-given right to get something for nothing, especially if it's on the Internet. At least the man was honest, didn't give me a lot of bull, promise me he'd try to do something about new copyright law."

"That's our boy, honest as the day is long. Winter days, that is. In Nome."

"Still riding the same horse, John? John, *good.* Senator Harrison, *bad.*"

"Senator Harrison, a sorry piece of—Henry, I can bring him down."

Henry nodded. "The business about this nonprofit, supposedly nonpartisan association he's got going? The one that you say is making a pretty fair profit on top of being totally under Harrison's control? His, and his contributors? What's it called again?"

"*Your America, My America.* You know how it goes, Henry. Grab a title touting truth and family values and character and mom and apple pie, and all that good knee-jerk stuff. Sounds so patriotic on the TV commercials. Not that he'd call it the rich old boys organization to screw and destroy anyone who's against us and line the pockets of anyone who's for us, right?"

"You'll never be mistaken for an optimist, John," Henry said with a sigh.

John shrugged. "Henry, at least ninety-five percent of politicians are good, loyal men and women who want nothing more than to serve their country. Whether I agree with how they want to go about it isn't the point. That's why we have more than one party, and everybody gets a vote. Most of our leaders are honest. Harrison is as crooked as a dog's hind leg, to quote my Aunt Marion. Him, I'm bringing down.''

''So? Is that it? You're going to go with the follow-the-money angle? You've got collaboration? Reliable sources? In plain words, do you have more now than you've already shown me? Because that wasn't enough. It has to be solid, John, or he'll bury you, and Brewster Publishing along with you. Still, I really couldn't see you going any other way, not without opening your mother's reputation to a lot of talk you couldn't want.''

''Actually, Henry, I *am* going with the woman angle. But not in any way you might think. It's sleazy, sort of sick, easy for the public to understand. I don't know if it's true, but I've got it in black and white, just enough to ruin him. And you're going to love it.''

John sat back, looked at his friend levelly. ''I know you, Henry. You're fair, you're honest. You're even kind of cute,'' he added, grinning. ''But, Henry, for something like this, you'd run over your own grandmother. Are you ready? Because I may need your help to play this out the way I want to . . . the way Jane and I have decided to play it.''

''You and *Jane?* John, if you've corrupted that sweet little—''

''It was mostly her idea, Henry. We were up half the night, working the angles. The woman has depth, Henry. And a mean streak. And freckles, and this *honesty* that's amazing, and the way she *eats?* Well, never mind that. God, Henry, I have to face it, I'm crazy about her.''

''You're—'' Henry sat back, goggled at John. ''You're kidding, right? You do know she's not your usual playmate?''

''I know it, Henry. With Jane, a man has to be willing to play for keeps. That's why I'm taking it slow, although it's killing me. She's the first woman I can see as the mother of my children. Other than Aunt Marion, I can't think of anyone else who'd be able to control my kids, if they're anything like me. Damn it, Henry, she's even got me picking up my own clothes. I'm not really clear on how it happened, but I'm doing it.''

"You? Picking up your own clothing? Johnny-boy, I was your roommate through four long years of college. I think I saw the carpet twice. It was green, wasn't it?''

"There was carpeting?'' John asked with a grin, putting down his empty mug. "Now, let's get down to business. We're going to bring Harrison down. Down hard. You wanna play?''

Henry sat up, smoothed down his unruly shock of red hair, and straightened his bow tie. "Who else is on the team?''

"Jane, me . . . Brandy Hythe, if my private research is anywhere near correct when coupled with the way she looks at Harrison when she thinks no one else is looking. I can't tell you how glad I am that she's not his latest lover. Anyway, Jane's feeling her out now. You, if you sign on with us. Jane's cousin. And one other, a sort of backup, but I'm not sure of him yet, so we'll let that alone for now.''

"I'm not very physical,'' Henry said, patting his soft belly. "Would I have to be physical?''

"You'll be mostly our idea man. Henry, you've been finding any plot holes in my work since the beginning. If there's a flaw in our plan, you'll find it and suggest a workable alternative. I trust your brain, Henry. I'm not nuts enough to want to depend on your left hook.''

"Good, because I don't have one. What do *you* have?''

"I thought you'd never ask.'' John reached into his inside pocket and pulled out two stapled pages he had folded lengthwise. "I've got this.''

Henry looked at the papers, sighed mournfully, then slowly reached out a hand to take them. "I just know I'm going to hate myself in the morning,'' he said, then began to read.

* * *

John paced the hotel room, waiting for Jane to return. She'd left before him, and he'd finished with Henry an hour ago. Was it true? Women just talked longer? Aunt Marion would say that was because women had so much more to say.

He rubbed his palms together, looking around the room for something to do. Something *constructive* to do, as Jane called it. He'd already straightened the desk, committing all their notes to memory and then destroying them. Earlier, he'd wiped his computer clean of everything about Harrison, Brandy, Dillon, anybody—first putting it all on a floppy disk that was now in Henry's possession for safekeeping.

That had been Jane's idea, and since he hadn't been able to come up with anything better, he had gone along with it.

Because, once he'd told her about the break-in, they'd agreed that they couldn't be sure Kevin the Bum wouldn't be back for an encore room search.

Kevin the Bum would find one really neat room, and unless John wanted to scrub the tub or something, it couldn't get any neater. He'd even refolded all his underwear, which he could only consider a temporary mental aberration brought on by too much Jane in his life.

Could he have too much Jane in his life? John didn't think so.

But the rest had been his idea, he reminded himself and his ego. A trip to a small downtown shop with a photocopying machine, the packet of grape jelly and the local newspaper he'd swiped from a room service cart in the hallway, the smiling appeal to one of the courteous housemaids to please replace something he had taken to his own room by mistake.

Sometimes his own brilliance frightened him, John thought with a smile. A wicked smile.

He heard the key card in the lock and quickly went over to sit on the edge of his bed, picking up the remote as if caught in the act of turning on the television. "You back?" he said casually, not turning his head as she came into the room and put down her purse.

She sat down. Next to him. Right next to him.

They had been up half the night, sitting like this, talking, scheming. Two "pals," planning the downfall of one of the most powerful men in America.

They had been all business. Okay, *she'd* been all business. He'd spent at least some of the time just watching her mouth move, counting the new freckles on her nose, and wondering how her breasts would feel if he were to touch them through the soft cotton of her pajamas.

"You're not going to believe this," she said, pushing her hair behind her ears. "I mean, you are just *not* going to believe this."

"Probably not, since you don't seem to be telling me anything."

"Oh," she said, shaking her head. "I'm sorry. I'm ... I'm just so ... so flabbergasted. Brandy Hythe is a really nice woman."

"And I'm not going to believe that?"

She gave him a small shove on the upper arm.

She did that a lot now. Touched him. He didn't think she even realized she was doing it. She didn't seem to realize a lot of things, which was why John had spent at least fifteen minutes of their late night in the bathroom, taking a very cold shower while reciting lines from *Macbeth*.

"You're not going to believe what Brandy told me." She shook her head. "That poor girl. Harrison's been blackmailing her."

Okay, so his libido could return to the back burner, which was where it probably belonged. "Come again?"

"Blackmail, John. Brandy, whose real name is Helen Sanchez, by the way—"

"Yes, I know that. I've done some research myself, remember? Helen Sanchez, of Bayonne. Brilliant student. Won the Mirabelle Harrison scholarship, which explains her connection to the senator. She only got involved in a campus drama club her last year and sort of fell into her career. I, um, I only pretended not to know about her that first day because I didn't want you to think I was some sort of groupie."

"You're an idiot, and you're interrupting," Jane told him rather primly, getting to her feet. "I have Brandy's permission to tell you this, but it isn't easy. I wish I could just say that you were right, she has no great love for the man, and leave it at that." She turned to look at him. "How did you know that part? How did you find out?"

"Research?" John offered innocently, but Jane's stern glare told him he wasn't going to get away that easily. "Okay, okay, so I bought some information from Brandy's former secretary while I was following a lead from my student's information. But that didn't mean they hadn't been lovers, at one point. I couldn't get that out of the secretary. Sue me."

"Somebody will, someday, if you don't stop doing things like that," Jane warned in fine nursery school teacher fashion. "Anyway, Brandy owes her scholarship to Harrison, her career, too, if you stretch it out a bit. But Harrison wanted more. He wanted to get himself a Hollywood connection and picked Brandy as his best candidate."

John nodded. "Young, beautiful, from New Jersey, squeaky clean, which is rare these days. It makes sense."

"Yes. And she was fine with that, for a while. Very idealistic. But when she realized he wasn't going to push any of the programs she's interested in, that he stood for a lot of things she couldn't stomach, she tried to back off. So he set her up."

John lay back on the bed, reached for a bag of roasted peanuts, then sat forward once more. "Set her up?" He cracked one open. "How?"

Without missing a beat in her pacing, Jane picked up the waste can and placed it on the floor between John's legs. "For the shells," she said, then added, "Gimme one."

"Only if you sit down next to me. I don't want shells on this nice clean carpet."

"You didn't vacuum the carpet," she said, then sat down. "I think I like you better with a little more Oscar Madison and a little less Felix Unger."

"In that case," John said, and flipped an empty shell across the room, to land on top of the desk. "Okay, enough diversion, enough stalling. I know this is hard for you, Jane, even if Brandy gave her permission. Why not just say it and get it over with?"

"Okay." She took a breath, let it out slowly. "Harrison invited her to his farm several times a few years ago. Just to be nice, he said, give her a break after shooting one of her films. She said she went a total of three times, the last two pretty much out of duty, because she really didn't like the man, but didn't know how to say no. He'd always called her one of his most successful *projects,* which bothered Brandy, but she did feel she owed him."

"The man has more strings than a puppet master," John said, shaking his head. "What happened at the farm? I know the place, by the way. Forty acres, a couple of horses, and a few chickens. The rest is all house, tennis court, indoor pool. The guy really knows how to rough it."

Jane nodded, biting her bottom lip. "It was in the pool. Brandy went for a swim, late at night. She was on the swim team at college . . . but you probably already know that, too, Mr. Smartypants. That's probably why we always find her at the pool. She likes the water. Anyway, it was dark, with only the lights inside the pool itself, so she stripped out of her suit and swam in the nude. She'd done that each time she visited the farm, locking the door to the pool house behind her, sure she was alone."

"I think I'm starting to get this," John said, snapping another shell. Pulverizing it, actually.

"Six months later, when Brandy declined Harrison's invitation to sit on the podium with him while he gave a speech on the greenhouse effect—knowing he was just going to

blow more smoke, and not really *do* anything—an envelope
showed up in Malibu. There . . . There were pictures.''

"Special low-light camera, everything set up ahead of
time . . . what a prince.''

"Brandy says she can't afford to have those pictures out
there. In the tabloids, on the Internet. It's bad enough they
already have her picture on some sites, stuck on the body
of some other woman. Some other nude woman. Did you
know they can do that?''

"I've heard,'' John said, brushing shell fragments off his
thighs and standing up. "So why now? Why is she telling
you this now?''

"Well, for a while, she felt that she could make some
difference, convince Harrison to change his position on some
political matters. She said she was going through her dumb-
as-dirt stage,'' Jane said, smiling wanly.

"Yeah. We all have one of those.''

"But then she won the Oscar last year. She's not the
starlet she was when the pictures first arrived four years
ago. She's already half decided to go to the newspapers
about the photographs, beat Harrison at his own game. Harrison can smear her, but he can't ruin her; and she's sick
and tired of lending her name to the man when she knows
he isn't worth . . . spit.''

"Said 'spit,' did she?'' John laughed, then sobered.
"Gutsy woman. So she's on board?''

"Definitely. I . . . I told her that if this works, she'd
have nothing to worry about, that Harrison wouldn't have
anything to gain by releasing the photographs.''

"True. And if he did, all she'd have to do is tell the
world they were taken without her permission, by the senator
himself. She'd still have to face that Internet and tabloid
crap, but it wouldn't gain Harrison anything. It would cost
him, and once we're through with him, the last thing he'll
need is more adverse publicity.''

"It's coming together, isn't it?'' Jane said, closing the
bag of peanuts and returning the waste can to its spot beside

the television cabinet. "What about Henry? Did you sell him? I know how badly you want to write this story."

"He says it will make a great book," John told her. "Sure, the newspapers will have it all first—correction, Molly will have it first—but we can get a book out there in six months, tops. I've got everything but the contract. But that's just a detail."

"I know. You're going to sell a book, John, and I think that's wonderful," Jane told him, reaching up to pat his cheek as she walked by, heading for the bathroom.

He really had to tell her the truth. Soon. As soon as they had Harrison on the ropes. Anything sooner would just complicate matters.

Jane was still heading for the bathroom. "Oh, I told Brandy we'd meet on the beach. There's a cookout planned for this evening, you know. You can call Henry and let him know. Oh, and would you ask him for his copy of *Shallow Ground* if he's through with it? He said he'd loan it to me."

"You finished the other one?" Good. He could put it somewhere, the book and the photograph on the back cover. Somewhere like a Dumpster in downtown Cape May.

"Um-hmm. Good book. But I did guess the ending a little sooner than I really wanted to, losing some of the suspense."

He grabbed her elbow just as she was about to disappear into the bathroom. "You guessed the ending? When? Where?"

"John? What's the matter? Don't tell me you read it, too, and didn't guess. It was so obvious. He never should have dropped that clue about the pattern of the broken glass in the ambassador's office. Not so soon. I immediately knew the glass had been broken from the inside, not the outside."

"Really," John said, releasing her elbow. "Not many people would pick up on that."

"I've been reading mysteries and thrillers since I was old enough to reach them on the shelves. Saturday nights alone, John, remember?"

He nodded, smiled weakly. "Go take your shower. What time do we have to be on the beach?"

"We have an hour," she told him, then closed the door.

Moments later he heard the shower turn on. He raced over to the nightstand and picked up his book. Where had he mentioned the pattern of the broken glass? Chapter Fourteen? He began paging through the book. Damn. Why hadn't Henry caught that one?

Aubrey Harrison leaned a shoulder against the doorjamb, looking in at his nephew . . . his nemesis, at this point. The bungling fool whose own ambition could have ruined everything. "So now you're telling me you've found it?"

Dillon stabbed his fingers through his hair, then nodded. "I don't understand it. I looked through this pile three times. Four. And it was here all the time, stuck to the back of a section of the Sunday paper I must have kept for some reason." He sniffed the stained page. "Grape jelly. I don't eat grape jelly."

"No. You decorate with it," Harrison said, pushing himself away from the doorjamb. "Come on, we have time for another drink before we have to go down to the beach."

Dillon followed his uncle into the living room of the suite. "We can't get out of this? Eating on the beach? Open fires? Sand all over the food? Gnats? I'd rather stick bamboo shoots under my fingernails."

"*I'd* rather stick bamboo shoots under your fingernails. But don't worry, Dillon, we're not eating on the beach. Well, we are, but not with everyone else. I've arranged for our party to be served in the gazebo. You saw it? Lovely little open-air building someone set up just at the edge of the beach."

"Our party? You mean sweet little Janie, the sexy starlet, the professor, and the bow tie? Sounds like a bad episode of *Gilligan's Island.*"

"Hardly, Dillon. No, we'll be joined by the esteemed gentleman from Pennsylvania, Congressman Patterson. Artemis Slade, our friend representing big oil. And bringing up the rear, America's favorite newscaster, the inimitable Mr. Sampson. Sans wives, of course. They've all been sent off to Atlantic City for the day.''

"You want to meet with them all at the same time?" Dillon asked, accepting a glass of scotch on the rocks. "Isn't that dangerous?''

"I don't think so. They all want the same thing, power. Makes the world go around, Dillon, my boy. They know the president will have enough of it to spread around to all of them. I've halfway promised Patterson a cabinet post, but he's worth it if he can deliver Pennsylvania.''

"And Slade? Easing of off-shore drilling restrictions?''

"I thought that would be enough," Harrison said, standing at the window, looking out over the ocean. "But now he's making noises about the federal government withdrawing any backing for alternative energy research and development for five years. That could be sticky.''

"Especially with Sampson's sponsor. Agri-business means corn, and corn means alternate energy source, remember?''

"Which is why both men are here with us, Dillon. I know you wanted them here this week to talk money, but I want them here to talk to each other. Between them, they should be able to work out a compromise that's fair to both of them . . . and beneficial to me.''

"To *us*.''

"Whatever," Harrison said, lifting his glass in a mock salute. "Tell me more about Romanowski. Everything your man found out.''

Dillon sat on the couch, laying one arm along the back. "I already told you everything. He's investigating you. That's no surprise, now that we know he's J. P. Roman. He's been painting you in fairly broad strokes for his last two books. Nothing actionable, but he cuts it pretty fine. Still, we've lucked out, Uncle. He's too busy boffing our little nursery school teacher this week to bother us. You know these writer types. All talk, no real action. He won't come after you, Uncle, confront you directly, either about your politics or his nutso mother. He doesn't have the balls.''

Harrison turned away from the window. ''You love to talk crudely, don't you, Dillon? Must be the boys' school education. Very well, I'll forget Romanowski. Happily. However, speaking of *boffing,* what about our little lady of the nightclub? Did you make sure she knew I couldn't meet with her as promised?''

Dillon held up the stapled and jelly-stained pages. ''I've been a little busy, Uncle.''

''Damn it,'' Harrison said, putting down his empty glass with some force. ''Learn something, nephew. Never disappoint a lady.''

''That was no lady,'' Dillon said, smirking.

''She thinks so. They all think so,'' Harrison said, and he was deadly serious. ''I never, never ever, let them go away mad, not since Romanowski's mother. I got lucky there; she had that breakdown, never went to the media with anything. You'd better hope this one doesn't come back to bite us in the ass.''

''You're overreacting.''

''And you, nephew, are an ignorant cretin,'' Harrison said without emotion. ''Find her, give her my regrets, my sincere apologies, and one of those bracelets we keep around here somewhere. That way, she'll have something romantic to tell her grandchildren someday.''

Dillon rolled his eyes. ''Yeah. Right,'' he muttered under his breath, heading back into his bedroom. ''I'll be sure to put that right at the top of my to-do list. Sure, like I have time for the bastard's little playmates.''

Chapter Fourteen

There was something rather disappointing about fires dotting a wide beach when the sun was still shining overhead. Even less romantic was the permit for open fires tacked to one of the gazebos, and the pair of fire trucks standing by about two hundred yards down the beach.

But, hey, it made for good photo-ops. Great for the "back to basics" big shots trying to look human, and great for the small group of placard carrying protesters chanting that open fires destroyed the ozone layer. Just an all-round good time.

John sat with Jane, Henry, and Brandy, all of them camped around the upwind side of their own fire, which was putting up a lot of smoke and not a lot of flame.

"Anyone remember their Boy Scout fire-starting training?" John asked as the four stared at the pitiful fire and the hamburgers that were sort of just sitting there in their wire holders, looking gray.

"I never joined," Henry said, nursing a beer from a can. "My father said I wouldn't like it."

John looked at Jane.

"What?" she asked, sounding a little miffed. "You want me to say I was a Camp Fire girl, don't you? Well, I wasn't."

"So you never did the sign up and get badges in making baskets out of twigs routine? Why don't I believe that?"

She squirmed a little as she sat, bare legs folded Indian style. "Okay, okay, so I was a Brownie. And then a Girl Scout. But I got my badges in child care and sewing, not campfire cooking. And I quit when I was fourteen, and Molly screwed up my cookie order so badly I was going to get drummed out anyway."

She put down her head and ended quietly, "Or maybe charged with a felony. We were never sure."

"Molly?" Brandy took the wire holder from Henry and turned it over, held it closer to the fire. "That would be the reporter, right? Have you contacted her yet?"

"I tried, but she didn't answer at Kiddie Kare. I left messages on her cell phone and with my parents. But Mom and Dad are on their way to the cabin for the Fourth, so that probably didn't do me any good. I'm giving her time to get back to her apartment in Washington."

"She probably burned rubber all the way out of town the minute the kids were gone and the doors were locked," John said, and Jane glared at him. "Hey, not that I would, but you said she wasn't really cracked up about doing the baby-sitting thing, right?"

"No, she wasn't," Jane admitted. "But she also wanted to stay in touch with me, and she hasn't, even after you stopped the switchboard from holding all calls to the room. Or used the cell phone, and I've kept it on constantly."

"Your cousin, Janie—how reliable is she? I mean, not that I don't trust your judgment, but so far . . . ?"

Now John got more than a stare. He got daggers. "Molly is very responsible." She then answered Brandy. "Well, sort of responsible. I mean, she's . . ." She turned back to John, eyelids narrowed consideringly. "How badly do we need her?"

"You think she's bailed?"

Jane bit her bottom lip. "I don't know. This was so important to her." She sighed. "But, then, everything's important to Molly, at one time or another. What are we going to do now?"

Henry raised one hand, as if wishing to be called on. "Yes, Henry?"

"Well, I don't want to intrude here, John," he said, smiling at Brandy in a way that made John want to hug the little guy, tell him to go on, have his dreams, but don't go nuts with visions of shoes and rice.

"Oh, intrude, Henry, intrude. That's why you're here."

"All right. I'm sure you've noticed that there are about six different news vans parked around the hotel, and just as many print reporters wandering around looking for stories. Can't we just pick one?"

Jane looking appealingly at John—she always looked appealing to John. "But Molly—?"

"But, Jane? You said you can't get her on the phone, remember?"

"But she—oh, never mind. If she calls, she calls, but we can't depend on her. Henry's right, we have to pick someone else."

"I already have," John told them all as some hamburger fat finally melted into the fire, causing flames to shoot up. With any luck, they'd be eating by midnight.

"Who?" Brandy asked before Jane could do more than twist her hands in her lap, either feeling embarrassed about her cousin or doing her best not to sock John in the nose. He wasn't sure which and frankly didn't want to ask.

"Who else but the unhappiest man at the party?" John said, getting to his feet. "Excuse me, I'll be right back, with our unhappy man tagging along if I'm right. Just go with the flow when I get him here, okay? Follow my lead, as soon as I figure out how I'm going to lead him. Brandy? You've done improv?"

"Tops in my acting class."

"Good." John dusted sand off the seat of his shorts and

walked toward the news vans, the knots of reporters and cameramen and whoever stood around, shuffling their feet, smoking cigarettes.

He found his quarry standing by himself, for even the guy's cameraman had deserted him for greener pastures, or a better brand of beer. "Jim?" he said as he approached. "Jim Waters of *Live at Six?* Am I right?"

Waters threw down his cigarette and ground it out in the sand before taking John's extended hand in a quick, rather limp shake. "Yeah. What of it?"

"Nothing, really. I just wanted to say how professionally you handled that interview in Senator Harrison's suite the other night. And the networks picked it up. Good job."

Waters sniffed. "Yeah. Good job. And the only one I'll get to do all week, unless anyone thinks covering this god-awful back-to-nature cookout is worth more than thirty seconds of air. What a load of horse hockey. CNN already packed it in for the night. I'd be gone, too, if I had anywhere else to go."

"Cut you off, did they?" John asked, already knowing the answer. He had seen the network vans, the network reporters. "That's probably because the President will be here tomorrow. The media's bringing out their top guns."

Waters pulled a small silver flask from his back pocket, took a drink, then offered it to John, who declined as politely as possible. "Thirty years. Thirty years I've been doing this. Wichita. Mobile. Albany. I'm in Philly now, big damn market. *Big* damn market. But not good enough for this. Do a little human interest piece for us, Jim. Take the cameras to the Cape May County Zoo, there's a freaking new bird there. Give us a color story to fill a couple of minutes, but then go away, let the big boys do the real work. Thirty damn years."

Ah, yes. A bitter man. Just what John needed.

"Jim," he said, putting his arm around the man's shoulders. "I think you should meet a few of my friends."

"Why would I want to do that? Besides, if one of them

isn't named Johnnie Walker, I'll take a pass, thanks anyway," Waters said, turning his now empty flask upside down.

"Jim, Jim, Jim," John said, sort of steering the man back across the beach. "You don't know it yet, but you're about to become the luckiest man in the world. The President? Small stuff. He's coming here to wave the flag for the Fourth, that's all. He's not making any big speeches or anything, and he'll only be here for about an hour, tops. *You,* however, are going to get the scoop of the week. Of the year, Jim. If you're game."

He stopped, took his arm away, gave the man a big smile. "Are you game, Jim?"

Sometimes these things were just *too* easy. . . .

Henry stood up as John and Waters approached. "Mr. Waters? It is Mr. Waters, isn't it? I recognize you from the news program." He walked over, extended his hand. "Good to meet you, sir."

"Henry Brewster, owner of Brewster Publishing," John said by way of finishing that particular introduction. "And I'm sure you remember Jane Preston from the other night? And not that Brandy Hythe needs any introduction."

Waters shook hands with all of them, looking a little confused even as he tried to look sophisticated and less in the bag than drinking an entire flask of Johnnie Walker actually made him. "A pleasure," he said, then pulled up some sand and sat down at John's invitation. "What can I do for you all?"

"I believe you were talking about air time?" John said, also sitting down once more, folding his long frame into what could only be a comfortable sitting position for people with shorter legs. "First, Jane would love to talk more about child care, if you're interested."

"Nah," Waters said, accepting a beer from Henry. "That's yesterday's news. You either talk when the story's new or forget it. Sorry."

Jane actually looked miffed for a moment; then her features smoothed as she seemed to realize that she had never wanted to do any interviews in the first place.

John looked at Brandy, nodded his head.

"Would an interview with me help you, Jim?" Brandy asked in that low, sultry voice.

Waters's lips sort of worked, and he swallowed hard. "I could do that," he said, nodding . . . and hyperventilating only a little bit. "You'd do that?"

"For you? After Jane told me how nice you were to her?" Brandy said, smiling. "Of course I would."

John held up one hand in a big okay sign behind Waters's head. Brandy Hythe wasn't just another pretty face . . . fabulous body . . . great pair of legs. . . . Yeah, all right, back to the matter at hand.

"Well, great," Waters said, fishing in his other back pocket for a small notebook. "Tomorrow? How about twelve? Noonish, that is. Whenever you want." Then he frowned. "Oh, no, wait. It can't be tomorrow, not here at least. I don't have clearance to be on the grounds tomorrow, not until after the President leaves."

"Man, they are screwing you, aren't they, Jim?" John said commiseratingly. "Tell you what. Senator Harrison is making an announcement on Friday—we're not sure of the time yet, but I'm sure you'll get notice. How about you and Brandy get together, oh, about an hour earlier? That way, you and your cameraman can finish with Brandy and then swing straight into the press conference. Sound good to you?"

Waters nodded. "Sure. Fine. Gives me some time to get some file footage, a little background. You're a New Jersey native, right? Where shall we meet?"

Still out of Waters's sight, John held up his arms and moved his upper body about, as if dancing with an invisible partner.

"Born and bred," Brandy said, turning on the charm even more. "I've only done one interview so far this week, but I know where they're held. Just outside the hotel ballroom, in the rear, on the verandah. I'll meet you inside the ballroom, about an hour before the senator's press conference.''

John gave her another okay signal.

Waters nodded again, scribbled in his notebook, and then sort of sat there, smiling at John, who was now wearing his poker face. ''That it? That's my big story? Another puff piece? Thanks, and all of that, but go to hell, mister.'' He turned to Brandy. ''No offense, Ms. Blythe, and I do want the interview, but the guy promised me a big story. You're a big star, but not a big story.''

John looked at Jane. ''Don't you hate it when a guy looks a gift horse in the mouth? I know I hate it when a guy looks a gift horse in the mouth.'' Then he turned to Waters. ''Just be there, bozo, okay? You and your trusty microphone and camera. I'll tell you about your big scoop then. Hey, it's not like you've got anything else going, right? Unless you'll be too busy at the zoo?''

Waters got to his feet. ''You're all nuts, you know. Intellectuals? Give me a freakin' break . . .''

John called after him, ''But you'll be there?''

The newsman gave a wave without turning back as he walked away in the twilight now that the sun had finally dipped below the horizon. ''Yeah, yeah, I'll be there.''

John turned back to the group, taking a hamburger from Jane, who had taken over the roll of cook. ''That went well. No onions, right?''

''Sorry. Just ketchup. We're roughing it for the cameras, remember?''

Henry took a bite of his hamburger, then wiped ketchup from his chin. ''Came out of the little packet too fast,'' he said apologetically. ''That did go well, though, John. Now we've got a reporter and a cameraman. But we don't have Harrison.''

''We will,'' John said. ''Tell him, Jane.''

Jane, who was in the process of licking ketchup from her fingers—was there no mercy in this world?—held up one finger, swallowed, and then said, ''Brandy is going to tell

Harrison that she has called a reporter to tell him about the pictures. She'll phone his suite about an hour before Harrison's own news conference and tell him he and Dillon have five minutes to come down to the news conference area—the ballroom, I mean—and tell her why she shouldn't do it. Molly was going to be hiding in the room somewhere, behind a screen or something, listening to and recording everything, but now Mr. Waters and his cameraman can be there instead. And we've got him!''

"No," Henry said, sounding quite firm. "There's no reason for Ms. Hythe to reveal that there are photographs of her. I thought we were going with the other thing.''

"We are, Henry, we are. It's just that Brandy's provided the perfect way to get Harrison where we want him, when we want him. Any flaws?''

Henry chewed on his hamburger. "No, I don't think so. As long as Harrison plays along. Otherwise, you've done all of this for nothing, and Miss Hythe will still have to tell about the photographs. Do you really think the man did it? I mean, I know what I read, but did he really *do* it? And if he did, shouldn't we be going to the police?''

"All things in their time, Henry. First, we have to get the man to announce that he's not going to run for president. After that, just about everything is negotiable.''

"Whatever you say, John," Henry said, shrugging. "Now, if you'll excuse me, I think I want to go inside. They say this is a week of mental reflection, invigoration, contemplation, and revelation. I've already had one revelation. I don't like eating out-of-doors.''

"I'll go with you, Hank," Brandy said, getting to her feet, where she stood towering over Henry by a good six inches. "Will you buy me a drink?''

"Would I—*me?*'' Henry shot a quick look to John, who nodded. "I'd be delighted, Ms. Hythe," he said, holding out his arm to her.

"Brandy. Call me Brandy, Hank. Tell me, do you always

wear bow ties? My father always wore bow ties. I think it's so . . . so refined.''

John and Jane watched the mismatched pair walk back toward the hotel, their forms fading into the rapidly descending darkness lit only by flambeaux lining a temporary wooden boardwalk.

"She called him Hank, just like one of the big boys. That's so sweet," Jane said, watching them go.

"That's one word," John agreed, getting to his feet and extending a hand to her. "Her father, by the way, sold ice cream out of a truck he drove through the suburbs. The bow tie had to be part of his uniform.''

"You're such a cynic. I didn't need to know that, John," Jane said reprovingly, ignoring his outstretched hand.

"You're right. Sorry. Come on, let's go. Everyone else is leaving. Soon there won't be anyone here except the firemen and the protesters. As it is, we'll probably be at the end of the line for the buffet I heard has been set up inside, for anyone who didn't want to play Boy Scout out here. One hamburger just isn't going to do it for me, Jane.''

"Oh, but I'm not ready yet," she said, digging into the beach bag she had brought with her.

He sat down. "What? You've got a jar in there, and you want to catch lightning bugs?"

"Don't be facetious," she said, reaching into it. "Brandy and I took a long walk, to talk, and I stopped in a grocery store to pick up a few things for tonight. See? Graham crackers, chocolate bars, and marshmallows. I brought enough for everybody, but they left before I could say anything.''

"I don't get it," John said, still watching as Jane unearthed two fairly long twigs from beneath the towel she had been sitting on. Nobody else had thought to bring a towel, but Jane had. Of course she had. Bless her neat little heart.

"Sure you do, and don't be silly.''

"First facetious, now silly. I'm so glad to know how much you admire me.''

"Oh, hush. Now, here's a marshmallow. Put it on the stick, John, and hold it over the fire."

"We're roasting marshmallows? You're kidding." He laughed. "Man, I haven't done this since—since I can't remember. I used to toast mine over the gas stove in our apartment, until Aunt Marion showed up and called me a firebug. I like mine on fire. You know, all black and crusty, and oozing inside and—"

He broke off, snapping his mouth shut. Oozing? Jane was going to eat a sticky, oozing marshmallow? In front of him? Did the woman think he was a eunuch?

"I don't like mine that way," she told him, holding her own stick over the dying fire. "I like mine an even golden brown, all over. But definitely melted inside. Careful, John, you're getting too close to the flame."

"Tell me about it," he muttered. If they were in a room, he would be looking around for the nearest exit. He hadn't led a blameless life, but what had he ever done to be tortured this way?

"Okay, done enough," Jane told him a few minutes later, handing him her stick. "Here, hold this while I get everything else ready. It will only take a moment."

He didn't know what the hell she was talking about, but he did what she said, watching as she broke two of the graham crackers in half, then did the same with one of the chocolate bars. She placed half a chocolate bar on half a graham cracker. Centered it neatly.

"Now, you put my marshmallow on top, and I'll cover it with the other graham cracker, and you can pull out the stick."

"You went to some high-class French culinary school, didn't you, Janie?" he asked as she helped him perform this minor surgery on the marshmallow.

"Don't be silly. These are s'mores. Everybody knows about s'mores."

"Everybody does now," he said as they repeated the

assembly with the second marshmallow. "So now what? How do you eat one of these things?"

What a glutton for punishment! He had to ask. . . . And she, bless her innocent little self, had to demonstrate for him.

First, she gently squeezed the two graham crackers together, so that the heat from the marshmallow melted the chocolate a little, and the marshmallow itself sort of flattened and expanded, hanging over the edges of the graham cracker.

She disposed of the excess marshmallow with her tongue, gave the crackers another squeeze, and started on the melted chocolate.

The rack. Truth serum. Hanging a person up by his thumbs while listening to Lawrence Welk music. Those were the favorites of torturers.

He knew a better way.

All they had to do to get any secrets, all secrets, was to tie a man down and show a film of Janie Preston eating a s'more.

He took it for as long as he could, and that wasn't long.

"Okay. That's it," he announced, tossing his own s'more over his shoulder, onto the sand. "Jane Preston, I want to go to bed with you. Deal with it."

She halted in midlick, and looked at him. "What . . . What did you say?"

"I said," he gritted out from between clenched teeth— hell, all of him was clenched, one way or another—"I want to make love with you. To you. Several times. In, oh, so many ways."

"Now?" she asked, actually licking some chocolate off her fingers.

"No, in September. Yes, Janie, *now*. Here. Now. Better in our room, I grant you, but I'll take you any way and any-place I can get you. How's that for desperate?"

She wiped her hands on an edge of the towel she sat on as she looked at him. As she smiled at him. "Never write another love story, John. You're not very romantic."

"You want hearts and flowers? Tell that to someone who hasn't seen you eat."

"What? Oh." She dipped her head. "Sorry. S'mores tend to get . . . a little messy."

"Godzilla raging through downtown Tokyo tends to get a little messy. You, Jane, are tramping all over me like a dozen Godzillas."

She put everything back in the beach bag, stood up, picked up the towel, folded it neatly. She was driving him nuts . . . totally nuts! How else could a neatly folded towel react on him like some damn aphrodisiac?

"Are you sure, John?" she asked him, hugging the towel to her chest protectively. "You aren't just being nice, knowing I wanted a little . . . adventure in my life?"

"Nice? *Nice?* I'm not nice, Jane. And you're not nice." She frowned in the darkness, and he raked a hand through his hair. "Okay, so you're nice. I'll give you that one. But you're not my pal; I'm not your pal. We're two adults, sharing a room, and trying to pretend we're nice, and we're pals. Well, pal time's over. If I don't get you into my bed in the next"—he shot a quick look at his watch—"ten minutes, I'm probably going to do something inside me some permanent damage. And it'll all be your fault."

She lifted her chin in what had to be her best schoolmarm style, looked at him, then said, "Tough."

He followed after her as she walked back up the beach toward the hotel, trailing after her like some overgrown puppy. "Tough? What do you mean, tough? Is that no? That's no, isn't it?"

"Actually," she said, not slowing her steps, "it's maybe. I mean, yes, I'm interested. I won't lie and say I'm not, because we were both here on the beach the other night, kissing each other, so we both know what might happen . . . and want it to happen. But you couldn't be less romantic, John. And you want to be a writer? Can't you at least say one nice thing to me?"

"You're right. I went a little berserk. I can only plead

temporary insanity. But if you'd been the one watching—
okay, okay, scratch that. I apologize.'' He took hold of her
shoulders, turned her to face him. ''Jane, I want to kiss you,
to hold you, to . . . to learn you. I want to see your face as
I come to you. I want to hear your soft sighs. I . . . I want
to make love with you.''

He held his breath.

Jane blinked a few times, and then she smiled. ''I want
to make love with you, too, John,'' she said at last. ''Thank
you.''

Thank you? The woman said thank you? God, he was
crazy about her. Or maybe he was just plain crazy.

Either way, he grabbed her hand and led her toward the
hotel, ready to steamroll over anyone who got between the
two of them and the door to their hotel room.

He wasn't her type.

Yes, he was.

He was too big, too hairy.

She liked big. She thought hairy was cute.

She didn't used to, but she did now.

He was only after a fling.

Hadn't that been just a small thought, hidden deep in her
own mind, when she had agreed to help Molly?

Well, sort of . . . maybe. . . .

Don't lie to yourself, Jane, you know that's true.

So was this a fling? Was it something more, hold the
promise of something more?

How would she know if she didn't try it?

John was lightly rubbing his thumb against her palm as
they stood waiting for the elevator along with another couple.
She had to concentrate to keep her knees locked, to remain
upright.

Her blood hummed through her veins as she smiled
politely at the middle-aged couple. *Oh, people, if you only
knew what I know. Hello. This is the esteemed Professor*

Romanowski, and I run a day care and nursery, and we're on our way upstairs to bang each others brains out, thank you, and it was so nice to meet you, too.

Not that she would ever say such a thing. She had only just begun to *think* such a thing. Had she really thought *bang?* My goodness!

She would have said hello to the couple, but her tongue—probably thankfully—was pretty well stuck to the roof of her mouth.

"You have some chocolate on your chin, dear," the woman said.

"Why, yes, she does. Here, sweetheart, let me get that for you," John said as Jane went to wipe her chin, bending down and licking the chocolate from her skin. Two licks, with the tip of his tongue.

The older woman's eyes went wide behind her bifocals.

"Um . . . thank you, Professor," Jane managed.

"My pleasure, Ms. Preston," he answered from somewhere below her. He was tall—he used to tower over her—but now she was floating somewhere near the high ceiling, watching herself, watching him, her body no longer her own.

"We . . . We could take the stairs?" she managed at last, because the woman was now staring at John, smiling as if he was the most interesting person she had ever met and she would like to take him apart and examine the pieces. One particular piece, if the level of her stare was any indication. Only moments earlier, John had all but ripped the beach bag from Jane's hand and was even now holding it in front of him, poor man.

"Good idea," John said, pulling her away from the elevator just as the woman said to her husband, "Jonathan? Did you bring those lovely blue pills with you, dear?"

Jane tried to keep up with John's longer stride as they walked down the hallway to their room. He already had the key card out of his pocket, and his breathing seemed to be a little heavy for a guy in such good physical shape.

She was pretty sure she wasn't breathing at all. Might not even remember how.

Door, open. Lights, off. Beds—right over there. His was closer. They fell onto his bed.

Jane jumped off again. "Get up," she ordered.

"What?"

She motioned with her hands. "Up, up. I want to take off the bedspread."

John looked at her for a few moments in the darkness, muttered something, and suddenly the bedspread was on the floor, along with the blanket, the pillows, and the top sheet. All removed with one sharp jerk of his hand. The bottom sheet was almost completely ripped from the mattress.

"Happy now? And if you think I'm folding any of it, you've just lost your mind."

She nodded. "Sorry. It's just that my father—well, after what he said, I—I mean, you really don't want to know what could be—and we just almost proved what he heard was right, you know, and—"

"Did I ask why? I don't think so," John said, falling back onto the bed and holding his arms out to her. "Come here."

"O-kay," she chirped quietly, no more Miss Neat-girl. Then she took a deep breath and launched herself onto the bed.

John lay on his side, one strong arm beneath her back, supporting her. His mouth was on hers, at first gently, and then with more force, more abandon, as she opened her own mouth for him. She moaned a little, but she would pretend she didn't hear herself do that.

He was big, so big. Her hands could barely cup his shoulders. Deltoids? Were they the deltoid muscles? Did she care?

His hand was on her breast now, cupping her, as he slid his mouth to her throat, whispered, "You're so small. I don't want to hurt you."

Jane arched her neck. Small? "Molly says she knows a surgeon . . ."

He pulled back, looked down into her face. "What the hell are you saying—don't you even *think* about it. You're perfect, Jane. Perfect. It's just that I'm so damn big, and you're so damn small . . ."

Okay. He hadn't meant her breasts. He had meant her. Wasn't he wonderful to believe that her sort of rounded figure was small? And hadn't he picked one heck of a time to start thinking of her as fragile?

She wasn't fragile. She didn't break easily. She didn't want to be treated like some easily broken doll.

So she moved, turned onto her side, pressed herself against him, chest to groin. She could feel his arousal. Satellites a thousand miles in space could probably see it, like they could see the Great Wall of China.

Stop it, stop it. Stop thinking!

"We seem to fit where it matters," she said, grinning nervously. She was such a loose woman. . . . Shame on her for enjoying the feeling so much.

"We do, don't we?" John said, stroking her hair, moving his hand lower, trailing down her throat, skimming over her upper chest . . . finally sliding beneath the neckline of her light sweater, her bra. His mouth sought hers again, and she gave herself up to his kisses, the sensations shooting through her, moving her, pushing her closer to him so she could feel more of him, burrow into him and never, never ever be without his strong arms again.

He was a world, just as she'd thought. And she wanted to explore him, claim him for her own. She'd never felt more protected, and yet so free. She could give herself to this man, body and soul, and he'd keep both safe for her, wrapped in his strong arms.

Which was all well and good . . . for a while. But Jane realized that kisses weren't enough. His hands gentle on her body weren't enough.

She wanted more. Needed more.

"Don't hold back," she whispered as he ran his fingers over her bare midriff. "Please, John. Don't hold back."

And, just in case he needed a little more reassurance, she put both her hands against his chest, straightened her elbows, and pushed him onto his back, following with the rest of her body, straddling him as she dipped her head, bit his bottom lip.

She, at last, and about damn time, was woman—hear her roar!

John seemed to get the message.

The next few minutes would always remain a sort of giggling blur for Jane; but then they were both naked, and she could feel John's hairy legs against her smooth ones, and the sensation was a sensual tickle, as was the feel of his chest hair against her newly sensitive nipples.

He kissed her, his perennial five-o'clock shadow rubbing against her chin, but that, too, felt good.

Everything felt good.

And then it felt better. . . .

Chapter Fifteen

John looked at his hand as it rested on Jane's back. He knew his hands were big, but he hadn't considered ever giving anyone a massage with just one hand. But, with Jane, two would be too many. Which was nice, because it left his other hand free to massage . . . other places.

"Hmmm, I guess it's time for me to say that I'll give you an hour to stop that," Jane said, then sighed in unabashed contentment.

He pulled her back against his chest as he lay propped against the pillows he had retrieved sometime during the night. When was that? Oh, yeah. Right after they had sort of toppled from the bed and landed on the floor. That had been . . . interesting, to say the least.

How had they done that? Had it been when he had knelt there, leaned over her and . . . Or maybe it was the third time, when she attacked him after he'd moaned comically that he'd be a dead man if he didn't get some rest, and soon.

"John?"

"Hmmm?" He stroked her bare hip, loving the smoothness of her skin. "You rang?"

"Several times," she said, giving his chest a playful slap. "You know, there are some times I wish I kept a diary. Last night's *Dear Diary* entry would have made a real zinger."

"Yes, I suppose so. Dear Diary, last night neat, sweet, petite little Janie Sunshine killed a man."

"Oh, I did not," Jane said, sitting up, pulling the sheet with her. Modest, now? God, she was terrific. He would lay eight-to-five odds that if she got up to go to the bathroom, she would first slip her feet into her slippers. The same woman who, at about three this morning, had kissed her way down his body and ... no, better not go there. He wasn't a teenager anymore; he needed to think about other things, like his galloping heart rate.

"Really?" he teased. "Then explain, please, why I can't feel my legs."

Tucking the sheet—which had never before been tucked to such advantage—around her breasts, Jane scrambled down to sit at the bottom of the bed. "I suppose I'll just have to leave you alone now, to rest, you poor old thing." She took a deep breath, let it out slowly. "And they call us the weaker sex."

John looked at her. Hair mussed delightfully, cheeks still rather flushed from their last round of lovemaking—no, never their last, they'd only just begun—those crazy freckles dancing across her nose. She had freckles in lots of places, he had found out. ... And he'd kissed most of them. But, then, just as he had told himself, they had time. They had the rest of their lives. He would find them all.

"So, pal of mine," he said, grinning. "How do you like your fling so far?"

She dipped her chin a little, then grinned at him through her eyelashes. "You're looking for compliments now?"

He shrugged. "No," he said quietly, suddenly serious. "I think I'm looking for a lot more than that. As a matter of fact ..." he continued, hardly believing what he knew he was about to say, "I think I've found everything I've ever been looking for, even though I didn't know I'd been looking."

He waited as she digested what he had just said.

She tipped her head to one side, blinked at him. "Are you . . . Are you saying what I think you're saying? Because you don't have to say it, John, not if you don't mean it. I'm a big girl. I knew what I was doing last night. Well, most of the time. There are a few moments where I think my mind left my body, to tell you the truth. But, honestly, you don't *have* to say anything."

He pushed himself away from the pillows. "You don't want me to say anything?"

She rolled her eyes. God love the girl, she actually rolled her eyes. "I didn't say *that.*"

"Then, you wouldn't mind if I told you that you're the most beautiful, wonderful, fantastic woman in the world and I really, really think I want you in my life?"

Her smile was slow, but it grew. "And you tried to write a love story? John, just say it. Please. I would really like you to say the words. If you mean them."

He tried to open his mouth, but couldn't. He had never said those words, never thought he would. Here he was, a man with a damn impressive vocabulary of over ten thousand words, and he had never said those three certain words in a row.

This was hard.

And then, suddenly, it was easy. He didn't know why, but he felt a blossoming deep in his gut, a warmth that had nothing to do with sex or desire. It was a purer feeling, deeper, more profound. He felt good; he felt a little light-headed. He felt. . . . He felt *sure.*

John suddenly believed in happily ever after. In goodness and purity and blue skies and little children giggling and long walks and growing old together, all that good stuff. The cynical part of his brain, always the largest part, said, *Sure, you're the Grinch, and your heart just grew three sizes today.*

And the optimistic part of his brain, which had been hiding behind a door for a very long time, came out, hammer in hand, and beat the cynical brain cells into a jelly.

"I love you, Janie Preston," he said, surprising himself with how strong his voice sounded. He was grinning like a loon, and he knew it, and he didn't care. "Damn it, woman, I'm in love with you."

John and Jane stood next to their bicycles and watched the President's helicopter take off.

"I wish I could have seen him. I don't agree with him politically, but he is the President, and this was an historic visit in its own way," Jane said, cupping a hand over her eyes to watch as the huge helicopter swung out over the ocean, then headed inland, toward Philadelphia, where the President would make a three o'clock speech in front of Independence Hall.

"It's like football, sweetheart. Unless you can be fairly close to the fifty-yard line, you'll see everything better at home, on TV."

"I suppose so," she said, smiling at him. She was smiling a lot this afternoon. "And there's always film at eleven."

"True. Or *Live at Six,* except Jim-bo won't be reporting the story."

"Do you think he'll show up on Friday?"

John nodded, as he got on his bike, and they pushed off down the sandy street edging the beach. "It's not as if he has anything else to do. Where are we going?"

Jane looked back over her shoulder at him. He looked so sweet, practically dwarfing the largest rental from Congress Hall's bike rental shop. "Well, I wanted us to go see the DoWop Preservation League and all the Miami Beach-type classic motels in Wildwood, but that's too far away for a bike ride."

"The Do-what?" He pulled his bike alongside hers as they stopped at an intersection. "What in hell is that?"

"Let's see if I can remember it word-for-word from the tour guide. Okay. The DoWop Preservation League, located in Wildwood as I said, is dedicated to the education of the popular culture and architecture of the nineteen fifties."

"The fifties? There was architecture in the fifties? I thought there were just boxes, piled on top of other boxes."

Jane looked ahead, saw the sign she'd been looking for, and steered the bike onto a smaller path. "A lot you know, Professor. The UN was built in the fifties."

"I rest my case." John pulled in beside her, put down one foot on the path, and rubbed at his other knee, as both his knees seemed to hit the handlebars with depressing regularity.

"Frank Lloyd Wright designed in the fifties."

"I rest my case again," John said, stepping away from the bike, putting down the kickstand. "Give me stone, and brick, and great carved woodwork, and gargoyles, and turrets. And ivy."

"You live in an older house?"

"No, I live in a bunch of boxes stuck to the side of a hill."

Jane pushed down her own kickstand, and they left the bikes where they were and went on foot down the path. "Why would you do that if you don't like modern architecture?"

He took her hand in his. His hands were so large that she had to wrap her fingers around his at his ring finger in order to get a comfortable grip. "I don't know. The view, I think. I was a sucker for the view. But you know something? I just realized that I don't have many neighbors, and none of them are close. On top of that, the driveway slopes too much, so I couldn't put up a basketball hoop. And there's hardly any level ground anywhere, so a swing set and jungle gym are out. Nope. The house goes. We'll let Aunt Marion stay there if you don't want her to come with us, although I'm betting you'll love her. I know she's going to love you."

She looked up at him, shook her head. "What *are* you talking about?"

He stopped, put his hands on her shoulders. "I think, Jane, I'm asking you to marry me."

"Oh." The word came out very quietly, and she could feel her cheeks beginning to burn. "That's nice."

"Nice? *Nice?* Damn it, Janie, we've got to make a vow never to say that word again."

"Yes, John," Jane said, pressing herself against his broad chest, wrapping her arms around his waist.

"Yes, John, what? Yes, John, we won't say nice again, or yes, John, I'll marry you?"

She had her ear close against his heart and could hear its rapid beat. What a great big wooly teddy bear he was. "Oh, John, yes. Yes, I'll marry you." Then she took a breath, let it out slowly. "Eventually."

He disengaged himself and looked down at her. "Eventually? What the hell does that mean?"

"It means, John, that we haven't even known each other a week. I love you, I really do—"

"That's the first time you said it, you know. Back in the room, you didn't say it."

"I know. I wanted to, and I wanted to hear you say it, and I did say it now. But ... But now that I've thought about it more, we're probably rushing things. I mean, what do we really know about each other? We probably need ... more time."

John gave a short laugh, looked up at the sky. "I don't believe this. For the first time in my life I—and the woman says *eventually?*"

"Please, John, don't be angry. You know I'm right."

He glared at her, opened his mouth, then shut it again. "Okay," he said shortly. "Okay, you're right. So now what do we do, play True Confessions?"

She gave him another hug. "No, silly. We're two people getting to know each other better. We'll just ... talk. But not now, all right? It would feel funny if we talked now. Like an interview. Let's just go see the shipwreck.''

''There's a shipwreck out here?''

She took his hand and pulled him along with her. ''There is. The HMS *Martin,* part of the blockade during the war of eighteen-twelve. There's another ship somewhere around Cape May, the *Atlantus*—that's with a U, not Atlantis, Atlan*tus.* It was an experimental ship built during the first world war. They built it out of concrete. And then they wondered why it sank.''

''Just like Atlan*tis.* You like history, don't you, sweetheart?''

''I do. Do you?''

''I'm not sure. We could go back to the hotel room and try to make some?''

''Oh, John,'' she half sighed.

''Oh, Janie,'' he teased right back at her. ''So?''

''You're going to make me say it, aren't you?''

''If you're embarrassed, you can just nod,'' he said helpfully.

So she nodded, and he scooped her up into his arms as if she weighed less than a two-year-old and carried her back to the bikes.

The shipwreck could wait. . . . They were going to go make history.

John was singing something Elvis in the shower, perhaps in homage to the DoWop Preservation League. He didn't do Elvis any better than he did Springsteen, bless him, but Jane still smiled as she stood in front of the dresser and combed through her hair.

They had called down for Room Service last night, and again this morning. And if it weren't for the fact that they had already planned to meet with Henry and Brandy for some more planning, they probably wouldn't have left the room all day today.

They'd gone out on the balcony after dark last night, John in a pair of shorts, Jane wrapped in the top sheet from her bed—they'd used both beds last night, one way or the other—and watched the fireworks display over the beach and ocean.

"And to think I was going to light sparklers with my parents, then watch the concerts on PBS and be in bed by eleven," she'd said, leaning back against John's bare chest.

He'd nuzzled her throat, said something about the best fireworks sometimes being indoors, and she had missed the grande finale on the beach, gladly exchanging it for the private explosions of color behind her eyes as John loved her, held her, showed her just what the word *celebration* meant. . . .

Jane saw the pink flush rise in her cheeks and turned away from the mirror, knowing she had to concentrate on something other than the fact that John couldn't seem to keep his hands off of her. . . . And she couldn't keep hers off of him.

And they had talked, at least she had. He asked such good questions and seemed so interested. So she told him more about her childhood, about her parents, about Molly.

"Molly." Jane put down the comb and grabbed the phone, pushing in Molly's home number.

"Hi, talk to me. Then I'll talk to you, later. Just wait for the little—"

Jane hung up, didn't bother leaving a message. She had already left five.

She tried the cell phone number, not really believing she would get an answer there, either, but Molly picked up on the second ring.

"Molly?" Jane practically crawled into the phone. "Where are you? Why haven't you called me? You have to get down here. Tonight, tomorrow morning at the latest."

"Oh, I don't think so, Janie," Molly answered, sounding distracted.

"What do you mean, you don't *think so?* Molly, I've got

your scoop. Bigger than any announcement you might have wanted. Much bigger. *Pulitzer,* Molly, remember? Save me, Janie, save my job! Am I ringing any bells here, Molly? And where are you? You didn't tell me where you are." Jane narrowed her eyelids. "Are you in Cancun?"

"Cancun? Are you kidding? That's totally out of season, Janie. Oh, look who I'm saying this to—a woman who drove down to Disney World in *August.* Why not just stick on some mouse ears, turn on the oven, and melt yourself? And you went with your parents, too. You need help, Janie, you really do. Serious help. You've got to break out. Speaking of breaking out—how's the prof?"

"Molly," Jane said, sitting down on the side of the unmade bed, "you're not going to deflect me with smart remarks. Where are you, and why aren't you coming here?"

"I'd tell you I was in Paris, but you wouldn't believe that, because the cell phone would be out of range."

"It would?"

"Darn. One opportunity missed. I keep forgetting that you're locked in Fisher-Price land and don't know about grown-up toys. And, speaking of grown-up toys once again, you didn't say—how's the prof?"

Jane's head snapped up, and she looked toward the bathroom door. She didn't hear John's bad singing anymore. She didn't hear water running. He'd be out here any moment, and she'd have to tell him Molly was being difficult, that she was being . . . being Molly. "He's fine. He's, um, he's downstairs, giving a seminar. Look, I have to go now. When can I expect you?"

"Ah, honey, sweet, sweet Janie, you can't," Molly said. "I'm afraid I made other plans. Oh, and I quit my job at the newspaper. There was no future in it."

"You *quit* your—what plans?"

"Saving the reputation of Preston Kid Kare, of course."

"That's Kiddie—what about my reputation!"

"I told the professor most of it, so I'm sure he can explain.

I just want you to know that no sacrifice of mine is too great for my dear cousin Janie.''

Jane was positively panic-stricken. "Your idea of a sacrifice is going two weeks without a pedicure. What's going on?"

"If I tell you, you'll come here, so I'm not going to tell you. And now I'm going to turn the power off on this cell phone. Oh, and Janie? Thanks. Thank you *so* much. I think my name's going to look great in lights."

"No, wait. Lights? Molly? Molly! Damn it!"

"Problem, sweetheart?" John said, walking into the room, clad only in a small white towel, which would have been an enjoyable sight if she wasn't so upset. "I don't have my contacts in yet, so you look a little fuzzy, but I think that's a frown. A beautiful frown."

"You talked to Molly? You never told me you talked to Molly. What did she say?"

He rubbed his hands through his damp hair and sort of squinted at her. "She swore me to secrecy. Sorry."

She held up the phone, then replaced it on the hook. "She just unswore you, so tell me what she said."

John sat down beside her, then sighed, as if collecting his thoughts. "Okay. Somebody interviewed an uncle who thought he could use your place to—I don't know—to store a couple of kids for two weeks in July, starting this past Monday, I think, but the person who interviewed him and said yes thought he meant August. When I talked to Molly, she was waiting for the guy to show up and tear down the building. Did he?"

"But we're closed. She had to tell the man we're closed. What else could she have—omigod." *I just want you to know that no sacrifice of mine is too great for my dear cousin Janie.* "Oh, she wouldn't." Jane looked at John hopefully. "Would she?"

"Would she what?"

"Take care of somebody else's kids for two weeks," Jane said, her words computing about as well as if she had been speaking Japanese. . . . And she didn't speak Japanese. Okay, Honda. Mitsubishi. But that was it.

No, Molly wouldn't do that, wouldn't do anything like that . . . unless there was something in it for her. What could be in it for her? What was that about her name looking good in lights?

The phone rang, and Jane pounced on it. "Molly? Talk to me, Molly."

"I'm sorry, the operator must have given me the wrong extension," a woman's voice said, a very pleasant, cultured, and slightly southern voice.

"Who . . . Whom did you wish to speak to, ma'am?" Jane asked, looking at John, who made a sudden stab at grabbing the phone from her hand.

"Why, John Patrick, of course. Is this his room? John Patrick Romanowski? J. P.?"

Jane shifted her eyes to the left, looked at John, who sort of waved to her. It was a pretty sickly wave. A really guilty wave. "John Patrick? I . . . I didn't know he was John Patrick. Just . . . just John. J.P., you said. Yes, he's here, just a moment."

She handed him the phone, listened to him say hello to his Aunt Marion, and then got up and walked to the far side of the room.

John Patrick. She hadn't even known his middle name. She had gone to bed with a man and hadn't even known his middle name. She had said I love you to a man and hadn't even known his middle name. She had—John Patrick?

John Patrick Romanowski.

J. P. Romanowski.

J. P. Roman.

No.

Impossible.

I'll kill him.

Jane swung into action, heading for her suitcases in the bottom of the closet, where she had packed away the book she'd finished reading. Dropping to her knees, she unzipped one suitcase, then the other. No book. Where was the book?

"Where's the damn book!" she all but shouted as she got up off her knees and approached the bed just as John was hanging up the phone.

"Book?" He asked it innocently, but she knew better. *Now* she knew better. "I still don't have my contacts in, but I know you at least *sound* sort of homicidal. Anything wrong?"

She waved a finger at him. "Henry Brewster. Henry Brewster, who doesn't like being alone in social situations. I asked you how you knew that, and you told me he phoned the room and told you."

John shrugged, pulled his contact lense case out of the nightstand, and began deftly inserting the cleaned lenses. "It was a reasonable assumption? Look, Janie, sweetheart," he said a moment later, batting those big blue-green and now focused eyes at her, "I was going to tell you. I just hadn't gotten around to it yet. We were sort of busy, remember?"

Jane held out her hands, palms forward. "No. Don't talk. I'm talking."

"Got it, teach." John shook his head, then sat down again. It was hard to look humble at six feet, six inches tall, but he was doing a pretty good job of it. And it cut no mustard with her!

She began to pace, all five feet, three inches of her, slamming her feet down hard with each step. "I've got to think. Everything's making sense now. The nerd! And I almost fell for that one. The confidentiality agreement. Knowing about Henry. Knowing about the *senator!* All this information you had. From a student? I don't think so. That never sounded right. And the topper. J. P. Roman would like nothing better than to bring down someone like Senator Harrison."

"Yes, that's—"

She held up her hands again. "Ah-ah-ah. Me talking, you sitting."

"Yes, ma'am. Sorry, ma'am."

"And that ridiculous business about writing a love story?"

"True. That part's true, sweetheart. Henry can tell you. I write a lousy love story." She glared at him. "Okay, shutting up now."

"You were going to *use* me. Just like Molly was going to use me. Except she's off on another Toad's Wild Ride, and we're . . . we're . . ."

John stood up, wrapped his arms around her, pulled her against his chest. "We're here. You. Me. And I love you. I'm sort of afraid of you," he added, his tone amused, "but I love you. Will you forgive me for not telling you sooner?"

Jane thought about it for a few moments. "Yes, I think I will. As long as there are no more secrets." She pulled back her head to look up into his eyes. "Are there any more secrets?"

"Just one," he said, sitting down, dragging her onto his lap. And then he told her about MaryJo. . . .

"So now she knows everything?" Henry said, nursing a cold beer in the Blue Pig. "Good. I was starting to get confused as to who knew what."

"You should have seen her when Aunt Marion called, Henry. She's little, but she's mighty. Trust me, there's nothing fragile about Janie Preston, soon to be Janie Romanowski. Hmmm, I wonder what her middle initial is."

"Probably *D*, for delusional. She really loves you?"

"Enough to cry when I told her about MaryJo, then get so angry I thought she was going to go down the hall and personally rip Harrison's head off and feed it to him."

"Good. I like her. So, now that this Molly person is totally out of the picture, are there any changes in the plans?"

"I'm not sure. I think we can count on Jim Waters showing up, but I don't like putting all our eggs in one basket."

Henry nodded. "True. Nothing like having a great unveiling and nobody there to see it, hear it."

John drained the last of his beer. "We could change our plans. Instead of using Brandy to lure him, we could send some sort of note. Threaten him somehow with what we know. Have some sort of cloak-and-dagger midnight meeting, bring a tape recorder?"

"That's called blackmail, John. It's also called thirty to life if we're wrong and those papers don't end up meaning anything. I really hope they're real, because otherwise, Brandy's dead-set on going through with it, telling the press about the photographs." He shook his head. "The man never should have told her he was going to okay more offshore drilling in California and wanted her on his team. That was the topper for her."

John looked at his friend, momentarily distracted. "And how is Brandy, *Hank?*"

Henry blushed, from his bow tie to his slightly receding hairline. "She's fine. Why do you ask?"

"Oh, no reason," John said, relaxing back in his chair. "I just wondered if I scented a little *romance* in the air?"

Henry began lifting his glass, replacing it, making a pattern of wet rings on the tabletop. "We're having dinner later. Not here. She's got a limo coming, and we're going up to Atlantic City."

"Oh, my. Oh, my, oh, my. Really? Hank, you dog, you."

"Mind if I sit down, gentlemen?"

John looked up to see Dillon Holmes already pulling out a chair and easing himself into it. "Yes, as a matter of fact, Holmes, we do mind. Go away."

"There's nothing I'd like more, J. P., but I think it's time we had a little talk."

John decided to ignore the J. P. part. "About what?"

"About your . . . playmate."

John's fingers tightened around the handle of his beer

mug. "Careful, cockroach. Otherwise, I might have to step on you."

"Yes," Henry said, leaning forward, his voice low. "I've seen him do it, you know. He's ... He's rather *big*. Big men are usually very gentle, and John is by and large a levelheaded man, a good man. But when a good, gentle man gets angry, a *large,* good, gentle man? Well, I'd apologize, if I were you."

"Certainly," Dillon said smoothly. "I apologize, J. P. I'll even leave. Right after I ask you to please remind Ms. Preston that the photographs are still in my possession, along with a copy of the original hotel registry for room two-seventeen."

John kept his expression blank. He and Jane were going to be married ... "eventually." The photographs wouldn't mean anything. But Dillon Holmes didn't need to know any of that. Let the man think he still held the upper hand. "Go on."

"There's really nothing much else to say. Oh," he said, pushing back his chair and getting to his feet, "just one more thing. I don't eat grape jelly, J. P., and I don't read the local newspapers. You should have gone with orange marmalade and the *Wall Street Journal.* Plot flaws. They're the very devil, aren't they? Good day, gentlemen."

"What's he talking about?" Henry asked in confusion.

John leaned an elbow on the table and dropped his chin in his hand. "He knows we saw the papers and then put them back. We're screwed."

"Yes, that's rather obvious from your expression," Henry agreed. "He knows, so he'll be prepared. Now what?"

"We could still drop back to Plan B and go with Brandy?"

"No," Henry said firmly. "I won't allow that."

"Neither would I, Henry, neither would I."

"So we stick with Plan A and hope they haven't figured out a way to counter it?"

John thought about that for a moment, worked on it, chewed on it, as he would a plot point. "He threatened

Janie. He wouldn't have done that if he wasn't worried. Guys like Holmes, like Harrison, they're used to getting away with things. They threaten, and people cower. Blackmail works for them, Henry, it always has. But what if we're too pigheaded to care about blackmail?''

"Shouldn't that be Janie's decision?''

"She wants Harrison on a spit, Henry. She won't back off now. But you're right. Maybe it won't play out the way we hoped, not now that they're forewarned, may even have thought up some logical explanation that makes us look like idiots. Maybe we should just anonymously leak the photocopy to the media camped outside.''

"Quoting what source? With what collaboration? No, John. It would make a stink inside the media, but nobody would ever print it, ever touch the story, not even the tabloids. Harrison would sue them to hell and back.''

"And maybe even come off looking like the poor victim. You're right, Henry. We stick with what we've got. Call their bluff.'' He pushed back his chair, stood up. "And now, if you don't mind, I've got a date.''

"Janie, of course.''

"Of course. We're going to a place called Wildwood, to visit the DoWop Preservation League.''

Henry rolled his eyes. "Sure you are.''

"Hey, *Hank,* some people go to Atlantic City, and some of us go see the DoWop. It's what makes the world go around. See you tomorrow? The press conference is set for five, so we'll see you and Brandy at four o'clock, in the ballroom.''

"We'll be there,'' Henry agreed. "Just you make sure Jim Waters is there, too.''

"Did he buy the threat?''

Dillon Holmes walked past his uncle and sat down on the couch. "Of course he bought it. He's one of the good guys, remember? Or at least he thinks he is. Wave some tail in front of a good guy, and he rolls over and plays dead.''

"Again with the crude," Harrison said, making a face. "A simple yes or no would have sufficed. Now, about what we'll say if he goes through with it. Let's hear it, Dillon, and you'd better have it right." '

"Right? I wrote it, didn't I?" Dillon laid his head back against the cushions and recited, singsong, "We don't know what it is, a copy also was sent to us through the mail. Someone sick and twisted is obviously trying to play on the senator's genuine grief, shame, shame on them, but we're standing here now to say that it's nothing more than a vicious pack of lies meant to derail the candidacy of the most honest, upright, and moral man ever to seek the office. And it's about time America turned its back on the politics of personal destruction and said, 'No more!' God, I think my stomach just turned. That's a first. I mean, you practically *invented* the politics of personal destruction, Uncle Dearest."

"Never mind the sarcasm. Just practice your sorrowful and humble and yet outraged look, okay, and we'll get through this. I still can't believe that you would actually have—"

"Right. Stick with that bunch of crap, Uncle. Pretty soon you'll even believe it, if you don't already. Except we both know the truth."

Harrison poured himself another double scotch. "I just want tomorrow *over*. I want to get out of this hick town, away from these blathering idiots and their high public ideals and sneaky backroom deals. I need to *relax*."

"And yet you do it all so well. The king of the backroom deal," Dillon said, saluting his uncle facetiously.

Harrison turned toward his nephew. "One more thing. The girl, Dillon. Did you talk to her? Do you have her number? I need to relax. Maybe she's free tonight."

"For crying out loud, keep it zipped, just one more day.

Please. Then we'll be back in Washington, where you can trust the talent.''

"You're right, you're right," Harrison said, then downed his scotch, not looking at Dillon. Very carefully not looking at Dillon. "One more day."

Chapter Sixteen

Friday dawned sunny and warm. Outside.

Inside, it was still dark . . . and hot.

John raised his head, looked down at Jane, and then rolled over onto his back. "Okay, that's it. I'm officially awake."

"I thought you were," she said, snuggling against his shoulder. "Very awake." She smiled as he rubbed a hand over her upper arm. It was a casual gesture, not one of passion—and she had certainly learned what the touch of passion felt like. It was just John, being with her, lying with her, sharing with her.

She loved the sex. No question. But she loved him more, loved these moments more.

"Tell me again," she said, looking up at him.

"I love you," he said, picking up his head just enough to plant a kiss on her forehead.

"And how much do you love me?" she persisted, because each time she asked, his answer was different. He loved her so much his teeth ached. He loved her so much he would shave his beard five times a day if she asked. He loved her so much he would give her the last of the Rice Krispies if there was only enough for one of them. He loved her so much he would allow Molly to be maid of honor at their wedding.

"I love you so much . . ." he said now, with a crooked smile, "I'd give up this whole idea if you wanted to quit now."

Jane shifted on the bed, wrapping the top sheet around herself as she sat up and knelt on the mattress. "You're kidding. You'd give it all up? The whole plan to knock Harrison out of the race? After what he did to your mother, to you? Knowing what a no-good person he is?"

John shrugged. "I didn't say it would be easy, but yes, I would."

She shook her head. "All right. My turn. I love you so much, I'd never ask you to do that. Never."

He pushed himself up against the headboard. "I knew that," he said, then ducked as Jane grabbed a pillow from behind her and started beating him with it.

The pillow fight led to tickling, the tickling to other sensory investigation. . . . And it was after nine before they got downstairs for the tail end of the breakfast buffet, eating fairly cold eggs and limp bacon, and smiling secret smiles.

"Hi, mind if I interrupt the lovers?" Brandy said, pulling out a chair and sitting down. She looked wonderful this morning, but then, she always looked wonderful. Jane would have hated her if Brandy wasn't so nice, or so brave.

"How are you doing?" Jane asked as she noticed Brandy's hand shake slightly as she lifted a cup of coffee to her lips.

"A little stage fright," Brandy said with a blinding smile. "Okay, a lot of stage fright. I know I said I've done improv, but in this case, I'd really like a script."

John sat back, laid his napkin on the table. "You know, Brandy, that's not such a bad idea."

"A script? You're kidding," Jane said, looking from one to the other. "Oh, wait a minute. John? Do you mean someone should *act out* the papers?"

"Hey, I think I like this. It would have to be a man,"
Brandy said, pulling her chair closer. "I mean, I could do
it, but the whole impact would be softened unless it was a
man."

Jane nodded her head. "She's right. But two men. One
to do the introduction and wrap-up, and one to do the message." John looked at her strangely. "What? Hey, I've put
on a few shows in my time. Christmas pageants, the annual
Easter Bunny Extravaganza. I know how to do it. Of course,
I guess no one wants to be dressed like an elf or a bunny,
huh?"

"I love you," John said, leaning toward her to kiss her
cheek.

"Oh, brother. Amateurs," Brandy said with a laugh. "I'm
working with amateurs. And soppy amateurs at that."

"No, no," Jane protested. "You have nothing to worry
about. All we need are two male voices. Right, John?"

"And you're looking at me?" John said, picking up his
napkin again. "I don't do readings. Not my own work, not
this. All that emoting, putting passion into the words? Forget
it. Bad idea."

"Oh, all right, don't go nuclear on us. You could do the
answering machine part, and the narrative. It's just reading,
not acting out lines," Brandy said excitedly. "And Hank
can do the rest. He acted in high school. He told me so."

John's laugh rang through the room. "He told you about
that? They did *Arsenic And Old Lace*. He was a corpse. He
didn't even have any lines."

Jane bit down on her lips to keep from laughing. "You're
making that up."

"Yes, I am," John admitted. "He had two lines, and he
blew both of them, to hear him tell it. I can't believe he
told you that, Brandy."

Jane watched the woman's eyes go rather soft and dreamy.
"Oh, we talk constantly. Hank's such an interesting man.
Very well read—"

"I can't argue with that one. There are times I think he

wishes he was Pinocchio, so his nose would grow and turn the pages for him,'' John interrupted. "Go on. Tell us more about *Hank*. This is . . . Well, this is fascinating. Really.''

"Don't, Brandy,'' Jane said, patting the woman's hand. "John is enjoying this entirely too much.'' She turned to glare at him. "Shame on you.''

John held up his hands in surrender. "Okay, teach, I'll go to my corner now. But seriously, Brandy, how would we work it if we tried to put it on as a sort of script?''

"I don't know, but Jane's idea sounded good. Do you have a copy with you?''

"I made five, mailed two to myself at home, just to be safe,'' John said, reaching into his slacks pocket and pulling out two much-folded papers. "Here you go. It's quiet here now that the seminars have started up, so we can practice. I'll start.''

Jane watched as John unfolded the papers, cleared his throat, and read quietly: "The following is a word-for-word transcription of a telephone message I, Dillon Holmes, Special Assistant to Senator Aubrey Harrison, received on the date listed below. The machine is my home answering machine; the caller is Senator Harrison. His is the voice on the tape. For purposes of personal security, the tape is in a safety deposit box, and I have the only key.

"The transcription follows: *You have one message, received at eight-twenty-three p.m., Tuesday, November twenty-third.* Message follows.''

Then he handed the papers to Brandy.

Brandy wet her lips, took a breath, and began to read, using all the emotion and inflection anyone could ask for:

" 'Dillon? Dillon, are you there? For crying out loud, where are you now? You told me you'd be home. You know, nephew, the idea was that you were to take care of me, be on call for me. It's bad enough you look like your father; do you have to be as brain-dead as your mother?

" 'We've got a problem, a big problem. The bitch is threatening to divorce me, and name Gloria in the suit.

Gloria? Hell, that was a dozen women ago. I don't know how she found out. Adultery, can you believe it? She wants to sue for adultery! I told her nobody does that. So she says yesterday—get this—she says, okay, then I'll say you beat me.

" 'Beat her? Hell, I would, but I don't want to *touch* her! Damn dumb drunk, got her head in a bottle all day and night. Can you see her as First Lady? It's a joke! But it's every day now, threat after threat. Tonight's the worst, Dillon. She's back on the Gloria kick, and I think she means it this time. Where the hell are you? Damn, I hate these machines.

" 'Anyway, she says she's got some sort of proof of the affair with Gloria, about Gloria's son—my son, damn it— and if I don't give her the divorce and damn near every cent I've got, she'll go public with all of it. I know the kid isn't mine, and so does Marcia. Hell, I stopped seeing Gloria a year ago. But proving I'm not the father is as bad as having to say, yes, yes, I slept with the woman.

" 'And then more women will come forward. You know how it is, every damn one of them waving her hand in the air and saying he screwed me, too, he screwed me, too, put my picture on the cover of the *National Enquirer,* give me a jeans commercial. Do you know what that would do to my campaign? Campaign, hell. She'll destroy me.

" 'Dillon? I'm telling you, boy, what we need is for that drunken slut to have an accident. I don't know—drive off the road, fall down the stairs. Something. She's in the bag all the time. Why can't she have an accident?

" 'Okay, okay, I'm calming down. She just gets to me, you know? Call me tomorrow, we'll figure something out. And for God's sake, erase this message. Surprise me, do one thing right.' "

Finished, Brandy handed the papers back to John, who read the rest: "As stated above, the day of the call was November twenty-third. November twenty-fifth, on the eve of her forty-third birthday, while I, Dillon Holmes, was in

California, Marcia Harrison was found at the bottom of the stairs in the Harrison mansion in Georgetown. Her neck was broken, and she was very, very dead.

"I draw no conclusions, and have no knowledge of any criminal wrongdoing, except to say that Senator Harrison's phone message seemed like the ravings of a very agitated, desperate man. A man whose problems all seemed to solve themselves two days later. For the sake of my mother, the senator's sister, and because it could have been a coincidental tragedy, I have not made this public until now, for I now believe Senator Harrison did, in fact, murder his second wife."

Jane rubbed her upper arms, because she had goose pimples crawling over her skin. "It sounds worse out loud," she said, looking at John. "Let's do it."

"I agree," Brandy said, reaching across the table to steal John's last piece of bacon. "The plan stays basically the same. I call Harrison and tell him to get down to the ballroom. Hank says Dillon let it slip yesterday that they know we have at least seen this, so they'll be expecting something, but not lights, camera, action. We get the reporter and his cameramen, I do a little bit of an interview while we wait for Harrison and Dillon to show up, and then we swing right into our reading, the camera already rolling. They say a picture is worth a thousand words. We've got a great thousand words, and with Harrison's face in camera, do you know what else we've got?"

"Yes? What else have we got?" Jane asked, figuring she was supposed to be playing the straight man here, to Brandy's version of *All The President's Men.*

Brandy broke off a bit of bacon and popped it into her mouth. "Oscar material."

"So much for that old saying," John said as he and Jane walked along the shoreline.

"What old saying?" Jane was stepping carefully, because

a storm out at sea had churned up quite a few broken shells that had been deposited on the beach with the last high tide.

"Time flies when you're having fun. Do you know it's only two o'clock? We've still got two hours to kill before the big unveiling."

"We could go swimming. It would only take a couple of minutes to go back to the hotel and change into our suits."

"No, I think we should just walk. Here, and maybe around town. Keep our eyes open. I don't know why, but it sounds right."

"Here's a novel idea. We could go to one of the seminars. I feel a little guilty that we haven't participated more. In fact, the only person I've really talked to was that nice Bruce Hendersen, today at lunch. Although he didn't say much."

"He was an escort," John told her, squeezing her hand.

Jane sort of danced in front of him, to look up into his grinning face. "No. You're kidding. He was an escort?"

John turned her around and began walking back up the shoreline. "He was an escort. She wasn't at lunch, but good old Bruce is here with Dr. Leticia Ralston, genetic engineer. He's her arm candy."

Jane shivered. "I don't like that term," she said primly, then looked toward the blankets and sun umbrellas and everyone who had taken the last afternoon of the retreat for some sun and surf. "Oh, all right, I'll admit it. I'm nosey. Who else?"

"Okay. It'll pass some time." They walked another twenty yards or so, and then John inclined his head to the right. "Three o'clock, the blonde in the purple one-piece."

Jane turned her head, looked at the tall, well-built woman just then spreading sun screen on her long, long legs. "Paid escort? How do you know?"

"Look at the man approaching the blanket, carrying two cans of soda. The one in the plaid shorts."

"Got him," Jane said, watching as the man, clearly thirty years the woman's senior, clumsily sat himself down on the blanket. "Who is he?"

"Jeremy Proctor. Professor of Sociology. He wrote a very good book a few years back. Nice man, but not married. And not dating, either."

"And you know this how?"

"Okay, okay, I'll admit it. Henry told me. He's Proctor's publisher. So, now that I've reached the limits of my knowledge on the subject, what do we—hold it."

John stopped dead, and Jane did, too, first looking at him to try to figure out where he was looking from behind his sunglasses, and then scanning the beach herself. "What? I don't see anything."

"I do. Let's be casual, play it cool," John said, taking Jane's hand again and starting to cut across the beach, back toward the hotel. "See? We're walking, we're talking . . ."

"We're considering an adjustment in our medication . . ." Jane said, keeping a polite smile on her face.

"Cute. Just play along, sweetheart. You can't know how I've been hoping for this. Almost there," John said, and then suddenly he took a hard left, and the next thing she knew, he was kneeling on somebody's blanket.

"John! What on earth do you—*Kevin?* Is that you?"

Kevin, looking very much the vacationer in his Hawaiian-print swim trunks, mirror sunglasses, and zinc oxide white nose, smiled up at Jane. "So much for my latest disguise. But I couldn't resist, you know? That damn trench coat was *hot.*" He took off his sunglasses and looked at John. "All right, give. What gave me away?"

"Your ears," John told him as Jane also sat down, grabbing herself a corner of the blanket. "Did the other kids call you Jughead?"

"Dumbo, and it still hurts, so have some sensitivity, please, and stop grinning," Kevin complained, reaching in an insulated bag beside him and coming up with three cans of soda. "Drinks, anyone?"

John shook his head. "You're playing it pretty cool for a guy who steals key cards and ransacks rooms."

"Ransacks? Oh, come on, John, I didn't ransack. I was

very neat, and I deliberately left you a clue, so you'd know I'd been there and not get too sloppy with whatever information you already had. You did pick up on that, didn't you, J. P.? Oh, and I only gave him what he already knew. See? No harm done.''

''John,'' Jane said, putting a hand on his arm. ''Don't hit him.''

''I was thinking more of strangling him, actually.''

''Yes, but then he can't talk to us, can he?'' Jane put in reasonably. She glared at Kevin. ''You said *him*. You're working for Dillon Holmes, aren't you?''

Kevin reached up and scratched one of his Dumbo ears. ''You'd think that. Harrison and Holmes think that. My boss, however, thinks otherwise.''

''Your boss,'' John said, tipping his head to one side. ''Okay. So I'm not nuts. I did figure it right, finally. Good. I'll take that soda now.''

''Me, too, I suppose,'' Jane said, her expression thoughtful. ''Are you a reporter, too, Kevin? Is that what John found out?''

''I don't think so, Jane,'' John told her. ''You're not a reporter, are you, Kevin? And you're not a bum or a burglar. You're a Fed.''

Jane felt her eyes grow wide. ''A *Fed?* As in *Federal Agent?*'' She sat back on her heels. ''No.''

''Yes,'' Kevin said. ''Give the man a cigar. Did you take it, by the way? I've been looking for months. I couldn't find it in your room. I'd really love to see it.''

John shrugged, then reached into his pocket and pulled out the folded papers. ''Here you go. Knock your socks off.''

''John? If you give it to him, then we can't—''

''You can't do anything anyway, Ms. Preston,'' Kevin told her as he read the pages. ''We've known about this for months, ever since Holmes quietly started testing the waters to see if he could gain anything with a blockbuster scandal *on* Harrison that he couldn't get *with* Harrison, although no one knew the exact contents.''

He refolded the pages, handed them back to John. ''This changes nothing. Old news, folks. He's slime, but he didn't kill his wife.''

Jane felt all her excitement melting away, to be replaced with frustration. ''Maybe not him, but maybe Dillon Holmes. Yes? No?''

''No to both. The beauty of it is only in the eye of the beholder, that being that each man thinks the other did it. That much I have figured out during my investigation. They're pretty much blackmailing each other, Harrison using all of Holmes's considerable insider power, Holmes hoping to be the power behind the throne when Harrison's in the Oval Office. Oh, and in case you're wondering, you can't be prosecuted for sleeping around. At least not again, seeing how sordid we all looked the last time, like a prurient bunch of damn Peeping Toms.''

John rubbed at the side of his neck. ''How? How do you know neither of them pushed her? And while we're at it, what the hell are you doing here in the first place if you know Harrison didn't murder his wife?''

''I'll answer your second question first. I'm here because Harrison is going to run for president and—at least in the beginning—we heard there was evidence that he may have murdered his wife. It's not the kind of thing you announce unless you've got rock-solid proof, and we didn't. We don't. Which answers your second question.''

''Only in your mind,'' John said, then took a swig of soda, made a face. ''Cripes, it's warm.''

''Which is as far as we got—warm. Nothing hot here, John, sorry. Harrison hid the fact that there was an autopsy, didn't even ask to see the results, probably because he figured they would show his wife was drunk. He just paid somebody off to lose the report. Poor bastard. Good politician, Harrison, but not exactly a brain trust, you know? Although, to be fair, he also may have thought it would show some other bad stuff, too.''

"But it didn't? So you don't think anymore that the senator pushed his wife down the stairs?'' Jane asked, still worried about Brandy's reaction to all of this. Would she insist on going forward with the information about the photographs? That didn't seem fair, to have to hurt herself to expose Harrison.

"Nope, no more," Kevin said. "And not for a long time. You see, the autopsy results, when we finally got to them—I have many talents—showed that the woman had a massive heart attack. She was dead before she began to fall. End of story, at least that part of it. Still, I'd always wanted to see what Holmes had hanging over Harrison's head. Just curiosity, you understand. That, and the private joke."

"Let me guess. You federal types are giggling up your sleeves at the idea that Holmes and Harrison each think the other did it.''

"Bing-o. Hey, in this business, you take your jollies where you can get them.''

Jane's spine sort of collapsed on itself as she slumped and closed her eyes. "We were so *close.*''

"And you're such *amateurs,*'' Kevin said, saluting them with his soda can.

"So why are you here? Why are you pretending to be on Holmes's team?''

"Can we say graft? Kickback? Influence peddling? *Real* high crimes and misdemeanors? Oh, I think we can, and that's why I'm sticking around, playing at Holmes's gofer. The pity is, we'll probably not be able to break the whole story for, oh, another two years or so. It's sad, but it takes that long to get all our ducks in a row.''

"So," John said, "in the meantime, Harrison announces, gets the nomination, and could already be in office by the time you're ready to go public. Are you sure you don't want us to at least leak this thing to the press?''

Kevin shook his head. ''Too easy to find the autopsy report. Harrison admitting he cats around is good, granted, but it's not enough when balanced against poor widowed senator is unjustly accused of murder. Okay, I've shown you mine; now maybe you'll show me yours. Will you tell me what you guys were planning?''

''We'd rather not,'' John said, getting to his feet. ''Come on, Jane, we've got to find the others, call it all off.''

''Call what off? There's more? What?'' Kevin asked, grinning. ''I so love conspiracy theories. Oh, wait, I think I've got it. You were going to do some big unveiling at today's news conference, weren't you? That's so cute, even precious. It's almost like Woodward and Bernstein playing Mickey Rooney and Judy Garland, saying, 'I know, let's put on a show!' ''

John sort of growled.

''Good-bye, Kevin,'' Jane said, as John helped her to her feet. ''And thank you so much for this lesson in how our taxpayer dollars are spent.''

John still held her hand, but Jane had to half run to keep up with him as they left the beach and entered the hotel.

''Henry's probably in the Blue Pig,'' John said, heading in that direction. ''Let's hope Brandy is with him. I don't want to have to tell this story twice.''

Jane pulled on John's hand, so that he stopped. ''John, we can't let Brandy say anything about those photographs. That's what she's going to want to do, and we can't let it happen.''

''I know. The question is, how do we stop her?''

''First, I'd say we don't tell her *yet*,'' Jane said, frowning in thought. ''Which means we don't tell Henry yet either, because he'd tell her. If there was only some way to get both of them away from here.''

John put his arms around her, picked her up a good foot

off the floor, and kissed her square on the mouth. He then set her back down, saying, "You're a genius."

"Yes, I know. It's why you love me," Jane answered, only slightly bemused. "What did I say?"

He took her hand once more. "Just follow my lead, because I'm going to be winging it. I can do that, you know, I'm a writer. I'm a great liar. Later, I'll sulk for a few hours, knowing we missed a great opportunity to bring that bastard down, and you can do your best to cheer me up—I have several suggestions in mind as to how—but for now we've got to protect Brandy. Do you still have that cell phone?"

Jane reached in her purse and drew it out, handed it to him. "Who are you going to call?"

"Jim Waters," John said, removing the newscaster's business card from his wallet. He dialed, hit Send, and put the phone to his ear. "One ring . . . two rings . . . Jim, hello, so glad I caught you! It's John . . . John Romanowski, remember? No? On the beach the other night? Tall?" he said, holding a hand above his head. Then he sort of winced at Jane. "Hairy?"

Jane clapped a hand over her mouth to keep from laughing out loud. John glared at her.

"Okay, so you remember now? Yeah, yeah, that's me. Good, good. Look, change of plans. Brandy can't meet with you until *after* the senator's press conference, okay? Same place, different time. You got that? Great! Boffo! See you later, alligator."

"Boffo? See you later, alligator?" Jane repeated as John hit the End button, then returned her cell phone. "I thought you gave up the nerd act."

"He thought I was Brandy's agent, doesn't even remember my name from the other night, so I played along, did the Hollywood thing," John told her as they headed for the Blue Pig. "And, I'll have you know, the man came right back with 'after while, crocodile.' No wonder he's not network."

"Okay, so now we're rid of Mr. Waters. How do we get rid of Brandy?"

"Same story. But this time it's Jim Waters who changed the schedule. Once the network cameras are packed up, I'll tell her the truth."

Jane pulled him to a stop again. "That's brilliant, John, really it is. But it's only a stop-gap, and you know it. Brandy will just pick another time to make her statement."

He shook his head. "I know. I think I'm going to have to show her everything I've got on Harrison's little organization, all of it, and promise her I'll make it public, soon. A hell of a lot sooner than the Feds, that's for sure."

"Putting your own head on the block if you can't prove it," Jane said, her stomach plummeting to her toes. "You could lose everything."

"In which case you could never be accused of marrying me for my money," John said, giving her hand a squeeze. "Come on. We break the news of the time switch to Brandy and Henry and grab something to eat, because I have a feeling we're going to miss dinner. What time is it?"

"Nearly three," Jane said, looking at her watch. "The announcement is set for five. Will we watch?"

"From our room, on television. All four of us. The networks are carrying it live. I don't want Brandy anywhere near a microphone until we tell her what's going on."

The Gang of Four—or the Amateurs, as Kevin called them—gathered in Brandy's suite at four-thirty.

Brandy busied herself filing her nails, then applied light pink polish.

Henry read a book.

John paced.

And Jane hoped for a miracle.

"It's time," John said at last, using the remote to turn on the television set. "Prepare to be nauseated."

A podium had been set up in the dining room because it had begun to drizzle outside, and about twelve different microphones were taped to the thing as Dillon Holmes smiled into the cameras.

He introduced his boss in no more than ten thousand well-crafted, sincere words, and then stood back to allow Harrison to step to the podium. And then there he was, in all his silver-haired, teeth-capped glory. He waved to the crowd, acknowledged the applause, thanked the invited guests.

And then he paused. Dramatically. Jane had to hand it to the guy; he knew how to be dramatic.

Everybody knew what was coming. And, for once, Aubrey Harrison kept it short and sweet. "Today I announce my candidacy for President of the United States! You will hear me make promises, and I'm here to tell you that I *keep* my promises!"

And then Jane's wish came true.

"Sez you!" a female voice screamed from the cheap seats. "You don't keep your *dates.*"

Dillon Holmes was back at the podium so quickly anyone could believe he had flown there. "If we could please have that woman removed?"

"Oh, no, you don't. Three hours! Three hours I waited, and it was raining. I gave up my ride and had to walk home when I finally figured out he wasn't coming."

Harrison tried to put his hand over the microphones; but there were too many of them, and some picked up the words, "I thought you said you called her. Jackass!"

John sat down on the couch beside Jane, whispered, "Ask me if I believe in Santa Claus, sweetheart. Just ask me, because I'll tell you yes."

"Shhh," she said, waving a hand at him. "Look—they've turned the cameras around. Who is she?"

As if she had heard the question, the young woman said into the hand mikes that were now pushed in her direction, "My name is Sheila Nesquith, and I'm a hostess at—well, never mind where, because I quit this morning. Last week-end, Senator Aubrey Harrison invited me back to this hotel, where I spent the night with him. And I can prove it."

Someone darn near dropped a boom mike on the girl's head. Flashbulbs popped. Huge television lights were being dragged into place. The entire ballroom was in turmoil.

All while Ms. Nesquith grinned into the cameras, her wad of bubble gum visible thanks to her wide smile.

"Yes! You go, girl," Brandy said, punching a fist into the air. "Damn, ruined my nails," she added, looking at the polish smeared onto her palm as she unclenched that fist. "Oh, who cares? Hank, honey, turn up the volume."

"Yes, certainly," Henry said, doing as she had requested.

At this point, a man in his fifties or so, wearing a navy pinstriped suit, his shoe-polish black hair slicked back, stepped in front of Sheila. "My name is Frederick Blake, Esquire, and I am Ms. Nesquith's attorney. Now that we have your attention, I have a statement."

But Sheila obviously wasn't done. She stuck her head back toward the microphones and yelled, "I'll teach you to stand *me* up! You're screwed, buster!"

"Charming girl," Henry said, wincing.

The dining room erupted again as forty reporters all asked their questions at once.

"You think I can get book rights?" Henry said, pulling his overstuffed armchair closer to the set.

"As long as I can play her in the feature, Hank," Brandy said, slipping onto the arm of the chair and putting her hand on his shoulder.

"Quiet, children," Jane said, taking command. "He's saying something else."

". . . proof. Proof that Ms. Nesquith, admitting her culpability in obtaining employment by misrepresenting her age, is indeed"—he paused for effect—"seventeen years old."

"Get out," John said, looking at Jane. "She's seventeen?"

"Makeup," Brandy said, nodding. "Good body, tall, strong features. She could get away with it. She looks twenty-one, definitely. But I'm too old to play her, darn it."

"Furthermore," Attorney Blake said, once the furor had

died down once more, "we have proof, solid, incontroversial proof, that Senator Aubrey Harrison did, indeed, engage in sexual acts with Ms. Nesquith. Although, in fact, legally, in many states of this great union, the term would be statutory rape."

Another uproar from the peanut gallery, before one voice rang out over the others. "What proof?"

"God love him, it's Jim Waters. See him?" John said, slapping his knees. "He's the closest one to her. Sometimes being stuck in the back row pays off."

"Our proof," Attorney Blake continued, looking straight at Waters, whose face was now the only reporter face in the frame, "is in a safe place. As soon as the local police are notified, which my associate is doing now, the evidence will be taken to the police laboratory for analysis. DNA, that sort of thing."

"What on earth is he talking about?" Jane asked, confused.

"Well, um," John began, and Jane noticed that the man was actually blushing. "I could be wrong, but I think the lady took a souvenir. And I don't mean a copy of the room service menu."

Jane shook her head. "No, I still don't understand."

John looked to Henry, who was showing an intense interest in his shoe tops. "Well," he said, trying again, "if I'm right, I think she took—"

"I got the condom, baby!" demure Ms. Nesquith shouted into the phalanx of microphones. "I got *both* of them! You are *so screwed!*"

"Oh," Jane said as Attorney Blake grabbed his client by the shoulders and pushed her into the hallway. "Oh, that's gross."

"Is it?" John asked. "Although I'd like to think of it as poetic justice."

"Ho-ly *shit,*" Brandy said, collapsing into Henry's lap. "Please, please, Hank, let me play her, make it part of any deal you can make. I *love* this girl!"

"Come on," John said, helping Jane to her feet as the camera swung back to the podium, the empty podium. "Let's get out of here."

Jane went willingly, only glancing back at Henry and Brandy, who made a very odd, yet very appealing couple, as John pulled the door closed behind them.

Once out in the hallway, John turned and put his hands on Jane's shoulders. "He's done, Janie. Finished."

"Yes, I know. How do you feel?"

He shrugged. "I'm not sure. I've wanted to see him go down for a lot of years. I thought I'd feel more than I do. Yes, I'm glad it happened, but mostly, all I want to do is go back to our room and make love to you. Does that make any sense?"

"It does to me," Jane said, putting her arm around his waist as they walked down the long hallway to their room.

On the way past the bank of elevators, the doors opened, and Dillon Holmes stepped out. To say the man looked harassed would be a major understatement.

"Dillon," John said, smiling. "Going to your room to pack? Or would this be more in the line of a rat deserting a sinking ship?"

"Go to hell, Romanowski. And take your bimbo with you."

"You know, Holmes, Jane here is a wonderful woman. A *nice* woman. She doesn't have a violent bone in her body. Fortunately, or unfortunately, depending on who's doing the looking, I do."

Jane didn't even have time to register John's movement before Dillon Holmes was lying on the floor, holding onto his nose as blood spurted down his face, onto his suit. "Do broke it, do broke my node!"

John slipped an arm around Jane's shoulder once more, and they walked on down the hall. "You know something, sweetheart?" he said as she slid the key card into the door.

"You're glad you did that?" she asked, grinning up at him.

"Oh, yeah," John said, his grin wide and almost childlike. "Oh, yeah. Now I need only one thing more to make this the best day of my life. Quick, sweetheart, what's a good opposite for *eventually?*"

Jane laughed as he lifted her high in his arms. "Why, Professor Romanowski, I think that might be *immediately.*"

"Give that girl an *A,*" he said as he stepped inside the room and kicked back with his foot, closing the door.

Dear Reader,

Well, now that Jane and John are settled, is anyone wondering just what has been going on with Molly? Could it be that everything at *Preston Kiddie Kare* is just hunky-dory? Could it be that Molly has neatly and efficiently solved every little problem and is now headed back to her Washington, D.C. town house for the holiday celebrations in the nation's capital?

Or could it be that Molly has just happily landed herself in yet another briar patch? Hmmmm. . . . Could be.

And here he comes now. . . .

We first encounter Dominic Longstreet as he bursts through the doors of *Preston Kiddie Kare,* in search of someone to murder.

What he finds is our very own Molly Applegate, who has taken over the running of the day care. But only for two days, remember, prior to the Fourth of July, at which time the establishment closes for nearly two weeks.

But Dominic thought his niece and nephew—eight-year-old Little Tony outside, getting nauseous on the swings, and nine-year-old Lizzie inside, on one of the computers, probably hacking into the Pentagon—were safely enrolled for all of this week and the next, while their parents cruised the Greek Isles.

Anyway, he locates Molly and starts in on her, both barrels.

He is angry. He is incensed. He is—Lord, but the woman has great legs. . . .

"I mean it," he says, dragging himself back to attention, "I have a contract, an agreement, whatever you want to call it. It's too late to make other arrangements, and *somebody* is going to watch these kids for the next two weeks or I'm going to sue. You got that?"

"You're Dominic Longstreet, aren't you?" Molly responds, crossing those long legs as she sits smiling at Dominic, obviously not too upset over the idea that her cousin's place of business might become the object of litigation. "The Broadway director? You do musicals. I saw *Felicitations* last year. Wonderful fun, really."

"Yes, thank you. *No*, I'm not thanking you, damn it! And not that it's any business of yours, but I've planned to work on my new show here for the next month. I already have the cast in place; they're rehearsing even as I stand here talking to—oh, hell, woman, I don't have time for this. *Do* something!"

Well . . . With Molly, it's pretty easy to guess what happens next.

She volunteers to move into the Longstreet mansion and lend her "considerable expertise in the area of child, er, child *management*" to the man for the duration.

It doesn't matter that everything Molly knows about child care could easily be put in a thimble, with room left over for the entire ensemble cast of *Les Miserables*.

Because she is going to be hobnobbing with actors and producers and—oh, she's always wanted to be on the stage. Didn't she spend a month last year as a singing, rollerskating carhop? That had been fun. The manager nearly wept when she quit, moved on to her dog-walking job (that one didn't last long; do you have any idea of the size of the pooper-scooper bag necessary to pick up after six dogs?).

Be that as it may, and getting back to the singing and rollerskating—it wasn't as if Molly didn't have talent. And then there's the great man himself, Dominic Longstreet. What a hunk, only to be considered a bonus in her overall plan.

So Molly closes the day care at the end of the day, packs up Tony and Lizzie, and heads to the Longstreet mansion on the outskirts of Fairfax County.

On Molly's side, this must be yet another lark, another adventure, another summer romance in the making.

For Dominic, as the days go by, this must be madness—this must be desperation and/or aberration—because he's very sure *This Can't Be Love*.

Yeah. A fat lot *he* knows. . . .

Look for *THIS CAN'T BE LOVE* in February 2004

Kasey Michaels

New York Times *best-selling author Kasey Michaels has a knack for whacking her readers in the heart—and the funny bone—with her witty tales of unexpected love. Now she delivers a whole new twist on sexual tension, as mystery writer Maggie Kelly sees her fantasy man come to life . . . right before a couple of her colleagues meet very untimely deaths. . . .*

Maggie Kelly is nothing if not resilient. She bounced back after getting fired from her old job as a writer of historical romances, reinventing herself as a mystery author. She bounced back when she discovered her lover—who also happens to be her publisher—cheating on her. And she bounces right back into her smoking habit whenever she tries to quit. But something just happened that's got tough-talking, quick-thinking Maggie swooning into her super-soft sofa cushions.

Something in the form of an incredibly sexy Englishman by the name of Saint Just. Alexandre Drake, Viscount Saint Just, to be exact. Tall, dark, handsome, with an accent to die for and charm to spare, he's everything she's ever dreamed of in a man. There's just one problem. He *is* her dream man. He's every woman's fantasy. He's the character who's made her a best-selling author. He's not real. No, he's not real— but he is, for some reason, standing in the middle of Maggie's apartment. With the adorable, bumbling sidekick she created expressly for him right by his side—and eating that piece of fried chicken she was saving for lunch.

What's a savvy, New York City writer to do when faced with the figments of her imagination—in the flesh? Well, short of checking herself into Bellevue, she'd better get used to it, because these guys aren't going anywhere—at least not until they've given Maggie a little unsolicited editorial advice regarding her latest telling of their adventures. Still, it's not the worst thing in the world to have a roomie as gorgeous as Saint Just—even if he *is* somewhat arrogant— and prone to leaving the cap off the toothpaste.

But just as Maggie's getting used to her new houseguests, things start to get quite a bit more complicated—in the "homicide" sense of the word. It seems her ex-lover, Kirk Toland, ever the inconsiderate cad, has had the nerve to die right there in her living room ... of poisoning ... after eating a dinner Maggie made. Her cooking isn't *that* bad— is it? And if that weren't weird enough, Toland's death is soon followed by the murder of a colleague whom *everyone* knows Maggie hated.

So, the mystery writer has become the murder suspect. And the only sleuth who's really on Maggie's side is the one she invented. . . .

Please turn the page for an exciting sneak peek of
MAGGIE NEEDS AN ALIBI,
coming in paperback in June 2003!

Prologue

It all began innocently enough. A desire to explore a larger world, that's what he'd said. A chance to step out, expand our horizons, spread our wings, and all of that.

I gave my approval, not that the man had applied for it, and came along because . . . well, that's what I do. Besides, I will have to confess to some curiosity of my own, most especially about the food. The food really interested me.

So we were off, or out, or whatever the vernacular. He thought it would be informative. He said it would be educational.

I supposed it might be fun, a bit of a lark.

Nobody had mentioned murder. . . .

Chapter 1

Rock music blared from the speakers on either side of the U-shaped workstation, aimed straight at Maggie Kelly's desk chair.

M&Ms were lined up neatly to the right of the computer keyboard, color-coded and ready to eat. Maggie was up to the reds, with the blues always saved for last.

A half-eaten cinnamon-and-sugar Pop Tart topped off the full trash basket shoved under the desktop. An open bag of marshmallows spilled over dozens of scribbled 5x8 file cards to Maggie's far left. The bag of individually wrapped diet candies, more a fond hope than a brave supermarket aisle life-changing epiphany, hadn't been opened.

Towers of research books littered the floor like literary Pisas. Others lay open around the base of her chair, scattered about like fallen birds, their spines cracked and broken.

A Mark Twain quote scribbled on a Post-it note was stuck to the edge of the huge, hutch-top desk: *"Classic:* A book which people praise and don't read."

There were two ashtrays on the desk (sugar fixes always to the right, nicotine fixes to the left, as a person had to have *some* order in her life). One ashtray was usually reserved for the cigarette that was burning, another for the butts. One fire in the waste can had been enough for Maggie to set up this, to her, quite logical system. Today, however, both ashtrays overflowed with butts, while a used nicotine patch was stuck to the larger ashtray.

The entire room, from noise to clutter to smoky haze, advertised the fact that Maggie Kelly was wrapping up the manuscript for her latest Saint Just Mystery.

And, sure enough, in the middle of the mess, dressed in an old pair of plaid shorts, a threadbare T-shirt with *F-U University* printed on it, topped by a navy-blue full length bathrobe that should have hit the hamper a week ago, sat Maggie Kelly herself.

Thirty-one years old. Short, curly, coppery hair with really great, wincingly expensive dark-blond highlights. Irish green eyes; huge, round horn-rimmed glasses falling halfway down her rather pert nose. Unlit cigarette dangling from a full, wide mouth just now curved into an unholy grin. An All-American, cheerleader type . . . with an attitude problem.

That was a quick snapshot of Maggie Kelly, the quintessential "successful writer at home." Five feet, six inches, one hundred sixteen pounds of *New York Times* best-selling author.

If she stood outside her Manhattan apartment with her empty teacup in her hand, she'd probably snag a quick five bucks from pitying strangers in ten minutes, tops.

Two Persian cats lay at her feet, snoring. A black one, Wellington, and a gray-and-white monster named Napoleon. Napoleon was a girl, but that knowledge had arrived after the inspiration for her name, so Napper was stuck with it.

Maggie dragged on the cigarette, frowned when she realized she hadn't lit it, and rummaged on the desktop for her pink Mini-Bic. She bought only throwaway lighters, one at a time, always swearing she would quit smoking and wouldn't need another one. She was beginning to think she was the

one faithful consumer standing between Bic's lighter manu-
facturing division and Chapter Eleven.

She lit the cigarette, squinted as smoke invaded her left
eye, and collected her thoughts. After a few moments, her
fingers punched at the keys once more as she hunched forward, eyes shut tight as she concentrated.

Maggie was on a roll. She could creep for chapters, that
damn "sagging middle" she slaved over, but the end always
came to her in a rush. The faster she wrote, the harder she
hit the keys. She began chair-dancing, moving to the rhythm
of Aerosmith at its most raucous, and the keyboard practically winced.

*Saint Just, she pounded out, damnable, damned sexy
quizzing glass stuck to one dazlzing blue eye, pivoted
slowly to face the earl. "One of the people present in
this room knows precisely what happened here the
night Quigley was murdered. Actually, not to be
immodest, two of us do," he drawled in his maddeningly arrogant way that melted the innocent (at least
the females) and inspired dread in the guilty.*

Pause. Open eyes. Hit Save. Read. Correct the spelling
of dazzling. Eat two red M&Ms. What the hell, eat the whole
row. Smile as the next song begins. Keep to the tune, keep
to the rhythm.

Maggie tapped both barefooted heels against the plastic
rug-saver beneath her swivel chair while doing her best to
"Walk This Way" while sitting down. She could do that
today. She could do anything. She was Maggie Kelly, writer.
And, hot diggity-damn, by midnight, she'd be Maggie Kelly,
a writer having written.

*"For the remainder of our assembled company, my
good friend here, Mr. Balder, will help demonstrate
as I explain. Sterling, if you please?"*

"Again? I'm always the corpse. Don't see why, but

all right,'' Sterling said, walking toward the fireplace to join his friend.

"Ah, very good. Now, if everyone will refresh their memories of the evening poor Quigley met his Maker? Just here, I believe. Sterling?"

Sterling Balder sighed, split his coattails, and lay down on the floor, crossing his arms over his ample belly.

"So there he is, poor Quigley, his lifeblood draining away. Sterling, please try not to look so robustly healthy if you can manage it. Be more desperate, if you can, knowing death is imminent but wanting to tell everyone who did the dastardly deed. Ah, wonderful. And now we need someone to play the murderer. My lord? If you would please be so kind as to take up a position providing a clear shot at Sterling? Pretend he's still upright, as he's looking quite comfortable down there, and we don't want to disturb him.''

"Me? Why me? Surely you don't believe . . . you don't think . . . what utter nonsense!'' Shiveley backed up a pace, trying to straighten his spine, and failing miserably. He cast his panicked gaze around the crowded drawing room, looking for allies, seeing only unsmiling faces. Condemning eyes. "What are you all looking at? I would never do such a thing. He was my very closest, dearest friend.''

"Really? And who would say otherwise? But to get back to the murderer. Fortunately for us, your dearest friend had time, as he lay dying, to employ his own blood to tell us all who killed him. That's it, Sterling, pretend to write on the marble hearth. I commend you, you're really getting into the spirit of the thing. Shiveley? Now come, come. Be a good fellow and pretend you're the one who fired the fatal shot.''

"Oh, very well, but I'm doing this under protest. You're an ass, Saint Just. Always poking about, pre-

tending to be a Bow Street Runner. As if the word flowers means anything to anybody.''

Saint Just watched as Shiveley walked to precisely the spot he had concluded the murderer had stood that fatal night. How very helpful of the man, for Saint Just had come into this gathering tonight still unsure of Shiveley's guilt. It was so pleasant when one's hypothesis is proved correct.

''Yes, Shiveley, flowers,'' Saint Just said, shooting his cuffs, careful to contain his glee that Shiveley was behaving just as he'd hoped. He winked at Lady Caroline, wordlessly assuring her that there would be ample time for their assignation later that evening. Wouldn't do to ever disappoint a lady. Especially one of Lady Caroline's talents, who had just lost a bet.

''Excuse me. Where was I? Oh, yes. No one knows what it means. At least, not until one expands their imagination to include sources of flowers. Sources such as the markets in Covent Garden. Flowers. So much easier to spell out in blood than Covent Garden, I suppose, although dying utterances—or, in this case, scribblings—have this nasty way of being unnecessarily cryptic, don't they? Difficult to believe a man known best for his mediocrity could rise to such heights just as he was about to expire, but perhaps approaching mortality concentrates the mind. Still, I digress. Flowers, and Covent Garden. One word, to mean both place and person. Do you know, Shiveley, what I learned when I mentioned Quigley's name in the theatre at Covent Garden? Perhaps if I were to say the name Rose? Does that jog your

Aerosmith's Steven Tyler opened his larger-than-life mouth and screamed.

Maggie screamed with him. Some jackass was leaning on her doorbell. She hit Save—damn near snapping the keys in half—swiveled in her chair, glared at the door. ''Go away.

She's not home. She broke her leg and we had to shoot her.''

Wellie and Napper, who could sleep through Aerosmith at top volume and squared, woke at the sound of Maggie's voice and trotted toward the kitchen, believing it to be time for their afternoon snack, no doubt.

"Eat the dry stuff in the dish," she called after them, "and I'll open a can later." Damn it. The doorbell. Cats. Was it too much to ask to be left alone? She was just getting to the best part. So was Tyler: "Dream on, dream on . . ." She reached over to the portable stereo system sitting on the shelf of the desk unit and cranked up the volume.

"Had to shoot her? Maggie? Maggie, I know you're in there. Come on, sweetheart, open the door. Can you even hear me?"

Maggie's shoulders slumped. "Kirk," she mumbled as she turned the volume down a notch, angrily ground out her cigarette in the ashtray, and threw her computer glasses on the desk. On a scale of one to ten, ten being the highest, if anyone were to ask who she wanted in her apartment at the moment, she'd give Kirk Toland a One and killer bees a Six, with a bullet. "Go away, Kirk. You know I'm writing."

"I know, sweetheart, and I apologize. Maggie, this is embarrassing. I can't grovel out here in the hall. Let me in, please."

Kirk Toland groveling? Not a pretty mental picture. Besides, he wasn't supposed to be groveling. He was supposed to be moving on to greener pastures, and the blondes lying in the clover, waving condom packets at him. She pushed herself to her feet, aimed herself at the door, undid the three dead bolts and the security chain, and pulled it open.

"Kirk," she said shortly, then turned her back on him and headed for one of the overstuffed couches in the center of the large living room.

He followed her, like an eager puppy coming to heel, hoping for a treat. "Maggie," he said, his carefully cultivated Harvard accent evident in that single word—which was a neat trick if you could do it. Kirk Toland could.

Kirk Toland could do a lot of things. Tall, as trim as his personal trainer could get him, distinguished-looking at forty-seven with his just-going-silver hair and smoke-gray eyes, Kirk was handsome, twice divorced, richer than God, and pretty decent in bed. But not great, which was one of the reasons Maggie had tossed him out of hers. That, plus the fact that she didn't like threesomes, and Kirk's ego was always between the sheets with them. Kirk Toland, Maggie had decided two months ago, had been a prize, a rite of passage. And a complete mistake.

Unfortunately, Kirk Toland was also something else. He was the publisher of Toland Books, Maggie's publishing house. Which pretty much made it a little sticky to flat out tell him to take a hike.

Maggie had been tossed out of Toland Books once, and didn't much long for an encore. Six years ago she had been Alicia Tate Evans, historical romance author (three names are always so impressive on a book cover). She'd also been a historical romance author cut loose by Nelson ''The Trigger'' Trigg when Toland Books had brought the bean counter on board and he'd blown away more than three dozen midlist authors with one shot of his smoking red pen.

Alicia/Maggie had bummed for about a week. Her checkbook balance hadn't allowed for more of a pity party. And then she'd gone to work on reinventing herself. She turned her back on the genre that had turned its back on her and entered the mystery market. All she kept was her usual early-nineteenth-century English historical settings as she created Alexandre Blake, Viscount Saint Just, amateur sleuth, hero extraordinare, world-class lover.

And, damn, the switch had worked. Her editor had slipped her new pen name, Cleo Dooley (Maggie had decided that Os looked good on a book cover), past The Trigger, smack back to a spot on the list at Toland Books (See? Even Toland Books agreed on the Os). The tongue-in-cheek Saint Just

Mysteries had started strong and grown rapidly, so that her house had just asked for two books a year, and had put her in hardcover. The third installment made the extended *NYT* list; the fourth had climbed to number seven, stayed in the top fifteen for three weeks, and had gone *NYT* again in paperback. Her Alicia Tate Evans romances had been reissued, and this time hit the charts.

Maggie Kelly didn't need Kirk Toland. She didn't need Toland Books. But she felt loyal to her editor and good friend, Bernice Toland-James. Bernie liked Maggie's work and was a brilliant, insightful editor. And the topper—Bernie had been Toland Wife Number One and knew what a pain in the ass Kirk could be. You couldn't buy that kind of empathy in the open market.

Pulling the edges of her robe around her, Maggie flopped down on the couch and let the pillows envelop her. She watched, biting her bottom lip, as Kirk seated himself on the facing couch, careful not to lean back into the cabbage-rose jaws of life that regularly ate her guests.

"I really am writing, Kirk," she said, waving one arm toward the U-shaped desk and her very new, definitely unprofessional-looking computer, the one with the flowers on its cover. (Yes, and that had given her the idea for using "flowers" as the cryptic message—never look too deeply for the "why" of a writer; the answers often aren't that esoteric.)

The Aerosmith gang was still in good voice, still shouting and screaming, and obviously annoying the hell out of Kirk, God love them all.

"Writing? Yes, I can *hear* that. Could you possibly turn it down?" Kirk asked, inclining his head toward the portable stereo.

"Nope," Maggie said, feeling her mood brighten. "It's my muse, you know."

Kirk reached up one manicured hand and adjusted the knot in his tie. "Is that what you call it? I guess you know better than to call it muse-*ic*." And then he grinned, as if he'd just told a fantastic joke, and Maggie remembered another reason she'd broken it off with Kirk. The blue-blooded man's attempts at humor were so jarring and out of character, they were embarrassing—rather like being tied down and forced to watch George Dubya try to be coherent without cue cards.

"Very funny, Kirk. You crack me up, really. Did Socks let you in?" she asked, referring to her doorman, Argyle Jackson. Poor guy. He blamed his unfortunate yet inevitable nickname on his mother, whom he believed should have known better. "I've asked him not to do that. What did you tip him? Had to be worth at least a twenty to you."

"I could have had him for twenty? Damn. I did buzz, Maggie, not that you could have heard it over this noise," Kirk told her, shooting his French cuffs with the gold Gucci links. The man was forever fussing with his clothing, as if he couldn't get enough of touching himself, congratulating himself for being so perfect. What *had* she seen in him? "Anyway, you're right. When you didn't answer, Argyle was kind enough to let me in. Pleasant boy, Argyle, even if he is one of those light-in-the-loafers types."

Maggie winced again. What was that? Strike seventeen? There was so much she couldn't stand about Kirk Toland, mostly that she had been vulnerable enough, flattered enough, stupid enough, to have let him talk her into bed six months ago. "Socks is a nice guy, period. Try to get that straight in your very straight head, Kirk, okay? I mean, does Socks go around saying that we're pleasant types, even if we are heterosexual?"

"As I've explained to you before, Maggie, you make too much money now to remain a damned liberal Democrat. There's no profit in it." Kirk stood up, began to pace the Oriental carpet Maggie had indulged in after the sale of her third Saint Just mystery. "But let's not argue, all right? That's not why I came here."

"It isn't?" Maggie uncurled herself from the couch, stood up, and turned toward the hallway leading to her bedroom.

"Have you come for the rest of your clothes? I'll get them for you."

And that was her second mistake. The first had been letting Kirk into the apartment. The second was turning her back on him. She'd taken only three steps when she felt his hands come down on her shoulders. He turned her around, stepped closer to her, pelvis first, spreading his legs slightly as he planted his feet and smiled.

Nothing. She felt nothing. The strings of her heart did not go *zing*. She was free. Really free.

"You've *got* to be kidding," Maggie said, trying to peel his fingers from her shoulders. "One, are you blind? I look like I've been mauled by bears and then left beside the trail. Two, I probably smell like a bear. Three, we've been here before, Kirk, and we're not going here again. Got that?"

Kirk had great caps, and liked showing them off. He did so now, his smile part indulgent, part determinedly sexual. "Maggie, you don't mean that."

She pushed herself away from him, delighting in the knowledge that Kirk Toland meant nothing to her, less than nothing to her libido. "What is it, Kirk? You can't lose? You can't be the one who gets his walking papers? Do I have to take you back so that you can drop me, tell everybody you dropped me? What? Work with me, Kirk. Give me a hint here, okay?"

The caps disappeared as Kirk turned angry. "It's my reputation, isn't it? It's Bernice, and the rest of them. Damn it, Maggie, don't listen to them. I love you, don't you understand that?"

Aerosmith was really on the ball, as "Same Old Song And Dance" began blaring out of the speakers.

Maggie wrinkled her nose. "Actually, Kirk, no. No, I don't understand that you love me. I don't know why. Maybe it was the picture in yesterday's *Daily News*, showing some blonde with a really horrific glandular problem leaning her boobs all over you. Maybe it's the fact that we were together for four months and you cheated on me for three of them.

Maybe I'm afraid you haven't had all your shots. No matter what, it's over, has been over for two months, never should have started in the first place.''

For a Harvard man, Kirk Toland could be as thick as a Gallagher's filet mignon. He took another step toward her; she backed up two, amazed that she didn't feel trapped, panicked. "It's my age," he said, nodding. "Sixteen years, Maggie. That's not so much. And I'm certainly not lacking for stamina, right?"

"You're a fricking god in bed, Kirk," Maggie lied sincerely. "Never had better. I'm a hollow shell without you. There, happy now?" She neatly sidestepped him, headed for the front door of her apartment. His clothes could rot in her closet.

He tagged along behind her, amusing her. She was beginning to warm to the doggy analogy. Here, boy. Wanna go outside?

"Then we'll have dinner tonight?"

Correction. He could be as thick as a McDonald's milkshake, and twice as full of empty air. "No, Kirk, we will not have dinner tonight. I told you, I'm wrapping up my book. A three-alarm fire wouldn't get me out of this apartment tonight, or for the rest of the week, while I reread, print out the pages. You know the routine, right?"

"Friday, then? Saturday? We could fly to one of those islands, maybe one with a casino? Anything you want, Maggie. Anything."

"Really? How about this. I want you to leave, Kirk," she said, opening the door. Then she caved. She always caved, damn it. Big mouth, no follow-through. "Tell you what—I'll see you at the party I'm giving next Saturday night to celebrate getting this book out of here. Not this Saturday, Kirk, *next* Saturday. Can you remember that? Is that a deal?"

She watched, amazed, as Kirk digested this information, thought about it. A party? He liked parties. Sit up, boy, give me your paw and I'll give you a treat.

And, once everyone went home, he could have a party of his own, with just he and Maggie. She could nearly read the words as they crossed his forehead, like a ticker tape of lascivious thoughts.

"Kirk? This isn't a test. Just answer yes or no."

"Deal." He leaned down, his handsome face slapably smug, and aimed a kiss at her mouth. She turned aside, so that the kiss landed on her cheek. "I'll get you back, Maggie. Believe me when I say that. I don't lose."

"Uh-huh. Sure. See ya," she said, quickly closing the door behind him, then glaring at it as she threw the dead bolts, shot home the chain. "Creep."

"A first-rate suggestion, my dear, if Mr. Toland in fact heard you. Quite an insupportable person. He definitely should be crawling away on his hands and knees, preferably over shards of broken glass."

"Not that kind of creep. I meant—" Maggie's hand stilled on the security chain. *"Who said that?"*

"And now an excellent question, and so much more commendable than a maidenly scream. Please accept my compliments, Miss Kelly, but then, I already know you've got bottom. As for who I am, if you were perhaps to turn around, I do believe all your questions would be answered quite at once."

She was hearing voices? This was good. Not. How could she be hearing, talking to, voices? Who was in her apartment? How did he get in? Maggie froze, her back to the room. *Don't wanna look, don't wanna. Stupid fingers, stop shaking. Turn the locks, turn the damn locks. Get me the hell out of here.*

"I reiterate, Miss Kelly," the fairly deep, highly cultured, damned sexy, and scarily familiar male voice continued in a remarkably pure British accent, "if you were to turn around? Mr. Balder is poking about in your kitchen, impervious to my suggestion that he behave. Therefore, we won't wait on the man, if that's all right with you. So, if you will simply turn around, allow me to introduce myself? Formally, that is. As it is, we've been rather intimately acquainted for several years.''

The dead bolts were open. The chain was off. Maggie's hand was on the doorknob. The man wasn't coming after her, grabbing her; he didn't seem to be threatening her, unless he was planning to talk her to death. She could be out of the apartment in three seconds, four if she stumbled. If her damn feet would even move.

And then it hit her. The voice had said ''Balder.'' It had, hadn't it? Still with her back to the room, and doing a pretty good mental imitation of an ostrich pretending that lion lying in the tall grass didn't exist, Maggie croaked, ''Balder? As in Sterling Balder? *My* Sterling Balder?''

''I do believe my dear friend prefers to consider himself his own man, Miss Kelly, but you're quite correct, your Sterling Balder. Ah, how pleasant. It appears I've found the correct knob on my first attempt. I should be complimenting myself. I've come to harbor a certain appreciation for Mr. Aerosmith, thanks to you, but that particular composition is rather jarring. Frankly, I much prefer selections from *The Scarlet Pimpernel*. And *Phantom of the Opera* has a certain panache, don't you agree? I notice you prefer that music when you're orchestrating my romantic seductions.''

It took Maggie a moment to realize that the stereo speakers had indeed gone silent. Which was rather unfortunate, as now she could clearly hear the beating of her pounding heart, on top of the amused male voice that showed no signs of falling silent anytime soon.

Swallowing hard, and feeling herself caught between episodes of *America's Most Wanted* and some of the screwier *X-Files*, she turned toward her desk. Slowly. Tentatively. Keeping her gaze on the parquet floor as long as she could before raising her eyes an inch at a time . . . until she saw the pair of shiny, black, knee-high boots.

''Oh boy,'' she breathed, pressing her back against the door, her hand still on the doorknob. *X-Files*. Definitely *X-Files*.

The boots were attached to legs. The legs were encased in form-fitting tan breeches.

"No. This isn't happening. I'm working too hard. Or maybe it's nicotine poisoning from smoking too much. Am I drooling?" She wiped at her chin. "You drool with nicotine poisoning, right? I don't know about hallucinations, but I could buy it if you're selling. Because this is *not* happening."

She dared herself to look higher. There was a white-on-white waistcoat beneath a dark-blue superfine jacket. A gold-rimmed quizzing glass hanging to the waist from a black riband. A fall of lace at the throat, repeated at the wrists.

There were *hands* at the end of the lace cuffs.

Maggie closed her eyes, took a deep breath, lifted her head—and stared straight at the man standing beside her desk.

And there he was, in all his glory. Alexandre Blake, Viscount Saint Just. All six feet, two inches, one hundred and eighty-five pounds of the well-built hunk of her imagination, come to life. She recognized him at once. After all, she had created him.

Hair as black as midnight, casually rumpled in its wind-swept style, à la Beau Brummell. Eyes as blue as a cloudless summer sky, as mesmerizingly blue as Paul Newman's. Those winglike brows, the left one currently raised in wry amusement, rather like a refined Jim Carrey. Her creation did wry amusement well. He also excelled at sarcastic, insulting, inquiring and, most of all, sexy.

His head was well shaped, his face longish, with a strong, slightly squared jaw, his skin lightly tanned. Full lips patterned closely on Val Kilmer's sensuous pout. Slashes in his cheeks and fascinating crinkles beside his eyes when he smiled, both copied from a younger Clint Eastwood, when old Clint was knocking all the women dead in his spaghetti Westerns (put a thin cheroot between this guy's teeth, have him crinkle up his eyes, and the entire female population of Manhattan would melt into a puddle). Peter O'Toole's aristocratic nose. Sean Connery's familiar, and only slightly more British, bedroom voice. A composite for her readers to fantasize about as their husbands or boyfriends watched television in their boxer shorts and scratched their butts.

"No. It's not possible."

"I beg to disagree, Miss Kelly. It is very possible. I fear I shock you, and make no doubt that you are experiencing some difficulty in believing the evidence of your own eyes. But please do try to come to grips with the obvious. I am Saint Just. *Your* Saint Just, if that makes any of this easier."

She took a single step forward. Blinked.

He was still there. Worse, his smile crinkled the skin around his eyes, serving to produce those sexy cheek slashes. The man was a god. No, scratch that. The figment of her imagination was a god.

She'd been working too hard. She'd been under way too much pressure. Smoking too much, eating and sleeping too little. Because this couldn't happen. It just couldn't.

"Ah, we're alone now that odious man is gone. Good. The fellow's pushy and revolting, and all of that."

Maggie's head snapped around to see yet another Regency-era dandy advancing on her from the kitchen. Again, recognition was simple. This could only be Sterling Balder, Saint Just's good friend and compatriot. She'd invented Sterling Balder because every hero needs a sidekick, a foil, someone to talk to so he isn't talking to himself. Preferably, a hero needed a slightly bumbling friend, as bumbling, adorable sidekicks made for the best theater. So Maggie had made Sterling short, plump, balding (Balding, Balder. Get it?), and rather delightfully dim-witted. Her readers loved him; he even had his own fan club.

But he shouldn't be in her living room, damn it, holding the KFC chicken leg she'd been saving for her lunch.

"Delighted and all of that, Miss Kelly," Balder was saying as Maggie tried to hear him through the sudden ringing in her ears. "We've been waiting for ever so long to meet you, haven't we, Saint Just? Do you mind? I have a question for you, not that I'm not completely grateful that you've allowed me to be a figment of your imagination and all of that. But, and here's my question, Miss Kelly—couldn't you have figmented me just a tad *thinner*?''

It was perfect. A perfect Sterling Balder question, right down to his self-conscious overuse of the phrase "and all of that." Maggie would have laughed, except that her gums were now going numb, along with her lips, her forehead, and three-quarters of her body.

"I—I created you," she said, her voice coming to her ears from far away as she stared at Saint Just once more. God, he was gorgeous! She really did do good work. "But you're in my *imagination,* not my living room. Who gave you permission to drop in for a visit? It sure wasn't me! But no. I take that back. You're not *really* here. You can't *really* be here."

Saint Just raised his quizzing glass to his eye, put one foot forward, one hand on his hip, and struck a pose. A perfect Saint Just pose based on a perfect Beau Brummell pose she'd seen reproduced in one of her research books. "Far be it from me to point out the error in that statement, Miss Kelly," he drawled in that wonderful young Sean Connery as James Bond voice, "but we most definitely are here. Now, if I may brook a suggestion, might I say that Sterling and I are most happy to excuse you while you . . . forgive me . . . *freshen* yourself?"

"Yes," Balder said, nodding. "Not to be insulting, but you do look a trifle hagged, and all of that. Probably do you good, a wash and a brush-up."

Maggie looked down at her body, winced, pulled the edges of her robe around herself. She did it without really thinking, but simply responding to Saint Just's arrogant remark on her appearance.

Arrogant. Yes, she'd made Saint Just arrogant. She'd had to, as no character is perfect, not even the perfect hero. In the end, she gave him a few other less than kind characteristics.

Arrogant, a bit sarcastic, perhaps a tad overbearing. More than slightly proud, a completely confident man who didn't suffer fools gladly. Those were the defects (could they be strengths?) she'd picked for the Viscount Saint Just. Not that it mattered. All she had to do was shut down her computer and he'd shut up, go away. At least that's the way it was *supposed* to happen.

And that was the way it did happen, damn it. Saint Just and Balder were not in her living room. They couldn't be. She was dreaming, that's what she was doing. She'd locked Kirk out, then lain down on the couch and fallen asleep and begun to dream.

"Ouch!" Okay. So pinching herself didn't wake her up, banish these imaginary intruders. Clearly she had to find another way to wake herself up, regain her sanity.

Maggie lifted her chin, just the way defiant heroines did, and commanded herself to walk forward . . . to put out one trembling hand . . . to poke a hole straight through the washboard-flat belly of this absurd, absurdly handsome figment of her imagination.

But before she could touch him, that figment of her imagination took hold of her hand, bowed over it, turned it at the last possible moment, and planted a kiss in her palm.

More By Best-selling Author
Fern Michaels